Graham Sheppard

POTENTIAL

Limited Special Edition. No. 19 of 25 Paperbacks

Born a war babe in Shepton Mallet, Somerset in 1944, Graham spent most of his formative years in Barnes, SW London, where his parents ran a tobacconist and confectionery shop.

Running was an early attraction when winning the half-mile at his secondary school, but with the River Thames only yards from his front door, his sporting interests switched in his teens to rowing, reaching the semi-finals at Henley Royal Regatta in 1970. Running was always an interest however and Graham completed the London Marathon four times in his 40s.

Taking the opportunity of an early retirement in 1997, after 34 years working for the Sun Life Assurance Society, the idea was to finish writing his novel, *Potential*, a task only completed last year. The era and background of *Potential* have seen many changes throughout the years but the main characters are as you meet them today.

Graham currently lives in Cambridgeshire with his second wife, Ellie. His sporting activities these days are centred around table tennis, playing in two local leagues.

Graham Sheppard

POTENTIAL

AUSTIN MACAULEY PUBLISHERS™

LONDON · CAMBRIDGE · NEW YORK · SHARJAH

A CIP catalogue record for this title is available from the British Library.

ISBN 9781528909846 (Paperback)
ISBN 9781528959407 (ePub e-book)

www.austinmacauley.com

First Published (2020)
Austin Macauley Publishers Ltd
25 Canada Square
Canary Wharf
London
E14 5LQ

A big thank you to Steve Little for all his work and effort in editing my manuscript in its early form. Also my thanks to my editor, Elaine Denning, for her sincerity and kind words that I found so encouraging in the early stages and her final critique which taught me so much.

Thanks also to Bob Littlechild, Graham Pack and Richard Mussett for their expertise on various subjects and Linda, Helen, Gill and Vanessa at Sun Life Assurance Society for their encouragement so many years ago.

Also my brother, Malcolm, who was such an inspiration in my competitive years of sport. Nicknamed 'Driftwood' for his dedication to the River Thames and rowing, his successful career was highlighted with two gold medals in the World Veteran Rowing Championships of 1973.

Part 1
From Little Acorns

Chapter 1

"It's really quite spooky out there," observed Rachel Forbes, her nose almost pressed on the windowpane as she tried with difficulty to assess the state of the fog. It had grown progressively worse during the night, the thick layers which clung tenaciously to the house, obscuring any signs of the garden below.

"I can't even see the tubs on the patio anymore," she added, wiping the glass with the tips of her fingers where her breath had condensed in a light film.

"Yes, you're right, the worst I've seen in the eight years I've lived here," David Lucas confirmed from the comfort of his bed.

He could not resist staring at his girlfriend as she glided across the bay windows at the far end of his narrow room, fascinated as she was by the prevailing weather conditions. There was an innocence about her he found so appealing. Framed by the window, she wore only a pair of thin white panties, her slim lithe body with finely muscled back, trim legs and firm buttocks creating a picture of sensuous delight.

All of a sudden, she turned and smiled, sensing, as she did so, the adjustment of his gaze to her eyes. It was only the second time she had shared his bed in the three weeks they had been dating and a slight awkwardness still persisted. The first time occurred only a week ago when Tom had spent the night at his friend's house.

She shivered involuntarily as the chill of the room caught her by surprise.

"Come and get into bed before you catch pneumonia," he said with affection, his lifting of the duvet, an invitation she could not resist. Her eyes lit visibly as she moved towards him. With feline grace, she slid on to the sheeted mattress, immediately feeling the warmth of the cover as it fell cosily around her. They manoeuvred themselves to face each other, his mouth finding hers with a gentleness that begged a response.

"I think I love you, David Lucas," she sighed, her eyes twinkling with a seductive glow. It was the first time she had spoken of love and instantly, a sense of caution bit his mind. For a fleeting moment, he was lost as, once again, a flush of guilt shaded his thoughts. Was it unfair to commit to this relationship in his current circumstances? She sensed his hesitation and instinctively raised her hand so that her fingers caressed the fine hairs of his chest. Any negative thoughts he may have had were immediately dismissed.

"Love you too," he responded, the words slipping with little effort from his mouth. They kissed again, more passionately this time as she slithered down the bed in complete surrender to his body. Without thinking, his hands moved to her breasts.

"D…a…d!" It was not a yell of panic, just a loud vibrating call that echoed around the walls of the room.

They both froze together, their hearts stopping for a split second before returning to their natural rhythm. With an extravagant sigh, he sat up. Rachel followed, drawing her knees up to her chest and giving him the cutest of looks.

Then it came again, seemingly much louder and stronger than the initial outburst.

"D…a…d."

As their eyes met, they both burst into fits of laughter. Cut off in the throes of their passion, the inappropriateness of the lad's timing seemed so comical.

"Shush," David gestured, putting his finger to his lips. With his other hand, he tried to muffle her reaction, but alas, to no avail. He could see her eyes welling with tears of laughter as she tried to control her emotions.

Pulling himself together for just a moment, he raised his head to the ceiling in mock annoyance. "Thank you, Son," he half whispered. "I knew I could rely on you. And your timing is, as usual, spot on." This only set Rachel off again in a further spasm of giggles. Unable to control herself, she fell away from him on to the pillow, clamping her hands firmly to her mouth in an effort to stem any sound.

Addressing the door, he took a deep breath before adopting a serious tone that belied his amusement. "Coming," he shouted as he prepared to leave the bed.

It was much colder than he had expected, the central heating not having sufficient time to complete its initial work. Sorting his pyjamas from an untidy pile on the chair by his bed, he deftly slipped them on before grabbing his dressing gown from the hanger in his wardrobe. A quick check of his appearance in the mirror and he padded barefoot to the other side of the bed where he could see Rachel still in a state of unrestrained mirth. He had to smile as he watched her shoulders shaking.

"You get your money's worth when you stay here," he whispered as he bent down and placed a light kiss on her head.

"I know," she said looking up at him fondly, her eyes moist with the tears she couldn't control. She watched, even more amused, as he tiptoed with clumsy strides towards the door.

Once outside in the landing, he took a deep breath. He was not finding his current situation easy. There was a guilt factor in his actions which he found impossible to ignore.

Gripping the handle firmly, he opened his son's bedroom door as quietly as he could, expecting to find him sitting up in bed. Instead, he was seated at his computer with his back to him, unaware of his presence. He waited a few seconds, savouring the enjoyment the boy was deriving from the frenetic use of the mouse in his hand, the slight twitching of his hunched shoulders emphasising the tenseness of the motor racing game on his screen.

"Morning, Tom. Winning, are we?" The question was asked with a certain tenderness. The boy immediately swung around, his eyes lighting with affection as the brightest of smiles splashed warmly across his face. Not for the first time David felt a slight jump of his heart with the reaction.

As he had done so many times before, he marvelled at his son's fine features. He seemed to be growing more like his mother each day. The shock of curly blond hair, neat and easily manageable, complementing the eyebrows of the same complexion; the finely chiselled nose, full mouth and the high cheekbones. God, he looked so many years older than the eleven he had experienced. He was surely a lad to be proud of.

"Hi-ya, Dad," Tom drawled in a faked American accent, the origin of which David had never understood but guessed had been picked up at school from the various children who had spent their holidays visiting Disneyland in Florida. Several times, he had hinted to the lad that he would take him there, or maybe the European version in Paris. Perhaps, one day, he would be able to save enough money for the treat. His business was beginning to expand and he could see this as a possibility in the next year or two.

"How are you? Did you sleep well?" he enquired.

"Fine, thanks. I'm sorry if I woke you up but I thought I could hear you moving." The cheeky smirk he tried to hide told David enough to know that there was more behind his robust yell than the usual morning greeting. He wondered just how much he was able to hear through the meagre wall that divided the rooms.

"Look, Son," David said with some difficulty. "When it was time for Rachel to go home last night, the fog was so bad she had to stay."

Tom never said a word, just stared at him with the same blank expression he would throw out when he thought he was fooling. He felt guilty and ashamed, and stupidly, annoyed at himself for his confusion, all at the same time.

He was only too aware that Tom was not willing to accept Rachel as his girlfriend. He had made that plainly clear only last week when he had introduced her to him for the first time. Frankly, he was both appalled and embarrassed by his behaviour but he had made up his mind not to make an issue of the situation, especially as Rachel had told him to be patient.

When he had first mentioned he had a girlfriend, Tom appeared to take little interest but at the same time, there had been nothing negative in his response. He had taken this as an acceptance and asked her to join them for a meal. It had been a big mistake.

The evening was a complete failure. Apart from a strained hello, they could get little out of him. Rachel had tried her hardest to make conversation but his short and curt answers left much to be desired. All evening, he picked at his food and finally, announced he was going to bed on the excuse of a headache.

Fortunately, Rachel had taken it well, dismissing his reaction as typical of any boy who had lost his mother only eighteen months ago at such a young age. His feelings for her had only strengthened with her understanding and compassion.

"Will you give me a game, Dad?" his son's voice brought him back to reality.

"Not just yet, Tom, Rachel and I are about to have a cup of tea. I'll give you a game later," he said with little enthusiasm, avoiding the look of scorn that flashed to his son's eyes. "See you in a while, okay?" Not really waiting for a reply, he closed the door prematurely and took a further deep breath. It took him a few seconds to regain his composure. By this time, he was ready to face his next adversary.

Before he reached the kitchen door, he could sense the boiling agitation from within, the escaping whimpers assaulting his nerves like a screeching chalk on a blackboard. No sooner had he turned the handle than the door burst open and sixty pounds of Labrador threw herself at him, almost knocking him off his feet. He struggled to reach the light switch.

"Down, Tammy, down, girl," he pleaded in vain, attempting to ward off the barrage of juicy licks that were soon being plastered one after the other across his cheeks, all the time her front paws resting on his chest. Despite his pleas, it took several minutes for her affection to recede, her interests only switching to the joys of the garden once the bolts had been released on the back door. As it opened, the freezing air washed over him like an avalanche. He held his breath with the sudden impact.

"Cats," he shouted, at the same time filling his lungs fully with the invigorating air. Tammy took off into the gloomy darkness with her usual enthusiasm.

Peering down the garden, he had a feeling the fog was beginning to lift. The outline of the pond, only a few metres away, was, all of a sudden, just visible, the dew crystals on the ice shimmering sullenly under the searching rays of the kitchen light. On the bank, he could just make out the old plastic gnome maintaining his lonely vigil, the line of his fishing rod buried solidly in the icy water.

Quickly closing the door, he was at last able to give his full attention to the job in hand. Within a few minutes, the kettle had boiled and it was only a few more before two mugs of steaming hot tea were ready on the tray. He could not remember whether Rachel took sugar, so found a small bowl in the cupboard and half-filled this before sticking a spoon in the middle. An unopened packet of custard creams completed his presentation.

Pleased with himself, he returned to the garden. Opening the door, there was no sign of Tammy. He called her twice, on each occasion aware of the resonance of his deep voice in the still of the morning atmosphere. It was really quite eerie and he shuddered with the realisation. Weirdly, the spell was broken with Tammy's return. Like a ghostly phantom, she emerged from the grey backdrop, panting heavily as she zigzagged a path in his direction. When close by, she paused to sniff at some distracting odour.

"Come on, girl, let's get inside, it's freezing out here," he cajoled her.

Running straight to her water bowl, she proceeded to lap at the contents in her usual enthusiastic manner so that drops splashed untidily over the clean floor.

"God, you're a mucky bugger," he told her, throwing a paper kitchen towel over the mess, whilst at the same time patting her head fondly. "Right, in your basket then. I'm going back to bed."

With the tray in his hand, he made for a return to the bedroom. No sooner had he reached the half-landing than his attention was drawn by a long low whine at the foot of the stairs. He twisted round to see Tammy lying motionless on her stomach, her head resting in a doleful pose on her paws, those big sorrowful eyes staring straight at him, sad and unblinking. He could not help but smile at her dramatics.

"You stupid dog. I'll try and take you for a walk later, if you're lucky," he laughed. Her tail immediately gained momentum at the personal address.

Entering the bedroom, he noticed Rachel had moved to his side of the bed. Huddled under the duvet and facing away from him, all he could see was the long honey coloured tresses of her hair spread loosely across the pillow. Carefully, he placed the tray on the bedside cabinet and picked his way to the other side of the room, keeping his weight on the balls of his feet to minimise any sound.

As he had suspected, she had fallen asleep. Breathing thinly, she looked so beautiful. The closed eyelids, the short cute nose, threatening to rise at its extremity and her lips, the first feature he had noted of her, so full but somehow shaped to perfection.

Standing there, studying her features, he had to wonder once again if it was a mistake in developing their relationship. Was he ready for it? More to the point, was Tom ready for it? Under normal circumstances, he knew he would have had no doubts but he was just not sure he was doing the right thing at this time. She was such a sweet and lovely girl. The last thing he wanted was to lead her on and subsequently hurt her.

As he sipped his tea, a fresh idea came to him. His eyes returned to Rachel as he gave it further consideration. Her breathing had become much deeper, now a regular rhythm of short rasping breaths. The night of passion and little sleep had taken its toll on her. He smiled wryly on reflection. It took just one further look to convince him and with that, he came to the conclusion she would not wake for some time.

An impulse to tackle his morning run, an event that had become as regular as brushing his teeth, was too strong to ignore, even in the forbidding conditions thrown up by the weather. He had not missed a morning outing for as long as he could remember. Hopefully, if Rachel should wake before his return, she would understand. If not, he would put the blame on poor Tammy, telling Rachel it was imperative she has a walk first thing in the morning. His main concern was that Rachel would wake, leave the bedroom and bump into Tom, a meeting he would prefer not to happen in his absence. He could only hope on that one.

With little further thought, he decided his shorter run along the riverbank, taking less than forty minutes, would be ideal. After a quick visit to the bathroom, he was back in the bedroom to don his shorts, vest, socks and tracksuit. Finally, he was ready.

As it had done for some time now, the idea of a run awoke in him a new spirit, a release of energy that gave him a zest for the day. It was the inspiration he needed.

Before leaving the bedroom, there was one final task. Opening the drawer on the cabinet by his bed, he withdrew a small writing pad and a biro. Quickly, he scribbled a short message. Pulling the top sheet from the pad, he left it on the cabinet. Fast asleep, Rachel looked even more beautiful, he thought to himself. *Love you*, he mouthed in silence.

Passing Tom's door, he gave a quick knock and pushed his head inside. He was at his desk still engrossed in his games.

"I'm going for a run. Be about forty minutes," David addressed the lad's back.

"Okay," came the response. From the tone, it sounded as if they were back on good terms. He was not usually a lad to sulk. He closed the door.

"Dad."

Opening the door again, he stuck his head back inside. Tom had swung round to face him, a pleasant smile on his face.

"Yes."

"Will you give me a game on the computer when you get back please?"

"Of course," he told him, their eyes locking with familiar respect before he closed the door again.

Once Tammy knew she was going for a walk, there was no controlling her. Before he had reached the bottom of the stairs, she was pirouetting in circles, her tail thrashing the surrounding furniture with wild swipes. No sooner was he with her than she was up on her back legs licking his face.

"Right, you lucky girl, you're going to get your walk." She barked in response and he quickly wrapped his hand around her snout in protest. "If you wake Rachel," he told her, "your walk could get the chop, so I would behave if I was you." His words had little effect as he continued to wrestle with her collar.

"This is more physical than running," he told her as he finally completed the task. Dragging her into the kitchen, he set her free. She immediately ran to the back door and started scratching furiously to be let out.

"No," he shouted with some concern. "We won't have a door if you keep that up much longer." The rather distressed state of the panels on the oak door endorsed his statement. Looking around the kitchen, he spied his trainers at the side of the fridge. *They were beginning to look a little threadbare,* he thought. He had been running regularly now for nearly two years and these were only his second pair.

At last, fully kitted, he picked his phone off the kitchen table and made for the bolts on the door, shunting them open with a forceful tug. Once again, the cold air surprised him with its icy cut. At his feet, Tammy sprang away with a mighty thrust into the surrounding mist, disappearing within seconds. He could see down the garden for three or four metres. He would have to keep his wits about him on the farm lane but he couldn't imagine there would be much traffic in these conditions. In any case, he would hear it and move off on to the fields if necessary. Once he reached the riverbank, he would be safe.

Approaching the gate, a slight breeze caught him unawares so that he pulled the collar of his tracksuit tighter around his neck. It was much colder than he had imagined. In every direction, all he could see was a wall of fog, the dense clouds swirling around with menace like huge monumental waves. One moment they would appear so dense he could see very little in front of him and then, as if by magic, it would clear in patches, the lane before him and the surrounding buildings lifting out of the gloom. There was a feel about the whole thing that was quite weird.

To acclimatise to the unfamiliar conditions, he decided to walk to the first bend in the lane, some hundred metres from the house. Off to his right a line of old elm trees suddenly came in to view, their dark arthritic branches appearing from nowhere in a ghostly salute. There was a feel about the whole thing that was quite fascinating, the land secretive and strange in its new form.

"Come on, Tammy, let's go," he shouted to the nothingness surrounding him, at the same time breaking into a run that he could maintain comfortably for several miles. In a matter of seconds, she was by his side, jumping up and licking his hand, and then she was off again, disappearing into the gloom as quickly as she had appeared. Running freely, he felt an affinity with nature that he had never before experienced. It was really quite invigorating.

Chapter 2

Sean Nolan was a rogue, an out-and-out scoundrel who had spent the majority of his sixty-five years as a petty thief, poacher and prison inmate in roughly equal proportions.

Over the past forty years, he had relived a nightmare many times. It came to him again during the night, so vividly that he whimpered fearfully for several minutes before the climax tossed him from his sleep into consciousness, his head in turmoil with the reaction. The dream was always the same, only sometimes more frightening than others, his father dying in his arms following an attack from an enraged homeowner whose property they had ransacked with little thought for the consequences.

Despite the chill of the caravan and his inadequate sleeping bag, he was drenched in his own sweat. He shook his head to clear his mind. The two blankets he had thrown over the sleeping bag for extra warmth lay crumpled on the floor.

Life had not been good to him after his father's death. For his part in the bungled robbery, he had served two years in borstal. On his release, he had returned home to his mother to find she had taken up with a market stallholder. The new man in her life soon made it clear that he was not wanted.

For a while, he tried to settle in a job as a farmhand with a little poaching on the side, but the old life, with its financial rewards and excitement, beckoned like a strong magnet and it was not long before he was back in the burglary trade.

Only this time, it was not so easy. Now known to the police, they were regularly on his doorstep. His father's associates were wary of him after the publicity of the case and their help soon dwindled, leaving him with the problem of disposing of the stolen goods through new and untried sources. It was a risky business and failed badly.

At first, he had been under the apprehension that he could outwit the law. A big mistake, as he soon found out; being blessed with only the minimum of brainpower was too much of a handicap. He was caught time after time and put away for increasing periods of internment. On one occasion, he served two years for a crime he had not committed.

The result of this was that he hated the police with a vengeance. In fact, he hated people in general. The two relationships of any significance he had developed in his life, both with local women, had failed miserably. Both had left him whilst he was serving time at Her Majesty's pleasure, so that he trusted no one.

In recent years, he had tried to mend his lifestyle, realising his old body could no longer cope with the hardships of everyday prison life. His extended coughing fits and breathing problems had confirmed his suspicions that his days were numbered. Nevertheless, he would delay his visit to the doctor until the forthcoming summer had run its stay. The cancer which was surely ravaging his body would remain temporarily unleashed.

Unfortunately for Sean, spring was still some weeks off and the prospect of several more weeks of harsh weather still lay ahead before there was any chance of tasting the change.

Today, in particular, was one of those days he would gladly have forsaken, preferably tucking himself up in bed with only the old oil heater, his radio and Castro, his seven-year-old Rottweiler, for company.

But it was not to be. He had promised John Howarth, the farmer who owned the land where he had been residing for the past two years, he would run his stall at the Wisbech Sunday Market whilst he went off to visit his family up north. John was known to be a mean hard-hearted character with a temper that fizzled at the slightest provocation and Sean valued his current position too much to risk any disharmony by refusing.

Part of the farmer's income was derived from the breeding and sale of pigs to the wholesale market of the food industry, and it was Sean's job to raise them on the twenty acres of land where he resided in his old caravan.

Sean enjoyed his new life overseeing the mating, birth and growth of the piglets. He had become quite fond of the animals, especially the young ones in their early days when he was able to pick them up and fondle them lovingly whilst they squealed and squeaked in resistance. With each litter, he never ceased to be amazed at the rate with which they grew, often from just a pound at birth to a good two hundred and fifty within six months.

In return for his work, he received a cash payment of fifty pounds a week, together with the use of the caravan and his quarter acre of land where he would grow a few crops. John Howarth also paid his electricity bill so that, taking in to account his old age pension, he was probably in the best financial position he had ever been in his life.

Although dilapidated and draughty, the caravan did at least give him a roof over his head. There were times, especially in the summer, when sitting outside in the warm sunshine, he felt satisfied with his lot in life. He had even purchased a very comfortable reclining armchair from the Wisbech Auction House for a mere fiver, which he kept outdoors and covered with a good strong waterproof sheet when not in use.

At first, the pungent smell of the pigs had been a little overpowering but even this had diminished with time so that he was now unaware of the scent he carried with him.

After struggling with the lacing of his boots, he was forced to rest for a few minutes to catch his breath. On the floor, Castro was gnawing at a large bone that still promised a sliver of meat. Sean swung his foot forward with a mind to clearing it from his path. Castro growled menacingly. With surprising alacrity,

Sean was on his feet and before the dog had time to assess the situation, he felt his master's firm boot on his snout.

"Don't you snarl at me, you damned animal, or you will be outside in the cold," he threatened. The dog backed off, still snarling, his upper lips drawn back to expose a row of discoloured teeth.

It was almost two years since Sean had saved him from certain death at the hands of his previous owner, a travelling gipsy, after he had fiercely bitten the man's son on the calf, opening up a nasty wound. Following a severe beating with a thick stave, which Sean had witnessed in shock, the man had left him in a pool of blood, hardly alive. Later that evening, Sean had returned and carried him away in an old wheelbarrow. Painstakingly, he had nursed him back to health. The beating had done little to improve his temperament but he had proved to be a suitable companion.

Taking the last swig of whiskey from the bottle, he belched freely before slinging the empty bottle on the bed. Thankfully, it was Monday tomorrow and his Social Security payment would allow him to restock.

Pulling on his thick coat and scarf, he thought he was prepared for the elements, that was until he opened the door. It was much colder than he had imagined and the fog was seriously more dense than it had appeared through the windows of the caravan. When he had last looked out, only twenty minutes earlier, he had been able to see the wooden fence that encircled the field quite clearly but now it had almost disappeared.

Again, he cursed his ill-fortune in having to commit to such a task in these insufferable conditions. *It was possibly the harshest day of the winter,* he thought to himself. A good three-mile walk to the town with little chance of sitting down all day and then the return journey home in the dark seemed the worst of ordeals, especially in his current state of health.

Standing at the door of the caravan, he sniffed the air, his chest tightening with the slight exertion. Bolstering his courage, his hands went to his pockets to find his old woollen gloves. Once out, he stretched them lovingly over his fingers. At least, he had fed the pigs their grain and given them fresh water, doubling their portions so that a further feed would not be required on his return.

It was his plan to follow the river path all the way to town. He imagined it could be slippery in places so he would have to take care. It was easily the shortest route and being only seven o'clock, he had, fortunately, allowed himself ample time. Climbing the riverbank, he was soon aware of the cold savaging his old bones. Once at the top, he stopped, just for a moment, to catch his breath. Meanwhile, Castro had run ahead and was looking back awaiting his next move. Resigned to the challenge ahead, he followed, his legs already paining him with every step.

Chapter 3

On the other side of town, no more than a couple of miles as the crow flies, another sixty-five-year-old was assessing the morning and the weather that came with it. Although born in the same year as Sean Nolan, he was a much healthier individual in both body and mind.

If anything, pride dominated Charlie Greaves life, a pride in his physical condition, a pride in his achievements and most of all, a pride in his social standing. Charlie was a Fenman, born and bred, tough, ambitious and hard working.

Although he had overslept, Charlie's desire to run this Sunday morning was neither blunted nor threatened by the weather. On opening the curtains in his bedroom twenty minutes earlier, the sight of the Spartan elements, with the shroud of fog pressing at the windows, had immediately infused in him a warm desire to tackle the elements. After a quick wash, he was soon dressed and ready for the challenge. As usual, he would breakfast on his return.

His only concession to the severe conditions was the thicker tracksuit top which he now pulled over his head before opening the front door. The quick cold stab from the weather took him by surprise but instantly, he was into his routine of warm-up exercises, stretching and bending on the lawn to loosen the muscles that had served him so well in the past. Occasionally, a sharp flash of pain in his back as he forced his fingers to the ground reminded him the accruing years were beginning to take their toll. Ten minutes of exercises and he was more than ready for the test ahead.

Squaring his shoulders, he broke into a jog that would take him through the back streets of Wisbech to his old grammar school just outside of town where his real work would begin in earnest.

Amidst the enveloping fog, he was in his element. It fed him with a strange exhilaration, a conflict with nature that warmed his heart. He had always loved a challenge and here it was, right on his doorstep. Something new, something different, a challenge to be met with the brashness that was the foundation of his very existence.

In no time, it seemed, he had reached his old school. With the weather conditions as they were, there was little traffic. Standing in front of the tall metal gates of the vast grounds, memories of his happy school years flooded back as they often did. Faces and incidents of the past, school chums, bullies, teachers, sports days and academic achievements always seemed to cram his mind at this point.

Marking time to keep warm before setting off for the four miles of country roads to the village of Wisbech St Mary, a fresh idea filled his mind. It was an instinct that appealed to his current mood. Rather than take the road, he would follow the river path and the farm lanes that would bring him out just the other side of the village. If the conditions were too bad, he could always come back via the road.

He was less familiar with this route, a course he only occasionally took in the summer when he had become bored with his regular routine. Today, the adventure suited the feeling of reckless abandon that currently consumed him.

With a fresh sense of purpose, he set off, his breath breaking in descending clouds above his head with the effort. In no time, he dropped into a comfortable stride, a loping rhythm he felt confident he could maintain for the distance. Immediately, he realised the fog was much worse closer to the river than the conditions he had experienced so far.

At first, he was mesmerised by its density, fascinated by its parting on his approach, like the Red Sea before the Israelites. After a while, he became more accustomed to its behaviour, relaxing his whole body and allowing his legs to glide smoothly over the terrain. As usual, it was a wonderful feeling. To Charlie, running was one of life's great pleasures. A sense of achievement to start the day on the right note.

Within a few minutes, he had covered the farm lane and was soon pulling away from the firm surface to tackle the grass of the riverbank. The fog appeared even thicker here, coming and going in gushing waves. At times, he was forced to slow down as he hit a particularly bad patch. Cutting his stride, he bowed his head to concentrate on the ground immediately at his feet. Once safely past and his confidence restored, he lengthened his stride again to eat the new ground with each calculated pace.

Chapter 4

"Don't get lost," David said with a touch of humour as he encouraged Tammy through a sizeable gap under the bottom rung of the old style. Once clear, she was away, immediately dropping her haunches over a patch of decaying ferns before disappearing completely into the gloomy undergrowth.

He had been running seriously for twenty-five minutes and was now relaxing as he idled for a while to collect his thoughts. Perched astride the top rung of the stile, his legs dangling loosely, he surveyed the misty panorama with a tinge of trepidation. Allowing his eyes to judge the conditions, he was aware that since approaching the river, the fog had grown much worse, its thick layers seemingly clamping themselves to the vegetation in all directions. Visibility was now down to only a few metres in places. To add to this, it was freezing, the glacially cold air biting at his exposed cheeks with little sympathy. Isolated by the elements and void of any noise, it was a strange eerie sensation, like being a deep-sea diver lost and alone on the bed of an ocean.

Wrapped up in these thoughts, a shiver running down his spine prompted a decision to move on. He had been resting longer than he had intended and his legs were beginning to stiffen. It was time to make for home. In one easy movement, he lifted his trailing leg over the stile and jumped lightly to the ground. The cooked breakfast Rachel had promised was now his main incentive. A pleasant thought of giving her a quick ring and hearing her voice was warm in his mind but he decided she may still be sleeping and he did not want to wake her.

"Here, girl," he called to Tammy through the gloom, her tell-tale brushing of the bushes confirming she was close by. When she finally appeared, like a phantom from the mist, her eyes were fired with a certain awareness, her tongue lolling casually from the side of her opened jaws. No sooner had she reached him than she was up on her back legs in her traditional greeting, her dirty paws resting on his chest. He noticed her nose was embroidered with scraps of dirt.

"Where have you been?" he questioned her in a companionable tone. "Chasing rabbits, by the look of you."

Her tail wagged freely as he brushed the particles away. Once done, she dropped to the ground, took one look behind her as if she could not be parted from her new found pleasure any longer and strode off back into the mist, disappearing in a couple of steps. David had to smile at her carefree manner.

Now his turn to make a move, it was only a few paces before he was back in his stride, soon finding the economical rhythm he was confident he could maintain until his return to the cottage.

How he loved running, the cold air hitting his face, the ease of his movement as he eat the ground. He often wondered if he would have taken it up so seriously if not for Natalie's illness. Watching her condition gradually deteriorating had a strange effect on him so that he started to crave his morning runs as a therapeutic retreat from the life he was witnessing. Up until then, he had always kept himself reasonably fit with the occasional jog around the park when the feeling took him. He had tried a fitness course at the local gym but the strict indoor regime of weights, cycling and rowing machines had never appealed, especially when compared to the freedom and advantages of the outdoors.

In the beginning, he had taken it fairly gently, just jogging for a mile or two, often three or four times a week, but as time passed, he found that he wanted more. Often, he would force himself on, pushing his body beyond the pain barriers, the aching in his chest at times almost unbearable. Yet, he persevered, mentally setting himself fresh targets at each outing, sometimes a lengthy sprint at the end, or a greater distance. Much to his delight, his body responded willingly, offering a little more with every effort. After six months, he could run a good five miles at pace with little strain. The pleasure he derived from this achievement was immeasurable.

In time, he bought himself a stopwatch, thus adding a further dimension to his newfound passion. Delighted with the results as he gradually eroded his best times, he would increase the distance so that on weekends he was achieving ten miles or more. He was amazed at just how quickly his strength and stamina improved. The more training he put in, the easier it had become. Much to his delight, he found he could run with comfort for longer distances at speed and still sprint over the last three or four hundred metres.

With luck, he would be home in ten minutes. He had chosen the lower path beside the river in preference to his regular route along the crest of the flood bank, believing it would be less exposed and therefore, more friendly in the tricky conditions now prevailing. Within a few strides, he wondered whether he had made the right decision. The ground had become badly rutted by the weather with deep furrows moulded into the earth by the draining rainwaters. Every few metres tufts of long grass protruded dangerously from the soil, intermingling with the surfacing roots of the various willow trees that grew in profusion along the bank. The morning frost added a further hazard to the treacherous terrain.

Now concentrating at every step, he was forced to slow down to a walk at several points, his only distraction being the rhythmical crunching of his heavy steps on the frozen ground underfoot. Occasionally, he would raise his sleeve to the corners of his eyes to clear his vision as the wind whipped a continuous stream of tears down his cheeks.

Yet, despite the elements and the accompanying difficulties, he felt content with his decision to tackle the morning as he had. He only hoped Rachel felt the same. At best, she may still be sleeping, he surmised.

With only the long bank and a mile of farm lane to negotiate, he felt secure in the belief that he would be home very shortly.

It was then, out of nowhere, a bloodcurdling cacophony of frenzied animal noises assaulted his ears. He froze mid-stride, his action killed by the sheer reaction of his startled senses. Guttural sounds of the most horrific intensity issued from the shrouds of fog, enhanced by the no less savage implications of physical contact as the dying vegetation gave way to the crushing might of heavy bodies thrashing against the ground. It was the most horrendous and chilling sound he had ever heard: like the death throes of some ravening monster issuing from the soundtrack of a terrifying horror movie. Occasionally, amid the pandemonium, he could just make out the distressed yelps of Tammy. It sent a cold shiver down his spine.

"Tammy," he yelled without thinking, his voice quivering with anxiety as he rushed forward in blind terror towards the sounds of combat.

He had taken no more than a dozen paces when his foot caught a clump of weeds, throwing him off balance, so that his legs splayed wildly beneath him. In correcting his movements, he had taken his eyes from the path ahead. Carried by his own momentum, he looked up, just too late to avoid the hanging branch of the tree which struck him heavily on his forehead knocking him with some force to the ground. Dazed but conscious, he lay still for just a few moments until the sounds of conflict again focused his mind. Without a thought for his own condition, he was back on his feet. Disorientated, he staggered forward blindly, still confused by the pandemonium of activity that appeared so close.

Almost immediately, without warning, the ground evaporated under him, throwing him forward. His legs jellied. For a split second, he sensed he was flying through the air, the shiny blackness before him rapidly apparent as he hit the water. The icy impact quickly restored his senses so that he was aware of the current grabbing at him and carrying him along with some force. At first, he thrashed his arms about in wild abandon before breaking into a more subdued breaststroke. Although he could see very little, he sensed the current was tugging him to the centre of the river.

Telling himself to stay calm, he changed direction and swam towards the bank, already aware that the coldness of the water was drawing the strength from him. The tide was strong and appeared to be rising fast. On reaching the bank, he attempted to pull himself from the water but the sheer steepness of the slippery sides offered little opportunity. His fingers dug into the mud but drew away helplessly as he applied the weight of his body. After several attempts, he was exhausted. Realising he was growing weaker, he felt at any moment he would faint.

At the mercy of the current, he feared for his life when, out of the mist, the sight of a fallen tree, its branches dangling loosely in the water, offered some hope of survival. Carried towards it, he could see a branch just riding above the water level. As he struck it, he threw all his remaining energy into lifting himself up. He partly succeeded, so that his chest and upper torso were now clear of the water with his legs still dangling.

For a moment, he enjoyed the temporary relief, a moment to collect his senses, but aware at the same time, the rise of the tide would not be far away.

Terrified by the situation he found himself in, he looked about for some sign of escape. It appeared that the branch supporting him had partly broken from the bole of the main tree close to the ground so that it hung with little strength above the water. Three or four metres from the bank, it appeared to be his only option. He would have to clamber along it if he could. He just had to try.

Summonsing all his strength, he reached out the length of his arms, grabbed the underneath of the branch and pulled with every last ounce of energy in his body. It lifted him sufficiently so that his legs were now clear of the water. Totally exhausted, he lay still, unable to do more at this stage until his body recovered.

At this moment, he remembered his phone. If he could only lift it out of his pocket and call Rachel, maybe she would be able to send help. He prayed it would still work after being immersed in the water. With difficulty, he rolled over slowly so that he was now lying on his back. Painfully, he moved his hand to his side and slipped it down to his pocket. Numb from the cold, he had little feeling. He pushed his fingers into the pocket and tried with difficulty to grip the phone. Gradually, he eased it out until it was free and in his hand. Carefully, he drew it up to his face.

Once at eye level, he held it with both hands and felt for the buttons. As he was about to push the first digit, the phone slipped from his grasp. He grabbed for it as it slid across his body. Feebly, he made contact but his lifeless hands were useless as he watched it drop off his chest, hit the branch and bounce into the water to vanish immediately. Panic-stricken, he felt desperate at the loss.

It was then he thought he heard noises from the bank. Patiently, he listened. Was it a human cough or similar throaty utterance? It definitely sounded like it. Although difficult to judge in the desperate conditions prevailing, he thought he caught a glimpse of a slight movement along the bank. It was enough to raise his hopes.

"Help," he yelled in a voice so weak that he was not sure that it had left his throat. He repeated it immediately, with much more force. He waited for a reaction but none came. His last thought, before a deep blackness suffused his brain, was the certainty of death.

***

It didn't take long for Sean Nolan to realise the day was likely to be a lot tougher than he had imagined. As soon as he could find a safe passage off the exposed higher ground and on to the flood plain, he took it. Although the new path was a little more protected from the wind, it was still unbearably cold, so cold that it was penetrating the several layers of clothing he had considered adequate for the conditions.

Within half a mile, he felt tired. So it was, when he came to a large tree with several of its branches drooping close to the ground, he found one that provided a temporary seat where he could take a short rest. No sooner had he pulled out an old handkerchief and dabbed his eyes than he was startled by the fierce sounds of a dog fight some distance ahead. Wild, aggressive, brutal Castro was on the attack. He sensed it straight away, so that he jumped up and broke the fog hastily in the direction of the rumpus. He had only taken a few steps when he was aware of the unmistakable sound of a loud and emphatic splash ahead as if a heavy bulk had hit the water. With it, the fury of conflict instantly ceased. He stepped up his pace as best he could.

A further twenty metres and his breathing caught up with him. He had moved too fast and wished he hadn't. With his hands on his hips and wheezing uncontrollably, he bent forward in surrender to the pain that racked his chest. In this state, he was attracted by a noise from the murky depths of the river. Only faintly at first but gradually increasing in volume, it was the sound of an animal frantically paddling in the water. You could hear it snuffling and gasping for breath as it forced its way towards the bank and climbed the side. After a short moment of suspense, Castro's head appeared over the ledge and with little effort, he pulled himself up to the path. Water was dripping freely from his stocky body. Without pausing, he shook himself violently, so close to Sean he felt the spray hit his cheek.

"What have you done?" Sean questioned him as he noticed a fleck of blood on his left ear. He bent down to inspect it, only to find it wiped off easily between his fingers leaving no wound on the dog whatsoever.

"Looks as if you came off best with whatever it was you had the fight with," he addressed Castro. Only seconds later, out of nowhere, what sounded like a human voice, weak and quivering, came so softly to him from the direction of the river that he was not even sure he had heard it. He felt suddenly alarmed. *Was it a strange spook of nature,* he asked himself, with the river whispering its presence so close on one side, the spread of the willow above and all around, the restless fog, seemingly creeping closer, filling every nook and cranny.

When it came again, just a little stronger, he had no doubt. Shocked but inquisitive, he moved warily towards the bank, clambering clumsily under a low branch to reach the nearest point where he considered it safe to stand. From here, looking out towards the river, the glassy movement of the water caught his attention as it glided under the branches of the tree. He raised his hand to his rheumy old eyes and rubbed the sockets gently to clear his watery vision.

Through the veil of mist that surfaced ahead, he could just make out the form of a body, a man by the look of it, lying across a fallen branch of the tree that was dangling in the river. He appeared to be staring in his direction but there was no movement. Squinting, he looked again, his attention drawn to the rising water level which seemed to be almost upon the body.

For a moment, Sean gave the matter some thought, his mind temporarily disturbed by the unexpected dilemma before him. His deliberations were, however, short-lived.

"Come on, boy, let's get away from this. No concern of ours," he said grimly to Castro who was again preening himself after his soaking. The dog pulled himself from his task and was soon lumbering with careless strides along the path as Sean followed.

Within minutes, Sean had dismissed the situation from his conscience. The police would have got involved and that was definitely a no-go, he told himself. The man was probably dead by now. Besides, he had a job to do and at least a further two miles to cover before he reached Wisbech.

Chapter 5

Finally, Charlie reached the stile, one of the few landmarks he was familiar with. In three easy movements, he was over it, jumping clear and already running as he started his ascent of the steep grassy bank that followed. It was slippery and treacherous but his trainers found sufficient purchase to allow him to climb comfortably. By the time he reached the top, he was blowing hard but still felt full of running. Within a few strides, his heart had settled to the easier terrain of the level higher bank. The path was much narrower here, falling away on both sides, to the river plain on his left and the farmland on his right. He restrained himself to take more care.

It was at this time he was aware of dogs barking excitedly in the distance. Muffled by the fog, the sound was almost imperceptible and he dismissed it immediately.

He was amazed at how good he felt, his breathing relaxed and controlled. It was at times like these that he would find himself reminiscing on those wonderful years of the past when he was king of the track, the crowd's adulation ringing in his ears as he performed some miraculous sprint along the final straight to collect one of his many Championships. With these thoughts egging him on, he lengthened his stride, increasing his pace for some fifty metres in a flush of enthusiasm, that was, until his heart reminded him he was not the young man of old. Dismissing his fantasies, he quickly dropped back to a more sensible pace.

What happened next took him by surprise, so much so that his thoughts were instantly frozen. Seemingly, out of nowhere, a dog barked so close and hysterically, it gave him the feeling it was upon him. He came to an immediate standstill, his senses razor sharp as he expected an attack of some sort. Around him, all was still, only the freezing fog, floating aimlessly before him, showed any signs of movement. He waited, his mind openly alert as he probed the stillness for another indication of the animal's whereabouts. Nearby, there was some movement in the undergrowth. He was not sure what to expect. Long seconds passed but nothing appeared. With his patience ebbing, he decided to change tack.

"Hello," he said, almost in a whisper, feeling slightly stupid as he addressed the wall of fog in front of him. With no response, he then whistled in the hope of a better reaction. He sensed that whatever it was, it was still present.

Suddenly, as if by magic, the fog seemed to clear close by, so rapidly that Tammy appeared before him like a ghost. A frantic apparition of activity, she bounded towards him. He was not sure whether she was going to attack and prepared himself to respond, marking her snout as a target for his trainer should she make the attempt.

But she stopped, just in front of him, her eyes staring wildly, before breaking into a series of frenzied pirouettes. Jumping up and down and prancing about, to Charlie, it seemed an act of madness. She looked bedraggled, her wet coat clinging to her skin. Just below her left eye, he noticed a nasty wound. It looked raw, the blood still trickling down her snout only serving to enhance her image of insanity. All the time, she was barking so loudly he feared it would split his eardrums.

"Good dog. What's wrong?" he asked in an effort to calm her. It seemed to have the opposite effect, her excitement only increasing.

He had little experience of dogs or their mannerisms. His father had had two on the farm but they had been kept outdoors in a kennel and he had shown little interest in their welfare.

He moved towards her and she quickly spun away, taking just a few steps before turning to face him, at the same time refocusing her eyes to his. He moved towards her for the second time and again she reacted in the same way, enticing him forward, just a few steps at a time. Once more and the penny finally dropped. At last, he had cottoned on to her demands. She wanted him to follow her.

There was such gravity in her behaviour, a wild intoxication of anxiety and frustration he felt sure something was amiss.

"Come on then, show me," he challenged, moving towards her with purpose. Tammy didn't need a second prompt. She was away, disappearing from his sight in a flash. Charlie ran forward in pursuit, blindly searching in her wake for the direction she had taken. Cautiously, he followed the path along the top of the bank, his senses honed for a clue to her whereabouts. Floundering in the depths of the fog, he tried to keep calm but frustration soon got the better of him.

"For Christ's sake, where are you?" he yelled fiercely.

Descending the steep bank could be tricky, he soon realised. He was not sure how slippery it had become with the morning frost clearly a problem. Leaning backwards and bending his legs at the knees allowed him to keep his balance. Slowly at first, he took each step before allowing himself to move more freely. A few steps and he worked out that planting his heels into the tufts of grass was the safest way to stay on his feet. Finally, he reached the flood plain. Conditions here were unfortunately no better. A combination of uneven ground, decaying vegetation and long grass forced him to move slowly. Only Tammy's continuous barking some way ahead kept him focused in the right direction.

A desire to solve the mystery of this enticing dog's behaviour was now the carrot that had him hooked. He was determined to stick with it, whatever was asked of him. At this point, Tammy's barking seemed louder and more intense, giving him the feeling that maybe the chase was coming to an end. Just when he was about to stop and take stock of his whereabouts, she appeared just a few metres ahead, staring straight at him, her face keen and intelligent.

Without hesitation, he moved towards her and once again, she disappeared before his eyes. In the hushed silence that now followed, he sensed they were close to the river and cautioned himself to take more care. The atmosphere carried with it a certain deadliness, an aura of menace and mystery.

In response to his apprehensions, her barking returned with a vengeance. Far more agitated than her previous bouts, she was going at it non-stop, a certain gravity apparent in her pitch.

He sensed the outcome could be imminent as a large tree took shape before him, its vast branches breaking from the mist like a huge predatory bird of prey. It was here Tammy was holding court. Standing high on the lower branches of the tree, her back to him, she was barking furiously at something in the river.

As he closed in on her, for the first time, she didn't run away. The branches of the tree dipping into the river were so deeply entwined, both on the ground and above, that he had difficulty in reaching her. Ducking under one branch and then another, he finally drew up to her side, running his hand across her back in a gesture of friendship as he did so. Only when she moved was he aware of the seriousness of her plight.

"Bloody hell," he swore impulsively, his eyes popping from his head at the sight of a track-suited body resting precariously on the branch of the tree some distance from the bank. What was even more alarming was the sight of the rising tide lapping only inches below the comatose figure.

"Hello, can you hear me?" he shouted in a fit of panic, hoping for some sign of life but there was no response.

Aware of the perilous state of the situation, he rushed forward. Pushing Tammy to one side, he grabbed a loose branch for support as he made his move along the holding branch over the water. Taking one step at a time, he nudged slowly forward checking his balance at every stage before taking the next. Gradually, he had eased his way along until he was only a couple of metres short of the body. At this point, the situation was more difficult. There were no branches to aid his balance.

Falling to his knees, he decided this last phase had to be undertaken with greater care. Stretching his arms forward to take his weight and then drawing his knees forward one at a time, he crawled unsteadily along the branch. There was barely enough room for both his knees side by side. The dark glaze of the water gliding swiftly past so close was awesome. Ignoring it as best as he could, he concentrated on each move.

Half a dozen and he was almost within touching distance. The face was turned towards him. For the first time, he could clearly see he was a male, quite young, middle twenties, was his assessment. The face looked completely drained of any colour. What with his hair, wet and dishevelled, plastered untidily to his head, he looked a sorry sight. He had doubts as to whether he was alive.

He was lying on his back, cradled by several smaller branches, all connected to the major one he had descended. It looked as if he had pulled himself up from the water and presumably passed out.

Once he had reached the body, he was eager to check whether he was alive. Moving in close, he lowered his ear to the man's mouth in the hope of catching some sign of his breathing. He was immediately rewarded with just the slight feathery wisp of a sound giving him hope that his actions had not been in vain.

"Thank God," he mouthed to himself

Now came the biggest challenge. Somehow, he had to pull him along, keeping balanced on the branch. He could only do this by standing up, which he did, with some care. Steadying himself before reaching for the man's arm, he bent down and gripped the right hand in his two. Shocked at first at how cold it felt, he prepared himself for the first phase. Pulling as gently as he could, he was surprised at how easy it was. Just a few inches but nevertheless, it was proof that, with care, the manoeuvre was possible.

Once more, he gripped the hand and pulled, drawing the body with him as he eased backwards just one more calculated step. Again and again, he executed the same movements, pausing after each one, until he was halfway towards the bank. Here, he took a breather, allowing himself a few moments of respite to relax his muscles. From time to time, the water licking at the branch created a sucking noise, chilling his nerves. On the bank, he could see Tammy watching his moves hawk-like, pacing backwards and forwards, and barking at him from time to time in frustration.

"All right, girl," he told her. "Will be with you very soon, hopefully."

Satisfied with events so far, he took a few deep breaths before applying himself to what he hoped was the final instalment, at least as far as the rescue from the river was concerned. Using the same strategy, just a short shuffle each time, with the utmost care it took only a few moves to reach the bank. No sooner was he there than Tammy was upon them, licking the man's face so enthusiastically he had to push her away.

"You'll kill him with love, girl, if you're not careful," he told her in fun. The tail wagged in response. For the first time, he tried to examine the wound below her eye but she shied away fiercely each time his hand drew near. *At least, the blood looked to have gelled,* he noted with some satisfaction.

Feeling the firm ground underfoot was a relief but he soon realised he was about to face his next challenge. After the twists and turns of following Tammy, he was lost as to his whereabouts. Presumably, if he followed the river, he would come to the stile by the farm lane but he could not remember whether there were any houses close by. Then, of course, there was the flood bank to negotiate. If he left the man here and went for help, he was not sure he could find him again with any certainty, especially in current conditions.

What's more, there was the man's health to consider. He looked terrible. His face now a deathly pallor and the eyes, sunken so deeply in their sockets, gave the impression that life was slowly draining from them. It was obvious he was in need of urgent medical attention. If the fog was not bad enough, there was now the fog of confusion to deal with. Should he leave him here and go for help alone, or should he attempt to carry him, at least to the farm lane.

He sighed inwardly, facing, as he was, a decision that could make the difference between life and death.

He cursed not carrying his mobile phone but it was a habit he had adopted many years ago when the pace of his business had been more frantic. The remoteness and solitude of his runs were an ideal antidote to the pressures of everyday life, a feeling of freedom from the troubles of the world whilst he was enjoying himself doing what he loved best.

There was no let up from the grip of the fog. Wreathes of it still surrounded them with visibility a little more than a few metres.

A sudden tinge of cramp in his right calf encouraged him back on his feet. He stretched his toes painfully before the spasm subsided. Tammy came again to her master's side and stood over him. With a look of anguish, she gently nuzzled the side of his face.

"What shall we do, girl?" Charlie asked her earnestly, her ears stiffening in response.

What came next was a blessing in many ways, the man coughed harshly, a raw chesty exhalation that confirmed his desperate condition. With his eyes still closed tightly, his lips started to twitch. He murmured something. Just a few weak incoherent sounds and then he went quiet again as if the effort had tired him.

If nothing else, it had the effect of firing Charlie. Abruptly, he made up his mind as to his course of action. Placing his arms under the man's back and legs, he snatched him from the ground in one momentous lift. Staggering to catch his balance, he straightened up, letting the breath flood from his body with the effort. He inhaled sharply several times before making a move.

It took just a few steps to realise the monumental task that lay ahead, each one a raw demand on his strength and energy. With the man in his arms, he moved unsteadily, taking each step with caution. After fifty metres, he was forced to stop, his arms feeling as if they were being pulled from their sockets. For a brief moment, he contemplated lowering him to the ground but his fear was that if he did, he would not have the strength to lift him again. Resigned to continue, he took several deep breaths and then staggered on, his chest aflame with his tortured breathing.

Hugging the bank, he continued very slowly before changing direction and moving away from the river. It was a mere whim, he was really trusting fate to lead him from this nightmare.

When he slipped only seconds later, a feeling of desolation overcame him. Under the severest of pressure, his strength was rapidly flagging, a surrender to the weariness of his body imminent. He came to a halt, gasping for the breath his lungs demanded. The need to release his load was almost too strong to ignore.

With a mammoth sigh, his eyes fell to the face of the young man whose life was in his hands. It was a strong face, he mused, with a promise of good breeding and dignity despite his current apathetic state. Just for a moment, his mind played havoc with him, his thoughts throwing up the memories of what he considered to be the blackest day of his life. It was the day his son, Daniel, only eighteen months old, had passed away.

For the umpteenth time in his life, he wondered what the lad would have looked like, should he have lived. He imagined him at twenty-eight, tall and handsome, maybe something like the man in his arms. It was these thoughts that strengthened his commitment.

Staggering forward again, almost immediately his prayers for some sort of relief were answered when the dark outline of the flood bank emerged from the veil of fog. A dirt track to the left caught his eye and he made for that. Once there and facing the steep bank before him, he knew climbing it in his current condition, with the man in his arms, was an impossibility. He had to be sensible. Spent of energy, he lowered the man to the ground.

Convinced that he must now be close to the farm lane and hopefully, houses and people, the only sensible move was to leave the man and go for help. He was pleased to see Tammy had taken up sentry duty next to her master, stretching out lethargically beside the static body. Hopefully, she would stay with him. She could be a huge asset in finding the place again on his return.

"Well done, girl, look after your master until I get back," he told her, "I won't be too long." Tammy looked up to him and whimpered, the hint of sadness in her eyes clearly visible. She watched him go, following his every move until he finally vanished from sight.

Chapter 6

Rachel awoke calmly from a pleasant sleep, her mind still active with the potency of her exquisite dreams. She had imagined herself walking hand in hand with David along a white sandy beach, the sun shining brightly in a pastel blue sky and the surf breaking calmly around their bare feet in a creamy froth.

With a deep breath, she came fully awake, immediately feeling the bed for the warmth of the man she soon realised was not there. She stretched her arm out and as she did so, her hand touched a mug on the bedside cabinet. Her hand circled it. It was cold. She had obviously slept for some time. Raising herself from the duvet and stuffing two pillows behind her back, she caught sight of a note alongside the mug. Smiling to herself, she unfolded it. What she read gave her a deep thrill.

Taking Tammy for a walk. Won't be long. Looking forward to your breakfast. Love you, Dave xxx.

She read it twice more in quick succession. For the first time in a long while, she thought her life was taking shape. Loving David had come so naturally and with such an intensity that she had quickly dismissed her two previous relationships as mere infatuations.

In a moment of reflection, she pondered briefly on the fateful circumstances that had drawn David and her so miraculously together. If she had not fallen for the charms of Tony Southern, her previous boyfriend, she would not have left her family in Tunbridge Wells three years ago, at the age of nineteen. Together, they had made the move to Cambridgeshire as part of a promotion he had been offered with his company.

She had found it difficult to settle at first but had persevered for Tony's sake to try and make a go of it. They were happy and it appeared to be working, that was until she came home one afternoon to find him in bed with a cute little sixteen-year-old from his office. She had been devastated.

Her immediate reaction had been to run home to her parents. Fortunately, she had stopped herself, steadied herself in fact, quickly aware in going home she would be saying goodbye to the newfound lifestyle she was then relishing, an independence she valued more than she could have imagined.

By the morning of the following day, she was already chasing the local estate agents for rental properties in the county but a safe distance from Tony. By the afternoon of the same day, she had settled on a comfortable little flat in Wisbech, a pretty market town known as the Capital of the Fens.

She found herself sharing with Vanessa, a girl with a sparkling personality and a verve for life that left you breathless. For almost a year, most evenings were spent chatting into the early hours of the morning and nearly every weekend was filled with a party of some kind. Finally though, she realised her new lifestyle was changing her personality. She was drinking too much and had even started to smoke in company, a habit she had previously detested. At first, she excused her behaviour as a social function, a part of growing up. Deep down, she knew she was not really happy with herself in this new climate and again, thoughts of returning to her parents and the other life of coveted security, began to tug at her emotions.

For some reason, she blamed her job for her then melancholic moods. Her work as a trainee accounts clerk in a firm of electrical fitters no longer satisfied her ambitions. It had become stale and boring. What she needed was a more demanding challenge, something interesting that would test her capabilities more fully.

She smiled bemusedly to herself as she remembered reading David's advert in the local paper for an office manager and nursery administrator. There was something about its simplicity that appealed to her then current mood.

Nervous but confident at the interview, she was soon aware David was struggling more than her. His rouged complexion, the beads of perspiration on his brow and the continuous amount of *ums* between sentences gave her the impression that he was on unfamiliar ground as an interviewer. After a while, she found herself wanting to make his job easier and assist him with his ordeal.

Once they were over the business side of the questioning, she saw a rapid change come over him. As he relaxed, the conversation moved on to more personal subjects, his love for sport, films, books he had read and, of course, his son. It was then she saw his true personality. When his eyes lit up as he digressed on some private story and followed it with an engaging smile, she had to admit she found him adorably handsome.

A distinct shriek of '*Yes*' from the adjoining bedroom brought her reminiscences to an abrupt halt. She imagined Tom had achieved another maximum score on his computer game and no doubt they would be hearing about it later.

Buoyed by a feeling of deep happiness, she jumped out of bed and made for the bathroom. In no time, she had showered and dressed. She wished she had some fresh clothes to wear but told herself you can't have everything. Life was good. Before leaving the room, she tidied the duvet and picked the note off the cabinet, reading it one final time before popping it into her handbag.

Once in the kitchen, it didn't take her long to find her way around. She switched the television on, flicked through the channels, and settled on a programme displaying the work of shepherds and their dogs in the north of Scotland. Anything to do with the country and the outdoor spaces, always interested her. She watched for a few minutes before concentrating on the task at hand. Opening the fridge door, she was amazed at the quantity of food in stock. A reasonably large fridge, it was filled to capacity. Had it been David's intention for her to stay the night right from the start, she wondered with a bemused smile.

A quick glance at her watch told her it was twenty to nine. She could not be sure of when she had fallen asleep but thought it must have been about half past seven. He could be back at any time, she surmised contentedly.

The fry-up would only take twenty minutes so she would wait for his return before starting. In the meantime, she placed six rashers of bacon under the cold grill, diced the mushrooms and put them in the frying pan with the sausages. She would add the tomatoes later and finish off with two eggs apiece. She was cooking for her man and his son, and she was determined to excel herself.

She soon found herself humming to a familiar tune on the television, one she had always liked, but had not heard for some time. She could not remember feeling happier in her life.

Another fifteen minutes passed and she was beginning to fret a little over David's return, especially considering the conditions outside. She had looked through the window a couple of minutes ago and thought it was getting worse if anything. To help settle her mind, she made herself a cup of coffee and sat sipping it whilst watching the news which had just started.

Only when the face of a young German boy came on the screen was her attention fully focused. He had been rescued from under twenty foot of snow after being buried for two days. The accident, in the Alps, was described as the worst avalanche tragedy ever. Interviewed by a reporter, the young lad, only eight years old, looked so excited, so vivacious, she was immediately captured by his spirit.

At this moment, Tom entered the kitchen. Rachel looked up. "Good morning, young man," she said as brightly as she could.

Closing the door behind him, he strutted in an arrogant fashion across the room between her and the television, his eyes set straight ahead, not the merest indication from him that he was aware of her presence. As if the electric current had been tripped, a tenseness descended on the room, an atmosphere so thick you could almost touch it.

It was as if she didn't exist. She felt embarrassed, awkward and would gladly have ignored him, but she couldn't. If David and she were to be together, she had to win this battle and it may take time.

"Does your dad always go running for this length of time?" she asked.

Without checking, he continued his passage to the fridge, opened the door, pulled a carton of orange juice from the door shelf and moved to the cupboards where he withdrew a large glass and filled it almost to the top.

"He said he would be back about half eight," he mumbled, without looking up.

"What time did he go out?" she asked.

"About half past seven." The tone of his voice was devoid of any warmth. With the glass in his hand, he passed her again and made for the door.

"I'm doing a fry-up for breakfast when your dad gets back." She found herself raising her voice in frustration as he disappeared out of the room. She may just as well have spoken to herself.

Chapter 7

Released from his burden, Charlie climbed the bank wilfully. Close to collapsing, he knew he had to somehow keep the adrenaline pumping, feeding his body with the impulse it badly needed. By the time he reached the top, he was breathing heavily with the effort. Never had he valued keeping himself in good shape more than he did at this moment in time.

Only a few metres on and the old stile was a welcomed sight as it appeared murkily from the gloom. Clambering over it with little of the ease he had given it on the outward journey, he had finally reached the farm lane.

Looking ahead, the scene was bleak, yet he felt sure there were houses somewhere as the road branched away from the bank. He could not remember how far. He attempted to run but his legs wouldn't let him. Instead, he slogged along, trying to lift his leaden feet with every step as he tacked from side to side, his mind fuzzy and unfocused.

Finally, he caught sight of a faint glare ahead, just off the lane to the left. At first, it appeared as a mere pinprick peeping sullenly from the grey surrounds but grew stronger on his approach, eventually throwing its illumination over the walls of an old cottage. One by one, various elements of the property emerged from the surrounds. The front garden looked forlorn, both plants and weeds long dead under the icy winter onslaught.

But to Charlie's tortured brain, it was like a beacon, a greeting of warmth and hope that could release him from the traumas of the current situation. The gate gave way easily under his body weight as he fell against it and staggered up the path, his legs crippled with fatigue.

At the weathered door now facing him, he pushed the bell button down firmly twice in quick succession. Inside the house, the rings echoed warmly. Long seconds became minutes in his mind as he tried to be patient, tried to relax as far as his condition would allow him. He felt shattered, his body completely exhausted.

"Surely, someone must be at home?" he said aloud in a pugnacious tone, at the same time pressing the bell button again so viciously it rang with a monotonous continuity. For a moment, he feared the worse but then a faint movement from within gave him some hope. There was the soft shuffling of someone approaching the door.

"Hold on, I'm coming," a deep male voice called out with measured calmness. At the same time, he could hear a bolt being noisily released.

The door opened to reveal a bespectacled old man, in his eighties, Charlie guessed, his head almost bald, with a smattering of liver spots that reclined noticeably on his shiny scalp. The friendly smile that had at first greeted him dispersed rapidly through the phases of welcome, surprise and awe. Later that day, he was to wonder just what an appearance he had presented to warrant such a reaction. The man's eyes surveyed him in total disbelief, all the time his mouth agape.

"Please help me," Charlie pleaded, leaning on the door jamb for support as a bout of dizziness nearly brought him to his knees. The old man rushed to his assistance, grabbing his arm and levering him up before guiding him forward into the warmth of his hallway.

"This way," he said positively, taking the first door on his right which opened up to a cosy lounge. For a few moments, Charlie was unaware of anything, his head swimming in a kaleidoscope of frantic patterns. The warmth of the open fire hit him like a furnace, only adding to his distress. He felt his legs start to buckle.

"Right, sit down here," the old man said, standing over a well-worn settee, "and I will go and fetch you a glass of water." To Charlie, the words seemed fluffy and distant like an echo. He sagged gratefully into the comfort of the awaiting seat.

When the man returned a few minutes later, a glass of water in his hand, Charlie was perched on the front of the settee, his legs spread wide with his head resting forward, supported by his hands. The old man tottered forward holding the glass with his arm outstretched.

"Here you are, drink this and you will hopefully feel better," he said with sympathetic charm. Charlie sipped it slowly, immediately feeling some relief as the wave of nausea began to recede. It took him just a few minutes to recover. Once back in command of his faculties, the plight of his young man was again his priority.

"Thank you," he addressed the old man, forcing a wisp of a smile to his lips. "But it's not me who needs help. I pulled a man from the river. He's unconscious and needs medical attention. Can I use your phone please?" There was an urgency in Charlie's voice that set the old man's heart racing.

"Shall I phone for you?" he asked on seeing Charlie's condition.

"That would be great," Charlie replied with some relief. "You will be able to give them better directions than I will. The man is with his dog, just down the bank, the other side of the stile, at the bottom of the road. Hopefully, I will be okay in a few minutes and I will be down there to meet them."

"Right, I'd better get going," said the old boy with a sense of purpose. Hiding the stiffness of his limbs as best he could, he shuffled heavily out of the room.

For a few moments, Charlie took stock of his strength. He felt much better, which was a relief. It was the bullish tones of the old man as he addressed the emergency services that caught his attention. He was all ears as he heard him giving them strict instructions as to the whereabouts and requirements. He had no doubt they would be here as soon as possible.

Returning to the room, the man was all too eager to share his call with Charlie.

"The ambulance is on its way, but the young girl said it may take a while with the fog." The smug look that now adorned his face was confirmation that he was pleased with himself.

"My name's Harry, by the way, Harry Bowater." Charlie took the proffered hand and shook it warmly.

"Thank you so much for all your help, Harry. Mine's Charlie." The handshake was renewed briefly. "Hopefully, together, we have been able to save the life of a young man which will make all our efforts worthwhile."

"I sincerely hope so," Harry said with sincerity.

"And now, I must get back to him."

"Are you feeling better?" Harry asked.

"Yes, I think so," Charlie said as he prepared to leave. Harry followed him to the hallway, holding the door open and waving warmly as he set off down the lane.

Once in the fresh air, Charlie felt a little stronger. Reaching the stile, however, made him realise just how tired he really was. He clambered over it once again and made for the climb up the bank, all the time his heart banging in his ears, knowing at any moment he could be facing the truth of his decision to leave the man. *Did he get it right?* Any moment now, he would know.

By the time he had reached the top, he was puffing freely, but it didn't matter. His stride lengthened as he freewheeled down the far side, almost falling as he collected speed. Mercifully, he stayed on his feet to reach the level ground, his emotions fraught with anxiety as his target came into view. He really didn't know what to expect.

The scene that greeted him was very much as he had left it, Tammy still sitting beside the comatose body of her master. *Was he still alive?* Charlie rushed forward.

On his approach, Tammy jumped up, her tail wagging with prodigious swipes. He fondled her ears briefly on passing before moving quickly to the man. As before, he bent down and listened for his breathing. With relief, he heard the faintest of sounds, so soft that it was barely audible. The emotion struck him at this point, so poignant he felt his eyes welling with the reaction.

He immediately pulled himself together, aware on looking at the young man and the fog still ever present, his task was, by no means, at an end. He decided to return to the road to await the ambulance.

Once there, he was unable to relax. Several times, he walked down the lane and back again before the soft drone of a siren seeped faintly through the fog. At first distant, it rapidly grew more resonant, eventually penetrating the fog with an acute clarity. He watched as the intermittent blue glare of its beacon strengthened to his sight. As it approached, he placed himself in the centre of the lane and waved both his arms frantically above his head. The driver flashed his lights in acknowledgement as he drew to a standstill. Opening his window, he stuck his head out and gave a cheerful smile.

"Good day, sir," he said warmly.

"He's just beyond the stile on the other side of the flood bank," Charlie indicated, pointing his arm in the direction. Charlie moved to one side as the ambulance was manoeuvred smartly off the lane on to the grass.

Wasting no time, the two medics were quickly out of their vehicle; one had a large holdall slung across his shoulder while the other carried a lightweight stretcher. Tensely, Charlie led them beyond the stile and over the flood bank.

"He's in a bad way," Charlie warned them as they climbed the steep bank and descended the far side.

Ignoring Tammy, they rushed straight to the man. In seconds, the younger paramedic, a wiry individual with wispy blond curls cascading over his forehead, had his bag open and a pulse reading was in progress. A series of methodical tests followed, each one performed with strict precision and care. Whilst he was working, his partner, a more sturdy man in his forties, stood behind him, watching attentively, ready to offer assistance should it be required.

The presence of these two professionals had a calming effect on Charlie. For the first time in what seemed an eternity, he felt he could relax and let someone else shoulder the responsibility. As his anguish gradually dissipated, he took a seat on the frozen ground. Oblivious to its icy feel, he realised for the first time just how exhausted he was. Tammy came to him and he did his best to comfort her.

"Hopefully, your master will be okay, old girl," he told her as he roughed the fur around her neck.

It was a good ten minutes before the men completed their work. After lifting their patient off the ground and placing him on the stretcher, the younger one stood up and addressed him.

"He has seriously bad hyperthermia owing to the cold," he explained. "And we need to get him to the hospital pronto. We have given him an injection but it is the hospital care he must have. Are you okay if we leave you?"

"Yes, I'm fine, thank you," said Charlie. "Are you taking him to Kings Lynn?"

"Yes, sir."

With this, they raised the stretcher and walked in measured strides towards the bank, the younger one taking the lead. Tammy immediately rose and was about to follow when Charlie caught hold of her collar.

"Not you, girl, you're staying with us," Charlie told her. Taking note of the situation, the two medics stopped abruptly, the older one turning back to him.

"I found a lead in the chap's pocket," he told Charlie. "I think I've left it where he was lying."

"That's great," Charlie agreed. "I'll go and have a look."

The lead was lying on the grass as the medic had told him. Maintaining a firm hold on Tammy's collar, Charlie slipped the hook into place. He would take her to the police station before making his own way home. He turned to Tammy who was busy preening herself. "Come on, girl, let's get you to the police station." Realising they were on the move, her tail swished her pleasure as she yanked Charlie from his standing position. Immediately, he threw all his weight against her so she came to a sudden halt, her head looking back with an enquiring stare.

"Steady, girl," he told her. "This old man's a little weary at the moment." She seemed to understand and started again at a gentler pace. As he walked her to the police station, his thoughts were buried deeply in the events of the day, a feeling of well-being ever present for his contribution.

Chapter 8

Rachel was finding it impossible to concentrate. With yesterday's paper in front of her, she was browsing the pages with little focus, scanning the headlines of each article and the first two or three lines before moving on to the next. Every few minutes, she would raise her eyes to the clock on the wall. It was now half-past nine, and two hours since David had left. She found it hard to believe he would be running for that length of time, especially as he knew she was here. The cooked breakfast she had promised him just before they went to bed was a further incentive.

And why hadn't he phoned her? She sensed something was seriously wrong.

For the second time in the last half hour, she went to the front door, opened it and stood in the chilly air taking in the eerie scene before her. The fog may have thinned a little, the hedge, the wall and the metal gate at the end of the front garden just appearing faintly. There was no movement, no sound. It was frighteningly calm. She was alert to any noise, praying at any moment she would be rewarded with some small indication of his return, but it was not to be. Returning to the kitchen, she made herself another cup of tea and took a seat by the table.

With her mind freewheeling in a maelstrom of fears and anguish, her imagination was running free. *Perhaps he had been attacked?* She gave it some thought but soon dismissed the idea as she could not imagine any potential thief going out in such conditions, especially in this rural area, with the intention of robbing anyone. Surely, they would go where there were more people? Besides, Tammy was with him and she wouldn't let anyone hurt him.

Maybe he was ill? This seemed a possibility but he was young and in good health so it seemed unlikely. He would phone her in any case.

Another half-hour passed and she could stand it no longer, her nerves were shredded to ribbons. Finally, she picked the phone up and dialled 999. Immediately, a distinct female voice came on the line.

"Do you want police, fire or ambulance?"

"Police, please," she said as calmly as she could. There was a slight pause while she was connected.

"Police, can I help you?" This time it was male.

"Yes, please. My boyfriend left the house two hours ago for a short run and hasn't returned," she told him. "I wondered whether you had received details of any accident in this area."

"Is it possible that he has called in to see somebody or gone off somewhere?" the voice asked.

"No…no, I don't think so. I was going to cook him breakfast and he was coming home to that, so I don't think it's likely that he would have gone elsewhere." She felt slightly foolish with her reply.

"I'll have a check for you, madam. Just hold on a minute."

"Thank you," she said as the phone went quiet. Pressing it against her ear, she was aware of her heart beating a rhythm in her chest. She was not sure whether she wanted a positive or a negative response. Her nerves were at snapping point. After a couple of minutes, the voice returned.

"Hello, there. Well, nothing has been reported in the way of accidents I can tell you. If you would like to leave your number with me, I will let you know if something comes up."

"Thank you, that's very kind," she said before leaving him her mobile number. Once she had turned her phone off, she felt a sense of relief in one respect but alarmed in another. The fact that he had been missing for some time with no attempt at contacting her, as far as she could see, was a major mystery.

By eleven o'clock, she had lost count of the number of cups of tea she had made and partly drank. From the latest one, she had just taken a few sips and it was now standing cold on the table. Lost as to what course of action to take, she felt so helpless.

Tom had come down twice in the last hour on the pretence of collecting another drink but she suspected that he was at last worried about his father's continued absence.

On his last appearance, she had questioned him as to the route his father took when he went running with Tammy.

"As far as I know," he said, for once in a polite tone, "he takes several depending on how long he wants to run." It was of little help. In the circumstances, with the weather so bad and her lack of knowledge of the local geography, she could see no sense in going out to look for him on her own.

Should she phone the police again? She badly wanted to, but felt they would contact her if there was any news. She would give them another half-hour before phoning again.

When the door opened and Tom appeared for the third time, she was almost relieved. He gave her the now familiar sulky stare before dropping his eyes and making for the refrigerator.

"Hello, Tom. What do you think we should do about your dad?" she asked in a serious tone. "It's now over three hours since he went out."

As before, there was no immediate response. He poured himself another orange juice, closed the fridge door and then turned towards her.

"I think we should go out and walk along the lane to the river," he began, as though he had given the matter some thought. "He may be ill and passed out somewhere."

For the first time, she sensed the anguish in his voice. The fact that he was now concerned gave her some comfort. They at least had a common bond, albeit quite fragile she would imagine, but it gave her something to work on.

"Do you have a torch?" she asked as he sat on the chair tightening the laces on his trainers.

"Yes, Dad's got one he keeps hanging up under the stairs. I'll go and get it."

When he returned, he had a thick coat on and was holding a large metal torch in his hand. He flashed it on and off a couple of times to check its efficiency. The beam was wide and strong. She was impressed.

After snatching her mobile from the table, she followed him to the front door, grabbing her coat off the hanger in the hallway on passing. Outside, the sharp chill caught her by surprise. As she had driven her own car to the house the previous evening, a journey taking no more than ten minutes, she had not bothered to wrap up too thoroughly. Shivering beneath her coat, she now wished she had brought her scarf. Fortunately, she had a pair of gloves in the pockets and quickly slipped these on.

The visibility had improved little in the last few hours so that the surrounding fields still appeared as just a blank grey mass, invisible from the farm lane. As they walked steadily to the riverbank, some eight hundred metres on, Tom kept his distance from her, always leading by a couple of metres as she tried with difficulty to close the gap. She found herself breathing quite heavily with the exertion. She kept her annoyance to herself.

Finally, as they reached the bank, Tom came to a halt and turned towards her, his hands pushed into his pockets in a cocky stance as he set out his thoughts.

"We can either stick with the farm lane which follows the river to Wisbech on the left or go over the stile, up the bank, which leads to Guyhirn, on the right," he announced.

"What do you think is the most likely route he would have taken?" she asked. He took a few seconds to consider before replying.

"I don't really know," he said. "But cos it's foggy, he'd probably stick to the lane." It was a sensible decision and she decided to go with it.

"Okay, it's off to the left then," she said with a spark of enthusiasm. For the first time, she took off ahead of Tom but it was not long before he caught and passed her, again keeping his distance to her side. Occasionally, her eyes fell on his silhouette as he strode comfortably before her, his easy youthful movements reminding her of David. She so badly wanted to be his friend, to share a life she knew was so important to his dad.

Twice, she slipped on an icy patch where trickles of water issuing from the bank had frozen. Her shrill cries of shock on both occasions had little effect on Tom who continued walking at a relentless pace.

It was a further half mile before the emergence of another lane joining the bank lane added another possible option to David's route. Rachel sighed in frustration.

"This one services a couple of farms," Tom explained as he changed direction to pick up the new lane. "There is another lane that joins this one which branches off in the direction of our house. I think there's a chance that Dad could have taken this," he said with such conviction she felt she had to go along with it.

Tom raced ahead. After running for a few strides, she caught him up and settled a couple of metres behind. It was then that her mobile warbled into life. She rummaged through her pocket and pulled it out, her finger immediately finding the speak button as she put it to her ear.

"Hello," she said.

"Miss Forbes?"

"Yes, yes," she replied nervously.

"It is Sergeant Allan from the Wisbech Constabulary here. I can tell you that a man has been picked up from the river bank in a state of unconsciousness half an hour ago and has been taken to the Queen Elizabeth Hospital in Kings Lynn."

"Is it David?"

"I'm afraid I know little else but there must be a good chance in the circumstances, madam. I suggest you go to the hospital as quickly as you can."

"Yes," she said shakily. "Thank you."

As she lowered her mobile, an outpouring of relief overcame her, so poignant that the tears flooded from her eyes. At least he was alive. On hearing the sound of Rachel's mobile, Tom had turned and come to her. In her high state of emotion, she threw her arms around him and hugged him to her.

"Your dad's been found and is in the hospital," she said. He wanted to reciprocate her actions but he controlled himself and pulled away in embarrassment.

"We'd better get off to the hospital," he said, rather sheepishly.

"Yes," she replied after her initial reaction but quickly realised there may be bad news to come.

Chapter 9

No sooner had the figure materialised than, without warning, it disappeared before it had taken any distinct form. Almost immediately, it came again, this time more vividly than before, the image sucked from his brain with frightening clarity.

She stood alone under the branches of a tall oak tree, the dappled shadows giving her a mysterious, yet charismatic presence. On the ground around her feet, the bluebells were so thick and lush they appeared as a mist. She was smiling sweetly, the same familiar smile that had captivated him so forcefully when their eyes had met for the first time. It lit her face infectiously.

Wearing the short grey skirt and the blue cotton top she had bought for their engagement celebrations, she looked chic and demure. The boots had been a later accessory. She had treasured the outfit through the years, promising him she would always keep her figure trim so that she could wear it forever. It had held a special place in both their hearts.

A loose lock of fine blond hair straggled her forehead in the slight breeze. She looked so serene, so beautiful that it squeezed his heart with little mercy.

Suddenly, as if summonsed, she took a few steps towards him and came to a halt. She raised the palm of her hand to her mouth and kissed it gently, closing her eyes for a few brief seconds as she did so. Then, turning the hand dramatically towards him, she blew the kiss in his direction. A smile returned to her face, so rich and expressive that it seemed to eclipse her whole being. She raised her hand once more and waved with such tenderness before turning around, and moving slowly away along a path through the surrounding foliage. He watched in fascination, until he could stand it no longer.

"Natalie, don't leave me," he pleaded in an act of despair as he struggled to go after her, but he could not move, his feet seemingly rooted to the ground as if by shackles.

She appeared not to hear him and continued, each step carrying her further away into the distance. Finally, when she reached a ridge where the path fell away behind bushes, she stopped, just briefly and glanced back at him over her shoulder. Her eyes twinkled adoringly as she waved again in his direction. Then she was gone.

"Natalie, Natalie," he yelled like a maniac, surging forward with all his strength. Miraculously, she reappeared as if she had jumped in space, so that she was suddenly right in front of him. She was, however, less clear, her features blurred and indistinct.

"Nat, I love you, please…please don't leave me again," he cried in confusion. She was now so close. He tried to rise, tried to touch her. He made contact. The face was warm and soft, her features suddenly focusing clearly before him. She looked different, her eyes were not as he remembered them, the hair was darker. The features were not hers. He was totally lost. He started to panic and then it hit him. It was not her.

"God," he moaned, in shock, his lips trembling visibly as he closed his eyes and covered them with his hands. It was several seconds before he opened them again, hoping he could recapture the faded image, but somehow, he knew it was gone forever.

The face before him was young, beautiful and smiling but it was not Natalie's. She was bathing his forehead with a cool flannel.

"Where am I?" he asked, scanning the brightly lit room through an overbearing fuzziness.

"You're in a private room at the Queen Elizabeth Hospital in Kings Lynn," the nurse told him. "You have been unconscious for quite some time. Apparently, you fell in the river, and were pulled out by an elderly gentleman who then carried you to a point where you were picked up by an ambulance and brought here. You have been suffering from a bang on the head and hyperthermia as a result of the cold. You are very lucky to be alive, as I understand it."

"I don't remember," David moaned, still struggling to make sense of everything around him. With difficulty, he made a concerted effort to focus his eyes on a chair standing by the door at the foot of his bed. The double image swayed to his initial examination. It scared him at first and he closed his eyes. When he opened them again, the image was stable. Thankfully, he stared at it for a few seconds, all the time his brain recharging as a state of normality gradually returned.

"Everything will come back to you in due course, young man," the nurse said playfully, emphasising the final words with deliberate sloth. She was probably younger than him.

"As I said, you were very lucky, the ambulance men said the guy that rescued you was not young and they were amazed that he was able to carry you."

David was deep in thought for a minute, his head cradled in his hands.

"Do we know who he is?" he asked.

"I don't think so, but I understand he was taking your dog to the police station after the ambulance left him so I would imagine the police will have his details." At the mention of Tammy, David showed renewed interest.

"Is Tammy all right? Where is she?" The nurse had to smile at his rapid recovery, as confusion turned to understanding and the questions began to flow. She gently pushed a thermometer into his mouth whilst dropping lightly on to the edge of his bed. Her hand went up to his forehead.

"I believe she is fine and will be found at the local police station." To make herself more comfortable, she adjusted her position on the bed, leaning over towards him whilst she tidied the sheets and blankets.

Deliberating on the information she had given him, David was still puzzled. With his lips sealed tightly around the thermometer, he could not speak and could only watch her as she fussed around his bed.

Untroubled by his searching gaze, she checked her watch before reaching towards him for the thermometer.

There was no warning for him or her. He felt the surge in his throat at the same time as he panicked, the milky vomit flooding from his mouth in unrelenting spasms. Quick as she was, the first heavy spurt landed just above the hem of her white tunic, the liquid spew running freely down her tights as she leapt for the bowl on the bedside cabinet. In a flash, she had it under his chin, catching the next burst as it left his mouth.

Oblivious to her own predicament and the acrid stench that now filled the room, she calmly reached for a pile of paper towels, pulling one off the top and dabbing his chin with calm efficiency.

"Don't fight it, let it come," she enthused. "You will feel much better afterwards."

He gagged involuntarily, spitting the dregs from his mouth. It was fully ten minutes before the feeling subsided but when it did, he felt better. The nurse offered him a glass of water and he sipped it gratefully. The throbbing in his head was still there but a lot less severe. He felt exhausted. Leaning back on to his pillow, he closed his eyes and drifted into a peaceful sleep.

When he woke again two hours later, he felt a little better. The throbbing in his head was still present but had receded somewhat from its initial intensity. The worst feeling was exhaustion, as though all his strength had been extracted from his body. It was a strange feeling, one that he had never before experienced.

After a few moments of muddled reflection, he pushed himself free of the sheets and sat up. As he did so, the door gaped open and Tom rushed in. Without stopping, he ran forward and threw himself with all his might at his father. His knees landed on the bed, his arms immediately encircling his neck, so tight that he thought he may have to prise them off.

"Dad, are you all right?" he asked in such a serious tone he had to break his hold to look him in the eye. The force of contact had done little for his headache but his show of affection did wonders for his depression.

"Yes, Son, I'm fine…honest." In the eighteen months since his mother had died, he had seen few tears but they were there now, slithering in full view down his cheeks. He pulled Tom to him, kissing his neck and fondly massaging the back of his head with his hand.

"I thought you'd died," he cried pitifully against his neck.

"Takes more than a dip in the river to kill me, Son, don't you fret."

"I love you, Dad."

"Love you too, Son."

As he hugged him even tighter, Rachel came through the door, anxiety etched clearly on her face. Slowly, he raised his hand behind the boy's back and gave her a gentle wave.

"Hello," he said calmly, gesturing her forward.

With Tom in such an obvious state of distress, she felt awkward barging her way towards David. Aware now of Rachel's presence, Tom was not willing to give way.

"Hi there, how are you?" she asked sheepishly as she approached his bed.

"I'll be fine, they tell me. Just a little weak at the moment." Realising Tom was not ready to release his hold, he tapped him on the back of his head with his hand.

"Here, Son, let Rachel have a little room please?" With some reluctance, Tom dropped down off the bed and stood to one side, scowling openly as she moved closer. Under the boy's scrutiny, she could do no more than lean forward and kiss David's cheek like some indulgent aunt. She really wanted to throw herself at him as Tom had done and give him the biggest of hugs, telling him she was so relieved that he was safe, but it did not seem appropriate in the circumstances.

"I was looking forward to your breakfast," he said jovially to break the strained silence that followed. The catch of his eyes reinstated her confidence.

"Yes, I had it all ready," she said smiling openly and taking a deep breath in an effort to restore her calm. "Unfortunately, it's still in the pan as we left in rather a rush." She laughed and he laughed with her.

"Next time, hopefully," he responded with a comforting look.

Conversation flowed with little restraint from then on as each was eager to relate their tale of the day's adventure. Rachel pulled a chair to the bedside and Tom took a seat on the end of the bed, a dour expression set on his face. Occasionally, David tried to draw him into the conversation with a casual question but he showed little enthusiasm, his response being no more than a nod or a couple of words at best. Rachel readily ignored him, channelling her concentration on the questions David was throwing at her, one after the other. After half an hour of continuous chatter, David showed signs of tiring. He yawned helplessly.

"I think I'm going to have to take a rest," he told them as his hand went to his brow. His eyes closed briefly before he forced a smile.

"I'm beginning to feel a little groggy again," he apologised.

"We had better leave and let you get some rest," Rachel told him, rising from the chair, "I'll stay with Tom tonight. The nurse seems to think they may let you home tomorrow so we will come and fetch you as soon as we hear from them."

"I don't need anyone looking after me," Tom chirped up curtly.

"Yes, you do," David cut in, his tone laced with a rare tinge of anger that his son immediately picked up on. He jumped off the bed in a positive huff and made for the door.

"Aren't you going to say goodbye then?" he addressed the boy's retreating back as he flew through the door leaving it to slam with a solid crash.

David looked exasperated and spent.

"I'm sorry," he said wearily, "to put you through this but he's too young to look after himself." His eyes were half closed from the pressure of the head pain that had returned with interest.

"Of course," Rachel told him. "Don't worry, he'll be fine. I'll fix him up some food as soon as we get home." With this, she kissed him fondly on the forehead.

"Love you," she said.

When she reached the door and looked round, she noticed his eyes were already closed.

Chapter 10

When David next awoke, it was seven o'clock in the morning and he had slept a full twelve hours. Outside his room, he sensed a bustle of activity as the ward came alive for an early start.

Once breakfast had been served and eaten, a porter arrived with a wheelchair to take him to Nelson ward, one floor above. The ward was partitioned to provide several blocks, each one with four beds on either side. The porter, who introduced himself as Bill, pushed him the length of the ward before stopping at an area marked E.

On their arrival, two of the patients broke off from mundane interests to offer a welcoming smile. The others were either asleep, snoring peacefully or surrounded by friends and family, many of whom were strewn across the beds. Only a handful seemed fortunate enough to have found chairs. There was only one bed unoccupied in this division and that was at the far end in front of the window. He guessed it was his.

He thought how lucky he was to have been allocated a bed by the huge window which ran the whole width of the section.

"Thank you, Bill," he addressed the gregarious porter as he pushed himself from the seat of the wheelchair and stood before the window, pleasantly surprised at the panoramic view on offer. With the fog now almost cleared and some thin sunshine penetrating the passive clouds, he could appreciate the beauty of the countryside spread before him. Still feeling a little unsteady, he sat on the edge of the bed.

"Well, I'll be off now, sir, hope you are soon feeling better." They were Bill's final words before he reversed the wheelchair and made for the exit.

"Hiya, mate, in for an op, are yer?" the man in the next bed introduced himself. He looked a jolly individual despite his weight problem, his huge paunch perched on the bedclothes like a giant bubble. David noticed his face was in proportion to the rest of him, his podgy jowls collapsing untidily on to several tiers of fleshy chins.

"No, only in for one more night, I hope," he replied with an amiable smile. He wasn't really in the mood to chat and felt relieved when a nurse approached.

"Mr Lucas, I believe?" she enquired.

"Yes, that's right."

"Well, hop into bed then and we will get you comfy."

David did as he was told, sensing his neighbour's eyes on him the whole time as he climbed into the bed. As soon as he had stretched his legs out under the sheet, the nurse plumped up his pillows.

"I'll leave you to get to know Roger," she said with a bemused smile as she went about her further duties.

"She's nice, that one," Roger quickly confirmed. "Name's Susie, the same as my wife, so I can't forget it." A chuckle followed.

Over the next twenty minutes, David was treated to Roger's life history in full, so much so that he felt he knew all there was to know of his wife, his two children, his mother and various other members of his family. With his obvious breathing problems, David wondered how he could talk so fast and for so long.

It was, therefore, with some relief, when a stranger appeared and walked purposely towards them. Not recognising him, he imagined he must be coming to see Roger. Dressed in a smart leather coat, shirt, tie and corduroy trousers, he looked the part of a bank manager or a solicitor.

As he approached, he smiled warmly, his eyes catching his with some strength.

"Hello, there, you're looking a lot better," the stranger addressed him, his smile broadening even deeper as he offered his hand. Taken aback for a second, David had to think before his brain registered.

"You must be the guy who pulled me from the river," he gushed on realisation, before grabbing the proffered hand and shaking it enthusiastically.

"Yes, that's right, Charlie Greaves is the name," Charlie said, introducing himself and increasing his grip in response to the strengthening of the handshake.

"David Lucas, and thank you so very much." Their eyes fixed on each other with a warmth that took immediate effect, an instant fusing of a friendship brought about by the events of the past twenty-four hours. Both men felt a strange draw to each other, a force of nature that both found difficult to define. It was something special.

"Can you find a chair, Charlie? I think they're a bit of a premium in this ward." As David spoke, a couple rose and said their goodbyes to a patient at the end of his row. Charlie was quick to seize the opportunity and was soon pulling the chair up to the side of David's bed.

Roger, reading the situation, diplomatically turned to the far side of his bed, pulled a paperback from his drawer and started to read, a pretence to his eavesdropping that followed.

"Well, how are you?" Charlie asked once he had settled comfortably in '' chair.

"I'm fine now, thanks to you. A little tired but that's to be ex~

"It's your dog you have to thank, not me. If she had~'
persuasive, I would never have found you in the
thought she was going to attack me, she looked so a

David had to laugh at this. He couldn't imagine
Cuddly and over-powering at times but never aggressi

"You may laugh, but I can tell you it was quite a sh

53

"I'm sorry," David apologised. "But I just don't see Tammy as aggressive. She would lick you to death."

"I know that now but I didn't at the time. What with the fog and everything, she looked like a monster when she first came at me. She was wet, bedraggled and had a cut below her left eye which made her look even more fierce." David appeared to be concerned.

"Is she okay?" he asked, frowning.

"Yes, I took her to Wisbech Police Station and they said they would get their vet to check her over. I'm sure the wound had stopped bleeding and it will be fine." Hearing this, David seemed to relax again.

"What were you doing there, in any case? I can't imagine anybody being out in conditions like that."

"Same as you, presumably, I was out running." With this, something clicked in David's brain, a note of some recognition registering.

"You're not Charlie Greaves who used to run for England in the eighties, are you?" David asked excitedly. The local paper often ran articles on Charlie's coaching programmes in the sports column and David had become quite a fan since he had started running.

"I could well be," Charlie replied with a tinge of pride.

"Well, I always read your column in the local paper with interest and have used some of your tips from time to time."

"I'm glad to hear it," Charlie added with a keen smile. The rapport between the two men was developing strongly.

"So, tell me your side of the story," David requested, leaning forward towards his new friend. Charlie looked just as eager to relate all the details of an event both men would never forget.

Starting at the point where Tammy appeared from the fog, his storytelling captured all the aspects of the event in some detail, so vivid and dramatic in places that he had David's face contorted with various expressions of surprise and horror. A couple of times, David thrust his hand through his hair in wonderment, leaning forward towards Charlie as he did so, completely enthralled by the incredulous tale he was hearing. Although Charlie played down his more physical actions and the dangers involved, it was still very clear that he had acted heroically in a situation, which in the conditions, was life-threatening for both of them.

It was strange listening to a story where he was such a major player yet so oblivious to any part of it. Although looking extremely fit, it must have been a daunting challenge for Charlie to have carried him at all, let alone the distance he described. There was no doubt in his mind that Charlie had saved his life.

Only when Charlie had recounted the adventure fully and come to the end with his visit to the police station, did he explain that it was so lucky he had taken path along the riverbank and not followed his usual route along the main road isbech St Mary.

you had, I probably wouldn't be sitting here," David said thoughtfully.

Charlie nodded in confirmation. "I guess not," he said. "One thing I can tell you, however, is that, when I finally arrived home, I was completely exhausted. I fell into bed and didn't wake up for six hours. I felt as if my sixty-five years were finally catching up with me."

"Blimey, Charlie, you're good for sixty-five. I thought you were in your fifties." Charlie looked pleased with the compliment.

"That's what running does for you. Keeps you young."

"I agree. Since I started, I've felt like a new man."

"Do you go running often?" Charlie asked.

"Every day, now, if I can fit it in," David enthused. "I run for about forty minutes every morning during the week. Usually longer at the weekends."

"You must be quite fit."

"I just enjoy it," David shrugged with an air of satisfaction. "I've been doing it now for two or three years. I can honestly say that it has given me a completely new perspective on life. I started when my wife fell ill with cancer and it helped so much, just that short break each day, to handle the trauma of seeing her health gradually declining. When she died, eighteen months ago, I kept it up and it makes me feel so good." A sudden sadness in David's tone made Charlie realise he was digging up his emotions.

"I'm sorry," Charlie said, with feeling, rapidly eliminating the awkward pause that followed with a suggestion that was warmly accepted. "If you ever want to join me down my club, let me know. You'll be very welcomed."

"Wow, that sounds wonderful, I'll definitely take you up on that." David's reaction was so ecstatic, leaving Charlie in no doubt as to what it meant to him.

"I go down to the club three evenings a week and weekends," Charlie added. He was deeply impressed with the passion of this young man. He appeared so enthusiastic, his eyes sparkling as he fully digested the offer made to him. Charlie was about to continue when he was aware David's concentration was focused elsewhere.

"Hello, love," he said with some tenderness at the approach of a newcomer.

Charlie turned around and looked to see an elegantly slender young woman, smiling freely, her eyes on David, as she came towards them.

"This is Charlie Greaves, the man who saved my life," David explained with some relish. Charlie stood up as Rachel offered her hand.

"Wow, thank you so much," she said, her eyes burning into his with the strongest sense of gratitude.

"This is Rachel, my girlfriend."

"Pleased to meet you, Rachel." With the introductions made, she moved to the other side of the bed.

"You're looking better," she told David as she planted a firm kiss on his puckered lips.

"Yes, I feel it," he replied casually. "Where's Tom?" he then asked, a touch of anxiety in his voice as he realised his son was not present.

"He's gone to Danny's again," she said a little tensely. "He said you wouldn't mind. I'm going to pick him up on the way home. I'm sorry if that's wrong?"

"No, that's fine," David replied, aware of the awkward situation she had found herself in. Hopefully, he would be home tomorrow and life would return to normal.

"This is my son we are talking about," David explained to Charlie. "He is eleven years old and out of the blue, poor Rachel has been put in charge of him and she is probably finding it very difficult." Rachel said nothing but just smiled. "I'm sure you know what young boys can be like?"

"I guess I do with the large number that come through my care on the athletic track, although I haven't any of my own," Charlie replied, at the same time, raising his arm to view his watch.

"Well, David, I don't want to seem rude but I have to be in Wisbech in half an hour so I'm afraid I am going to have to take my leave of you." He stood up. "I hope you will take up my offer of joining us at the club. You never know you may well be a very talented athlete." It was said with true sincerity. Charlie pushed out his hand.

"I very much doubt it, I should think I'm well over the hill at thirty," David said jovially as he once again strengthened his grip on Charlie's hand. "Well, Charlie, I'm a little lost as what to say to someone who has saved my life. It doesn't happen that often. All I can think of is thank you, so thank you." Their eyes met with an intense bonding that both clearly recognised.

"I'm not really hero material," Charlie replied as graciously as he could. He turned towards Rachel.

"And nice to have met you, Rachel," She smiled fondly in acknowledgement. The couple watched his departure in silence.

Rachel was the first to speak. "What a charming man."

"A lovely man," David confirmed. "And do you know he was a top athlete? He used to run for England in the eighties…and he's the coach at our local athletic club…and he's asked me to go down and do some running at his club."

"Wow," Rachel said. "Quite a celebrity." She sensed that David was more than pleased with his new friendship.

"Well, have you missed me?" she asked in an effort to refocus his mind.

"Yes, of course," he said, locking his eyes to hers with fondness. "How is my lovely girl?"

"I'm fine."

"And how's life with that son of mine?"

"Getting there very slowly, I think," she replied with a sigh. "He seems to avoid me as much as he can. I picked him up from his friend, Danny, last night. He never said more than yes or no to anything I said to him, hopped out the car at your house, said he had already eaten and went straight up to bed."

"He'll come round, I'm sure."

Rachel was not so sure.

Chapter 11

"Hi, Charlie, it's David Lucas."

"Dave, how lovely to hear from you. How are you?" The warmth of Charlie's voice was so intense. "I've been meaning to phone you all week."

"I'm fine, Charlie, but bored stiff. I came home from hospital on Tuesday but Rachel insisted I have the week off so I've been sitting around basically doing nothing. I started reading a novel a friend recommended to me but I'm struggling with that. So, I thought I might take up your offer to join you down your athletic club, if that's okay?"

"That's great. I suggest you come down on Sunday morning about ten o'clock when I have the juniors. You can join in and get a feel for it."

"Suits me fine. My son's off to his friend's and Rachel is working this weekend."

"Okay, I'll see you Sunday then."

"Look forward to it."

Suddenly, the weekend ahead looked a lot more interesting.

***

When Sunday morning finally arrived, David was still on a high from his conversation with Charlie and the excitement of joining a bona fide athletic club. Passing through the rusty iron gates from the main road, he entered the Wisbech Harriers car park. Littered with shreds of discarded newspapers, bottles and several empty beer crates, he had to omit it was not what he had expected. Somehow, the club's connection with Charlie had thrown up a much more affluent image.

It was a few minutes past ten o'clock. At least twenty cars were parked haphazardly around the car park perimeter. He quickly found a space off to the left-hand side between two large puddles and cut his engine. Just for a moment, he sat in reflection. After the turbulent weather of the previous weekend, it was pleasant to feel the soft warmth of the shallow sun as it flooded through the windscreen.

As soon as he had locked his car, he followed the direction of an arrow on a battered signpost which indicated the path to the clubhouse and the track. A short climb over an undulating hill brought both into view. He stood for a few moments and surveyed the scene before him, squinting against the hazy sun as he did so.

In the foreground, the remains of an old spectator stand, badly weathered by the elements, stood feebly facing the track. From behind, you could clearly see several of its vertical slats were missing and others were hanging despondently from their fittings. It was obviously no longer in use.

On the grey cinder track, blotches of green every few metres marked the unwanted appearance of tufts of grass. The other side of the track appeared a little more promising. From where he was standing, another public stand, looking a little healthier than the first, possibly because of its fresh coat of white paint, dominated what he imagined was the home straight.

On the track in front of this, he immediately spied Charlie in charge of a group of youngsters. They were all exercising vigorously, running on the spot and kicking their knees high in the air. Even though a good distance away, he could hear the excited exchanges as they laughed and joked amongst themselves.

No sooner had he made his descent of the hill to the level of the track than Charlie saw him and waved enthusiastically. He reciprocated as he crossed over and approached the group.

"Okay, short rest," Charlie announced when he was a little closer. Much to his surprise, as they came together, Charlie opened his arms and swept him up in a bear hug, an unexpected action that fascinated the young audience who looked on in bewilderment.

"Hi ya, Dave, lovely to see you," Charlie whispered clearly in his ear before releasing him from his hold.

"Lovely to see you too, Charlie," David responded with a broad smile, once he had recovered from the shock and the strong waft of aftershave that accompanied his mauling. It was a further endorsement of the intimate tie developing between them.

"You look much better," Charlie said as he stood back a couple of paces and inspected him carefully.

"I feel it, thank you," David said with some pleasure.

Charlie then turned to his young group.

"This, ladies and gentlemen," he told them, "is a very good friend of mine, David Lucas, who will be joining us over the next few weeks in training, so I want you to be kind to him and help him when you can. He is a bit older than you but hasn't yet drawn his pension." There was a flurry of light-hearted laughter from everyone.

"Hello," David said, feeling slightly embarrassed as he scanned the whole group from one side to the other. There were about two dozen youths in total, a mixture of ages, sexes, heights, builds and colours. Boys outnumbered girls by at least three to one. They stared back at him, their faces registering a friendly acceptance, as they grinned openly in his direction.

"Right, back to work," Charlie said, clapping his hands sharply to regain their attention.

The group spread out surprisingly quickly across the inner lawn, each ensuring he or she had ample room to complete the familiar exercises that would follow.

"Dave, if you would like to join the group, we'll get going. These are just warm up exercises before we take to the track," Charlie explained.

David took a position at the side of the group, nodding at a tall black lad next to him, who responded with a toothy grin.

"Right, running on the spot…again," Charlie commanded. "Go." With this, all of them started raising their knees one after the other at a fairly casual rate. David followed suit.

"Now quicker." The pace increased.

"And higher."

"And now sprint for twenty." As they all attacked the target, you could hear bursts of heavy breathing from the less fit. A few were struggling to go the pace. A couple of young girls exchanged giggly comments before collapsing on to the grass. David had no problems, the exercise was well within his capabilities.

The remainder of the warm-up exercises consisted of a range of trunk curls, sit-ups, press-ups and squats, all of which were executed with exuberant energy and a general feeling of good humour.

David had little difficulty in working with them and soon found himself relishing the atmosphere of the team training therapy. There was a comforting feel in seeing so many youngsters throwing themselves into the programme with such vitality. He guessed they were no older than sixteen or seventeen; all of them had somehow discovered an interest in athletics and, best of all, were willing to forego the television, computer games, and probably, in some cases, their homework, to enjoy training through the harsh murky days of the winter months in the hope of bettering their performances.

Following a short break and sufficient time for even the most unfit to regain their strength, Charlie announced the next phase.

"I now want you all to jog a lap of the track and when you come to the final straight, I want you to sprint flat out to the finishing post. Okay, let's see you move." The response from the squad was a chorus of groans which brought a grin to Charlie's face. He caught the look of bemusement from David.

"Don't worry, Dave, I always get this. They love it really. How are you feeling?"

"I'm fine, Charlie, really enjoying it." It was the early impression that Charlie had read.

One by one, the group took to the track, some joining friends and running in pairs, some in larger groups, and others stretching out on their own. David fell in at the back, a few metres behind a trio of boys who were chatting casually as they trotted comfortably together. David made no effort to close the gap until reaching the final straight where he set about sprinting to the finishing post fifty metres ahead. He was amazed at how quickly he ate the ground between himself and the three boys, catching the first after thirty metres, and the other two together five metres before the line.

"Well done, David," Charlie encouraged him from the centre of the track.

"Right, it's time for some serious sprinting now," Charlie announced, again clapping his hands for effect. "Arrange yourselves in groups and line up at the start of the hundred metres." The obligatory groans followed.

"I reckon you should join the lads in the back row, Dave, as they are the oldest and the best."

By the time they had all arrived at the corner of the track incorporating the sprint start, the youngsters had arranged themselves across the eight lanes in four rows with the youngest in the front, working back to the eldest in the rear. David joined the six lads in the final row. They were big lads for their ages with two of them well over six foot.

"Done this before, mate?" asked Shane Widawe, the leaner of the two, a mixed race lad with a sharp striking face and happy features.

"Not exactly," David told him. "I've done a fair bit of distance running though."

"Well, this will give you a bit of speed then."

With a cheerful beam, the lad returned his attention to the proceedings on the track. In the front row, three of the eight were girls. Only one had kept her tracksuit on, the others jigging up and down in an effort to keep warm in the chill of the morning. All the boys had stripped down to their vests and shorts. Occasionally, they would share a few words with a colleague whilst watching Charlie's every move as he sauntered down the track to a position some eighty metres from the starting line. In his hand, he carried his trusty stopwatch. Once he had settled in his chosen spot, he turned and looked back down the track towards the eager group.

"Okay then, flat out to the finish," he shouted. "Remember to keep your arms and legs pumping and relax as much as you can." With this, all eight in the front row dropped down on one knee, leant forward and carefully placed the splayed fingers of both their hands just behind the line. It went quiet as everyone's concentration focused on the imminent event.

"On your marks," came the next command and as one they rose up like coiled springs on to their leading leg.

"Get set." Only a slight pause and, "Go." In a flurry, the youngsters took off, their arms flaying wildly as they came upright, found their balance and stride. From David's position at the back, he could see very little but it was not long before Charlie's dulcet tones spliced the atmosphere.

"Come on, Lucy, drive your legs. Now go for it, Tamara. Work your arms, Samuel." In no time, the leading runners hit the line and came to a standstill. Two of them tottered to the inside of the track and fell exhausted on to the grass. Others passed the line and stopped dead, immediately bending forward with their hands on their knees until the pain of their effort receded.

"Well done, everyone," Charlie praised, before giving his attention to the next group who were already in position, eager to start.

By the time it came to David's turn, he was feeling a flutter in his stomach, a touch of nerves that, at first, surprised him. He was enjoying himself so much that he queried this reaction. Maybe it was just the competition, he told himself, after all, he had little idea of his capabilities, especially at sprinting. In recent weeks, towards the end of his runs, he had sprinted the last two hundred or so metres and had maintained it powerfully until reaching his set target. Was running a hundred metres any different? He was about to find out. A tinge of excitement warmed his mood. He would give it his best shot.

He had removed his tracksuit. Oblivious to the chill, he took his position with the other six lads on the starting line. For no particular reason, he chose the outside lane. Down the track, he could see Charlie adjusting his stopwatch.

In no time, they were under orders and his nerves soon forgotten as his concentration kicked in, his senses pinprick sharp as Charlie went through his starting procedure.

"On your marks. Get set." The pause seemed extra-long. "Go."

Instinct took over. For the first dozen strides, he felt lost, his action rushed and clumsy amid the overbearing smoothness of the other competitors. He was amazed at how quickly they dropped him. Within twenty metres, all six had left him and were seemingly together in a line across the track ahead.

Charlie was watching the final group and David in particular with keen interest. Like David, he was not sure what to expect. So far, he had been suitably impressed with his performance. With his six feet two inches, broad shoulders and leanness of frame, he looked every part the athlete. He definitely moved well and there was no doubt that he had acquired a high degree of fitness.

Two of the lads beside him were quite useful and he would expect them to beat him, but, by how far, he could not say.

When he was dropped at the start, he was not particularly surprised but the two metres between him and the group opened no further over the next twenty. At this point, Shane Widawe, started to pull clear of the baying group.

It was on David, however, that Charlie's eyes were firmly fixed. Initially, he could see he was floundering with the pace, his movements uncoordinated and distressed, but then, before his eyes, he noticed the change.

As if he had been touched by the hand of God, there was a sudden surge of not only power and determination but, a fluency of movement that had Charlie mesmerised. In a few strides, he was eating into the deficit between himself, and the leading pack, passing first one and then another until only Shane remained ahead. By the time David reached Charlie's vantage point, he was at Shane's shoulders. Charlie was not sure who was the most shocked, Shane or himself, as he passed him, seemingly effortlessly, to hit the finishing line a good metre clear.

Once the impact of what he had just witnessed sunk in, Charlie quickly composed himself. Controlling his emotions as best he could, he made a conscientious effort to assess the situation. After all, the lads are only schoolboys and David is a fully developed male, possibly at the height of his power. But, at the same time, the boys, especially Shane, are very good. He was anticipating that the youngster would do well, in fact, have a chance of a medal, in the youth championships later in the year.

Shaking his head in confusion, he ambled over to the finishing area. He sensed an atmosphere of restrained tension from the group as the youngsters huddled together, talking excitedly about the spectacle they had just witnessed. Not one of them had ever seen Shane defeated over a hundred metres in the two years he had been competing at the club. An atmosphere of heavy elation hung in the air, as yet not released, but suppressed by etiquette and respect for the beaten warrior.

The two main players were in various states of recovery. Shane was standing with the other tall lad, Paul Harrison, who appeared to be consoling him in short breathy gasps as both tried to regain their normal breathing. Five metres ahead, David had dropped to his haunches taking sharp intakes of breath.

Charlie joined the group, smiling in his usual easy manner.

"Good run, lads. Good effort," he threw at Shane and Paul on passing.

"What was the time, Charlie?" Shane asked with some passion.

"Thirteen fifty-one for David, thirteen fifty-two for you," Charlie replied, picking the safe figures from his head. In the excitement, he had failed to push the button of his stopwatch. Shane looked confused as Charlie made for the victor.

Reaching David, Charlie put his hand on his shoulder as he bent forward in total surrender to his condition. "Well done, Dave, that was quite impressive."

When David finally stood up, he was pleasantly surprised to find Shane Widawe's outstretched hand in front of him, a gracious smile of friendship spread across his face.

"That was some run, man," the youngster told him with a look of admiration.

"Thanks, Shane. No one was more surprised than me, I can tell you," David replied as he shook his hand firmly.

"I hope we can do that again."

"I'm sure we will," David replied.

The rest of the morning was spent with some longer pieces of work and culminated with an eight hundred metres finale.

"This is to build your stamina," Charlie announced to the group as they all set out on the final two laps at a fairly steady pace. Charlie joined David at the back of the pack and ran alongside him.

"Have you enjoyed yourself, Dave?" he asked.

"Immensely, Charlie."

"Well, you'll be joining us again then?"

"You bet, you'll have trouble keeping me away."

"I'm down Tuesdays and Thursdays in the evening, and Saturday mornings if you're interested."

"No, I can't do that, Charlie," David answered in a more serious tone. "I have Tom to consider and on Saturdays Rachel needs my help at the centre. As much as I would like to, I am going to have to keep my visits to Sunday mornings only at the moment but I do go out running nearly every morning before I take Tom to school."

"That's fine, Dave. I don't want to push you but it will be nice to see you anytime."

"Thanks, Charlie."

"Are you going to join us for a drink?"

David gave the question a moment of thought. There was no particular reason to return home immediately, and he was enjoying the company and a change of scenery very much.

"Yes, that will be great, Charlie. I think I owe you a drink for a small matter of saving my life," he tagged on in a casual manner. "That sounds a bit dramatic," Charlie replied and they both laughed.

When they had all completed the second lap, some more seriously than others, they formed a circle around Charlie to await his final instructions. David was impressed with the mood of achievement that oozed so infectiously from every member of the group.

"Well done, everyone," Charlie began, his eyes scanning each of them in turn. "A good morning's work. I'll see you again next Saturday afternoon, hopefully. I'll see you two on Tuesday and Thursday," he added, directing a glance towards Shane and Paul who acknowledged with a nod.

"Right, have a good day." With this, they all dispersed rapidly in small groups, chatting excitedly as they crossed the track. Charlie and David watched them go.

"Dave, prepare yourself for your introduction to the clubhouse," Charlie said as he shepherded him towards the main stand. The flinty gleam in his eye had David wondering what was ahead. He did not have long to wait as they quickly passed through the arch in the centre of the stand to the grounds beyond.

"One of the finest pieces of pre-war architecture you have ever seen," Charlie announced emphatically with a flamboyant wave of his arm as they broke out of the exit to face the building ahead.

If David had been surprised by the car park, it would be true to say he was shocked by the sight of the clubhouse. It reminded him of an old army hut and in fact, as Charlie explained, that is what it had been originally, seventy years hence. Sealed with a dark brown varnish, it had been well preserved but just looked so dated compared to modern facilities. Tacked on to one side, an extension had been added, but again this looked falsely outmoded and crass.

"We are hoping for a grant from the Sports Council shortly," Charlie explained as he picked up on David's reaction.

"That's good news by the look of it," David replied, as politely as he could.

For the next half-hour, David enjoyed Charlie's company and the company of Roy Crowther, a retired runner who had taken up the duties of chief barman. Over a lager, they stood at the bar and chatted comfortably. Roy had a wicked sense of humour which kept them both amused. It was not until the main door crashed open and in rolled a rowdy group of runners that their friendly chatter came to an end. Their faces flushed by the cold, the stream of arrivals seemed to last forever as one after the other, they crowded through the door seeking the warmth of the clubhouse. David counted thirteen. They all seemed to be talking at once, the room immediately charged with an atmosphere of mega excitement.

"Hello, Charlie," shouted the first one through the door, a thin short guy with a bobble hat and glasses.

"Hi, Mike. Good run?" Charlie asked.

"Yes, mate. Think I'm going to have a good season."

"I certainly hope so."

One by one, they filed through the clubhouse in the direction of the showers. Each one seemed to have either a few words of greeting or a pleasant facial acknowledgement for Charlie on passing. As the last one left the room, David looked at his watch. "Well, I think it's time I made a move," he announced, turning to Charlie. "Thanks for today, Charlie, I've really enjoyed myself. I'll see you next week then?"

Charlie eyed him with what was now a familiar look, one that was reserved for the closest of family or a dearest friend. Instinctively, they both came together and hugged fondly.

"See you next week, Dave. Look forward to it."

"Cheerio, Roy, nice to have met you," David shouted to the barman as he made for the door.

"Cheers, Dave, see you again hopefully." No sooner had the door closed than Roy looked at Charlie.

"You like that boy, don't you, Charlie?"

"We have a special connection," was all that Charlie was willing to give away.

Chapter 12

For the next five weeks, David attended Charlie's sessions every Sunday morning, enjoying the company and competition of the youngsters who openly accepted him as one of them. They were a joyful bunch, full of spirit and energy that was infectious to say the least. It was on the fifth week that Charlie pulled him to one side after setting his pupils off on a lap of the track.

"Dave, I'm so pleased at the way you have taken to this and you're doing so well, you know?" Charlie began. "I'm going to ask a couple of my senior lads, Colin Baker and Neil Goodman, to join us next week, and see how you get on with them, if that's okay with you?"

"That's fine, Charlie. I'm sure they'll sort me out and put me in my place."

Charlie had been amazed at the improvement in David's performances. After the defeat of Shane Widawe, he had originally thought his talents lay in sprinting but this only led to confusion when he was able to test his ability over the longer trips of four and eight hundred metres. His times were good, very good, in fact. He knew his two senior runners would test his abilities to the limit and give a true indication of his talent.

As it happened, David struggled to cope with these elite athletes at first but as each weekend passed the gap between them gradually closed. On Charlie's advice, his early morning runs were revamped. Not every day, the five-mile slog, but intervals of sprinting, mostly around a hundred metres at a time with a few longer ones thrown in for good measure.

Not wanting to leave his bed earlier than the six-thirty that had become the norm, he measured the intervals along the farm lane from his house using the trees, fences and the few buildings as markers. They may not have been exact but they would do the job. By the end of the first week, he had settled into the new regime, enjoying the change of routine with some enthusiasm.

Within two months, he was pushing Colin Baker to a couple of metres over the four hundred, pushing him all the way down the home straight to the line. In the eight hundred, Neil Goodman was the reigning club champion at the distance. His tactics were usually to kick for home from a long way out, usually at least three hundred metres. Stamina and guts were his forte as he would often boast but very few were able to pass him in the final lap.

At first, David found it difficult to deal with Neil's final kick and was dropped four or five metres before picking up again, too late to close the gap before the finishing line. However, as the weeks passed and the benefit of Charlie's new routine kicked in, he was pushing him closer and closer until he finally had the satisfaction of passing him ten metres from the finish and coming home a couple of metres clear.

Sensing David's euphoria, Charlie had pounced with a request that David had found difficult to ignore. For weeks, he had been trying to entice David to join his group on Saturdays.

"Dave," he began earnestly. "We have a very special meeting coming up next Saturday here at the club. It is a friendly against a London club where the chairman and leading coach is an old rival of mine. At the moment, Colin, and Neil are doubling up in both the eight hundred and fifteen hundred and Neil is also doing the four hundred, which is his best event, but I'm still one short for the fifteen hundred. Is there any chance you could help me out, please?"

Staring deeply into Charlie's eyes, his first reaction was to refuse. It was, however, his debt to Charlie that finally did its bidding, his conscience playing its hand. He knew he just had to agree. As a smile broke the silence, the look on Charlie's face was a picture.

"Okay, Charlie, just this once then," he capitulated. "You never give up, do you?"

"That's a sign of a good athlete," he replied with a wry smile.

***

Charlie had been looking forward to this Saturday for some time. It was one of the highlights of his year and today was special; the club was celebrating twenty years since the event's inauguration. A friendly but competitive tournament, it brought together each year, the two clubs, the Spartan Athletic from London and the Wisbech Harriers from Cambridgeshire. The original idea, back in 1991, had been Charlie's but he had to admit without the help of his old friend and rival, Freddie Soames, it would never have got off the ground.

Unfortunately, over the years, Wisbech had only been successful in winning the event three times and there was now a gap of six years since the prestigious cup had held a place in the Wisbech trophy cabinet. In recent years, the London opponents had shown their superiority with devastating effect, monopolising nearly all the field events and most of the track.

This year, however, Charlie fancied the club's chances of taking a few events, a situation that would at least give him some satisfaction in partly deflating Freddie's huge ego. After the event, it was usual practice for the defeated coach to take the victor for a meal. With the loser paying, and it was usually Charlie, it was bad enough, but to have Freddie lauding the performances of his athletes for two or three hours was almost unbearable.

To add to his woes, Freddie had phoned him during the week to advise that he was now bringing his star performer with him, one Philip Rhodes, who had had a promising season last year and was tipped by many pundits as a hopeful for a medal in the Olympics next year. Philip's fame had grown rapidly since his final run last season when he had put in a time just a fraction of a second off the British record. Charlie had nobody to match that class.

Freddie had asked Charlie if he could provide pacemakers for his star who in return would make an attempt on the British record, obviously, a huge attraction for such a low-key event. Both Colin and Neil had offered their services, Colin to take the pace over the first two laps with Neil, hopefully, leading throughout the third. Both considered running against such a high profile athlete a huge honour and with their best events behind them, by the time the 1,500 metres was scheduled at the end of the afternoon's programme, they had nothing to lose.

As far as David was concerned, Charlie saw little point in making an issue of the situation. He had no idea of his capabilities over the distance and presumably neither had David so he might as well let him take his chance. He had found it difficult enough to persuade him to take part and the last thing he wanted was to frighten him off. Throwing him in at the deep end was probably a little unfair but he could see no real harm. If he was soundly beaten by such a competitor, it would be no disgrace.

Standing in the centre of the track, Charlie studied the sky with some concern. The bright expanse of blue sky that had prevailed all morning was broken in the distance by an ominous gathering of grey storm clouds. The weathermen had forecast the possibility of some thundery downpours and it looked as if they could be right.

Now, one o'clock, the day had gone well so far. All the club members who would be acting as marshals had arrived and hopefully, the first race would be off on time at two o'clock. In the past, most of the organising had seemed to fall on his shoulders but this year, thanks to a string of keen young volunteers, he had been able to delegate most of the marshalling duties. He was confident that they would carry out their allotted jobs competently and was free to enjoy the afternoon ahead in his role as senior coach.

Reaching into his tracksuit pocket, he pulled out a packet of mints. Quickly unwrapping one, he popped it casually into his mouth before returning his attention to the proceedings on the track.

"Well, well, if it ain't good ol' Charlie Greaves, the scourge of the Yanks."

Charlie turned abruptly to see the larger than life figure of one Freddie Soames, descending on him like a comic book hero, his hand thrust out in a gesture of friendship. Charlie's first impression was that he had put on a lot of weight since their last meeting only six months ago, so much so that his stomach bounced in time with each step he took. Charlie gripped the proffered hand warmly.

"Hi, Freddie, nice to see you."

"And you, mate. How are yer?"

"Fine, thank you."

"And how are the Fenland yokels? All set to chase us home again, I hope," Freddie said in a raised voice as if he couldn't wait to start the teasing.

"You might get a few surprises this year," Charlie countered with a degree of confidence that had little effect on Freddie.

"That's our Charlie, always the optimist," Freddie chuckled annoyingly.

With ten minutes to go before the first event, everything seemed to be in place. The spectators had spilt in groups from the clubhouse and were now filling the main stand. Inside the track, many of the competitors were warming up with varying degrees of leg exercises and sprints. Several families had settled around the verge of the track, setting up tables and chairs to enjoy the entertainment to the full.

Although taken seriously by all involved, there was somehow a light-hearted feel to the day, a relaxed friendly competition enjoyed by competitors, friends and family, which was the target Charlie had set out to achieve all those years ago.

For a few moments, he bathed in the atmosphere. It was just grand to see so many carefree and happy faces. The club members, for a start, disengaged as they were from their respective jobs or studies, were different people. Enthusiasm abounded as they tackled their athletics with a passion that was often diluted by the drudgery of their weekday lives.

All of a sudden, the start of the first event, the men's 100 metres, was upon them.

"Good afternoon, ladies and gentlemen. Welcome to the twentieth anniversary of the Greaves and Soames Cup Competition between the Wisbech Harriers of Cambridgeshire and The Spartan Athletic Club from London." A rather accentuated *hurray* from one of the competitors immediately triggered a round of applause from the crowd. George Saunders, the club treasurer, waited for this to calm down before announcing the first event.

Charlie watched the tall spindly Shane Widawe rise and touch his toes a couple of times before resetting himself in the starting blocks. He was very hopeful this young man could provide an early fillip to the afternoon's events. He had been working with him closely throughout the winter, concentrating on his starts in particular, an area where in the past his lack of application had left him vulnerable. The butterflies in his stomach started to flutter as the six competitors rose for the gun.

The muffled bang galvanised the attention of everyone present as the six runners sprang from their marks in unison. Shane's patience in training looked to be rewarded when he held a slight lead off the opening ten metres. One of Freddie's group, a tall gangly lad with little grace, went with him as they pulled a further metre clear of the chasing field over the next forty.

"Go on, Shane, now you've got him," shouted Charlie as all the runners bolted past him with Shane looking strong. He knew he finished well and was confident he had the race in the bag. From where he was standing, there seemed to be little change in the order until the final few metres where the tall visitor appeared to challenge strongly.

From the swell of chaotic shouting near the finish, it was obvious that some drama was taking place as the runners closed on the line, the name of Pete clearly audible in the dying strides. Once the race had climaxed, a handful of spectators clustered around the two principals in frenzied acclamation of their performance.

Charlie looked nervously down the track to the finishing line where the four judges were deep in conversation. Finally, an announcement was made amid the tense atmosphere now prevailing.

"In first place, Peter Jacobs. In second place, Shane Widawe…"

"Bugger it," Charlie swore uncontrollably.

"That's a shame, Charlie, I thought Shane had it sewn up." It was David.

"So did I," said Charlie, his tone not hiding his disappointment. Seeing David, however calmed his emotions. It was funny the effect this man had on him. In seconds, his melancholy petered out, blanked and replaced by new positive thoughts of the events ahead.

Only when he saw Freddie out of the corner of his eye, heading in his direction, did he quickly shepherd David away from the track towards the pavilion to explain his plans for his big race and the celebrated company he would be competing against.

"I'm going to punch that idiot in his fat gut shortly," he told David over a cup of tea in the recreation tent.

"Now, now, Charlie, remember it's a friendly," David said playfully. "And I thought he was a friend of yours?"

Charlie screwed his face up as if such a statement may not be entirely true.

The afternoon's events moved on in a similar vein to the first race. One by one, Charlie's hopes were scuttled. Sometimes, it was down to the smallest of margins but always in the Spartan's favour. Charlie was exasperated. Freddie was at his worst, hunting Charlie out at the end of nearly every event. At first, it was just playful ridicule but as the afternoon wore on, his behaviour became more and more overbearing.

Some pride was restored in the men's shot when Josh Jenkins, a local builder, excelled himself to win with a personal best throw of 19.62 metres to take the gold with the Spartans in second, third and fourth positions. No sooner had the event finished and the results announced before Freddie appeared. Expecting a little praise, Charlie lowered his head as Freddie whispered in his ear.

"Is that guy on drugs?" Charlie was so amused he couldn't stop himself laughing openly, so loud and genuinely that Freddie disappeared towards the main stand in confusion.

By the time David's event was announced, the whole scene had been transformed. For most of the afternoon, it had been bright and warm, the sun putting in some lengthy appearances between a few wispy cloud formations. Now, within what seemed just minutes, storm clouds descended over the track. Thick grey bulbous masses tumbled overhead like huge balls of fluffy cotton wool. With the coming of the clouds, the air cooled with menace, a lively breeze sweeping the area and dragging an assortment of empty drink cartons, wrappers and loose litter across the centre of the track towards the pavilion. Rain threatened as darkness descended.

Looking on from the hill on the far side of the track, David was fascinated by the change in the weather. He had a strange contempt for rain. When he was out running in the mornings, he would never let it interfere with his training. His only concession to its presence was a waterproof top. He actually found the freshness of a shower quite invigorating, especially when still a little sleepy in the mornings.

Earlier, he had watched with interest as Philip Rhodes made his appearance. After a preliminary consultation with Freddie, he had broken into a series of short controlled runs covering no more than fifty metres at a time, on each occasion taking lazy idle strides. More serious sprinting followed, usually over bursts of twenty or thirty metres. These were followed by a further session of stretching exercises. He calculated that the whole process had taken well over thirty minutes. He was impressed with the thoroughness of the warm-up and the man. About David's height, well-proportioned with a strong bronze tan, he looked every part the superstar. Oblivious to the weather, he appeared fully focused, like a man on a mission. Although David knew little of him, he found himself admiring the professional approach.

"I think you'd better get this race off before the heavens open up," Freddie bawled to Charlie as a gust of wind grabbed a deckchair and sent it sprawling across the grass.

"Yes, I know, George is just about to call them in," countered Charlie, as he received a nod from his chief marshal that he was ready to proceed.

"Ladies and Gentleman, this brings us to the highlight of the afternoon and we are pleased to have with us today, international Philip Rhodes, who will hopefully be representing the UK in the Olympics next year." A huge roar rose from the crowd, many of whom had now wrapped themselves in coats and jumpers as the wind persisted. Philip Rhodes raised his arm in acknowledgement of the generous response.

"Philip was to attempt a British record but I don't know whether this will still be on in the conditions?" George continued, trying to keep a little drama in the event, despite the unfolding situation. Philip gave no indication of his intentions, his poker face held firmly in place, his concentration seemingly focused only on the race ahead.

"Runners for the 1,500 metres, please line up." All eyes were on Philip Rhodes as he jogged purposefully forward. Charlie noticed Freddie exchange a few words on passing, no doubt reminding him of some prearranged plan.

As David left Charlie's side to take his place with the other runners, Charlie grabbed his arm.

"Remember what I told you, Dave. Colin is pace making for the first two laps and hopefully Neil for the third. You just run your race and see what happens. I'm not expecting a lot from you. Just do your best. Okay?"

"I'm fine, Charlie," David responded with a smile that disguised his nerves.

The runners came together at the starting line, a few nods, bemused smiles and sullen eye contact being the only exchanges. At one point, David briefly caught Philip's gaze and smiled involuntarily, only to be blanked with a glare that passed right through him.

After checking that all was correct, George lifted his pistol to the sky. An abrupt hush fell over the grounds. "Get set," he shouted in a raised voice followed after a short pause by, "Go!" as the pistol fired. Mechanically, Charlie and Freddie's fingers fell on their stopwatch buttons. The released runners shot into action with Colin quickly moving to the front at a strong pace.

No sooner had the report of the pistol blast died than a further crash, seemingly louder than the gun, boomed across the sky, vibrating the earth with a force that was both frightening and unreal. All around the track, the crowds stood dumbstruck, staring wildly at each other in disbelief.

With it came the rain. At first, just single heavy droplets, intermittently, but then more forcefully so that within seconds, it was falling with an intensity that blurred people's vision. Torrential rainfall flooded the track and the grass lawn interior. Across the grounds, people were racing in panic, young children dragged by their arms, the aged led firmly by their relatives, as they made for the cover of the pavilion, their seats deserted beside the track. Only the hardy and committed few were left to face the outcome of the race.

On the track, the runners were oblivious to the chaos, their concentration focused firmly on the task ahead. Colin had forced himself to the front from the gun at a reckless pace that he was unlikely to maintain for his allotted two laps. Behind him, in Indian file, Neil looked comfortable, as did Philip and David. The other two London runners filled the final positions. The order remained unchanged as they entered the home straight for the first time.

Standing by the finishing line, a sodden Charlie, rain dripping like a tap from his nose, bawled a few words of encouragement to his team.

"Well done, Colin, keep it going. Great, Neil, take it on after the next lap. You're moving well, Davy lad, stay with them," he shouted as one after the other passed him. There was no sign of acknowledgement from any of them, their eyes glued firmly to the competitor ahead, their minds focused only on the strategy of the unfolding race.

All the while, the rain teemed down relentlessly across the track in gusty bursts. Orchestrated by the wind, huge thick sheets thrashed the earth with a dull solid rhythm, a background noise that obliterated all other sounds. On the flooded track, the rain fell with such force that it created a myriad of small cascading fountains on the shiny surface, a shimmering pattern of aquatic animation.

David relaxed into the back straight for the second time, his legs almost propelling themselves with a natural stride that felt surprisingly easy. Ahead, he watched Philip loping along at a comfortable pace, his whole movement giving the impression of a finely tuned Porsche waiting to move up through the gears. Again, the order remained unchanged as the field approached the third lap.

In the home straight for the second time, Colin, aware that he had fulfilled his task as a pacemaker, made a passionate sprint for the finishing line before exiting abruptly from the track.

Left in the lead, Neil Goodman braced himself for the challenge ahead, determined he would hold on to the lead for as long as possible. Philip still moved menacingly behind him with David on his heels. The other two Spartan runners had been dropped by the pace and were by now a distance behind.

As they came out of the bend and into the far straight for the penultimate time, Charlie and Freddie appeared ahead, both pushing out on to the track for a better view in the murky conditions, their faces clearly animated at the performances of their respective players. With Neil almost upon them, they stepped back to clear the track.

"Well done, Neil, keep there, boy," Charlie shouted hoarsely, at the same time pulling the collar of his tracksuit tighter around his neck in some defence from the penetrating rain, a pointless effort in the freak conditions. "Great stuff, Davy. You're looking good," he added, without taking breath.

Just behind him, Freddie smiled with an air of indulgence. "In your own time, Champ," were his few words of instruction.

The rain kissed David's cheeks with a freshness that stimulated his mind and body. He felt good and with this, an urge to increase the pace came to him. He kicked with just a little extra effort and was amazed at the response. He was beside Philip, then, past him, now on the shoulders of the weakening Neil, who was throwing everything he had in an effort to hold on to the lead. Unfortunately, it was not for long. As he petered out, his stride faltered and his rhythm fell apart.

Heartily, David kicked again, this time leaving Neil in his wake, but drawing Philip in his slipstream as the two pressed on together. Moving into the home straight for the penultimate time, David was working harder to maintain the pace. So far, his body had responded to all he had asked of it. But could he keep it going?

Behind him, Philip accelerated to counteract his move and was now content to sit in the new comfort zone just a stride away, but not for long. It had originally been his intention to put up a fast time, somewhere near the British record, but the weather had put paid to that, so he had set his mind on a good workout run, increasing the pace over the final lap with a nice comfortable sprint along the home straight to victory.

With very few spectators left in attendance, there seemed little point in over-doing it. However, his intuition, his in-built knowledge of his own resources and experience, told him the pace was reasonably fast for the conditions. The pacemakers had thankfully done a great job, especially the one now in front of him but it was time to show him some real class, this country yokel, as Freddie would call him. He would now take him and leave him for dead. With these thoughts, the familiar feeling of invincibility overcame him.

Approaching the final lap, David caught sight of Charlie ahead on the bend. At the same time, he sensed a challenge from Philip as he drew level to his shoulder.

"Brilliant, Davy, brilliant, now go for it," Charlie bawled through the hissing rain. Just beyond Charlie, a more subdued Freddie checked his stopwatch with some surprise before preparing for his protégé's coup de grace. When the two runners were almost beside him, Philip's eyes caught those of his coach with a knowing glance. Freddie needn't have spoken but he did.

"Right, Champ, now's the time to go."

As Philip drew alongside, supposedly cruising in what seemed an effortless fashion, David didn't feel intimidated. If anything, the challenge invigorated him. Raising his head to the elements, he butted into the rain with fresh determination. Less than a lap to go and he still felt he had something to give. He knew he mustn't panic, just hold his pace and the coveted inside lane, and he was still there with a chance.

For the remainder of the bend, they were locked together, their arms and legs pumping in perfect symmetry, each testing the other for a sign of weakness.

As though draining the heavens, the rain was still bucketing down with unrelenting ferocity, soaking the runners to their skin so that their thin shorts and vests clung to their bodies like coats of paint.

In the back straight, they were still shoulder to shoulder, each man not prepared to surrender as they faced the watery track ahead for the last time. Philip, for his part, felt strangely thrilled by the unexpected challenge of this unknown stranger. There was nothing like competition to bring out the best in him. In a concerted effort, he injected a kick which gave him half a metre but no more. It was a move that broke David's concentration and his stride, just sufficient for him to catch the lip of the track and stumble, an error that cost him a metre and the inside lane. Philip swooped like an unleashed greyhound carrying him into the final straight just over a metre clear.

In a state of high animation, Charlie had followed the race as best he could in the poor conditions. He had attempted to read his stopwatch at various stages of the race but the heavy splattering of rain on the glass dial had made the task impossible. As he moved towards the finish, he saw David stumble on the bend and lose the advantage. He cursed only briefly as he watched in awe at his recovery.

Quickly recapturing his footing, David's only reaction was to push harder in the hope of closing the slight gap that had now opened up. Intuitively, he sharpened his pace, determined as he was to get back into the race.

Once on the inside lane, Philip felt secure despite sensing the presence of his opponent. His final kick was always a winner and he was confident it would carry him well clear down the final straight. He kicked, striding out with the grace and class of the athlete he undoubtedly was, his goal, the finishing line, now no more than forty metres ahead.

Working harder as he came off the bend into the straight, David could see he was holding Philip to the small margin that separated them. It was here that he made his effort. Mustering all his energy, he made one last surge. It took him again to Philip's shoulder but no sooner was he there than the Champ responded, his pride not allowing him to surrender as he regained the lead by no more than half a metre.

David pushed once more, gasping as he was for breath over the final strides. Through half-closed lids, he realised he was gaining, drawing ever closer, each agonising stride gnawing at the deficit between them. The pain grew worse, excruciating, searing his vision with a red mist of blinding agony. He struggled on, forcing his brain to respond, his legs feeling like jelly under him, the pain scorching his chest. And then, thankfully, it was over and he fell to the ground.

Charlie had run back to the finish, positioning himself so that he could watch the final throes of this unbelievable performance without hindrance. Mopping his brow to stem the dripping rain, he refocused his eyes on the beginning of the straight, not sure he could believe what he was witnessing. David was challenging the Champ. Bit by bit, he was clawing back the slight deficit, closing ever nearer to his celebrated opponent.

Charlie's heart raced uncontrollably upwards. His fledgling athlete humbling the Champ. It was beyond his wildest dreams. As they lunged for the line, there was nothing between them, both their faces contorted in masks of pain.

Then, it all happened at once. The two athletes flashed past the line, glued together like Siamese twins. At the same time, Charlie's finger hit the button of his stopwatch, and there was a cry of anguish, so raw and chilling, that it eclipsed all else.

Instinctively, Charlie glanced towards the sound to see Freddie fall heavily on to the sodden ground with a resounding crash that jangled his nerves. Like Charlie, Freddie had dashed from the far side, across the inner track, to reach the finishing straight before the runners. With his mind on the race, he failed to see the two loose hurdles lying flat on the wet grass. As his left foot caught the weighted stand protruding from the ground, the hurdle flew rapidly upwards, catching him at his knee so that he stumbled, his ankle cracking mercilessly with the reaction.

Charlie quickly dismissed the race as he dashed across the track to Freddie's aid. Arriving at his side, he could see he was in a bad way, his leg twisted at a frightening angle. He had crashed so quickly that his head hit the ground before he had time to put his arms out and protect himself.

"Are you all right, Fred?" Charlie asked with some concern as he squeezed his shoulder for a response. A long agonising groan issued from the ground before Freddie moved his head. When he did so, his face was covered in thick mud from his chin to his forehead, the whites of his eyes glaring forlornly from the slimy mask. Already, the right eye looked to be swollen from the bruising. Charlie moved to straighten his leg and Freddie immediately winced from the pain.

"I think it's broken," he hissed pitifully through clenched teeth.

"Can someone phone for an ambulance, please?" Charlie requested of the two stewards who had stayed at their posts during the downpour to marshal the race and were now approaching to investigate the state of the fallen coach. One of them immediately pulled his mobile from his pocket and dialled for the emergency services.

"Do you want to try and get up?" Charlie asked Freddie as a further mournful sigh came from the coach's mud-splattered lips.

"No, I'll wait for the ambulance," replied Freddie sharply, giving Charlie the feeling he was dreading any movement. By now, the rain had abated somewhat, so that only a slight drizzle was falling.

"What's up with Freddie?"

Charlie looked up to see Philip approaching. He had obviously recovered from his race and was just pulling his tracksuit top over his chest. He looked concerned.

"He thinks he's broken his ankle," Charlie answered with some feeling.

For a brief moment, Philip's eyes were glued to the distressed Freddie as he made his own assessment of the situation. "Doesn't look good, does he?" he said in a lowered voice, his face etched in sadness. Charlie nodded in agreement.

"We're waiting on an ambulance and we can't do anymore, so I suggest you go to the pavilion and get some dry clothes on, young man," Charlie advised.

"Okay," Philip said. "I'll come back when I've changed." Turning away from Charlie, he ran off at a leisurely pace in the direction of the pavilion.

No sooner had he gone than Charlie caught sight of David beside the track. Soaking wet, his hair hanging lankly over his forehead, he looked completely exhausted. However, as Charlie approached, there was a sharp rise in his demeanour.

"Don't think I quite made it," he said through a mischievous smile.

Charlie said nothing until he was right in front of him. He then threw his arms out, drawing him to his chest and kissed his sweaty neck playfully. For a couple of seconds, he held him there before gently separating, his hands on his shoulders so that their eyes held one another's.

"Dave," Charlie said with a look that spoke volumes. "You were absolutely marvellous." David smiled back coyly.

"I'm pleased with my performance."

"P...l...e...a...s...e...d!" Charlie shouted loudly. "P...l...e...a...s...e...d," he repeated, even more emphatically. "You should be over the moon. You have just given one of the best athletes in the country the fright of his life."

The short spell of euphoria was quickly broken by a further cry from the distressed Freddie who was trying to bend his knee in an attempt to assess his injury.

"Look, Dave, you go and get some dry clothes on before you catch pneumonia, and we will talk later."

"Okay, Charlie. Are you sure you don't want some help though?"

"No, I'll be fine, thank you, the ambulance will be here soon and we'll get old Freddie off to hospital."

David turned and started trotting towards the pavilion.

For the next twenty minutes, Charlie patiently waited for the ambulance. He could not dismiss the race from his mind. The fact that David had all but beaten Philip Rhodes was a miracle, an unbelievable event he could never have foreseen in any way. Philip was hailed by many as the new Sebastian Coe with strong expectations of winning a medal, possibly a gold, in next year's Olympics. The fact that the storm had interrupted the race almost from the start was not really an excuse for Philip to underperform. In any case, the conditions were the same for both runners.

Charlie's mind was working overtime, so shocked by what he had witnessed, he ran through the details of the race time and time again, trying, he guessed, to find some reason as to why Philip may have performed badly to allow David to push him so closely. Again and again, the faces of both men came to his mind as they put in their final effort towards the line. Both had given the race their best effort, he was sure. Lost in these thoughts, he was suddenly overcome by a flash of inspiration. Why hadn't he thought of it before?

In a flurry, he pulled his stopwatch from his tracksuit pocket and looked at the dial. What he saw was as big a surprise as the race itself. His eyes were transfixed to the figures before him. 03 36.92. The time was just unbelievable. Just eight seconds short of the British record. In those conditions.

Then, from nowhere, a siren split his concentration. He looked up to see an ambulance splashing through the puddles across the grounds in his direction. Immediately, he dismissed his thoughts for later consideration.

With the arrival of the ambulance, a group of runners from the Spartan Club filed out of the pavilion to check on Freddie's condition. As the two ambulance men went about their job of assessing Freddie's injury, they crowded around, talking noisily amongst themselves, much to the annoyance of the suffering patient.

Philip was amongst them so Charlie took the opportunity of having a word with him.

"How do you think the race went, Philip?" he asked casually.

Philip gave the matter a little thought before answering. The upheaval following the race had given him precious little time to reflect.

"I would say it was a good run in the conditions," he said candidly. "I must admit I was surprised that your guy pushed me so close. Who is he? I don't think I've come up against him before."

"His name is David Lucas and he only joined us a few months ago," Charlie answered, all of a sudden feeling a little cagey.

"Well, he's a bloody fine athlete, Charlie. I'll tell you that. Did you get a time, by the way?"

"No," Charlie lied, rather too emphatically and immediately reprimanded himself for his enthusiasm. "Unfortunately, Freddie fell just as you were finishing and in the ruckus that followed, I forgot to press the button."

"Shame, I reckon it could have been quite good, considering the conditions," Philip said, shrugging off his disappointment.

Within ten minutes, the ambulance staff had completed their initial assessment. Freddie was suitably subdued with some mild drugs, temporarily reducing the pain, the ankle was heavily bandaged and the patient was safely on the stretcher ready for transporting to the awaiting ambulance.

As Freddie came towards him, now sitting high on the stretcher with his entourage of Spartan followers shouting words of encouragement, he raised his hand in a sort of regal salute. It reminded Charlie of an old sixties film he had only recently watched on the television depicting the life of Cleopatra.

Controlling the smile that simmered on his lips, Charlie pushed forward to wish him well.

"Good luck, Freddie, old boy. Hope it's not as bad as you think," he said with sincerity.

"Can you stop for a moment?" Freddie requested of his two carriers. As they did so, Freddie raised his hand from the blanket and stretched it out towards Charlie who grabbed it heartily. "I'm so sorry to leave you like this, Charlie, and I'm sorry we can't lunch together tonight. I was really looking forward to that."

"So was I," said Charlie, lying for the second time in rapid succession and hoping his face hid his true feelings. "We'll make up for it some time, I'm sure, Freddie. Now, you look after yourself, mind and get that ankle better."

"And...Charlie," Freddie continued. "Thank that young man for his pace making with Philip. He ran a good race. I think the Champ must have been a little off colour today, but even so, he did very well." Controlling his emotions, Charlie found it hard to restrain himself, but was glad he did. He just smiled calmly at his old adversary as he was carried away, still waving graciously to his teammates.

That evening, as Charlie returned home, he was still in a state of high elation.

Chapter 13

"It's Charlie," Tom cried excitedly as he rushed into the lounge where his dad was finishing his evening meal. Quickly swallowing the final mouthful and dropping his tray and empty plate on to the carpet, David took the phone from his son.

"Hello, Charlie. What's up?"

"Hi, Dave, nothing too serious," Charlie said in his usual calm manner. "Would it be okay to come round and see you?"

"Yes," David confirmed, his voice not disguising the mystery of this unexpected call. "Do you mean tonight?"

"If that's okay?"

"Wow, it must be important."

"Well, yes and no," Charlie countered. "It won't take long, I promise."

"Then come when you're ready. You have aroused my interest."

"I'll see you very shortly."

"That's great. Bye."

A mere twenty minutes passed before the doorbell rang. Tammy was the first to respond, closely followed by Tom. No sooner had the front door opened than Tammy had forced her way through the gap between Tom's legs and the door, and was soon administering her usual greeting of warm and wet licks to the receptive Charlie.

"Hi, girl, lovely to see you," Charlie said as Tom grabbed her collar and yanked her back so that Charlie could enter. "And nice to see you, young man," Charlie added, addressing Tom. "How are you?"

"Fine, Charlie, thanks," Tom replied with a clear smile. He had taken an immediate liking to Charlie, not only for saving his dad's life, but there was a gentle and understanding side to him that had somehow appealed to his young instincts right from the start.

With Charlie leading the way, all three of them moved into the lounge where David sprung up from his seat to offer his hand.

"Hi, Coach, have you come to give me some tips on beating Philip?"

"I don't think you need them, Son, because the next time you run against him, you will beat him, I can tell you."

Charlie had never called him *son* before, but there was a pleasant ring to it and David found it quite warming.

"Do you really think so?" David replied, quite casually.

"Yes, I do." It was said with such emphasis, David realised that Charlie's mission may be of a more serious nature than he had imagined.

"Take a seat, Charlie," he said, directing him to the settee. "Would you like a drink?"

"Not at the moment, Dave, thank you."

"I'm going to play on my computer, Dad," Tom announced, sensing his presence was not required.

"Okay, mate, I'll come and give you a game later, won't be long," David replied.

"Hope I'm not spoiling your evening barging in like this," Charlie said with obvious sincerity.

"No, no, it's nice to see you, Charlie. You're always welcome."

"Right, I'll get to the point," Charlie began in earnest, pulling himself up so that he was perched on the edge of the settee facing David. "From your very first visit to the club, that day when you joined my juniors in the winter, I have been amazed at your performances." David looked pleased but said nothing. "You have an incredible amount of talent for somebody who has had no proper training or coaching. Your ability is natural and extraordinary." Charlie paused just slightly to let his words sink in. David's expression remained unchanged, only the intensity of his eye contact giving any indication of his feelings.

"You have great speed in your legs and I thought initially sprinting was to be your forte but in recent months, you have shown me you have stamina and pace as well. This is quite unusual. When I put you up against Colin Baker and Neil Goodman, I'll be honest, I never expected you to beat them but you have now done so on several occasions. They are not brilliant athletes but they are good, very good, in fact. Today, you were in a different class."

David was lost as to where Charlie's rhetoric was leading. Unable to absorb the significance of his praise to any degree, he listened patiently. He was building his presentation so well that David felt the stirrings of suspense gripping him tighter. Charlie read his mind, the knitted brow and thoughtful expression on David's face telling him all he wanted to know. He had built the suspense now he would deliver the knock out hopefully.

"Today, you took on Philip Rhodes, a young man who won the Paris Grand Prix last year and is hailed by Freddie as the greatest talent he has ever coached. And, what's more, you almost beat him. Many pundits have openly stated that they believe he has an excellent chance of winning a medal at next year's Olympic Games." Charlie took a deep breath.

"In another metre, I have no doubt you would have beaten him," he went on. "To say I was gobsmacked, would be putting it mildly. I was completely shocked, dumbfounded would probably be a better word. In fact, I have been in a trance ever since. I can't remember the last time I have been on such a high." Another short pause and Charlie continued,

"I spent the time whilst I was waiting for Freddie's ambulance trying to work out in my mind any good reason why Philip may have run so badly, if he ran badly at all. It was then the one thing, the one stupid thing that provided the cast

79

iron proof to how true the race had been run, came to mind. I had timed the race and in the confusion of Freddie's accident, I had completely forgotten this. I pulled my stopwatch out and unbelievably, the time for the race showed 3 minutes 36.92 seconds, only eight seconds short of the British record." Charlie's eyes were flaring with excitement now.

"Philip told me no time was taken?" David questioned.

"That's what I told him because I wanted to check my assessments before making any announcement," Charlie lied, as he had had no intention of telling Freddie or his charge of his discovery.

David was totally bemused. He had little idea of times but he could see from Charlie's elation that he felt it was something special. Neither spoke for some time, just eyed each other blankly as the implications of Charlie's words sunk deeper and deeper into David's mind.

Breaking the silence, David asked, "So where do we go from here, Coach?"

"What I am about to say may take you by surprise but I would ask that you give it some time to consider before making a decision. Is that okay?" Charlie's eyes held David's with an unwavering stare as he waited for his response. Not for the first time, David felt uncomfortable, not happy with the pressure the question may put on him. Finally, he answered in the only way he could.

"Yes, as far as I can see," he said, with nervous conviction, his brow furrowed deeper.

"Davy, I want you to consider becoming a full-time athlete; train two or three times a day, every day under my supervision. By next year, I'm sure you can achieve a standard that will put you in with a chance of gaining a place in the UK team for the Olympics."

As the penny quickly dropped and the full implications of Charlie's words became clear, David seemed to relax, his face breaking into a broad smile. At last, he could see where Charlie had been leading.

"Charlie, I have told you this many times in the past." It was said in a genial tone that could not offend. "I have a mortgage to pay and a young son to care for, just to mention a couple of my commitments."

Charlie raised his hand to cut him off. "Wait a minute, let me finish," he teased, a fresh smile spreading rapidly across his face.

"What I have seen of your ability, I am willing to back by providing someone to take over your work, to keep the landscape gardening and construction side of your business running, and, I promise to top up your earnings from this so that they are at least as good as you are currently bringing home."

If David had looked bewildered, he now looked completely shocked. He couldn't believe what he had just heard. This man, whom he had come to admire, trust and even revere was willing to sponsor him to participate in a sport that he enjoyed immensely but had never seen as anything more than a physical activity to keep himself fit and provide a little recreational relief from his daily routine. Charlie was asking him to become a professional athlete, to make running a major part of his life. For a while, he was both stunned and speechless as the full impact of Charlie's words filtered through his brain.

"I thought this may shock you," Charlie said after a while, only too aware of the magnitude of his request.

David looked up. "You're spot on there, Charlie," he replied, with a shallow smile.

"Well, I did say I wanted you to give it some thought. I do realise it is a lot for you to take in." Composing himself somewhat, David leaned back in his chair, looking completely exhausted by the weight of the conundrum that had been put upon him. For a while, he just stared at the ceiling deep in thought.

"You don't have to give me an answer until you have fully considered all the implications, good and bad."

"I think I'm the one who needs a drink," David said, jumping up from the settee and making for the kitchen. "Do you want one, Charlie?"

"Yes, I'll join you for a quick lager, if that's all right?" Before he had finished speaking, David had left the room.

A few minutes on his own in the kitchen gave him the chance to collect his thoughts to some degree, so that, by the time he returned to Charlie, a tray with two glasses of lager in his hand, he was able to offer a response that would hopefully satisfy him for the moment.

"Look, Charlie," he began, after passing him his drink. "You have given me an awful lot to think about. I need to discuss it not only with Tom but Rachel, who already plays a big part in the business and will be required to play an even bigger part if I'm not around most of the day. So, can you give me a couple of days to check out their reactions, and then I can make a decision and let you know?"

"Of course, Dave," Charlie answered warmly. "No hurry." It was as good a response as Charlie had hoped for at this stage. At least it wasn't a definite no.

***

The following forty-eight hours were some of the longest Charlie could ever remember. For the next two nights, he slept poorly as the events of Saturday afternoon replayed time and again in his brain. The desperate plunge to the finishing line by both athletes, the look of agony on their faces, Freddy's accident and the discovery of their fantastic time on his stopwatch; all combined to keep him from his sleep. On Sunday evening, he stayed up until 1 a.m., watching a film that held little interest in the hope of sleeping better, but once in bed, it was the same old situation with the elusive sleep escaping him for what seemed long and fretful hours.

When Monday finally arrived, at work, he was more tense than ever, treating each phone call that came to his desk as if David was on the other end of the line and grabbing at the receiver on the immediate sound of its ring. By lunchtime, he felt exhausted, the combination of lack of sleep and anticipation rendering him useless to his job. Nevertheless, he soldiered on, the belief that the call would come eventually, keeping him focused.

When, at last, David phoned, it was half-past eight that evening and he was at home. As he had done all day, he grabbed the receiver and put it to his ear.

"Hello," he said.

"Hello, Charlie, it's Dave." By this time, he was so uptight that a voice in the back of his head was assuring him the answer he so badly wanted was going to be a negative. For once, he was too nervous to speak. On the other end of the line, David was lost at the silence.

"Charlie, I want to take up your offer."

Charlie repeated the words to himself to make certain that he had heard them correctly before speaking.

"Are you sure?" he stammered as the relief filled him with the most wonderful elation he had ever experienced.

"Yes, I am," David laughed. "When do we start training?"

Part 2
Death and Glory

Chapter 1

It was well into the New Year. The weathermen had forecast a harsh winter and the gods were certainly delivering. A bitterly cold January ensued.

The lone runner trudged his weary path along the track, the teasing sleet stinging his bare face with every stride. Yet, the stronger the wind struck him, the more determined he became, so that he bent low into its path, not allowing his pace to slacken.

Once again, he sensed that his training was right, his body harnessing the ripening fruits of his work, his physical strength and stamina responding comfortably to his needs.

Ahead of him, through the turbulence of the falling sleet, he could just make out the silhouette of another human being, standing tall, watching him thoughtfully, his hands thrust deep into the pockets of his thick winter coat. David was nearing the end of his daily training session and welcomed the sight of this familiar figure, this colossus of a man who had transformed his life from mediocrity to one of daily achievement and purpose. Running had truly become his life and if he could believe Charlie, it would not be long before running was to become his passport to an exciting future.

He could hardly wait to sample the rewards of the programme that had been mapped out and executed so meticulously over the past six months. If everything went according to Charlie's plans, these would blissfully begin to materialise very shortly. In late March, only weeks away now, the competitive season would commence with a series of club meetings. These would be followed by the main meetings such as Crystal Palace where he would hopefully mark his card for a place in the GB Olympic squad. The really important day would be Saturday, June 21st, the British Championships at Birmingham, the one and only chance of selection for the British Olympic team. Just the thought of this day, and what it could mean sent a diverse flutter of excitement and fear through his whole body.

Then, if everything went to plan, there was the build-up to the London Olympiad in August, an event so breath-taking that it seemed surreal at this moment in time. The whole programme, if it materialised as planned, could only be described as mind-boggling.

Approaching Charlie, he prepared himself for his final effort, mentally tuning himself for the sprint that would lift him comfortably to the sprawling elm only fifty metres ahead where today's session would come to an end. Charlie was still working on his stamina and today was just another small brick in the wall they were gradually building.

Earlier in the morning, he had worked tirelessly at the gym over a period of some two hours with little rest, just part of a long routine that was now his life. These days, his body always felt weary, there being little respite from the endless round of weights, exercises and physical running.

It was part of the course, so Charlie told him and he had learnt to love it in a sadistic sort of way. If anything, it was a good feeling, a strange reaction that made him feel his body was alive. As far as he could see, there were so many positives in this new game. In the past months, he had discovered an inner strength of which he had been unaware, an inner strength that had surfaced and appeared to have, up until now at least, all the answers to the challenges that were put before him. He had surprised himself, so many times, with his own fortitude and will power. He was modestly proud of himself.

If he was truthful, it was the physical running that actually gave him the most pleasure. The gym and other aspects of his training, he tackled with the same discipline and enthusiasm but only because he realised that these routines, at times so mundane and boring, were gradually building the framework of his development, the bedrock of his stamina and strength that would hopefully carry him in to the future with all the success that Charlie promised. They were a vital part of the programme, of this he had no doubt. Once he was running, the ease with which his legs and lungs responded, the fluency and freedom of movement, confirmed the work that Charlie had so carefully prepared, was more than adequate for the job in hand.

It was only two-thirty in the afternoon, but already a premature dusky atmosphere prevailed, there being little light on offer from the murky grey clouds that tumbled endlessly through the overcast sky. Throughout this scenario, the sleet continued to fall with monotonous indifference, dampening the spirit of the day with what seemed an interminable bleakness.

Charlie's hand withdrew from his pocket the obligatory stopwatch as he cued David for his final sprint.

"Good work, Davy, now go for it, lad," he enthused.

Just for the briefest of moments, their eyes locked in what was now an intuitive understanding as David accelerated smoothly, maintaining his drive for forty or more strides until he reached his goal. When he did so, he pulled up comfortably, immediately floating into a more relaxed rhythm that allowed his body to commence its recovery.

He was tired, he had to be after such a strenuous session, but the satisfaction that accompanied this feeling touched him with its usual warmth of contentment. It was a couple of minutes before his heart was back to normal, but, as usual, he felt fulfilled. He turned and trotted back to where Charlie was standing. His mentor's broad smile confirmed his own intuition.

"Just under fifty-two minutes. Good time for the conditions, my boy. Well done." Beneath his woolly hat, Charlie's face looked gnarled and flushed from the cold, but there was no mistaking his upbeat mood.

"You're getting stronger all the time, how did it feel?"

"Good," David confirmed. "There was a harsh wind coming back but I just put my head down and pushed into it."

"That's all you can do in these conditions. I'm afraid the long-term weather forecast doesn't offer any respite either. Apparently, tomorrow we may get some snow early on and it's sub-zero temperatures again."

"That'll make a change," said David in his usual jubilant mood. "Throw it all at me, Charlie, I can take it." Charlie loved this natural exuberance. Over the months, he had noted how so often his mood changed for the better following a run and this pleased him greatly.

In particular, it stirred in his mind memories of the numerous times a run had had the same effect on himself over the years. He remembered fondly one occasion during his early years as a junior estate agent when all the staff had been called to the manager's office to learn that, with business at an all-time low, they were sorry to announce they had no option but to cull the staff by fifty per cent. Being the latest member to join the company and the youngest, Charlie imagined that he would be top of the list of redundancies.

The air of depression throughout the office for the remainder of that afternoon was almost tangible, the long faces and sombre atmosphere sealing the mood of disaster. When the hands of the office clock finally limped past the six-thirty closing time, the majority of the staff decamped to the local pub to drown their sorrows in a close-knit orgy of despair. Charlie had given his apologies for absence well beforehand, telling his comrades that his mother was ill and he had to visit her. If they had known he was out running across the countryside thirty minutes later, they may not have agreed with his therapy. Much to his surprise, he was one of ten to hold his job when the announcements were made the following day.

Without realising it, he found himself smiling as he contemplated that nothing had really changed. Running still had the same effect on him, even now, in the twilight years of his life. *Stupid old fool*, he chastised himself.

"Better get back to the club and get some warm clothes on," he instructed David on realising he had broken into a fairly brisk session of running on the spot to keep warm. In the conditions, David needed little encouragement. On Charlie's advice, he ceased the activity, smiled politely and pulled his tracksuit collar tighter around his neck.

"Yes, you're right, boss. It's a bit chilly. I'll see you later." Without further ado, he turned and moved off at a gentle trot, flapping his arms across his chest to generate some warmth as he did so.

The flowing effortless glide of his legs had Charlie's eyes glued to his receding outline as he climbed the hill ahead. Proudly, Charlie watched until he had passed out of sight. Only then did he set off for his car, the pain in his knee temporarily anaesthetised by the pleasantries of his thoughts.

***

Arriving back at the clubhouse, the old shack played its usual role in dampening David's spirits. Built in the early years of the previous century, the wooden army hut had been refurbished so many times there was little left of the original timbers.

As the door creaked his entry, he was disappointed to find the temperature appeared to have risen very little since they had left the premises nearly two hours previous. Despite the boiler working its heart out, it was still strikingly cold. Everyone knew the old boiler was on its last legs but with the club on the threshold of bankruptcy the purchase of a new one was hardly a priority.

It was a well-known fact, endorsed by the continuous issue of pleas for financial support from the committee and the rather tedious overplay of weekend raffles, that a crisis was imminent. The current exercise to try and sell off part of their land, in particular a corner of the car park, as a plot for building development was considered by many to be the final act of desperation. With the building industry in the doldrums, they had not, as yet, received a single offer.

What most of the members didn't know and the committee had purposely kept from them, was that the Inland Revenue were breathing very strongly down their necks for a sum slightly in excess of five thousand pounds. This rather frightening amount was in respect of overdue National Insurance contributions, which should have been paid several years previous, in respect of staff employed at that time. So far, they had been able to fob them off with partial payments on a monthly basis, but how long the IR would allow this to continue, remained to be seen.

The lack of a proper accountant had led to this rather unfortunate calamity, a matter which had been temporarily solved only in the past week by the offer of services from Geoff Stanley, a veteran member, now retired, but highly qualified, who had promised to take over the post for a minimum of two years. On top of this, a handful of the club members, including surprisingly two teenagers, had volunteered their services, also for free, at weekends, to man the bar and assist with keeping the facilities in a respectable condition. All these savings would hopefully help the club to reduce its running costs and, with a bit of luck, save them from extinction.

Stripping off his vest, the cold hit David like a punch; so much so that his arms were a mass of blotchy white goose bumps in a matter of seconds. He almost ran to the clubroom to find the thermostat. Quickly adjusting the dial, he added a further five degrees, guiltily wondering what effect his winter training outside of the usual club hours was having on the overall costs. Little did he know Charlie's generous offer to pay the club's heating bill for the whole year, backed by an immediate cheque at the time of one thousand pounds, had been gratefully accepted, the cheque banked by the committee without hesitation.

Back in the changing room, he tore off the remainder of his kit and hurried naked across the passage to the showers, grabbing his towel from his bag on passing. Giving the water a couple of minutes to reach an acceptable temperature, he jumped underneath the weak jet and was soon enjoying the refreshing spray. It would be a few minutes before Charlie joined him. In this time, he allowed himself to relax, his eyes closed tightly whilst he drained the tensions of the day from his body, luxuriating both mentally and physically under the hypnotic caress of the falling water.

"Have you warmed up yet?" Charlie's voice eventually interrupted his thoughts.

"Yes, I can just about feel my legs again," came his reply as he brushed the water from his face to see Charlie taking up the next cubicle. He was always amazed at the superb physical condition Charlie had kept himself, his body still lean and muscular despite his sixty-five years. Only the marked limp and slight hesitation as he stepped over the shower sill gave an indication that his body was finally succumbing to the march of time.

"How's Rachel, Dave?" Charlie asked once he had adjusted the shower to an acceptable setting. "How's she coping with the business?"

"Okay…I think, Charlie, she doesn't really say a lot, but I gather her plans for expanding the nursery business are working out. She's a go-ahead girl, that's for sure. Always thinking up new ideas. I'm lucky to have her. When she gets home, I think she's as knackered as I am. She cooks the evening meal for the three of us, and then we sit down and I fall asleep."

"That sounds exciting," Charlie said with a touch of sarcasm. "Never mind, once the season's over, you can sit back with your gold medal and your MBE, a national hero with a big bank balance. That should be incentive enough to make her realise it's all worthwhile?"

David had to smile at the flamboyancy of Charlie's words. He was sure Rachel had no such aspirations. In fact, he would go as far as saying that she possibly thought they were both mad in pursuing the dream Charlie had so convincingly mapped out. Yet, from the start, she had readily agreed and seemed happy to assist whenever she could to make a contribution in whatever way was necessary.

Right from the beginning, there had been a positivity about Charlie that would have been almost comical if not delivered with the sincerity of a man who believed a hundred per cent in what he was saying. At times, Charlie spoke as though he only had to train and turn up at the Olympic final to collect his gold medal. Of course, such faith was wonderful and from time to time, he found himself sharing his dreams. However, there was a limit to how far you were able to inflate your ego, especially when there was so far to go, so many obstacles to overcome and very little idea of the enormity of the target you are to achieve. He tried to keep some rational judgement to the task ahead.

But, whatever the future held for him, his new role as an athlete was one he was really enjoying. Above all, it was interesting, rewarding and had given him a new lease of life for which he was truly thankful. If, at the end of the road, he was not even good enough to reach the Olympic standard, he had lost nothing. In reality, he could return to his work and carry on where he left off, better for the experience.

"The fame and fortune sound wonderful, Charlie, but a little off my radar at this stage of the game."

"You *have* to believe me, my boy. If you don't believe in yourself, you have no chance. I'm telling you, *honestly,* that you have the ability to reach the top. Your training is going really well in the right direction and I can only tell you that I'm amazed at your development, especially your times and your performances, and I really mean that. I promised you right from the start that there is no way I'd bullshit you and tell you you're good if you're not. That's not my way and you can ask anyone that."

The sincerity of Charlie's words wedged a temporary silence between them. The funny thing was that he didn't have to ask anyone what they thought of Charlie. Almost from the time he had joined the club, one or other of the members, right from the very young to the hierarchy of ex-presidents and senior members, had been only too willing to confirm, without prompting, that he was a man held in high esteem by all, a man of high principles who spoke his mind with utter directness whatever the consequences. In fact, it was obvious that one or two had been on the receiving end of some of his stinging outbursts over the years but not one, seemed to hold a grudge.

"I don't doubt that, Charlie," David replied, his smile slipping even wider. The slight inflexion of tone was not only picked up but had the effect of irritating his mentor further.

"Anyhow, when you line up in the British Trials and win your place in the Olympic team, you will start to believe, I can assure you, young man."

From the starched tone of Charlie's voice, David realised he had to cease his baiting.

"Thank you, Charlie, for all you have done for me. Whatever happens in the future, I shall appreciate these last few months, not only because I have enjoyed working with you so much, but because I have discovered a part of me that I didn't know existed. I love what I'm doing and I will always give a hundred per cent, I promise."

His words struck home. Charlie found it quite touching. Reaching down to the floor, he retrieved the gel bottle that had slipped from his hand. Straightening up, he turned the shower off and shook the surplus water from his hair. Then, with no warning, he pushed a clenched fist slowly towards the centre of David's stomach in a mock punch.

"I've enjoyed it as well, my boy," he said fondly, a meaningful smile at the same time escaping his lips. "But we still have a long way to go. Don't forget that."

Chapter 2

Rachel was tired. Fridays were always difficult because she was on her own with no helpers. The week so far had, one way and another, been pretty horrendous. Today, however, was turning out to be the toughest of the lot.

No sooner had she arrived at the nursery, yanked the rusty iron gate open at eight o'clock, than she started the mundane round of watering the plants and seeds in the poly-tunnels. Whilst on this task, she made a thorough inspection of the plants, removing any dead leaves, pruning odd shoots and adding sticks to support weak ones where necessary. With twelve long display tables, this preliminary job could often take several hours to complete.

She was little more than halfway through the chore when the bell rang in the shop. She walked through to find a driver from their wholesale stone distributors waving an invoice at her.

"I have two dozen slabs on the lorry," he announced in a thick local accent.

"I'll show you where I want them," she replied leading the way to the outdoor area and pointing out a vacant patch on the patio where she was looking to build a new display. No sooner was she back in the poly-tunnels when two customers entered the shop and from then on, there was a constant stream, one after the other, throughout the morning.

She was pleased the business was taking off so successfully but today, she needed some time to organise a few jobs that could not be delayed any longer. Finally, after skipping her lunch, she was able to finish the watering. It was now two o'clock.

Just when she felt she was getting somewhere and was free to move on to the new tasks, there was, out of the blue, a power cut, throwing the shop into a dimness that was both eerie and depressing under the current weather conditions. Worse still, the cut took out her electric fire, her only source of heat, so that she had to throw her heavy jacket back on to keep warm.

The failure lasted almost an hour. It was not unusual this winter when power cuts had become quite commonplace, presumably because of the high demand for electricity in the atrocious winter conditions. What was worse, the fact that during this time, she decided to move half a dozen slabs outdoors to form a pile with the new delivery. They were all large, a couple of feet square, and very heavy. She was just able, using all her strength, to roll them edge-to-edge, taking care they didn't topple over onto her legs as she shuffled forward. Once alongside the new pile, she spread her legs above each one, bent her back to take the strain and lifted the block as efficiently as she could to lower it carefully on to the pile.

The latter part of the job was quite difficult but was going smoothly until the third slab when her back tweaked unexpectedly, sending a bolt of pain through her whole body. For a few seconds, she couldn't straighten up and then, when she did, she realised the sprain was bad enough to prevent her from doing any further physical work.

Frustrated, she made herself a cup of tea. Sitting and nursing it in her hand, she concentrated her mind on the evening ahead.

Since the beginning of David's new career as an athlete, the bedroom romps had gradually dwindled. Three months ago, when she had moved in with him, there had been a wild and wonderful sense of abandonment on the few evenings that Tom had slept at his friend's house. Gradually though, Tom asked to stay away more and more frequently, a request that David seemed happy to concede to, much to her surprise. Soon, he was spending most of the weekends with his friend, Danny, and often the odd weekday during the holidays. Both her and David had treasured the delightful thrills of an opportunity to be together, the uncertainty of not knowing when they may occur, spicing their appeal even more.

However, in recent months, the constant training had taken its toll. David had fallen asleep in the lounge chair time and time again during the evening, sometimes sleeping so deeply that he would not wake until after midnight unless she roused him. On the occasions she had, he had entered the bedroom like a zombie with a performance to match. She accepted that it was not his fault. He was obviously tired from the physical effort that Charlie was asking of him.

There were still times when he tried his best to satisfy her, throwing himself into the fray with a wild intimacy that left her tingling with sensation for hours afterwards. Even then, he would fall asleep almost immediately, leaving her to dampen down her excitement before sleep would finally overtake her. These times were now, unfortunately, few and far between. He had lost his libido and she knew she had to be patient.

Her relationship with Tom was another worry. It had not really improved, although David would possibly say otherwise, only because Tom led him to believe so. When the three of them were together, he treated her with false respect and affability, his manners soon disappearing once they were on their own. She found this pretence quite distressing.

His bad language was another matter that gave her some concern. When David was not around, he used the 'F' word continuously whilst showing off in front of his friends. It was a word that had been taboo in her family and one she subsequently detested, especially when used by someone so young. She had only heard David swear once in the time she had known him and that had been with the most genuine provocation.

She had pulled the boy up several times at first, a move she then regretted when realising he used it more and more just to annoy her. What to do about it was a problem, for she knew if she informed his father, he would angrily admonish him and the backlash for her would be aggravation from not only Tom, but his friends as well.

With these thoughts swimming around her head, she finished her tea and decided she would prepare a few more speciality pots. Valentine's Day would soon be around, followed closely by Easter, two special occasions that created a sizeable demand for the traditional daffodils and crocuses in presentation pots. She had already prepared half a gross but would, hopefully, need quite a few more. These would boost her takings during the spring months. Her ambition was to try and make the business financially independent, and not supported by Charlie. It was a long shot but she needed something to aim for.

Deep down in her heart, she did not believe that the aspirations Charlie openly broadcast would come true. Sport had never played a part in her life and she found it difficult to share the enthusiasm both men displayed. It was not that she wanted them to fail but just a feeling the whole thing was a little unreal and would just not happen. She knew that both would be disappointed but they would soon get over it, and then David could return to the business and they would be working together again, for part of the day, at least.

Returning to the poly-tunnel, her first job was to make room on her workbench. Next, she examined her box of daffodils for any sign of disease or damage. She removed a couple before deciding the majority were suitable for the job in hand. These would form the centrepiece of her display which would then be supported by a few crocuses and primroses, hopefully, giving the whole arrangement an attractive and distinctive appeal. A large bag of peat was at hand below the table so all she had to do was fetch the plastic pots and she could start.

In her flush of enthusiasm, the pain in her back was temporarily forgotten. Despite the chill, she removed her jacket and rolled up her sleeves before collecting the plastic pots. It was only when she bent down to lift them from the floor that she realised her back was not relenting. A flash of pain caught her sharply.

"That's a sight for sore eyes, hold it there, my sweetie, and let Jas enjoy the view for a little longer." She jumped up in an instant, the pain immediately forgotten on recognising the voice of Jason Phelps.

David's building work had been contracted out to Jason at the beginning of the Charlie and David union, and he would now call in most days on the pretence of learning whether any fresh orders were available.

Rachel had taken an immediate dislike to the man. His suggestive comments and repulsive behaviour made her skin crawl. She felt a flush come over her face as she attempted to hold his stare and keep her composure at the same time. From the sneer on his lips, she realised he was enjoying her embarrassment.

"What do you want, Jason?" she asked, her voice not hiding her contempt.

"Just thought I'd call in and see what's happening. Looks as if I picked the right moment." Again, she tried desperately to ignore the lecherous comment. The lustful raise of the eyebrows as if she was sharing some deep secret with him added further to her dislike for the man.

"Well, there isn't anything at this time," she told him, her voice raised unintentionally. "I told you I would let you know if anything comes in." She was trying her hardest to keep calm but this uncomfortable situation was getting the better of her.

"All right, my luvvie, keep your hair on." He moved closer to her, so close that she could smell the rank stench of his breath, a repugnant mixture of beer and onions, almost suffocating her as she tried with difficulty not to inhale.

"What's wrong? Your boyfriend too tired to keep you happy, is he? I saw him out on the road the other day. Old Charlie boy's certainly putting him through it; the poor sod must be exhausted when he gets to bed. A sweetie like you needs a little action. If you're not getting it regularly, you can always come round and get a little extra at my pad, you know?"

He tried to touch her arm. Her response was to step backwards, an involuntary move she wished she had controlled, not wanting to give him any further indication of the nervous state in which she found herself. As his hand moved towards her again, she pushed it away forcibly, the reaction sufficient to stop him in his tracks.

"Don't touch me or I shall tell Charlie," she threatened. She was not sure why she had chosen Charlie rather than David but it appeared to have the right effect as she noticed the slight check in his advance. She pushed her small advantage. "If he learns that you've given me any aggravation, you won't get any more work, that's for sure." Feeling she now had the upper hand, her confidence returned a little.

"I'll give you a ring if any new jobs come in."

He smiled crudely, signifying that her words held little threat, although she suspected otherwise.

"I'll call in next week, you may want to change your mind."

Not until his back had vanished through the exit and she had heard the bell confirm his departure did she start to relax. Even then, she had to move to the opening to convince herself he had actually left and was not lurking in the shop. On sight of the empty room, she let out a mighty sigh. To add to the pain in her back, her head had started throbbing with a dull ache that promised not to recede. She reached for her bag and withdrew a strip of paracetamol, forcing two from the package and swigging them down her throat with the help of a glass of water.

"What a day," she murmured to herself, her hand supporting her head in sympathy.

Chapter 3

"Don't be silly," Danny Gates said with some emphasis. "Even if yer get caught, which you won't, you always get off with a warning for the first offence." He gave Tom time to digest his words.

"My dad will go bonkers, I tell you. He's never stolen anything in his life."

"I doubt that," Danny replied with a touch of sarcasm. "I bet 'e did when 'e was a kid."

Tom was thoughtful for a few moments. He wanted to stand up for his father's good name but wasn't sure whether he should in the circumstances. He decided to drop it. Falling out with Danny, his best mate, was the last thing he wanted. They had been friends since their first day at Auriol Junior School when they found themselves seated next to each other in the big hall, listening to the warm introductory speech of headmistress, Mrs Hynes.

If the truth was known, on that day, they were both extremely nervous but neither would show it. Both had the bravado to cover it up. From that first day, there had been a mutual respect which had developed strongly over the years to create a formidable friendship.

"Look," said Danny directly, his impatience beginning to show. "If yer don't want to be a part of it, then chicken out, but there won't be a video to watch tonight, okay?"

Danny was pleased to see his words have the right effect as Tom immediately capitulated. Throwing his bag over his shoulder, he grabbed the collar of Danny's coat and yanked him forcefully forward, laughing as his mate lost his balance and almost fell to the ground in an effort to recover. "Okay, I'm with you, matey, just make sure we don't get caught."

"That's up to you, ye're the one who's doing the lifting, remember?"

They made their way through the throng of late shoppers towards Chantells, the town's main store which had proudly survived the economic gloom of the past three years. The current owners were in the process of purchasing the property next door, a family butchers who had been declared bankrupt six months previous. With this acquisition almost in the bag, the three directors would jointly own two thousand square metres of prime shopping area and were seriously considering the addition of a posh cafeteria to enhance the store's status.

"Yer know what yer have to do, don't yer?" Danny asked in hushed tones as they weaved their path around the central barriers erected only twelve months earlier by the Council to stop the motor traffic from parking in the square.

"No problems," replied Tom with a confidence now emanating from the adrenaline pumping through his veins in anticipation of the action ahead. A quick glance between them was all that was necessary to cue the commencement of their plan. They separated, Tom heading for the right-hand double door whilst Danny's target was the double on the left.

Inside and on his own, Tom found his nerves returning, so much so that he feared he might panic when the time came for him to play his hand. He reprimanded himself for his failings, instantly pulling himself together and forcing himself to relax and act as naturally as possible. He took a deep breath and felt better for it.

At the rear of the store, he stopped to investigate a geometry set in the stationery section, pulling it off its metal holder and examining it carefully before placing it back in position. Turning the corner, he found himself facing the display of DVDs and compact discs in the rather pretentious entertainment section. Beyond this was a more than adequate book section, both hard and paperback on display. The store prided itself in its comprehensive stock, generally keeping the top fifty sellers in all three items.

Tom flicked through the DVDs, calmly pulling one out and pretending to read the note on the rear cover before returning it to its original position. Finally, he reached the store's special offer of the week, the newly released video of *Death in Duplicate*. After only showing three months earlier in the local cinemas, it was probably a profitable move for the distributors to offer it to the video buying public, especially if the huge pile of DVDs at ten pounds each was anything to go by. It had done well at the box office and looked as if the DVD sales would go the same way. Satisfied with his preliminary inspection, Tom strolled calmly forward to investigate Danny's movements.

Security guard, Phil Jackson, had worked for Chantells for six years and considered himself a valued member of the staff. From the praise he continually received from brothers, Justin and Daniel Frost, the two main share-holding directors, he felt truly appreciated and in return was willing to fulfil his post as senior security officer, delivering the maximum proverbial pound of flesh whilst on the job.

Within six months of his appointment, he had been told by the brothers that the rate of theft had seriously reduced and the results had continued to please right up to the present day.

At thirty-six years old, he felt in his prime, topping up his physical condition every week with three to four visits to the gym depending on the freedom offered by his girlfriend, Lucy. He prided himself in being able to read a potential thief as soon as he or she came through the door. Just a glance from their eyes, the guilt written therein, the panicky drop of their stare or other giveaway signs in their body language were sufficient to set him on guard.

Today had been reasonably quiet but now a schoolboy had entered and given him a furtive glance followed by a sly nonchalant look back that he had immediately registered as suspicious. He had seen the lad before, he knew that; he usually came into the store with a school friend. Today, he was on his own.

As the lad strolled down the far aisle, Phil moved slowly but steadily along the adjacent parallel one. If nothing else and he should meet him face to face at the end of the row, the lad would realise he was under suspicion and hopefully, abandon any ideas he may have of thieving from the store.

Although he had taken his time, there was no sign of the lad as he reached the adjoining row at the rear end. Cautiously, he turned the corner to peruse his approach. Customers were beginning to disperse, and only a mother and her small child were browsing a railing of slippers down the front end.

Only when they moved away was he aware that the lad had been hiding behind them. The boy's sudden reaction was so incriminating that Phil would have put money on the fact that a pair of sports socks had found their way into the bag hanging, fully opened, at waist height from a strap at his shoulder. Furthermore, the look of fear that now lit the lad's eyes as he saw fourteen stone of security guard approaching was a positive sign of guilt if ever he had seen one.

Propelling himself down the aisle at speed to cut off any impulsive escape, Phil was suddenly confused by the lad's behaviour. Just as he thought he was about to make a bolt for the door, he changed direction and walked calmly towards him. And then, only a couple of paces apart, he flashed him a cheesy grin. It completely baffled him.

Despite a tightness in his gut, Tom had to smile as he watched with interest the antics of the security guard stalking Danny. The man reminded him of a lioness he had recently seen on a television nature programme pursuing its prey. Without realising it, he had transferred his weight to his toes so that he was rising at each step with the suppleness of a ballet dancer. From the cover of a broad display of boxed kitchen utensils stacked by the middle door, he had seen Danny saunter off along the furthest aisle and the guard tracking him in the penultimate one, presumably to cut him off at the far end.

At last, it was his turn to make a move. As he walked at a casual pace down the aisle, a young couple ran past him holding hands warmly. The store seemed to be emptying of customers which boosted his confidence a little.

Nervously, he returned to the entertainment aisle. The sight of a female assistant filling the shelves a short distance away initially paralysed him, yet, he checked himself immediately, realising that she was completely immersed in the job she was doing. There was no one else about. Calmly, he lifted the DVD case from the display and dropped it in his bag. With his heart now hammering in his chest like a tom-tom, he made for the doors.

You're over the worst, he told himself, *relax, keep calm and just walk out in the usual way. Don't look suspicious, whatever you do. Just act naturally.* Step by step, he reached the door, expecting at any moment for a hand to grab his shoulder and pull him back. Before he knew it, he was through, out in the open, the cold air kissing his cheeks, bringing him back to normality, his mind now honed in control as he crossed the square. Within a few strides, he felt he was safe.

"Are you following me, mate?" Danny enquired of Phil Jackson.

The security guard's face went limp with surprise, his professional training abandoning him for a brief moment.

"You think I've stolen something, don't yer? Well, I ain't, see, look for yerself."

With this, Danny pulled the flaps of his bag fully open showing it to be devoid of any contents except two exercise books.

"It's okay, Son," Phil said with a slight hesitation, at the same time clearing his throat with a wispy cough as he regained his composure. "I'm here to do my job, that's all. If you haven't stolen anything, that's fine." Danny was enjoying himself and in no hurry to bring it to a conclusion.

"Well, you shouldn't accuse people."

"I didn't accuse you, you challenged me, if you remember, Sonny," Phil retorted, feeling at last he was back on his feet and not prepared to let this youngster get the better of him.

"I've a good mind to report you to your superiors," Danny added.

"You can do what you like, young man, but I would advise you to leave the store and get off home."

Unfazed by the sudden change in tactics, Danny held his ground long enough to maintain respect, eyeing his adversary with a calmness that could only be interpreted as arrogance.

"Maybe next time," he said. Aware that it was time to make his departure, he closed his bag, raised his hand in a mock salute, turned and walked at a leisurely pace to the door.

It was Phil's turn to look bemused. As he watched Danny leave, the doors closing on his back, he could not help but smile at the lad's audacity. *Kids today,* went through his mind.

They met in the bus depot as arranged, both Tom and Danny still high on the emotion of their success.

"Told yer it would be a doddle, didn't I?" Danny said enthusiastically. "You should have seen the look on the guard's face when I squared up to 'im."

First Danny and then Tom related their different stories, each of them embellishing the details to spice up the adventure, both omitting any reference to fear or doubts. It took a good ten minutes for each to cover their respective episodes but once they had satisfied their egos, they took a seat at the bus shelter. Danny drew his mobile from his jacket and dialled a familiar number.

"Mum," he said after a few seconds. "Can you come to the bus depot and pick us up. We've finished our shopping."

Chapter 4

"I'm home," Rachel called aloud as she pushed Tammy to one side and kicked the front door closed with the sole of her booted foot. It had been a difficult day, a wearying day she would prefer to forget as soon as possible. She was glad to be home. After a couple of minutes, Tammy's attention had ebbed to a gentle tail wag.

Flushing the day's unsavoury thoughts from her head, she found herself quickly concentrating on the evening ahead. For several weeks now, Tom had spent almost the whole of the weekend, from Friday afternoon to Sunday evening, with his friend, Danny, and she had been led to believe by David that the same was on the cards for this current weekend. At first, when Tom had started sleeping at friends over the weekend, David had seemed on edge with the situation. She guessed he felt a little guilty, perhaps, with his new career in place, that he was not giving him enough of his time. She had to admit she felt a little discarded herself at the moment but realised that the running had priority for the next few months.

However, seeing the lad's jubilant return each Sunday evening, the proof that he had enjoyed the weekend, was sufficient to put David at ease. Confirmation of the completion of his homework was often a bonus. Whereas David had phoned him on his mobile no less than ten times over the weekend on the first occasion, she had noted only one call was made last weekend. She had to admit she felt so much better herself knowing David was happy with the situation.

Entering the dining room, she threw her two plastic bags with her purchases from the local supermarket on to the table. The room felt chilly. Looking through the glass panel of the wood burner, she detected a slight glow from the embers. Grabbing the metal hook from the hearth and yanking the doors open, she found only the tiniest remains of a charred log still smouldering in a bed of ash. It looks promising, she immediately told herself. She guessed David had filled it to capacity on his return, which was probably about two hours ago. She was always amazed at how long the burning process could last with the air vent closed. The basket at the side of the hearth was filled to the brim with logs, and she quickly transferred several to the fire and closed the doors. Within a few minutes, a satisfying whoosh accompanied the flow and she was soon rewarded with the first flame.

"Right," she addressed herself. "Now for David."

With luck, he had had a good two hours sleep and would hopefully be in the process of waking up fresh and energetic. As she climbed the stairs, her back reminded her of her earlier injury, yet, her enthusiasm quickly swiped it from her mind. She entered the bedroom. David was still fast asleep, lying on his back as was his natural position, his face serene and relaxed. The room was chilly, which was probably the reason he had pulled the duvet tight around his neck.

She lowered herself to the bed, so that she was balancing on the edge, all the time her eyes glued to the handsome features of his face in hypnotic fascination. At any moment, his eyes may open, she told herself, the thought sending a sudden stab of a thrill through her body. During her appraisal, he remained still, his breathing so shallow that at first she had to lower her head to catch the soft wispy murmur from his lips.

For a moment, she felt guilty in her desire to wake him. She pondered long enough to abandon her whim, deciding instead to cook their meal and wait for him to wake naturally. Once again, she realised the tremendous effort his new regime was extracting from him. Reluctantly, she left the room.

Back in the kitchen, she emptied the contents of her bags on to the worktop. Only briefly did she evaluate in her mind the calorific value of her purchases, a routine that had become as regular as brushing her teeth. From the beginning of David's new career, Charlie had given her a list of the foodstuffs that were to form his diet over the months preceding the Olympics. She practically knew the calorific value of every article on this formidable list. Casting her eye over the goods, she selected the packet of fresh chicken breasts, a bag of tomatoes and one of broccoli, and quickly dispensed the remainder into the fridge.

In the joyful mood she found herself, she had an urge to play the radio but thought better of it with David sleeping above. Instead, she started humming to herself, a ditty that came naturally to her but one that she would have to analyse thoroughly to decide its title. Whatever, she knew it was appropriate to her mood. Within a few minutes, her meal was well on its way.

"How's the prettiest girl in the world?"

The sudden impact of his voice took her unawares so that she jumped. She turned to see David leaning fully over the bannisters, such a look of pleasure engraved on his face, it squeezed her heart. She dropped the knife she was holding in the sink and ran towards him. At the same time, he descended the remaining stairs, his arms wide. She threw herself at him with such force, he overbalanced and fell backwards on to the bottom steps, her on top of him. They giggled in a foolish cuddle.

"Love you, David Lucas," she said in a hushed whisper as she felt his hands tighten around her hips, pulling her closer to him. Their lips met. They kissed passionately with a tenderness that had them both temporarily mesmerised. For a long moment, they were transfixed, the only movement being the insistent nudge of his lips on hers. Neither wanted to lose the magic of that special moment.

"Love you too, you beautiful creature," he said, finally breaking the spell. "How about an early visit to the bedroom as we have the house to ourselves?" The tone of his voice, the tinge of anticipation, immediately ignited her senses.

"That sounds fine to me," she said decisively, pulling herself away from him so she could focus clearly on his face. For the first time in several weeks, he seemed to be fully tuned to her needs. There was a feisty quality about him, a raw exhilaration that desired fulfilment. In his eyes, she read the intensity of his love, a sensuous promise, the scalding red fire of his passion and she could not wait any longer to quench it.

Warmly, she took his hands in hers and coaxed him to his feet. Playfully, he grabbed her, his tall frame masking her upper body. She felt his hands cup her buttocks firmly and then release them before slowly rising up her back, along her spine, until she could stand it no longer. Lustily, she responded, grabbing his neck for support and throwing her legs around his waist.

Instantly, it hit her, like a bullet in the spine, at first so sharp and fierce she shrieked in terror, the pitch so high he nearly dropped her in fright. Then as her legs fell to the ground, the pain came again, every movement as excruciating as the first.

Standing in front of him, she looked petrified, her face a mask of anguish as the pain streaked down her back in fierce stabbing unbearable flashes. In seconds, her mascara was washing down her ashen cheeks in black freaky smears. He was afraid to touch her.

"What's wrong?" he asked fearfully.

She was shaking, her movements so peculiar he feared she may have had a stroke. Beads of perspiration peppered her brow. He put his hand to her head and was amazed at how cool it felt.

"It's my back," she finally confided, whilst making an effort to relax her muscles and release the spasm. She was scared to move, the fear of further surges paramount in her mind.

"I did it this afternoon when I was lifting some heavy paving stones," she explained.

"Why didn't you tell me?"

"Because...because...I didn't want to spoil this evening," she cried huskily, the tears now streaming down her cheeks in torrents. Instinctively, his arms folded around her shoulders. Gently, he encouraged her to move, at first just half a step and then another until she realised the pain had partially receded, and she could move a little more comfortably. He escorted her to one of the armchairs and let her slide on to the cushioned seat.

"I'm sorry," she said, as he picked up a loose cushion and pushed it behind her back, ensuring she was adequately secure before replying.

"Look, love, it's not the end of the world. There will plenty of other weekends when Tom isn't around, I'm sure."

"I know, but I was so looking forward to it," she sniffed.

"So was I," he responded, his words so meaningful.

Chapter 5

The Birmingham Athletic Stadium was filled to capacity. The tickets for the British Championships and selection for the Olympic team had appeared on the market in December and were all sold within the month. The lucky holders were now enjoying the fruits of their purchases.

"He doesn't look as good as he did last season," Charlie remarked as he leant forward from his seat in the competitor stand and calmly folded his arms on the barrier in front of him. David was in no hurry to reply.

They were both studying Philip Rhodes, the London athlete and David's adversary from the memorable day last year, who had appeared at the track only minutes earlier. Almost immediately, the stadium cameramen picked him up and threw his image onto the giant screen at the rear of the track. A warm swathe of applause soon followed, which rapidly circulated the arena, much to the annoyance of one of the female high jumpers who had to delay her initial run-up until the adulation receded. Philip waved fondly to the audience before settling down to his lengthy warm up.

"Are we looking at the same person?" David eventually responded, without taking his eyes from the tall athlete in the navy blue tracksuit who was now gliding with languid strides past the stand on the far side of the track. As he considered Charlie's comment, the merest trace of a smile came to his lips as he realised only several minutes earlier he had thought Philip, the favourite for today's 1,500 metres, looked magnificent as he strode out purposefully over fifty metres along the inside track.

Following his initial work, Philip squatted on the ground beside his kit bag, removed his tracksuit top and then, in an exhibition of pure vanity, slowly peeled his vest off to reveal his lean and muscular upper body, bronzed to perfection by the French sun at Arles where David understood he had completed his recent training. This action was accompanied by a shrill assortment of whistles and catcalls that dissolved into laughter as Philip raised his arm in acknowledgement. Captured on the screen in close-up, his performance came over even more theatrical. A fresh vest from his bag, pulled dramatically over his bare torso, brought a further flurry of response before the excitement quelled to something like normality.

This was Philip's first appearance on English soil since his victory over Charles Boti, the Nigerian World silver medallist, at the Palace Championships last September. It was this performance, with a time only two seconds off the

British record, that many considered put him in with a clear chance of a medal at the big one.

The selectors had already announced that the first and second in each event at today's Championships would be guaranteed a place in the Olympic line-up, with the third place left to their discretion. Unlike the Americans, where all three places were decided at their Trials, the UK selection committee left a door open to proven athletes who may have suffered injuries or training setbacks and who could not, therefore, perform at their highest standard today but were, maybe, capable of returning to their best in the few months before the Olympics. It was a system that had proved invaluable in the past and the selectors had no intention of abandoning it in this vital year.

"Show off," Charlie muttered in a gruff rebuke, on watching with the rest of the spectators as Philip pulled the vest over his head. It was just loud enough to catch the attention of a couple of female competitors seated nearby. They had obviously enjoyed the exhibition and after catching Charlie's eye, giggled uncontrollably.

"Well, he has proved himself as the best in the country, so I suppose he can show off a bit," said David in Philip's defence, not wanting to aggravate too much Charlie's trait of knocking the opposition. It was something he had witnessed many times.

Besides, he was too nervous to want any form of confrontation, even leg-pulling, however light-hearted. He had always reckoned himself to be fairly laid back but the sheer significance of this day was getting to him. Up to a few days ago, he had been looking forward to Saturday, 21st May with an eagerness that surprised even himself. Usually, nerves were not a problem. In fact, he had given the day little consideration until the beginning of the week.

Charlie had driven him up to Birmingham on Tuesday. Purposefully restricting his speed to a moderate sixty miles per hour on the inside lane, it had been a leisurely journey. They had spoken very little, Radio 2 filling the interludes between the short spates of conversation. Generally, they had kept their thoughts to themselves and enjoyed the journey in a relaxed atmosphere.

They were booked in at the Royal Hotel, a City five star, where Charlie had provided him with a suite of two rooms of a standard well above anything he had previously experienced. It reminded him of one he had recently viewed on a television programme setting out the exquisite luxury of one of London's top hotels. The fact that Charlie had only booked himself into a single room increased his gratitude.

"You don't have to go to all this expense for me, Charlie," he had told his coach after viewing both their rooms.

"Only the best for my boy," Charlie retorted with an air of indifference.

"I'm quite happy to share a room with you, you know?"

"You wouldn't say that if you knew my habits, my boy. Apparently, I snore like a pig." With that, he dropped the subject.

On Wednesday, they had relaxed in the great city after an early morning visit to the training track where David put in a light session of sprinting and a couple of full 400 metres at half speed. Charlie had been satisfied with this and seemed more eager to draw him away from the arena than concentrate on any further work.

"This is the easiest day I've had for a long while," David had commented as they walked away from the track.

"If we haven't got your preparation right by now, you might as well stay at home, my boy," came Charlie's enthusiastic reply. "And your preparation is spot on."

Much to David's astonishment, Charlie then announced that he had a surprise for him. Once changed, they climbed into Charlie's car and took to the roads out of the City. At first, he had no idea of their destination but as the journey progressed south past Edgbaston, along the A38, the presence of special feature signs every mile or so rather threw up a strong clue.

Finally, they pulled into the car park of Cadbury World, a famous chocolate factory and one of the area's local attractions. He had remembered telling Charlie when discussing Birmingham some months before that this was one of the area's entertainments he had wanted to visit. Since childhood, he had always had a sweet tooth and chocolate was at the top of his favourites.

In the car park outside the impressive factory, Charlie could not resist the urge to tease. With a broad grin and waving a ticket frantically in the air, he announced. "Your fairy godfather has granted your wish, my boy. Let's go and meet Willie Wonka."

Laughing infectiously, David followed Charlie through the broad doors into the main factory. For two hours, like little kids, they wandered through the various departments watching the chocolate passing through its many processes. Finally, the tour came to an end at a giant reception area and shop where all the company's products were tantalisingly displayed to encourage their purchase.

Charlie quickly selected two enormous boxes of chocolates and before David had time to argue, had planted them in his arms. "One is for Tom and the other for you. But not until Saturday evening," was added as an afterthought.

It was just another simple gesture that endeared David even more to this remarkable and generous man.

Thursday and Friday followed in the same mould, each day offering what seemed to David the perfect relaxation after the strenuous physical activity of the previous months. They visited the City's museum and the Sarehole Mill in Hall Green, this famous magical construction being the inspiration for JRR Tolkien's 'Hobbiton' in his master classic, *The Lord of the Rings.*

Each day, he felt a little more uplifted. Physically, the few days respite from the rigorous regime of his full training programme left him feeling relaxed and refreshed, and surprisingly, stronger than he had felt for some time. It was yet another indication of Charlie's genius.

***

A squally breeze had hit the stadium mid-morning but once passed, the warm sun that followed, soon dispersed the skimpy clouds, bathing the arena in the afternoon with a calm and sensuous glow. You could sense the anticipation from the crowds as the day's events began to crank up. Already, the sprinters had opened the proceedings with three preliminary heats of the 100 metres. In the second, favourite, Ali Jamil from the Belgrave Harriers, had made a promising impression by pulling a couple of metres clear right from the start and then holding this advantage in what looked to be a fairly comfortable saunter to the line. The first two home in each heat were guaranteed their places in the final with the two fastest losers joining the line-up.

David watched with little interest, his mind only focused on his challenge ahead. The day was catching up with him and with it the nerves that were churning his stomach.

Since waking up, he had been plagued by a dreadful thought which he had found difficult to dismiss. It was a fear of the repercussions from the day's event, should he not be able to fulfil Charlie's ambitions. Would they split up and never again train together? Would Charlie walk away in disgust and their friendship dissolve at this point? Could this be the end to a way of life he had come to love?

A maelstrom of fear and worry set the butterflies fluttering, leaving him feeling queasy and lifeless. He tried to relax but it was useless. Whatever his thoughts, they were overpowered by the presence of the forthcoming event.

"The next event is the men's 110-metre hurdles…" the announcement from the loudspeaker jerked him back to reality. He took a quick glance at his watch. Realising he had less than an hour left before his race, a further flurry of nerves stabbed his stomach. He noticed Charlie was rifling through the pages of his programme, no doubt searching for some inevitable statistic. Seeing the indomitable Freddie Soames hobbling up the stairs towards them was the final incentive to make a move.

"There's less than an hour to go, Charlie," he said, as calmly as he could. "I think I'll start my warm-up."

"Take it easy, Davy, don't overdo it. You know what to do. The same routine we have followed for the past couple of months, old lad. Just relax and enjoy it."

Charlie's words had the opposite effect to calming him. Suddenly, all he wanted to do was to escape from the track and lose himself in his thoughts.

"Just run your own race sensibly and you will be fine. I know it," was added in a tone of confidence.

The amiable firm grip on his shoulder and the warm embrace that followed were almost a blur as he made his way to the changing rooms, and took refuge in one of the four toilet cubicles, thankful that he was at last alone. He felt nauseous.

Dropping the seat cover, he sat with his legs wide apart and his head between them, motionless for several minutes in contemplation. It wasn't until a throaty coughing spasm from outside eventually roused him from his troubled thoughts. He rose from the pan and flushed the loo, at the same time clearing his throat with an exaggerated cough.

Coming out of the toilets into the changing room, his attention immediately fell on the sole occupant seated in a position similar to his own just a while ago. The man's hands were covering his eyes. On David's approach, he looked up and forced a smile. David thought it looked a bit of an effort but responded with the same.

"Hi there," he said, breaking the ice.

"Hi, matey, you on the track soon?" the man asked, showing a sparkle of white teeth that lit his face.

David gave his watch a quick glance. "In about half an hour, I'm in the fifteen hundred."

"So am I," said the man, obviously, pleased with the discovery. "Which one are you then?"

"David Lucas from Wisbech."

"I was wondering who David Lucas was. James Thompson from the Devon Harriers." With the introductions over, both men raised their hands simultaneously and shook firmly.

"Glad to meet you, David," said James with warmth. "Now I'm familiar with all my opponents. I haven't met you before for some reason."

"I've been running in the Midland leagues mainly but very little down south, which is probably why," David explained.

"Are you nervous?" James asked.

"You're not joking, I can't ever remember feeling this tense in my life," David confirmed.

"Join the club, mate, that makes two of us." They looked each other in the eye, both searching for something further to say but lost for words. Realising their predicament, they both burst out laughing, killing any embarrassment at its roots.

"Are we really a couple of cowards?" James asked jokingly. At the same time, David's phone chimed in his pocket. "Excuse me," he said, extracting the mobile and putting it to his ear. "Hello."

"Hi, it's me." Rachel's passive tones always had a soothing effect on him and this moment was no exception. He was immediately receptive.

"Hi, love, nice to hear from you."

"I wanted to wish you luck. How long before your race?"

Realising that David was taking a personal call, James picked up his towel from the bench and with a gesture of farewell left him alone.

"About half an hour now," said David, making a further check on his watch. "In fact, I must get going with my warm-up."

"Are you nervous?" Rachel asked, sensing the tension in his voice.

"No," he lied. "Not really."

"I've got the TV on in the shop. This Philip Rhodes looks a bit of a dish, is he any good?"

"Oh, thanks, that's all I need," said David in a jovial tone. "My girlfriend falling for the opposition."

"Sorry, I didn't realise," she said. He sensed her laughing.

106

"He happens to be the favourite to win the event."

"Sorry," she repeated. Further giggling followed.

"No problem," he said, quickly dismissing her naivety. "Thanks for phoning, it means a lot to me but I really must get going."

"I know, love you and good luck again."

"Love you too. Bye."

As he shut the phone down, his thoughts jumped to Tom and he wondered whether his son was watching. The last time he had spoken to him, on Thursday evening, he had told him he was spending yet another weekend with his mate, Danny, but would ask the family to turn the athletics on in the afternoon. He wondered whether he would remember.

Over the last few months, what with his heavy training schedule, and dividing his time between his son and Rachel, he realised he had not been able to give the lad all the attention he would have liked. At the same time, Tom seemed to have become more independent, doing his own thing rather than relying on him. Hopefully, the change in their lifestyles would do him good. He was growing up, he told himself.

It was thoughts like these that had him pondering again on the future. If he didn't succeed today, he could be back doing his old job next week with his previous life back in place. Was this what he wanted? He knew it wasn't and shuddered in a further nervous spasm as the repercussions of his fears sunk in once again.

Fortunately, his warm-up had its usual calming effect. Satisfied his routine could not have gone better, he was almost relieved to hear the call for the competitors in the fifteen hundred metres to assemble in the main stadium.

Again, his stomach tightened, the dreaded nerves gripping him with a stubbornness he found hard to control. Relax, he told himself, but without success. Strangely, he felt weary but guessed it was only in his head, his nerves playing games with his mind. Angrily, he dismissed it. Once inside the stadium, he found himself concentrating on the proceedings which helped. Pasting a rather bleak smile on his face, he joined the other eleven competitors and their marshalling steward at the far corner of the track.

After a few minutes, they were shepherded to the starting area where they began removing their tracksuit bottoms.

James Thompson caught his eye. "Good luck, mate."

"And you," David replied.

A couple of the other competitors smiled in an amiable fashion and David responded likewise. Philip Rhodes seemed to keep his distance, locked in a state of concentration that David remembered clearly from their last and only meeting.

No sooner had he removed his top and checked his number was stuck firmly to his shorts than they were summoned to the start. After a little confusion, they finally sorted themselves into their respective positions and spread themselves across the track. The starter's assistant calmly walked forward checking that each competitor's foot was clear of the white line before raising his arm to the starter in confirmation. The scene was now set. The starter raised his gun to the sky, the audience hushed in expectation. "On your marks, get set." David sensed the static of suspense travel the line.

With the report of the gun, all twelve runners scrambled for their initial positions, each determined to hold the ground around them. David's size gave him an advantage but the firm jolt of an opponent's shoulder as his two neighbours jostled around him, caused him to surrender his momentum in fear of tripping. His inexperience shunted him back several places, leaving him in the rear of the group as they approached the first bend. There was only one behind him and he now moved to his shoulder so that he was temporarily boxed.

With the pace slowing on the bend, he found himself concentrating on the runner in front, keeping sufficient distance to avoid clipping his heels. Ahead of him, the green vest of Philip Rhodes appeared to hold an outside berth just off the leader. Feeling comfortable at the pace, he decided to stay where he was at this stage, rather than losing ground dropping back to go around the opponent by his side. It was evident that no one was going to cut a strong pace at this stage. As the field came into the home straight for the first time, he stole a quick glance at the giant screen, its image confirming the close bunching of the twelve runners.

There was little change up front, Ross Littlejohn, the tall Mancunian from Stockport, moving comfortably within himself, feeling confident that he could kick from the front when the time came. Behind him, Philip Rhodes moved like a hovercraft, carrying himself smoothly along the track on the outside of James Thompson. None of the field could fail to maintain this sedate pace.

Going into the second lap, David decided it was time to improve his position. To settle in the centre of the field was his plan, giving him the opportunity to cover any early breaks if necessary. With this in mind, he checked his position. He soon realised the move may not be quite as easy as he had originally thought. The runner at his side had fallen back and the one immediately in front of him had, unfortunately, dropped back with him, just a metre or so, so that he was still boxed. What made it worse was the runner behind him now moved to the inside of the track, putting David in an even more precarious position.

Now well into the second lap, the pace had increased a little but was nevertheless only moderate. David still felt comfortable but concerned with his pitch. On impulse, he nudged out to his right and on doing so contacted with his neighbour's shoulder. The response was, at first, a slight surrender, an action that was immediately repelled with a resounding thud as the man retaliated to hold his ground. He was obviously going nowhere. Panicking a little, the only solution was to slow his pace, hoping the opponent behind would keep his distance. Falling away from the field by a metre allowed his two closest rivals to go ahead. He was now last of the twelve with only six hundred metres to go.

Just at this moment, the pack accelerated. This took him by surprise. Winching his effort up a notch, he moved to the outside of his nearest quarry. With the injection of pace, all twelve runners had lengthened their stride. In the vanguard, Ross Littlejohn's plan to slow the field for the first two laps and then burn the last eight hundred appeared to be working. Previously, an eight-hundred metres runner, he now felt confident that he could stay the extra distance. The three-metre lead he had on Philip Rhodes as they hit the last lap looked promising.

The sound of the bell set the audience alight, manic shouting and chanting rising from the stands in anticipation of the mouth-watering possibilities of this final lap. Behind Philip Rhodes, the remainder of the field were in turmoil with several scrimmaging for the pace that was now beyond their capabilities. David started to move around the field only to collide with John Sutherland, a tall lanky runner from the Midlands, as he manoeuvred to overtake.

In a stride, he recaptured his footing but it took him several more to recover his rhythm. When he finally did, he sailed past John Sutherland, albeit two deep halfway round the penultimate bend. His long powerful stride was now eating into the pack, so much so that he had no difficulty in passing the next group in rapid succession. Moving to the inside of the track, he now had the main opponents in his sights.

At the head of the irregular procession, Ross Littlejohn was beginning to feel the pace, his legs no longer imparting the message of strength they had given until now. All of a sudden, he was feeling tired and struggling to maintain his stride. Behind him, Philip Rhodes, moving smoothly, was closing right up, drawing James Thompson with him together with two of the other competitors in tandem.

Just a couple of metres now separated David from his nearest opponent as he hit the final bend and was still gaining. His stride was strong and his confidence growing.

As Philip reached the straight, he opened up, overtaking Ross Littlejohn in a couple of strides and sprinting away with ease. Ross Littlejohn struggled on fiercely, not willing to surrender the coveted second spot without a fight. His legs felt leaden as he hit the final straight, causing him to stagger sideways as he set his sights on the finishing line, now a mere forty metres ahead. Charging in behind him, James Thompson took evading action, moving swiftly out to his right and taking the two other challenging athletes with him so that the four fanned out across the track in pursuit of Philip Rhodes who was by now striding unchallenged to his first British Championship and a place in the Olympic team.

Two metres down on the pursuing group, David was still full of running but with nowhere to go. The four ahead were spread so widely across the track that he feared an attempt to go around them would be a mistake. Intuitively, he stuck to the inside hoping a gap would open.

As he ran into Ross Littlejohn's slipstream, he sensed the man crack under the pressure of the sprint, his arms flaying uncontrollably with his effort as he fell slightly behind the other three. They were all sprinting for the line. Fortunately for David, the trio were too occupied with their final efforts to change direction and kept on in a straight line. David saw his chance. Gliding around the spent Ross he dived towards the gap on the inside of the track. By this time, James Thompson had gained a metre on the pair to his outside and was in a last gasp effort to reach the line. When David moved inside him, James was oblivious to his presence, that was until he felt his left foot snag, catapulting him to the ground. A further three strides, and David was over the line in second place and joining Philip in the Olympic team.

When David looked back and saw the forlorn James sprawled motionless on the track so close to the finishing line, a pang of guilt immediately slugged his heart. With little thought to his own condition, he steeled himself to face the aftermath and staggered back to the fallen figure. By the time he reached him, James had rolled over and was sitting on the track. His face said it all. It was something David would never forget. He looked so distraught, so disappointed and David could understand why.

"I'm so sorry," was all that David could say. He felt sick with guilt.

James looked up and tried to smile. "I don't believe it," he said, shaking his head.

"I thought there was enough room to challenge on the inside," David added, feeling worse than ever.

"There probably was. We were all flat out. It all happened so quickly," David found the words little consolation.

He had been unaware of the applause, first for Philip's swoop to the finish and then for the pursuing runners as they gave their all to reach the line. The spontaneous gasp of amazement that followed James's fall killed this instantly, leaving a lulling silence in its wake. The crowd had remained subdued ever since. As James looked ready to remove himself from the track, David offered his hand which he gratefully accepted and pulled himself to his feet. The crowd, looking for some slight relief after the drama, clapped heartily in recognition of this sporting gesture.

Side by side, both men walked the length of the track back to the exit, the crowd maintaining their applause in accompaniment. Both men had their heads bowed, their feelings mixed.

"Cheer up, champ," came a familiar shout from the stands. David looked up to see Charlie with a cheesy smile so wide and exuberant that he found it impossible to ignore despite the current situation.

Charlie had come to the front of the competitor stand and was now approaching with his arms thrust outwards. David went to him, leaving James to walk out alone.

With enthusiasm exceeding anything David had ever before witnessed, Charlie's arms seized him in a bear hug that lifted him clean off the ground.

"You did it, champ, you did it." Temporarily motivated by the euphoria of Charlie's mood, the reality of his actual achievement finally filtered home, the reward for all the hard work they had put in together. Forgetting the unfortunate event of the collision, he returned Charlie's affection with interest.

"But, what about poor James Thompson?" he questioned Charlie after a while. "I tripped him up when he would probably have beaten me."

"I don't think so," said Charlie with some conviction in his voice. "In my eyes, you would have passed him, the speed you were finishing. Anyhow, that's part of the game. We will never know. I'm afraid it happens sometimes and you can't do anything about it."

David found Charlie's words little consolation. A tap on his shoulder, however, refocused his mind. He turned around to see a beautiful young girl dressed in a tight fitting t-shirt and jeans standing before him, her smile both enticing and professional.

"James Duncan would like to interview you with Philip Rhodes if you could come with me, please," she requested.

A little surprised, he looked at Charlie, his mentor's immediate reaction of a nod of approval, being sufficient confirmation that he should follow the girl to his first television interview.

All of a sudden, the nerves returned, almost as severe as before the race. At the side of the track, he could see a small group of television personnel congregating around a well-dressed middle-aged man whom he recognised as James Duncan, the successful decathlon champion from the Seoul Olympics of 1988 who had recently joined the television company as a member of their sports team.

Philip Rhodes was part way through his interview as he approached.

"Well, Philip, were you aware of the melee behind you?" They were the first words David heard as he was shepherded next to Philip on the interview stand.

"I had no idea of what was going on. I was only focused on getting to that finishing line," said Philip jovially. Realising the stupidity of his question in the circumstances, James was pleased to notice David appear.

"Ah, here's the man who can tell us what happened. Welcome, David Lucas, runner-up to Philip and now a member of the Olympic team. David…how does it feel?"

Self-consciously, David pushed his hand through his hair before clearing his throat.

"It feels good," he said awkwardly. "But I could have done without the accident."

"Yes," James said, picking up on the opportunity. "What exactly happened?"

Unsure what was expected of him, David decided to tell it as simply as he could. "I saw an opening on the inside of the track and just went for it, I guess. It all happened so quickly."

Looking for a wider explanation, James pressed David with a more direct question. "Do you think it was your fault?"

"To be quite honest, I don't know, but if it was, I feel very sorry for James and apologise heartily. I only hope the selectors give him his chance by selecting him for the other place and then we can all perform again in August."

Taken aback by the sincerity, James looked pleased with his reply.

"Well, thanks for that, David. As we all know, your rise to the top of athletics has been meteoric to say the least and this must now be the icing on the cake?"

"Yes, it's all happened very quickly and it's really down to my coach, Charlie Greaves, who has planned the whole campaign. Without Charlie, I wouldn't be here."

"Well, I'm sure Charlie will be pleased to hear you say that."

Just at that moment, the big screen was showing the replay of the dramatic last strides of the race for the second time. Again, the crowd responded noisily at the moment of the critical collision.

Ignoring the interruption, James continued, "I'm sure the British public will be looking forward to your performances at the big one later in the year and thank you both for joining us."

Smiling respectfully, Philip and David thanked him, and moved away from the interviewing area. Once clear, Philip sidled up to David.

"David, for the record, from the replay it looked to me as if James came into you, so don't feel bad about it, okay?"

Coming from Philip, the words were appreciated and went a little way to diluting his guilt. In his own mind, however, there remained a vestige of uncertainty and he guessed there always would be.

Later that evening, he joined Charlie for an enjoyable and relaxing meal at a high-class restaurant in the City. Charlie, so enamelled by his success, mapped out the future in such promising detail he went to bed feeling the future months would unfold the greatest moment of his life and, as usual, he believed him.

Chapter 6

Rachel couldn't believe the speed at which the business was expanding. Since the New Year, she had increased her takings some thirty per cent on the previous year's figures and with David's agreement, had finally taken the difficult decision to employ a full-time assistant.

With the price of food rocketing, it would seem that everyone was looking to grow their own vegetables. Her plug plants of lettuce, sprouts, cauliflower, cabbage and the fragile beetroot had sold within a few days of display in the shop. She only wished she had prepared more. Even with regular daily watering, it took at least three weeks to grow them from seed to a suitable size for sale and it was now possibly too late in the year for gardeners to reap the full benefit. However, she reckoned she had nothing to lose in trying and had already set six dozen extra trays. Even with her summer plants, she had taken a chance and it had paid off so far. Mature chrysanthemums and daisies were selling at £ 3.50 a plant. Already, two hundred had been despatched to satisfied customers and she had at least another hundred ready in stock.

After speaking to David earlier on the phone, she had been distracted by her usual negative thoughts. Several times since David had started his new career as a full-time athlete, she had expressed her good wishes before a race with little sincerity, at the same time, secretly hoping, deep down, that this dream he shared with Charlie would come to an end so that their lives could return to some sort of normality. It often left her feeling guilty. She knew she was being selfish but she couldn't help it.

Right from the start, if she was honest, the idea of David running in the Olympics was much too ambitious in her opinion. She knew little about sport, especially athletics, but the prospect of someone of David's age and experience, being good enough to reach Olympic standard, seemed, in her eyes anyhow, unreal and ridiculous.

She had to admit she was amazed at Charlie's unshakable belief in what they were doing, especially as she understood he was a very knowledgeable coach with actual experience of Olympic competition. She was not sure David completely shared his confidence, but believed he was merely going along with his whims because of the debt he felt he owed the man for what he saw as saving his life.

With Charlie wholly sponsoring the exploit financially, she had, at first, thought the idea could do no harm to their long-term plans and was sure that within six months they would realise the futility of their efforts and abandon their scheme. However, this had not happened and here they were now, on the day of reckoning, with David and Charlie believing this to be the beginning to a whole new future.

"That was a twenty-pound note I gave you, young lady." The irritable tone of the grey-haired old lady standing before her, brought her quickly back to reality. The old girl had presented her with a trolley full of plants only minutes earlier, the cost of which she had calculated to be £ 7.51. With her mind elsewhere, she had only dropped £ 2.49 change into her waiting hand.

"I'm so sorry," Rachel stammered, at the same time scolding herself for not concentrating. The look of disapproval on the woman's face told her she thought she had purposefully tried to deceive her with the change. Not even checking the till, she frantically pulled a ten-pound note out and handed it over. Folding it carefully in two, the old lady stuffed it into her purse and without further eye contact, hobbled to the door yanking her wicker basket in an aggressive manner behind her.

"Silly old biddy," Rachel murmured in a state of annoyance, just loud enough to be picked up by her new assistant, Carol Thorson, who looked up from her job of rearranging the lower shelf of her window display.

"Thought I'd purposefully short-changed her, the old bat," she added, feeling some relief at getting the indignation off her chest. Carol smiled supportively. "How about a cuppa?"

Although only her third day of employment, Carol was quickly picking up on her little foibles. Rachel had warmed to her immediately, her sense of humour, and personality soon shining through her rather plain and austere appearance.

The next fifteen minutes gave them one of the few breaks from their customers, and they made the most of it by enjoying a cup of tea while nattering comfortably and keeping an eye on the old television set perched on a dilapidated table in the corner of the shop. It was tuned to the coverage of the British Athletic Championships at Birmingham.

Day by day, Carol had opened up with tales of her background, expanding on the history of her unhappy childhood, marriage to a drunk, subsequent divorce and the upbringing, on her own, of her two daughters. By the time she finished, Rachel felt her own personal worries were pretty insignificant.

Whilst washing the cups, Rachel saw a car enter the parking area; then, two more followed in quick succession. Within a few minutes, two couples had entered the shop and several more were perusing the plants outside. Rachel hoped the flow would subside quickly so that she could watch the race in comfort. A quick glance to the television screen told her the 1,500 metres was the next race on the track.

Carol was soon fully occupied with a lady and gentleman requiring advice on dealing with the weeds in their garden, and was in full flow explaining the different uses of the three brands of weed killer they kept in stock. Rachel tackled the second pair. This young couple were obviously in the early throes of gardening experience and were looking for some help with the development of a new rockery. Normally, Rachel would find this an interesting challenge but at this very moment, it was not what she wanted.

"What we are really looking for," said the young girl, rather sweetly, "is some advice on the sort of plants that will grow in a rockery." Her boyfriend backed her up with an enthusiastic nod, although Rachel doubted if he was really that interested. Out of the corner of her eye, she could make out the runners forming a line at the start. She would just have to forget the race, the customers had to come first.

"Rachel, I'll take over if you like?" Carol's interruption was so welcomed.

"Oh, thank you, Carol, that's brilliant," Rachel said in relief. Fortunately, Carol's previous customers had been quickly satisfied and were already making their way to the exit.

"Her boyfriend is just about to run in the Olympic Trials at Birmingham and it's on the TV," Carol politely explained to her young customers. They both smiled agreeably.

"I hope you don't mind?" Rachel added.

"No problem," said the young man, turning around with interest to view the screen. "Which one is he?" he asked.

"The tall guy in the middle of the pack with the number nine on his shorts," Rachel said, pointing to the screen. "I don't think he will win, but it would be nice if he does well."

Her sudden bout of pride came as a bit of a surprise and felt strangely warming. As she spoke, the race got under way. By this time, Carol had hived off the young girl and was firmly engrossed in discussing a colourful chart of plants suitable for her requirements.

The young man remained with Rachel watching the TV with interest.

"Doesn't look as if he's doing too well," Rachel said after a while, feeling she had to make some comment in the silence that now followed. David had fallen to the back of the field and looked as if he was struggling in her eyes.

The young man said nothing but found a seat on the edge of a couple of large wooden crates, where he made himself comfortable, his eyes glued to the screen. Nothing further was said until the third lap when David moved from the back of the field and started to pick off the field one by one.

"He's overtaking a few now," Rachel said with just a tinge of excitement in her voice. Realising that something special may be happening, Carol and her client moved back to the centre of the shop to join Rachel and the boyfriend. Even with Rachel's lack of knowledge, she could see that Philip Rhodes was going to win fairly comfortably but behind him, David was rapidly drawing into contention.

"He could come second," said the young man, for the first time showing some emotion.

"I think he needs to for a place in the team," Rachel added, nervously chewing her knuckle with the tension.

By this time, David was sprinting for the inner gap beside James Thompson. The carnage that followed as James stumbled helplessly across the track brought a gasp of astonishment from all four of them.

"Don't worry, he's made it," the young man confirmed almost immediately. "He's come second."

Rachel took a little longer to digest the situation. In her eyes, it looked a bit rough and David did seem to be involved in the fracas at the end of the race. She was not so sure of the outcome.

"Is there any chance of him getting disqualified?" she asked in bewilderment.

"No, I don't think so," said the young man with some confidence. "He didn't do it on purpose and there looked as if there was a big enough gap as far as I could see."

Feeling satisfied with what seemed a knowledgeable reply, the full reality of David's achievement finally hit her so that she started jigging around the floor in wild abandon.

"My boyfriend's in the Olympics," she stated so infectiously that all three shared her elation, smiling at each other warmly.

***

"He's really boxed in now," said teenager Josh Phillips as he sat watching the television screen in the clubroom of the Wisbech Harriers. Around him, some sixty or more members had congregated to watch their new star, David Lucas, hopefully gain a place in the Olympic squad.

The clubroom was full. Even the old and broken chairs, usually stored in the musty room behind the showers, had been retrieved and put to good use to accommodate the multitude of members who had arrived to see David perform in the British Championships. Several of the younger members found room on the floor, where they sat crossed-legged in front of the huge but outdated television set.

Chairman, Peter Joffre, was more than pleased with the attendance. He had counted sixty-eight members present only ten minutes earlier and believed a couple more had joined since. It brought back memories of the halcyon days of the past when the club always had several representatives at this prestigious event.

In recent years, the quality and of course, the quantity of their runners, had sadly declined. The emergence, thanks to Charlie Greaves, of David Lucas had been a godsend, bringing as it did, new life and enthusiasm to the club.

It was especially good to see so many of the youngsters taking an interest. Normally, at this time on a Saturday afternoon, they would be out on the track. However, today, he had noticed many of them training in the morning and were now seated in front of the television.

Knowing Charlie as he did for over forty years, he had become accustomed to his rather rash assessments and often flamboyant forecasts of the potential of runners in his charge. In the case of David, he was not sure. He had seen him run on several occasions and had to admit he had talent but whether he had the ability to reach Olympic standard, he had his doubts.

Looking at it logically, it seemed impossible to imagine someone of his age, with his lack of experience, could reach such heights in the short time they had been together. As he understood it, David had only been a part-time runner, just partaking of the sport for exercise, before his extraordinary meeting with Charlie. Anyhow, with the majority of the members repeatedly filling their glasses at the bar, he could only hope their new Messiah would continue the good work.

"He's clear now and making a move," said Brian Chapman with zest in his broad Fenland accent. On the screen, David was picking the rear field off one by one along the back straight until he was clear of them and now concentrating on the leading pack only five metres ahead. Momentarily spellbound, the whole assembly sat motionless as they witnessed David's long strides eating the ground.

You could feel the tension building as he seemingly glided into an attacking position. In the front row, the youngsters lent forward in anticipation, drawn to the television screen in total concentration, their crisps held in limbo before their mouths as they focused on the scene before them. Only the television commentator's measured tones filled the room as a hush of expectation hit the eager assembly.

Around the final bend, David had made his move to stalk the foursome immediately ahead. Most of the members were experienced enough to read that the winner's place was already in the hands of Philip Rhodes who had scooted clear of the field. It was the runner-up position now holding their attention.

Junior high jumper, Alesha Farquarson, was the first to break the silence, her words echoing so pertinently everyone's thoughts. "He hasn't anywhere to go," she almost cried as she clamped her hand across her mouth in an act of nervous tension.

Almost as she said it, the runner on the inside dropped away from the trio beside him, leaving the inside lane clear, and David saw his chance. "Oh my God," came simultaneously from two of the girls gripped with the drama as David passed the weakening runner in a flash of strides and pounced to the open gap. It now looked possible that he could make it. When he then collided with the runner next to him, the spontaneous gasp of disbelief was so forceful it was as though the whole clubhouse shuddered with the impact. No sooner had they caught their breath than David had made the finishing line and his place in the Olympic team.

"He's done it," someone bawled out.

As one, the room erupted in an ecstatic explosion of joy and excitement, everyone jumping from their seats. Several of the lads punched the air with their fists, whilst others hugged and slapped backs, females kissed fondly and the more staid shook hands with fierce intent.

"Looks like we have a new club champion," pensioner, Max Jones, said to Peter Joffre with the broadest of grins. They shook hands passionately. Peter immediately pulled his mobile from his pocket and quickly found the pad. With his index finger, he prepared his message.

WELL DONE, CHAMP AND CHARLIE. THE WHOLE CLUB IS HERE AND WE ARE VERY PROUD OF YOU. WE CAN'T WAIT FOR AUGUST AND THE OLYMPIC FINAL.

He knew what this day would mean to Charlie, a dream so long harboured, but now a possible reality. With these thoughts, he pressed the send button.

Chapter 7

Frank Lucas was not sleeping well of late. In fact, he had not slept well for some time.

This morning, he had struggled from his bed to fulfil his commitment of completing the construction of a large garden shed for a valued customer. He had arrived at the man's house just after nine o'clock.

As usual, he was enjoying the work on his latest undertaking. Some ten feet square and eight feet tall, built of quality wood, the shed was looking good, with three of the sides, the roof and windows completed, and only the door and the last few panes of tongue and groove still to be added. He was sure he would have it completed by the end of the day and collect the balance of his fee. However, by twelve o'clock, his strength had seriously diminished, he was feeling sick, and the pain in his gut was unbearable.

"I'm sorry, I feel terrible," he told Mr Gardner, after sitting on the garden wall for ten minutes with his upper body bent forward awkwardly. "I think I'm going to have to call it a day. If I feel better, I promise you, I will come back early tomorrow morning and finish off."

"You don't look very good," Mr Gardner confirmed. "I should get yourself down the hospital if I was you."

The kind words were welcomed but did little to improve his frame of mind in his current state. Letting people down had never been his way. Mr Gardner had commissioned him several weeks ago and he had promised him it would be completed by this weekend. What made it worse, the client had been recommended to him by a previous customer who had also been impressed with the quality of his work and his enticing quote, some fifty pounds lower than the three others he had collected.

With a rusty smile, he finally said his farewells, again promising he would be back in the morning if he was strong enough.

Once home and in the comfort of his sitting room, he felt a little better, the nauseous feeling gradually easing after he had taken a spoonful of the liquid morphine prescribed for his illness by his doctor. Fortunately, these still had some effect, relaxing him inwardly as well as reducing the pain.

It was six months since he had been told by the hospital consultant that he had the dreaded big C. The diagnosis of a large malignant tumour growing on one of his kidneys had followed a rather tedious series of tests and examinations over several weeks.

"I'm really sorry to have to tell you that you have cancer," were the words he would remember to his dying day, however long, or short that would be. At the time of the consultation, he could remember laughing nervously with the shock, trying to analyse the words before he had pulled himself together, just long enough to listen to the well-rehearsed presentation and make a hasty exit from the hospital building.

He had never classed himself as a serious drinker, his only participation being a glass or two of lager with a meal. That evening, he had found himself seated alone in a corner of the *Rose Arms*, a local pub at the end of his road, a pub he had only frequented twice in the two years since joining the community.

He had always detested whisky, ever since his mother had forced a rather large spoonful down his throat to cure a cold in his early teens. Within half an hour, he had downed two doubles before some sort of physic warning had told him to leave it alone. He was not sure why but had taken heed. From then on, it had been pints of lager, how many he could not remember.

By ten o'clock, he was seriously drunk but still, fortunately, in control of himself. He staggered the quarter mile to his home.

He had never felt as lonely as he had that evening as he opened the door to an empty house, his head in a turmoil of conflict over the events of the day and his life in general. His sleep that night was fitful to say the least, as, one after another, various deeds, some good, more bad, leapfrogged in and out of his mind. Finally he fell into a drowsy unconsciousness.

Much to his surprise, he awoke with a more positive outlook, his self-preservation kicking in with waves of optimism. He would beat it, no matter what, he told himself.

Within weeks, he was in hospital under the surgeon's knife having the kidney removed. During his convalescence, he had ample time to contemplate his life and his mortality, the former taking priority.

Nursing a plate of freshly made sandwiches on his lap and with a hot steaming cup of tea by his side, Frank had been able to make himself comfortable once the morphine had done its work and the pain receded. It was still his intention to return to his client first thing in the morning and finish the shed.

At least, he could now settle down and enjoy the athletics on the television. Originally, he had recorded the programme with the intention of watching it later that evening but now he was home, he could watch it live, which was a bonus in many ways.

It was the Olympic Trials at Birmingham and it would be interesting to see which athletes would be selected to compete in the Games in August. Athletics had always been one of his favourite sports and he had become quite familiar with some of the leading names over the years.

By four o'clock, he was fully engrossed in the programme, enjoying the effort all competitors were showing to secure their places in the Olympic squad. There was something very special in watching the youth of today vying for those few coveted positions.

A couple of fancied athletes in the earlier races, who would have been expected to gain their places in the team with little effort, had failed. He thought how disappointing it must be when you have given everything to secure a place at the biggest sporting event in the world and fail on the strength of just one performance.

His mind floated back for a few seconds to his own success at school when he had won the mile race from an older boy, whose name he could not remember. His opponent had been expected to trounce him. They had come down the final straight together and he had just pulled out enough to head him by a couple of feet. He could still remember the whole school standing by the trackside shouting their heads off. His two best mates picked him up and carried him shoulder-high around the track. It was a pleasant memory that had stayed with him through the years.

Returning from the kitchen with a fresh cup of tea, his attention was drawn by the presenter's voice announcing a competitor named David Lucas. *That's a coincidence,* he told himself as he dropped heavily into his armchair, spilling a few drops of tea on his lap in his haste. These he quickly dabbed with a tissue before leaning forward to concentrate on the screen.

His eyes had been failing of late so that he forced himself closer to the screen to improve the clarity of his vision. At the same time, the starter fired his gun and the twelve runners were on their way for the 1,500 metres final.

He watched carefully as the runners immediately clustered into groups of twos and threes after the initial scrimmaging to sort their positions. There was a fair bit of pushing and shoving as far as he could see. He was eager to spot the runner with the same name as his son, not that he thought it was he, but there was just some little fascination in hearing the competitor's name. David Lucas was probably a fairly common name, he imagined.

He was familiar with Philip Rhodes and his aspirations for the season. After all, they had been plastered all over the papers in the last few weeks. Ross Littlejohn was another who had had his fair share of publicity, performing at lesser distances in the past. These two led the field around the first lap. Halfway down the back straight the presenter gave a name call on the full field.

Frank watched with interest, his eyes taking in each competitor as the names were rolled off one by one down the field of twelve. Several were familiar to him. Paul Flannigan had done well earlier in the season. He was in tenth place. Then he called him. "David Lucas is one from the back and looks to be boxed in," the commentator advised, as the camera honed in on David for a close-up. Frank felt the muscles in his back straining as he pushed himself forward towards the television screen.

"My God!" he mouthed in utter disbelief. "That's my son!" His eyes were glued to the tall figure in blue as he tried to acquaint himself with his full features. Each time the television cut their shots to the front-runners, he swore his annoyance until the camera again panned to the whole field. There wasn't a further close-up of David but he had no doubt it was him.

The competitors were now moving on to the second lap. David was last but one and badly boxed in by the runners in front, behind and at his side.

"You've got to get out, lad," Frank murmured to himself as he realised the hopelessness of his son's position. Now agonising over every stride, Frank was totally engrossed in the race. He felt as if he was there on the track with him. Along the back straight for the second time, he was willing him to force a break from the encircling runners but it was not to be. *Surely, he's not happy to stay where he is?* Frank reasoned to himself. With no sign of a move on David's part, Frank was slightly consoled by the commentator's observation that it was only a moderate pace.

"Let's hope you can sprint, lad," he added out loud.

Approaching the third lap, there was the first sign of an injection in the pace when Ross Littlejohn took a quick glance behind, dropped his shoulders and lengthened his stride. Philip Rhodes covered his move immediately with a smoothly accelerated few paces to stay with him.

The rest of the field were caught off guard, losing a couple of metres on the leading pair, before picking it up. This caused havoc, with several less experienced runners panicking to match the new pace and others stumbling as they tried to extricate themselves from a dangerous position. David was one such competitor. From what Frank saw, he tried to force himself out by nudging the opponent at his side. It was soon obvious that this was not going to happen when the guy beside him, of a similar build, refused to budge.

"You bugger," Frank admonished the man in a fit of frustration. He now found himself willing David to make a break from the small group at the back. Thankfully, he was pleased to see him drop back to a position where he had more freedom to manoeuvre.

"Now go for it, Son, now go for it," he shouted at the screen, the volume of his voice raised with his enthusiasm. As if the telepathy had worked, David responded, coming to the shoulders of the runner ahead but just at the same time as the man had decided to make a move. They collided, David knocked sideways with the force of contact.

"Oh, God," Frank uttered in despair as he imagined the incident would put an end to any chance he may have had. Quickly recovering in what seemed a fraction of a stride, David was back in full flow and passed the man with apparent ease.

"One lap to go and now the pace has really moved up," the television commentator announced as Ross Littlejohn and Philip Rhodes still led into the penultimate bend. Frank could see that Philip had the race at his mercy any time he wanted to go. But his interest was now fully on David. Along the back straight, he was accelerating around the group to move into sixth position.

Frank felt his heart beating dangerously but could not restrain his emotions.

"Come on, boy, you can do it," he bawled wildly at the screen, now totally seduced by the unfolding drama.

Philip Rhodes eventually made his move at the final bend, pulling away from the field with majestic ease. Ross Littlejohn tried to go with him but looked more concerned to hold second place as he glanced back nervously at the pursuing field. Just behind him, a group of four were making their challenge, David amongst them. Mutely for a moment, Frank watched as the drama unfolded.

Leaving the bend for the final straight, the three closest pursuers to Ross Littlejohn fanned out across the track in an effort to pass the failing Ross and have a clear run along the straight to the finishing line. Right behind them, David held his position on the inside of the track. Frank could see his reasoning with such a short sprint to go. But would he get the opening he so badly needed?

As he witnessed Ross Littlejohn fall apart and the three runners at his side pull ahead, Frank could not believe the drama that opened up. The gap was now there but could David make it?

The question was immediately answered as David seemingly sidestepped the beaten Ross and threw himself at the gap. By this time, there was only one ahead of him, the two on the far outside having fallen slightly away. With only a couple of metres to go, David's momentum looked capable of taking the spoils. He had made the gap and was about to pass when the opponent to his side sprawled face first into the track leaving David a clear second.

"Yes, yes, yes. You've done it, my boy." Frank threw a punch to the ceiling, at the same time, releasing the air from his lungs in a rasping wheeze. He had to give himself a short time to recover, a slight dizziness reminding him of his condition. Without warning, he started weeping. He was surprised at his own emotion as the past caught up with him.

Chapter 8

"He should be 'ere soon," said Danny Gates in a casual manner, at the same time, twisting his wrist to check the time on his new sports watch. "He said about 'alf eight and it's now almost nine."

From his seat on a fallen tree trunk, Tom swiped another bunch of daisies with his stick and watched them disintegrate into shreds before replying.

"I'm not bothered whether he turns up or not. I don't particularly like him in any case."

"I've 'ad some good fun with Wayne in the past so if you wanna come along, I should show some respect, if I was yer."

Danny ignored the disdainful glare that came his way but instead focused his attention on the entrance to the playing field where he anticipated the appearance of his friend, Wayne Butler. They had been waiting in the council field behind the old disused church at Guyhirn since eight o'clock.

The daylight was drawing to an end. The magnificent sunset that had stained the sky only half an hour earlier with a wonderful display of crimson and pink shades had, by now, dissolved. It was still warm and soothing. There was something about this atmosphere that spurred the senses and Danny looked forward to the evening ahead with a tinge of excitement.

Another ten minutes passed before Danny's patience was finally rewarded. From the direction of the gate, there came a series of loud hoots, immediately followed by the appearance of a vehicle at high speed. Once in the field, it tore right at them across the grass, still at speed, only decelerating in the last few metres to swing to the right and miss the protruding stump of a tree by what must have been centimetres. From there, the car accelerated again and carried on to the far side of the field where the brakes were forcefully applied to send the rear in a spin of almost a half-circle before coming to a standstill.

Even in the failing light, you could make out the maniacal grin of the driver, his nose seemingly pressed on the windscreen as he prepared to take off again in their direction. The car appeared to have several passengers. Danny gave a wave of acknowledgement. Revving the engine angrily, the driver's foot came off the clutch. The front wheels spun several times before the tyres gripped the turf and the car shot forward, this time heading straight for Danny and Tom as they sat astride the branch of the tree.

"He's gonna try and frighten us," said Danny, anticipating his friend's antics as the car moved closer. "Sit still and don't show any fear."

Approaching thirty metres from the fallen tree where Danny was now sitting dangling his legs over the side, there was no sign of the car slowing. In fact, it still seemed to be accelerating. Another ten metres and Danny's wispy smile began to fade as his brain told him maybe his friend had underestimated the effect of the brakes. Instinctively, he rose to his feet on the trunk of the fallen tree as a precautionary move.

It was then that he sensed the brakes being applied. The trouble was, they seemed to have little effect, the car still careering towards him at what appeared to be a suicidal speed. The noise itself was frightening as the tyres bit into the turf, throwing clods of earth from the wheels. The car lurched forward, swerving slightly to the left and even more directly in Danny's direction. In a final effort to escape, Danny panicked, took a step backwards to another branch, lost his footing and stumbled, to land awkwardly on one leg before over-balancing in a heap behind the safety of the tree's barrier. In a final flurry of scorching brakes, the car skidded to a halt just short of the tree trunk.

No sooner had it stopped than the driver's door was slung open and a tall youth jumped out with a look of the utmost pleasure on his face. By this time, Danny had recovered some composure and was back on his feet hoping his fall had not looked too comical to the three passengers now standing before him. He was out of luck.

"Ha, yer chicken, thought I was going to hit yer, didn't yer?" Wayne challenged Danny who felt a slight flush of embarrassment come to his face. Fortunately, his defensive bravado soon clicked in before the full rush of blood took effect.

"I happened to remember when you hit that cyclist last year in Downham, that's what made me move." It was sufficient to kill the mirth as the smile was quickly swiped from Wayne's face.

"Hi, Tom," Wayne said with the hint of a sneer. "Didn't see you moving?"

During the exhibition, Tom had remained on the branch, not feeling any need to take evasive action, but he had not been as close as Danny and felt for his friend. He nodded dourly in acknowledgement of his name.

"He's got a tongue, I take it?" Wayne said, addressing Danny, much to the amusement of his two passengers who snickered openly.

"You bet," Danny replied with a plausible smile which he shared with a quick glance and a wink to Tom.

"So, what do you think of me machine then? Good, ain't it?"

The question was accompanied by an ostentatious wave of the arms that drew everyone's attention to the red, M registered, Vauxhall Astra Mark 2 which looked as if it badly needed a good wash, the dirt caked solidly across the whole of the bodywork and plastered around the wheel arches in thick stripes. On the front window, the arcs of the wipers were clearly etched across a wall of thick dirt.

"If I could see it, I'd let you know," Danny joked and they all joined in with a chorus of chuckles, Wayne included.

"Where did yer get it?" Danny asked.

"In the overhead car park at Wisbech. I'd only walked around for a few minutes when I saw this little treasure. No one about, waited a few minutes, then me hammer and screwdriver came out, and the lock gave way like opening a cupboard door. I just shouted *open sesame* and there we were, inside. Quick tinker with the wires and we were off."

Danny looked impressed.

"Well…who's coming for a ride?" Wayne addressed his entourage with a further show of flamboyant arm gestures.

In haste, the oldest and scruffiest of the two passengers, a sixteen-year-old nicknamed Pasty, so called because of his pale almost ashen complexion, regained his seat in the front next to Wayne whilst the other called Ryan quickly climbed into the back seat. Fearful of the repercussions that may follow, Tom would have preferred to have refused the offer, but not wanting to look a wimp he resigned himself to the ensuing trip. Danny looked delighted as his friend shrugged his shoulders in agreement and joined him on the back seat.

"Don't forget your seat belts," said Wayne in a voice strained by his efforts under the dashboard where his hands were busily manipulating the wires attached to the starter key.

"Don't wanna git done by the Old Bill, do we?" he laughed.

Tom looked over the front seat to see a faint spark as the two wires connected and the current surged, at the same time the engine throbbing in response.

"Right, 'ere we go," said Wayne in a fanatical chant as the car took off in an unbridled surge of power that caught Tom by surprise. Instinctively, he felt for his seat belt. Pushing his fingers down the crease at the side, he was relieved to feel the cold metal of the strap. Deftly he pulled it across his chest and secured it firmly.

"How about some lights?" said Pasty in a tone that couldn't hide his excitement. They had already reached the gate as Wayne flicked the switch. The road ahead was immediately illuminated. Not satisfied with this, Wayne clicked it on to full beam, lighting the riverbank at the far end of the short road. Neglecting the indicator, he took the left-hand turn to join the main road with little concern for any traffic. Tom felt Danny thrown against him with the force.

"Aren't you going to put your seat belt on?" he asked his friend with some concern.

"Nope," said Danny, his eyes not straying from the road as he leant forward resting on the back of the seat ahead. He was determined not to miss a single manoeuvre.

A mile along the road and they hit the outskirts of Guyhirn village, the speedometer already butting 60mph. Tom found himself gripping the door handle. Already, he was regretting his decision to join the ride. He was scared out of his wits and wanted to shout at Wayne to slow down but he knew his pride wouldn't let him. Once out of the village, it was only fields with the occasional fence picked out by the headlights.

A few minutes later, car lights appeared in the distance seemingly travelling at speed in their direction. As the car approached, the driver dipped his headlights, a peremptory gesture that Wayne would not be returning. Now fifty metres apart, the blinded driver flashed his lights furiously whilst reducing his speed in fear of losing the road. Unconcerned, Wayne roared with laughter and raised his hand in a V-sign as he passed the slowing vehicle touching a cool seventy.

"Up yours, mate," he yelled maniacally.

For the next five minutes, the car swooped through the countryside, eating the road in its path like a diesel express on a non-stop journey. Several times, Tom closed his eyes in dread as Wayne scorched round a bend on the wrong side of the road.

"We'll see their lights if anything's coming," he announced. By the time they approached the outskirts of Wisbech, Tom felt sick, his stomach churning with the jolting of the vehicle and the fearful awareness of his current situation.

***

PC John Hislop was having a good day. Only an hour earlier, he had visited a passing bookmakers to check on the results of his Yankee bet on four horses, each of which had run at the main afternoon meeting at Epsom. Two had won at good odds and the other two had been placed so his stake of a pound each way would give him a decent return.

He was not working tomorrow and this would give him the opportunity of watching the second day of the meeting on the TV in the comfort of knowing he would be well up on the week's gambling. Even better still, was the fact he and his colleague, probationer constable, Yvonne Foster, had only another hour before they could return to the station at the end of their eight-hour shift.

When he had joined the force at the age of twenty-one, he knew he was entering an occupation he had earmarked since his school days. Ever since PC Mathew Thomas had appeared at his school to make his presentation on the dangers of drugs, he had been hooked on the police force as his future aspiration in life.

He had been so impressed by the formidable presence and forthrightness of the man, not only his macho physical appearance but the remarkable self-confidence, charm and positivity in particular. He had been truly mesmerised for the full hour of the presentation. *That will be me in a few years' time,* he had told himself.

Once free of school and with six GCSEs to his credit, he had followed up with two years at college which rewarded him with three A levels and sufficient qualifications to apply to the force.

Much to his amazement, he came out of a stressful four-day assessment course with a pass to training school over a further ten-week period. Two years' probation followed before his first posting as a constable at Peterborough police station.

Right from the start, his fellow officers seemed to value his enthusiasm. He worked hard and within three years was promoted to the cars where he had spent an enjoyable eight years until the present time.

"Are we doing one more patrol around the farm lanes before we sign off, John?" asked Yvonne, interrupting his train of thought at the point where he had almost finalised his calculations.

He had taken to Yvonne right from the moment they had been introduced two months previous. What was more exciting was an inkling the attraction was reciprocated. Only the fact that his divorce was still raw in his mind had prevented him from asking her out weeks ago but he was sure the day was not far off.

The failure of his marriage, he put down primarily to his enthusiasm for the job and the unsociable hours that came with it. He didn't blame his wife of four years, Ginette, for throwing in the towel; he knew he had been less than committed.

"Yes, I'll pull off at Fallows Farm," he said putting his brain back into gear. "And we'll cruise round Red Grapes and the orchard, and see how the land lies." He decided he would wait until he was on his way home before attempting to calculate his winnings again.

They had received instructions to patrol the lanes around Red Grapes Farm and the adjoining orchard following break-ins the previous week when burglars had got away with several valuable antiques which included two firearms.

It was now dark, only the old Victorian lamps spaced at intervals along the wall of the riverbank giving any atmosphere to the quiet deserted street as John cruised towards the bend which would lead them from the river and away from Wisbech town centre. As usual, Yvonne sat relaxed but alert, seemingly enjoying each aspect of the unfolding shift, however dull, as much as he was.

Closing in on the bend, a flash of light signified an approaching vehicle. It was a familiar hairpin leaving Wisbech at the river, so tight and sweeping that several drivers had misjudged the length of its arc in the past, resulting in serious accidents, one fatal. The *Dangerous Bend* signs at both ends of the short bank road had done little to reduce the accidents.

Smoothly, John changed gear, reducing his speed. He was about to go into the bend when a car appeared at speed and looked to be coming straight at him. Instantly blinded, instinct jammed his right foot to the brake pedal as he swerved to the left. The sense of doom lasted just fleeting seconds, only the sudden jolt of the car and the acute impact as his side mirror disintegrated before his eyes, signifying any contact. Assorted pieces of metal and plastic cracked noisily against his window. No sooner was the other car beside him than it was gone in a flash, its horn sounding triumphantly like a serenading trumpet.

"My god," Yvonne yelled in wide-eyed horror as she caught her breath. "A bloody lunatic."

It took a moment for both to regain their composure. John looked glumly at the shattered remains of his mirror, the frame completely smashed and dangling by two loose wires.

"The bastard," he roared, turning his head to view the rear window through which he could just make out the lights of the offending car disappearing around the far bend. Throwing the car into reverse, his three-point turn soon had him in pursuit.

***

"Watch this bend, Wayne, it goes on forever," Pasty warned as they reached the corner by the river. On noting the *Dangerous Bend* sign, he closed his eyes tightly

"Don't worry, boys, you're in the hands of Lewis Hamilton of the Fens," Wayne bawled wildly at his four passengers. Hunched across the wheel, he could sense the fear within the throbbing vacuum of the car interior. This had the effect of heightening his bravado.

In the back, Tom was surprised to feel himself relaxing a little as gradually, bend by bend, he gained confidence in his errant driver. The fear of a head-on accident was slowly dissipating and was now replaced by a slight inkling of a thrill as he saw the tight bend ahead. Strangely, he realised he was beginning to enjoy the adventure.

Nevertheless, as his chest strained against the seat belt, he was relieved to feel the brakes applied just short of the corner. Wayne dropped calmly into second gear as he accelerated into the bend.

What happened next occurred so quickly that Tom was lost to the full event. All he saw was a light ahead, a flash of a headlamp, their car swerved sharply to the right, striking something with force before Wayne sailed forth with his hand on the hooter. He was not sure what was left in their wake. It seemed to happen so quickly it was over in a jiffy and they were gone.

"Yippee," Wayne yelled. "Got you, you bastard copper."

Tom looked across to see the bold smirk of satisfaction on the driver's lips as he studied the after-effects of his little scrimmage in the rear-view mirror.

They took the next bend at a similar speed in the direction of a roundabout and the town centre. Then, taking the roundabout anti-clockwise, Wayne swooped out of the first exit. Tom could only presume that he had checked for traffic. Every so often, he noticed Wayne snatch a glance in his mirror to check the road behind. On the straight road leading over the bridge, he was surprised to find Wayne reducing his speed and calmly cruising very slowly. But not for long, as he sensed his foot hit the floor, the exhaust burbled and they were accelerating again.

"Here they come," Wayne bawled to the windscreen with renewed enthusiasm. "Now I'll show the fuzz what a real driver can do."

Tom looked out the rear window to see the blue flashing lights of a pursuing police car clearing the roundabout and coming forward at speed. Its siren carried loudly to him despite the fifty metres between them. Fortunately, Wayne met the next roundabout clockwise, a wise decision considering a large articulated lorry was coming in the opposite direction and the wrong way was not an option. He shot off at the third exit.

The traffic lights, twenty metres ahead, turned to red but Wayne was not stopping. As he accelerated, Tom closed his eyes, not opening them until he imagined they were through and safe. When he did, he immediately took in the straight road ahead and wondered what chance their Astra had of out-running the police car. Again, a strange elation had come over him.

They accelerated for another hundred metres, when, without warning or signal, Wayne swerved right into a narrow road with cars parked nose to tail along its length on both sides of the road. They swished passed the cars to the next bend and found themselves facing another similar short straight before yet another junction. This time, Wayne did a left-hand turn. At this point, Tom stole a further glance through the rear window to see the beam of the trailing headlights just appearing. They had not gained he told himself with some relief

Wayne confirmed his thoughts. "Ha, yer losers, got yer just where I want yer."

Amazingly, or perhaps purposely, every road was short and narrow, one leading to another and then another. At each junction, John Hislop had little or no idea as to which direction they had taken. Now approaching the third junction, he had to slow down completely. There was no sign of the Astra. He took a chance and went left. Fortunately, his intuitive guess was correct as he caught sight of the tail light again just before it disappeared at a further junction.

Yvonne had passed details to her control room, requesting assistance, only to be told all cars were employed at a very serious accident on the main A47 and there was no one free. Not for the first time, she cursed the government's cut-back. The fact that they had still not come close enough to read the number plate was further frustration.

"Come on, slowcoach," said Wayne, smiling broadly, his eyes fixed impatiently on his mirror in anticipation of sighting his pursuer. Again, he was cruising, enjoying the chase, luring them to his web. Finally, the tell-tale beam in his mirror heralded its approach. As they turned the corner, he was away again, his foot hitting the accelerator. With the same calm deliberation, he took the latest bend, the tyres screeching as they held the tarmac. As quickly as he hit the new road with another straight parade of council semis, he had slowed to a crawl.

"Right, you lot, duck right down and don't come up 'til I tell yer," he commanded so fiercely that all four immediately disappeared out of sight. At the same time, Wayne swung the car calmly left through the gap between two brick posts, cutting his lights simultaneously as he crawled some thirty metres to a standstill in the interior of a metal built garage. Silently, he applied the brake before ducking down to join his passengers.

Bent fully forward in the cramped space of the surrounding seats, the youngsters waited in silence for the sound they knew must come. Tensely holding their breath, they heard the pursuing car take the bend, the spluttering exhaust firing noisily as it accelerated towards them. Onwards, it came for what seemed lengthy seconds but were mere fractions. Before they knew it, there was

130

a brief flash of light, it was past and gone, its sound rapidly receding into the distance.

"Okay, you lot, you can get up now," Wayne announced, his voice joyfully expressing the pleasure he felt in executing a plan so perfectly.

Tom was pumped up to the hilt. He had experienced the thrill of the chase, the excitement still gripping his chest like a clamping vice.

"Well done, Wayne," he shouted whilst leaning across the back of the passenger seat, his eyes still sizzling with the aftermath of the action. For the first time, Wayne saw in Tom's admiration a light of affection that had previously been lacking.

"You could go a long way, youngster," he said passionately, rewarding Tom with a rare wink.

"I was wondering why you came this way earlier," interrupted Pasty, also with similar respect that did not go unnoticed. "How did you know there wasn't a car in the space?"

"Number eleven, Buxton Road, my mate Ray's house. Phoned him this morning to tell him to leave his car on the road. I came this way earlier to check the space was free and he hadn't forgotten. Don't leave anything to chance, that's me, boys. Take note, a perfectionist, that's what I am."

Riding his ego, Wayne already had the car in reverse, just missing the pillar on the passenger side as he returned to the road.

"There's at least five roads ahead to keep the filth occupied, all short after Buxton here to keep 'em guessing, so it should be some time before they realise they're chasing a shadow."

The atmosphere was slightly intoxicating as they travelled back along the same route as they had come, all five talking at once, throwing in their own respective views on certain aspects of the chase. Tom was surprised to find Wayne keeping to the speed limit.

"Don't wanna attract the police, do we?" he laughed.

Fifteen minutes later, they were back in Guyhirn and approaching the playing field. Wayne stopped the car just before the gates and Pasty jumped out jingling a bunch of keys. The lights on a Renault Laguna parked on the other side of the road flashed their acknowledgement as the locks shunted open. Pasty opened the boot and extracted a green petrol can before running back to their car and dropping the can into the well of the front seat.

"Let's go, boss," he yelled with renewed passion. Wayne responded, hitting the pedal so that the car seemed to almost leave the road as it tore off. Flying into the field, he circled three times, much to the delight of his passengers who whooped with joy as they were thrown about with the centrifugal force. Their seat belts had been removed to increase the fun. In the back, Tom laughed along with the others at the mad antics of his driver as Danny and Ryan were thrown heavily against him. After a few minutes, the novelty wore thin.

"We're nearly out of juice," Wayne announced, giving the petrol dial an over exaggerated thump with his fist before applying the brake. Tom grabbed the back of the seat to save himself from catapulting into the front. Hearty laughs followed as they noisily exited, Pasty carrying the green can.

Once they were all out, Wayne grabbed the can from Pasty, quickly screwed the cap off and proceeded to sprinkle the contents wildly over the roof and bonnet of the car.

By now, the moon was throwing out a gentle beam, seemingly enhancing the stage on which they were all players. Already inebriated by the actions of the past hour, the aroma of the petrol seemed to add to their intoxication.

After opening all the doors and sluicing the seats thoroughly, Wayne dropped the front window and threw the petrol can in before slamming the doors shut. With a grin as wide as his face, his hand went to his pocket and he withdrew a box of matches. Animated by the adoration of his fellow passengers, he struck a match and theatrically flicked it through the open window.

The whoosh that followed seemed to move the air around them causing a rapid retreat from the vehicle.

"There goes any fingerprints or DNA, fellas," Wayne shouted exuberantly, at the same time jigging his hips in rhythmical movements as he danced around the car.

Immediately, flames licked into the sky, lighting the scene before them with an orange tinge that further enhanced their hypnotic mood. Within seconds, the front windscreen blew out as the flames escaped, spreading across the bonnet and beyond at a frightening speed. An acrid stench of caustic fumes and the resulting heat sent them all scurrying back further from the burning vehicle.

"Right, we had better make a move before the filth arrive," Wayne announced after watching for a few minutes. "Come on, lads, let's go," he said, breaking into a trot that soon developed into a more exhausting stride as they made for the field exit.

One by one, they followed in his wake, first Pasty, then Ryan with Tom and Danny chasing in the rear. By the time they reached the Renault, they were all seriously sprinting, trying to overhaul each other in a friendly but noisy dash. Tom soon left Danny behind but struggled to close the gap on the older boys. As each arrived at the parked car, they were puffing heavily from the exertion before regrouping for Wayne's final announcement.

"Have you enjoyed yourselves tonight?" he asked, his eyes flashing to all four in turn.

"Yes," came the chorus back to him.

"Well, we'll have to look for some further adventures," he said, feeling a little like his hero, Captain Jack Sparrow, from the *Pirates of the Caribbean.*

"Right, I'll give you a lift home, get in and don't wipe your dirty shoes on me clean carpet," he ordered with a dash of amusement in his voice. In an orderly fashion, they climbed into the Renault. Driving home at a gentle thirty miles an hour seemed a little tame after the excitement of the evening.

It was not until they had pulled up outside Danny's house, Wayne's foot impatiently playing with the accelerator pedal as the youngsters jumped out, that the driver threw a nasty spanner in the works.

"How did your dad get on today, youngster?" he asked genuinely, "I understand he was running in the Olympic Trials."

With these words, a bolt of guilt hit Tom's rampant mood. He had forgotten his dad's big day. His intention had been to phone him before the race. So much had been going on, it had completely slipped his mind.

Chapter 9

In many ways, Rachel was pleased David had decided to spend the Saturday night with Charlie in Birmingham. It gave her a chance to tidy the house and prepare dinner before his return. In recent months, she had realised how valuable Sundays were. Being able to rely on Carol to take over the garden centre was a godsend.

Furthermore, it was the only day of the week she had time to catch up on some of the regular chores; the laundering of the clothes for David, Tom and herself, the cleaning and general tidying of the house. The highlight of the day was the preparation of a roast dinner, which had become a regular feature with David and occasionally with Tom, if he was at home.

She didn't really mind housework if she had the time. Her fastidious nature, however, meant she had to do the job thoroughly, preferring to overdo the cleaning rather than run her finger along a shelf to find a deposit of dust, a situation which really depressed her. Ignoring it, was, for her, not an option, but recently she found herself wishing it was.

When it came to the garden centre, she had no qualms about her input. She enjoyed every minute of it and was getting such a kick from seeing the business grow. She did, however, realise it had taken over her life to a certain extent.

Originally, she had visualised it as being the bedrock of her future with David, so that, once his wild dreams of Olympic success were behind him, he would return to work with her in building a stable business. She had imagined him re-establishing the garden landscaping side where he had had such success and she would expand the shop and centre to provide a flourishing business that would give them a rewarding income for the future.

The events of yesterday had put a hold on that. Now that he had secured his place in the Olympic team, she was not sure what the immediate future held, but she was confident, long term, all her hard work would be rewarded.

Fortunately, she had slept well, so that she was feeling quite refreshed when the alarm went off at seven-thirty. The early hours of the morning had passed comfortably, two full washes in the machine and the dusting and hoovering of the downstairs' rooms already behind her.

Well on target, she felt she could allow herself the luxury of a short break and a quick coffee. Tom had phoned half an hour ago to confirm he would be home for dinner. Considering she had not seen him since he left for school on Friday, she was glad that he had made contact and would return hopefully before his dad arrived.

Surprisingly, he had seemed very polite for a change and she had immediately been asking herself why. She would have preferred to have David to herself but reconciled herself with the thought that the mood would be quite buoyant after his success at Birmingham.

Although David had not yet phoned her, she anticipated his return about one o'clock. When the doorbell rung five minutes later, she thought it must be Tom. The usual negative reaction came over her as she went to the door. It was strange the effect he had on her. Taking a deep breath, she opened the door.

The face that greeted her was most unexpected. It was that of a young lady, possibly a teenager and very pretty.

"Oh, hello," said Rachel, smiling warmly at the stranger.

"Hello," said the young girl in a slightly posh voice that complimented her classy appearance. "Does David Lucas live here please?"

"He's not here at the moment but I am expecting him back very shortly. Can I ask what it's about?"

Try as she might, Rachel could not avoid her eyes dropping to take in the full picture. The girl's slender frame draped in a black velvet skirt, pulled tightly at the waist by a decorative belt and the pure white lace blouse that was opened at the neck in a frilly collar, was enchanting.

"Yes, I'm sorry," the girl apologised. "My name's Gillian Radcliffe and I represent *The Wisbech Echo*. I was hoping I could interview David Lucas following his success in yesterday's Olympic Trials."

"Oh, I see," said Rachel, feeling herself relax slightly on hearing the explanation of the girl's presence. Muddled in her mind as to their plans for the rest of the day and the week ahead, especially after yesterday's outcome, she was lost as what to suggest.

"I'm sorry to call on a Sunday," the girl responded to the thoughtful silence that followed. "But I live locally and wanted to be the first to get the story. I can see it's inconvenient."

"No…no…it's not that," Rachel reacted, wanting to offer her some encouragement. "I'm sure David will be delighted you want to interview him but the trouble is that he's not back yet and at the moment, I'm not sure when he intends to get back and what his plans are when he does."

"That's okay, as I said, I'm sorry to have bothered you." The disappointment in the girl's voice was clearly obvious. Rachel felt for her.

"Look, when David gets home, I'll get him to give you a call and I'm sure he will be pleased to talk to you. How's that suit you?"

What had been a faint pout, immediately transformed to the broadest of grins that seemed to light up her face to even greater beauty.

"Oh, thank you so much," she responded excitedly whilst pulling a small notebook from her bag on which she scribbled her telephone number and handed the page to Rachel.

"There's my number, tell him he can phone me any time," she said. With this, she turned and took her leave down the garden path. Breaking her bouncy stride just before the gate, she turned and looked back at Rachel.

"Thank you again," she shouted so politely. If Rachel had needed a boost to the day, this was it. She had to smile at the coltish grace of the young lady as she closed the gate and skipped off down the lane to her parked car.

At last, she was able to relax and ten minutes later, a mug of coffee in her hand, she pulled the dining room chair out and finally, sat down. She had barely taken a sip when the doorbell rang again. She was sure it was Tom this time and she was right. With his usual lack of courtesy, he walked past her as she held the door open and went straight into the dining room.

"You could try *thank you,* considering I've just got up to let you in," she threw at him in annoyance. There was no reply. She followed him into the room.

"Did you see your dad's race yesterday?" she asked.

"Yes...did well, didn't he?" he openly lied. Following Wayne's reminder, he had immediately checked his phone to see his dad had finished second and secured a place in the Olympic squad. With the realisation, a sense of pride overcame him.

"Have you spoken to him since?" Rachel questioned further.

"Nope...so when's he coming home?"

"I haven't heard from him yet but I should imagine any time."

"That's good. We'll be able to hear what he has to say then, won't we?"

The chirruping of the phone was a welcome relief from the cat and mouse conversation in progress. Rachel picked it up hoping it was the voice she anticipated. Fortunately, it was.

"Hi, honey, how are you?"

"Hi, Dave, nice to hear from you." She felt the usual flutter in her chest. "Where are you?"

"Just hitting the A14 and should be about another hour or so. Look, would you mind if Charlie joined us for dinner as he's lost for something to do this afternoon and we're both feeling so high."

Not having seen David for most of the week, she had been looking forward to some time together. She had imagined Tom would take to his bedroom once they had eaten. This was really a situation she had been trying to avoid. Realising Charlie was probably sitting next to David and listening to every word, she hesitated for a moment. She would have loved to be able to tell David her true feelings but dared not.

"Yes, that'll be fine," she finally heard herself say. "By the way, a young girl called a few minutes ago asking whether she could interview you for the local paper. I told her you would contact her. She's very sweet and it would be nice if you can see her."

Rachel felt she had done her best to promote Gillian Radcliffe.

"Um, sounds interesting. Is she pretty?" David asked light-heartedly.

"Yes, very," she replied,

"And a good body?" he added as a further tease.

"Again, first class," Rachel replied, keeping the good-humoured banter going.

"Then, you had better give me her telephone number straight away." She read him the number from the slip of paper.

"It looks as if being famous is going to be fun."

"Don't let it go to your head," she told him, still maintaining an air of light-heartedness.

"I won't, I promise. There's only one for me and she's on the end of this line." She would have loved the conversation to have become more intimate at this point but the thought that Charlie was sitting next to him, possibly hanging on every word, made her feel a little self-conscious.

"So, I'll see you in about an hour."

"Love you," he concluded.

Rachel put the phone down and sighed. *I would have liked a little time to ourselves,* was deep in her thoughts.

Chapter 10

"Well, that brings me to the end of my little pep talk. I hope what I have had to say has inspired you.

"I know that all of you will have only one thing on your mind in the next couple of months. Train hard and give it your best shot, because I can assure you, it will all be worthwhile. When you enter that wonderful Olympic Stadium, you will face the most heart-warming atmosphere you will ever experience in your lives. Live the reality, my friends, enjoy every moment, and when you look back in years to come you will remember these times with pride and honour.

"I wish you all well with your training, and look forward to seeing each and every one of you performing with the skill and tenacity I know you all possess. Remember, you are here because you are the finest athletes in your country. You are here because you have outstanding qualities, so use them to your full advantage. Release your potential to the best of your capabilities.

"Your presence in the Olympic Stadium will be a pinnacle of your life, a one-off experience you will never surpass. You can do no better than a personal best. If all of you achieve this target, we, as a country, can achieve outstanding success. Good luck and thank you. I know you will make us proud."

No sooner had Sebastian Coe finished his well-received presentation than the whole assembly rose as one to honour this great man whose Olympic successes in the fifteen hundred metre races of the eighties were legendary. The first occasion, in nineteen-eighty, he had been a strong favourite to take his favoured race, the eight hundred metres, only to run a bad tactical race and finish third. Overturning his disappointment, he returned only five days later to take the coveted gold medal for the fifteen hundred metres and this, in an event in which he was given little chance with the strong favourite and victor of the eight hundred metres, Steve Ovett, in the field.

Four years later, when considered to be well past his prime and suffering a season of injuries, he surprised everyone by holding on to his title with a storming finish down the home straight. His career achievement of eleven world records is considered by many to be the finest ever.

Immaculately dressed in a light tan suit with a dark brown shirt and matching tie, Seb had lost none of the charisma that had been the hallmark of his career. Still slim and impressive, only the flecks of grey at his temples gave any indication of his fifty-five years.

Together, Charlie and David rose to add their applause to the resounding appreciation of the audience. David looked across at Charlie and smiled in mutual recognition of the man's outstanding attraction.

On the stage, Seb raised his arms in salute to the rapturous response that seemed to resonate in every crevice of the lofty assembly hall. As it continued to a deafening volume, he waved his hands up and down in a modest attempt to dampen the audience's enthusiasm. Realising this was not going to happen, with a broad smile, he took his leave from the stage followed by the delegation of top officials.

This had the required effect as the applause slowly receded to be replaced with the excited chatter of competitors and coaches leaving their seats and making for the exit.

"Well, that was worthwhile, I'm sure you'll agree, my boy," Charlie addressed his protégé.

"Superb, Charlie. If that doesn't inspire you, nothing will."

David had enjoyed every minute of the two-hour presentation by the six officials of the GB athletic team. Each one of the four men and two women had presented such a positive insight into their various areas of speciality that you came away feeling, as a member of Team GB, you would have the best support of any nation competing.

Even the transport manager, whose job it will be to see each competitor arrives at the start of their race with the minimum of hassle, made the audience feel the journey from the British camp, through the diabolical London traffic to the arena, would be a doddle.

David had enjoyed his first week at the Manchester training camp and looked forward to the second week with the same enthusiasm. The venue was magnificent; the stadium built some ten years previous for the Commonwealth Games had all the facilities you would associate with such an iconic complex.

He had gushed with amazement at the size of the gym and the accompanying equipment, then there were lecture rooms, a cinema room and a massage room, all of the highest quality.

The weather had been pleasant all week, dry with high temperatures, well above the average for the time of the year and he believed the same was promised for the following week.

Training with top athletes, and sharing your social life and ideas with people of a same ilk and interest did wonders for the camaraderie of the group. A few chose to alienate themselves from the main throng but, generally, most seemed to be stimulated by the exchange of ideas and social chatter.

He had a feeling the second week could be even better than the first, despite Charlie's absence for the first few days. He had made so many new friends since joining the squad he now felt completely at home in the routine of the track work and the occasional lecture.

In his mind, this was Utopia. His appetite for running was now insatiable, occupying his thoughts throughout much of each day and very often the night. It had taken over his life and, for the moment at least, with such a high profile event on the horizon, there was little he could do about it.

On several occasions, he had lived the final of the fifteen hundred metres in his dreams and on each occasion had awoken expecting to find the gold medal in his hand. His disappointment was always tempered with the thought that this premonition may come true.

Since the Trials, his confidence had grown in leaps and bounds, inspiring in him a feeling that anything was possible, even the gold medal. Charlie had been right all along. He was capable of achieving all the targets. The big difference now was that he believed in himself.

"I've really enjoyed this week, Charlie," he said as they ambled over to the cafeteria. Charlie smiled.

"It's a shame I have to go back to the office, but I'm afraid it's a necessity. Since the recession, business has been poor in the housing market and we have been losing money for some time. Do you know we have only sold twelve houses since Easter? That's how bad it is. This period of the year is generally accepted as a peak time and look at the results! I might have to sack a couple of the staff which is never very pleasant, especially in these times, with so few jobs around."

"I understand what you are saying, Charlie, and I'm sorry to hear it. Don't worry about me though, I'm fine. I'll join the lads in the evening, have a bite to eat in the canteen and be in bed by ten for my beauty sleep."

"How about Rachel? Aren't you missing her?"

The question had an immediate response from David, his face freezing with the depth of his thoughts. Charlie noted his reaction and wondered whether he was witnessing a sudden pang of guilt that he had temporarily dismissed her from his mind in the excitement of the day's events. He was faintly amused.

"Forgotten her, have you?"

"No," David said, noticing the smirk on Charlie's face. "Well, sort of...I guess."

Laughing openly, Charlie slapped him on the back.

"Don't worry, lad, I won't tell her," he said, his amusement obvious. "I understand. Remember, athletics took over my life as well." David found himself joining in with Charlie's mirth and smiled coyly even if he was the butt of his humour.

"Never mind, I'll pay her a visit over the next couple of days and see that she's okay to put your mind at rest."

"Thanks, Charlie," David said with sincerity. "I will phone her later but I can't really give her much time at the moment. I find all my energy is concentrated on running and training and I have just had to put her out of my mind temporarily. She's a wonderful girl and I love her dearly. I will make it all up to her after the Games, I promise."

"Ah, sweet," said Charlie mockingly. Davy had grown used to Charlie's leg pulling, especially where Rachel was concerned. There had been times when he had wondered whether Charlie was a little jealous of their relationship as he was on his own and this was the reason for the remarks that often came his way.

Only once had Charlie poured out his heart to him on his personal life. It had been after a particularly difficult day on the track, when his performance had been well below par. Charlie had joined him at the side of the track in an effort to console him.

"Don't worry, Dave, we all have bad days," he said in a light mood. "At least, you have Tom and Rachel to go home to."

There was a something in the tone of Charlie's voice that nudged a question from him. It was one he had wanted to ask for some time.

"Have you ever been married, Charlie?" he had asked, quite innocently.

With this there was a noticeable change in Charlie's mood. He paused thoughtfully before he answered.

"Yes, my boy, I was married once in the sixties," he replied, stretching his legs in front of him. Seemingly in deep concentration, his jaw muscles tightened as he focused his eyes on the skyline ahead before continuing. "I was married to a very pretty Liverpudlian girl called Janet whom I met at a disco in her city one evening after a local meeting. It was love at first sight for both of us and we were married within six months."

"That was quick work," David added in an effort to bring a little lightness to the melancholic atmosphere then prevailing.

Undeterred, Charlie continued. "On the day of the wedding, Janet announced she was pregnant and six months later, young Daniel was born. We were both over the moon. He looked a bonny baby but it soon became apparent he had health problems. At times, he would have difficulty in breathing and often turned blue following a coughing fit. There were many times when we feared for his life.

The specialist advised us he had a slight hole in his heart that would need an operation. Because of his age, this could not be performed until he was eighteen months old. Those eighteen months were so tense, so nerve-racking, the longest of my life," Charlie said, his voice strained. "Watching a child suffer with his health is the worst experience in the world for a parent."

Witnessing Charlie digging up the details of this period of his life was almost as painful for David. He was beginning to wish he hadn't broached the subject.

"Anyhow," Charlie continued, "when the time came for his operation, we felt quite confident in this day and age that it would be successful but, complications set in, and he died in the operating theatre."

"Oh, Charlie, I'm so sorry," Davy offered earnestly.

Temporarily lost in his grief, Charlie just had to continue, "He was buried a week later. We had a special little coffin built and I carried him from the hearse to the plot we had chosen beneath a large oak tree in the cemetery." With these words, he raised his eyes. A tear dribbled down his cheek.

"Charlie, I'm sorry I brought that up," Davy said truthfully, feeling so guilty with the situation he had created.

Pulling himself together, Charlie smiled. "Don't be, Dave it's good to open up sometimes. Just to complete my little story, which doesn't have a happy ending, I'm afraid, Janet and I seemed to grow apart after this. I think we were both so traumatised with the little lad's death that it took all the stuffing out of us. By the time we recovered, it was possibly too late. Silly perhaps, but one of those things, I guess. We split up amicably, as they say," Charlie sighed.

"God, Charlie, I'm so sorry I put you through that, I really am," David reiterated, his guilt multiplied with the look of grief now clearly written on Charlie's face.

He had avoided discussions involving Charlie's private life since that day. Charlie's leg-pulling concerning Rachel didn't really bother him. It was always good-natured, said in fun and if anything, probably added to the strength of their relationship.

Together, they climbed the steps and entered the noisy interior of the coffee lounge. Once inside, they made for a table in the centre of the room where a boisterous group of five, three men and two women, were in a lively discussion. As they picked a path around the tables, the familiar face of James Thompson looked up, beaming at them with his characteristic smile in recognition.

"Hi, Charlie and Dave, what'cha think of that then?" he asked in a jovial fashion, whilst grabbing a chair from the adjacent table and pushing it across the floor towards Charlie.

"Brilliant," Charlie answered, dropping on to the proffered seat. "Any of you want a drink?"

"No, I'll get them, Charlie," said a broad-shouldered giant on the far side of the table.

"I don't mind putting my hand in my pocket for you lads and lasses once in a while," Charlie countered.

"No, Charlie. You need a rest at your age," said the man with a broad grin. Beside him, a pretty blond giggled openly.

The man rose to his feet to display an imposing physique in a tight-fitting sleeveless vest. His unbelievably long hair was pulled back in a neat ponytail and what looked to be a week's stubble decorated his chin. With arms the size of most athletes' thighs and a body weight of some nineteen stone, Gareth Knott had once considered entering the Mr World competition.

His chances of winning such a title would probably be a lot better than his chance of a medal of any colour in the shot put, Charlie imagined. In an event in which the UK had struggled for many years to find success at the top, Gareth's throw of 20.15 metres at the British Championships, just within the Olympic standard, had given the selectors a slight hope their long term strategy in this event was going in the right direction. A medal, however, of any colour, was very unlikely.

"Mine's a pint of lager, thank you, Gareth," Charlie instructed.

"Pure orange juice for me, thanks, Gareth," David added. Gareth moved off with an easy stride that belied his huge bulk.

"Well, boys, guess you've enjoyed today's programme?" Charlie asked, scanning the group.

"You're not kidding, Charlie," said James Thompson with an enthusiastic grin. "I'm totally sold on our back-up team and everything that goes with it. I think I'm so lucky to have been picked to represent my country in such an important year. I'm sure we will show the world one of the greatest Games ever and to actually be a part of it, is a great honour. Roll on August, that's what I say!"

Charlie had really taken to James, not only for his natural personality and charm but his display of enthusiasm for life was a real tonic. There was an eagerness to him, an energy that was almost tangible, and Charlie really loved that.

The announcement, only four weeks ago, that he had been awarded the third and last place in the 1,500 metres was great news after the Trials calamity. It was immediately obvious he held no grudge towards David. He made it plainly clear he considered it an accident and no one was at fault. Charlie found it amusing to consider that such a situation could cement a friendship all parties now valued. James was a really nice guy.

Around the tables, the animated chatter and frequent peals of laughter highlighted the air of excitement that prevailed. Such an atmosphere of well-being was just what the Olympic committee were looking for and confirmed Charlie's thoughts that this fortnight was just the right preparation needed to bring out the best in all concerned.

"When you coming back to us, Charlie," asked the young blond, Suzanne, as she languidly combed her fingers through her long flowing hair. Charlie turned towards her.

"I hope to be back on Wednesday, Suzanne," he answered. "If my meetings don't go on too long."

The girl looked pleased. During the week, Charlie had become a popular figure with David's small group of training partners. Throughout the sessions, he had offered titbits of advice to several of them, and it appeared these had been put into practice and obviously gratefully accepted from the satisfactory response. Most of them had come without their coaches so Charlie's care and interest had been a welcomed bonus.

"How's your good lady?" James asked David when Gareth had returned and distributed the round of drinks.

"Fine, thanks, how's your wife and family?

"He's just heard he's about to become a dad for the second time," Suzanne interrupted in an excited voice before James had a chance to answer. Leaning forward across the table, David raised his hand to James in a high five. James met it with a flat palm in a loud slap.

"Congratulations, mate," he said with more than the usual enthusiasm.

The conversation flowed freely for the best part of a further hour, everyone contributing to the jubilant chatter. By this time, it was half past seven and Gareth decided to change the subject to one of the high points of his day.

"I think it's time to think about dinner, don't you?" he announced to an amused reception.

"Is food all you think about, Gareth?" Paul Matthews, an aspiring two hundred metres runner, asked.

"No, I think about girls as well…but food comes first," he replied to a burst of laughter from around the table.

Charlie was really enjoying the young company and the invigorating atmosphere but decided it was time to make his exit.

"Well, I must go," he announced. "I have a long journey ahead of me."

"See you Tuesday or Wednesday hopefully, Charlie," David shouted across the hubbub of chatter. "Have a safe journey."

"Will do, lad."

Before he had a chance to move away, Gareth grabbed him around the waist and lifted him a good foot off the ground whilst twisting him to and fro in a gentle bear hug. Finally, he dropped him back on the ground, seized his head in his huge hands and puckering his lips, administered a sloppy kiss to his pate.

"Take care, Charlie, you old devil," he said with a touch of fondness. The message was endorsed by the remainder of the table. Charlie made his way to the door to a chorus of good wishes.

"No chance of a quiet exit," he said as he opened the door and waved warmly at the youngsters.

He had always enjoyed his position as a joint partner in Ellis and Woods but at this moment, he would gladly have ditched it to stay in Manchester.

Chapter 11

Rachel always welcomed Mondays at the garden centre. It was usually one of the quietest days of the week and gave her a chance to relax a little. Today would have been ideal, if not for one little problem.

Just before eight-thirty, Carol phoned in. "I'm sorry Rachel," she began. "But I've been up all night with my daughter, Kelly. She's been sick several times and I feel I must take her to the doctor. I will try and get an early appointment, and be with you as soon as I can. Is that all right?"

"Yes, of course," was Rachel's immediate response on sensing the concern in her assistant's voice. "Make sure she's okay and get in as soon as you can."

"Thank you so much," Carol said, with some relief. She had been so reliable and such a good worker that Rachel was only too happy to agree.

At twelve o'clock, however, Carol phoned again. "Rachel, I'm really sorry. The earliest appointment had been at eleven but in the meantime, Kelly has been sick again and I have had to ask the doctor to call. I am waiting for him at this moment."

"Look, Carol, it's reasonably quiet today, so look after Kelly and don't come rushing in. I'm okay on my own so take the afternoon off and I'll see you tomorrow."

Carol was only too pleased to comply and thanked her for her thoughtfulness.

Up until late in the afternoon, it was one of the quietest days Rachel could remember, especially for June when the centre was usually humming with people seeking plants for their flowerbeds or to sow in their plots or allotments.

At least the weather had been pleasant with a cloudless sky and bright sunshine most of the morning. A few clouds had now appeared to spoil the heady atmosphere but it was still warm.

She was feeling a little isolated of late. David spent so much time away training and when they were together, he was usually so tired he seemed to find it difficult to concentrate on conversation of any length. She hoped he was not losing interest in her.

For the first time in her life, she felt she had found a soul mate, someone she had really bonded to, and something inside her, some inner feeling, told her this relationship was the one to give her the happiness she had always imagined.

She realised she was a bit of a romantic but, at the same time, she felt, from her experience of life, you must trust your feelings to a certain extent or you would just stand still, stagnate in a pool of mediocrity and never experience the wonderful opportunities life offers.

There were certain areas of your life where you had to take a chance and as far as she could see, relationships were one of these. There was a certain amount of luck. Life was all about risk. You had to accept that and pray you were a winner. Up until now, she didn't feel she had been that successful, so hopefully, luck would change in her favour for this relationship with David.

He had phoned her from Manchester last night just after ten o'clock, and they had chatted idly for a good twenty minutes before he had stopped her to say someone was knocking on his door and he had to go. She had heard nothing herself and was left wondering whether he was making an excuse to get rid of her.

These thoughts then stayed on her mind for some time, keeping her from the sleep she so badly needed. She really wished she could relax more.

Since David's new found fame, life had changed considerably and she knew she had to go along with it, to see it out until the Games in August at least, and maybe longer, who could say?

Almost weekly now, he was featured in the local paper in one article or another. Only last week, the Wisbech Echo had printed an article covering his daily diet, supposedly, an example to young budding athletes as to what the true competitor eats to stay fit and healthy. David was now a role model for the young.

She had to laugh when she went into town. From what she had seen in the market square, the fried chicken and beef burger outlets were crammed to capacity, attracting their fair share of over-weight and unhealthy looking youngsters. There were obviously still plenty to convert.

It would also seem his fame was now spreading much wider than the local press. She could quite understand the public's increasing interest in the situation, especially in view of David's late development as a formidable athlete. Thirty was an age when many athletes were considered to be past their prime, let alone making their debut in the biggest sporting event in the world.

Only last week, apparently a reporter from the *Daily Mail* had contacted him for an article covering his success and what it meant to the Wisbech Harriers. They had visited the club one evening during the week, and interviewed the chairman and several of the members to assess their various angles on his selection for the Olympic team.

Apparently, he understood the short clips of film taken had more than emphasised the poor state of the club buildings and facilities. She had found it quite touching when he told her he felt if nothing else came from his performance at the Games, he hoped the club would benefit in some small way from the publicity

Throughout their conversation, she had kept hoping he would just stop and ask her how her life was progressing but unfortunately, it did not happen. Under the pressure of his training schedule, he seemed to have forgotten her role at the nursery. He asked about Tom as he always did and she, as usual, had covered by saying he appeared to be fine.

Even when she had emphasised that he seemed to spend most of his time with Danny, there appeared little concern, so she just let it go. Tom's behaviour continued to worry her but there were so many other anxieties on her mind at this moment, it would just have to take its place with the other balls she had up in the air.

At least, her efforts with the centre were showing results. The bank balance was beginning to look reasonably healthy and she had so many plans for expanding in one direction or another. The trouble was, once in bed, exhausted and almost begging for sleep to take her, ideas for improving the business would tumble through her brain with mind-boggling clarity, one after the other, so that it was very often not until the early hours of the morning unconsciousness overcame her. She would often awake the next morning feeling as exhausted as when she went to bed.

Of late, she had revised her opinions of Charlie. At first, she had to admit she thought he was just a rich lonely old man with a dream of little substance which David had come along to set in motion. However, since the Trials, she had seen him in a different light. Whatever dreams Charlie had for the future, David now shared with him, she was sure. In fact, she was convinced David would follow him to the end of the Earth, if that was required.

She had to admit the fame had taken her by surprise, but she was gradually coming to terms with it. She was really proud of her partner and beginning to enjoy the little touches that came with it.

Whilst the Olympics had overshadowed everything of late, she strongly believed the future was about to open up a new and exciting life for all of them. The hard work she was putting in at the garden centre and the profits she anticipated she would generate, would be appreciated in due course, she was sure.

By the time she had taken another tea break and addressed a couple of envelopes, it was six o'clock. She quickly pulled her small red cash box from under the till. Withdrawing two-second class stamps, she stuck them carefully on the two envelopes.

Although the day had not been particularly busy, she felt tired. Absently, she yawned before deciding to attend to the till, add up the takings and be ready to leave on the dot at six-thirty.

Halfway through counting the coins, there was a sharp ring from the doorbell. As she looked up, her heart sank.

Falling through the door, a drunken Jason Phelps grabbed the wall to steady himself. He looked over and caught her wide-eyed stare, his mouth splitting open instantly in a fiendish grin.

"Hello, my sweetie, had yer on my mind all day, so thought I would call in and see how yer are. I understand your man's in Manchester so I thought yer might need a little company."

The pathetic slurring of his words confirmed he was hopelessly drunk. Remembering the last incident, she steeled herself to bluff a commanding position if that was possible.

"Looks to me like you've spent the whole day in the pub, Jason, so I would suggest you make your way home," she said as calmly as she could. Something told her the bold front may not hold up for too long today.

With his bleary eyes bulging from their sockets and targeted in her direction, he staggered forward, rolling sideways with every couple of paces as his legs gave way under his condition. She hoped he would drop to the ground at any moment but it was not to be.

In a few shaky strides, he made it to the counter where he held on hesitantly, catching his breath in noisy gasps. She felt herself slowly retreating, her back soon pressed tightly against the till. He steadied himself by gripping the counter. Pulling himself to his full height, his eyes looked blank yet threatening. She felt her heart ramming in her chest as more than a pang of concern overwhelmed her.

"I think it's time I taught yer a little respect, you snobby bitch," he grunted at her with menace as his eyes focused on the opened shutter of the counter. Reading his mind, she grabbed for the hinged shutter and in one deft movement, slammed it down with all her strength, leaning on her side of the wooden barrier with both arms in an act of defiance.

Her immediate thought that she had left her mobile in the poly-tunnel sent a shiver of fear through her body. She suddenly felt so vulnerable.

"Now, you get out of here, Jason Thomas, before I call the police," she shouted hoarsely. His only response was a sneer as he rolled precariously along the counter to meet her face to face, the waft of his beery breath catching her immediately with a nauseous response.

"Don't fight me, yer little minx, just enjoy me company," he added as he grabbed for her wrists. Alert to his sluggish movements, she had already withdrawn her hands and stepped back the few feet to the rear of her booth as he fell on the closed shutter. Angrily, he caught his balance and reached for the underside, throwing it skywards with all his force so that it somersaulted at the hinge and fell with a mighty crash against the counter.

With nowhere left to escape, she was now petrified. He read her fear, so clearly written on her face and with it his lips moistened to a malicious grin.

"Now I have yer, yer little bitch," he sneered as he moved forward.

"If you touch me, Jason, I'll scream," she threatened but to no avail as he continued menacingly towards her. There was little room in the booth but, intuitively, she still dodged to his right as he threw himself at her. There was really no escape. She was knocked against the rear wall with the impact of his body. She screamed helplessly as he seized her shoulders and pulled her back so she was now immediately before him, her face only inches from his.

She twisted her head to avoid the direct stench of his breath but he grabbed her chin and tilted her head back so she was forced to look into his lustful bloodshot eyes. At that moment, she knew her fate was sealed. His breath was so rancid she felt she would pass out.

"Relax, my dear," he said in an effort to calm her. In one last act of retaliation, she brought her knee up with all the force she could muster and aimed for his crotch but she missed, her knee deflected to his groin where it landed painfully.

"You cow," he growled with venom, drawing his arm back and swiping her with all his strength across her cheek with the back of his hand. The violence caught her by surprise, dissipating any fight she may have had left. Overpowered and helpless, she felt his hands roughly clamping her head before dropping to her breasts as he pressed his lips on hers. She shivered with the realisation, closed her eyes and thought she might faint.

Only seconds later, there was a violent reaction, so swift and decisive she sensed her attacker lifted bodily from her as if by a powerful crane. She opened her eyes to see Jason, a look of bewilderment spread across his face, being drawn helplessly backwards out of the booth, an arm tightly wrapped around his neck in the early throes of strangulation. Desperately, Jason tried to catch the sides of the counter as he was pulled through the gap, his efforts of no consequence to the strength of his tormentor.

Once clear of the booth, he was swung sideways so that he crashed to the floor in a heap. Through the gap in the counter, Rachel saw her saviour for the first time. It was Charlie Greaves.

"You dirty little shit," Charlie hissed, his voice carrying the malice she felt he was about to release. Even with the counter separating them, she heard the breath forced from Jason's stomach as Charlie's fist penetrated his solar plexus. As he straightened up from the force of the blow, Charlie swung a left that caught him cleanly under the chin, seemingly lifting him off the floor before he crashed heavily across a display of plastic seed boxes, scattering them noisily around the shop floor under the impact. Before he had time to move further, Charlie had grabbed his arm, and dragged him semi-conscious to the door where he picked him up and threw him fiercely through the opening on to the gravel beyond.

"If you ever show your face here again, I'll kill you, you little ponce. You're scum," Charlie shouted as his rage overtook him, his final words accompanied by a hefty kick in the ribs. He felt like adding a further but good sense prevailed. He stepped back, breathing hard, and turned to attend to Rachel's needs.

By the time he reached the booth, she had recovered a little and was standing unsteadily with her hand cupped to her mouth. On sight of him, she broke down, her face dissolving readily as tears somersaulted down her cheeks. He went to her fondly and she to him, immediately throwing her arms around his neck, all the time crying pitifully as she slowly expelled her anguish.

His hand went to the back of her head and he stroked her hair soothingly. The tears continued so that he pulled her closer to him in an effort to stem the long convulsive spasms of her sobbing. The throbbing of her heart seemed to resonate through his body. There was a tenderness in their embrace that reminded Charlie of a passion he had long forgotten, but obviously still yearned.

It took several minutes to calm her.

"I was so frightened, Charlie," she sobbed.

"He won't trouble you again, I can assure you," Charlie told her with a gentleness that took effect. As they drew apart, Charlie was aware of the wetness of her tears on his neck.

"I'm sorry," she said, realising his reaction and smiling for the first time.

"No problem," he replied readily. "There's something about rescuing a maiden in distress that gives a man a lift and I haven't done it for quite some time." From the passion of his words, she felt she understood.

Looking around the shop, he spotted the kettle and tea accessories on a side table.

"Would you like a cup of tea?" he asked.

She hesitated before looking at the clock. "I think I would prefer to go home if you don't mind. It's been a bit of a rotten day."

"I understand," he told her. "I'll drive you home."

"No, no," she said shaking her head. "I'll be fine, honest."

With streaks of mascara splashed across her cheeks, she looked anything but fine. Charlie realised there was no point in arguing, besides, he would have to ask her to drive him back.

"Okay," he conceded. "But I'll follow you home and make sure you're safe." She appreciated his concern. A little consideration was very welcomed at this moment.

Twenty minutes later, she was outside her house. Right behind her, Charlie drew up in his BMW and parked alongside. Wearily, she pushed the car door open and stepped out. She waited at the front door for Charlie to join her before inserting her key. As soon as the door opened, Tammy was out and in action. After jumping up at Rachel, she quickly transferred her attention to the visitor.

"Hello, girl, how are you?" Charlie greeted her, bending down on his haunches to face his second wetting of the day as Tammy's tongue lashed his cheeks. Once she had coated his face, a further battering followed as she attempted to drop on to his lap, knocking him off balance with the action.

"That's enough, Tammy," Rachel intervened, her only desire to get inside and relax a little after her ordeal. She caught hold of Tammy's collar and forced her into the hallway. Charlie followed and closed the door behind him.

He was surprised at the state of the lounge, the room looking a complete mess. An untidy assortment of cushions had been left lying haphazardly around the floor and settee whilst a pile of washing was slung over two chairs in a disorderly array.

The room appeared to need a good clean and tidy up which Charlie imagined would follow at the weekend before David's return. On several occasions, David had told him how fastidious Rachel was around the home so the scene before him was a little unexpected. He dismissed his imminent thoughts to concentrate on more pressing matters.

"Excuse the mess," she said with some obvious embarrassment.

"How's Tom?" he asked.

Her reaction to what he considered to be a straightforward question was strangely unsettling. He realised she had experienced a fairly heavy ordeal but was not prepared for the response that followed. She seemed to dissolve before his eyes to the same poor state he had witnessed less than a half hour before at the nursery. Tears welled her eyes and were again dropping freely down her

150

cheeks. He was lost as to any reasoning. Immediately, he went to her and cradled her in his arms.

"What's wrong?" he enquired, a little lost as to what direction this latest behaviour was leading.

"Oh, Charlie, you don't understand what I've been through," she cried. He could feel her whole body shaking as she wept. Giving her a little time to pull herself together, gradually, the crying came to an end. As though embarrassed by her actions, she broke free of his arms and moved to the settee. A box of tissues rested on the arm and she pulled one out and dabbed her eyes.

"I'm sorry," she said solemnly whilst taking a seat. Charlie followed, positioning himself so that he was facing her. He waited for her to begin.

"The truth is…" she began in an awkward manner. "Tom and I just don't get on. I have made out to David that we do, but really, I don't think he wants me here."

She swallowed hard and continued despite further tears dribbling down her cheeks. "I have told David everything is fine but the truth is that when David's here, he behaves as though he is quite fond of me but once David's not around, he treats me like dirt, swearing and shouting. He comes in with his friends and thinks he's big in front of them by treating me this way. They just sit around and laugh."

"Why don't you tell David?" Charlie asked. "Surely, he would put him right?"

"He's really tired at the moment with all the training and pressure of the Olympics so I have tried to keep it from him in the hope we can put it right in the future. He obviously thinks the world of Tom and I don't want to put a wedge between us. I don't know what I'm doing wrong with Tom but I just can't seem to get through to him. I want it to work and I have tried so hard."

Charlie sensed that she was at the end of her tether.

"Do you know he hasn't been home to sleep since Friday? He promised his dad he would walk Tammy every evening and there's been no sign of him," she continued. "I know he calls in during the day when I'm not here but I've no idea what he's up to. He's staying with his friend, Danny, presumably, but I'm not even sure of that. I don't trust that boy, he's a bad influence as far as I'm concerned. Tom could be up to anything as far as I know and what's worse…" Her speech disintegrated to further sobs despite her efforts to continue.

Charlie reached for the tissue box and offered her the contents. She took one and dabbed her eyes again before resuming. "Oh, Charlie, I make out to David that everything's all right when it's not and it makes me feel so guilty."

Getting her problems off her chest seemed to raise her spirits a little. She looked up to Charlie and forced a slim smile

"I'm so sorry to burden you with my problems, Charlie," she said huskily, "I know you must have a lot on your mind at the moment."

Charlie shrugged his shoulders as if to negate her concerns.

"I think you'll find a lot of young men of Tom's age go through a funny period at some time in their adolescent years and it would seem Tom's has come early. We have to remember he lost his mother just a couple of years ago and very often, this can play a big part in a child's development. David has told me that he has hardly spoken about his mother since she died so it could be he has bottled it all up, instead of letting it out."

Rachel's expression signified she agreed with his words.

"He's not a bad lad, I know," Charlie continued. "It could be he just needs a little fatherly attention. I'll have a few words with him, if you like?" The look on Rachel's face, like the sun appearing from a dark cloud, was sufficient confirmation she was in agreement.

"Oh, Charlie, that would be wonderful," she said with renewed enthusiasm.

"Now, I'm going to ask quite a big favour from you in return." It was spoken with a certain degree of emphasis and she immediately wondered what was coming.

"Yes, of course," she replied.

"I'm sorry to ask you to do this," he paused to find the right words. "But would you please not tell David about today's incident until he comes home at the weekend. I know the minute you tell him, he will want to comfort you and he can't really afford to lose this week. It is extremely important to him."

She immediately went quiet, whilst seriously considering the implications of Charlie's request. She badly wanted to share her nightmare with someone close. He realised he was asking a lot of her from the painful expression on her face. Finally, she looked as if she had come to a decision. She raised her eyes.

"Okay," she said, with some reluctance. Charlie felt relieved, but guilty.

Five minutes later, he was at the door saying his goodbyes when Rachel grabbed him fondly and hugged him for long seconds before planting a big kiss on his cheek. He studied her, a picture of youth and beauty, despite her recent ordeal. It stirred something inside him again, the bittersweet memories of a life he had left behind.

"Thank you so much, Charlie, for this and for all the effort you have put into David's career. He thinks you're a god you know? And, after today, I'm not far behind him." She was beaming now and Charlie lapped up the pleasure of it.

"If I had you to come home to, I'm not sure I would even be running," he said with that special sparkle in his eyes. He closed the gate and waved fondly as he pressed the key to open his car door.

No sooner had Rachel closed the front door than she ran upstairs to the bathroom, turned the shower fully on and stood beneath the scalding water for several long minutes in an effort to cleanse herself of Jason.

Chapter 12

Tom sat on the low coping of the old church wall overlooking the main road, his mind still alive with the excitement of the film he and Danny had spent the afternoon watching at the local cinema. It had finished only an hour ago. Bunking off school at lunchtime had been well worth it.

Entitled *Battleship,* it had been one of the most exciting war films he had ever seen. The action had started almost as the introductory titles came to an end and had been maintained throughout the whole film. Some of the scenes of the naval battles, full of action, violence and destruction, had been truly memorable. There were times when he thought the *Aliens*, a group of unknown origins seeking revenge on the human race, would succeed with their armada of battleships to wipe out the combined strength of the British and American navies. However, as usual, Liam Neeson, leading his trusted followers, overcame the odds and won the day.

A screech from a braking lorry brought him back to reality with a start. He looked down the road to see Danny returning from the shops with two bags of crisps in his hand. As he approached, he slung one to Tom's right-hand side so that he had to stretch out fully and nearly over-balanced across the back of the wall with the effort.

"Well held," Danny praised with a generous smile.

"Thanks, mate," Tom acknowledged, tearing the bag open and stuffing a couple of crisps hurriedly into his mouth. Danny joined him on the wall.

"Good film that *Battleship*, wasn't it?" Tom reflected.

"Yep, it were, some bloody good battles."

"I'd like to see it again sometime."

"I don't know whether I could watch it again," Danny said whilst giving the matter some thought. "Once you know the ending, it sort of spoils it. Anyhow, it will be out on DVD in a couple of months, so we can think about it then."

"I could watch that final battle scene again and again," Tom added. This seemed to bring the subject to a close as both of them concentrated on their crisps They sat in silence for a few minutes, just munching and casually watching the stream of traffic trundling along the road.

Tom was the first to open the conversation again. "What time did he say *this time*?" he asked, emphasising the final words deliberately.

Danny slung his head back and funnelled the remaining crisps into his mouth from the packet. Before answering, he screwed up the empty packet in his hand

and casually chucked it over his shoulder, at the same time wiping his chin with his other hand. "He said about five-thirty."

"It's already gone seven," Tom replied, after checking his watch. "Looks like another wasted evening."

"He'll come, he always does," Danny parried.

The next twenty minutes were spent discussing the virtues of various cars that caught their imagination as they motored past at steady speeds in the restricted area. With each minute, Tom's patience was ebbing. He was about to add further comment when the appearance of a Lamborghini smoothly cruising across their vision caused particular interest. Danny stood up and quickly moved to the kerbside to make a closer inspection. Turning to Tom once it had disappeared in the distance, he told him excitedly, "I'm gunna have one of 'em one day."

"You wish," Tom replied with a touch of sarcasm.

For a short while, the flow of cars were all fairly average in their estimation. That was until the gleaming bodywork of a metallic red Jaguar XJ Sports caught their attention. As it approached, its left-hand indicator signified it was pulling in. They both stood in awe as it drew into the kerb right in front of them. The front passenger window slowly wound down revealing a grin from a familiar face.

"Get in you two and be quick," Wayne Butler commanded. "I don't want to draw attention to the car."

The shock of Wayne's arrival was quickly digested as the thrill of the adventure ahead struck them both. Without further thought, they opened their respective doors and jumped in, Danny in the front and Tom in the back. Indicating, Wayne serenely joined the flow of traffic making its way through the town, the broad smile on his face painting the pride he had no intention of concealing.

"Cor!" Danny exclaimed openly, mesmerised as he was by the illuminated panel of knobs, screens, symbols and paraphernalia facing him directly on the dashboard. "W'ere the 'ell did yer git this from?"

It was obvious that Wayne was concentrating on his driving as he made no immediate effort to reply. Carefully, he listened to the engine as it nursed itself smoothly through the automatic gears and settled comfortably at the cruising speed of the surrounding traffic. It was some time since he had driven an automatic so he had to remind himself to keep his left foot redundant. Happy with the response, he relaxed before turning to Danny with a smile as smug as a cat that had got the cream.

"So what do you think, young 'uns? Ain't she sweet, eh?"

"It's amazing…terrific," Danny responded so enthusiastically that Wayne felt almost intoxicated by the surge of pride that overcame him.

"What can it do?" Tom asked from the back seat as he leant forward to make his presence felt.

"Don't know exactly," Wayne replied casually. "Believe it's got 400 horsepower under the bonnet and gets from 0 to sixty in five seconds when yer really put yer foot down." He wondered where he had drawn these statistics from but they sounded impressive, he thought.

The *wow* that came from Tom confirmed his assessment had hit the mark.

"I want to take it easy through the town. When we get out in the country, we can open her up."

"Where did yer git it from?" Danny asked for the second time.

"I was walking through the garage forecourt at the other end of town when I saw this little beauty pull in fer some petrol. I sat on the wall, and just looked casual whilst this geezer got out and filled his tank. Looked a real smart dude, he did. When he went to pay, I just strolled up to have a look and couldn't believe the arse hole had left his key on his seat. It was too much of a temptation and I just jumped in and was off. Laughed me 'ead off, I did when I looked in the mirror and saw the bloke shaking his fist at me. The wally," he added as an afterthought.

Again, Wayne gave Danny a quick glance for his approval and was immediately rewarded with a show of admiration he felt he truly deserved.

"The geezer won't take long to inform the police so we need to git out of town pronto. A car like this don't take much spotting."

Keeping his cool, Wayne calmly switched lanes to exit the dual carriageway and make his way to the A47. With his ego now peaking steadily, he was looking forward to the evening ahead.

***

PC John Hislop couldn't have felt better. It had been one of those perfect days when everything had gone right. Such days were not that frequent, so you have to make the most of them, he told himself.

In the morning, he had attended Court to give evidence on Michael James, a compulsive burglar he had the pleasure of arresting a couple of months ago. This petty criminal, with a list of thefts as long as his arm, had been arrested several times in the past two years but on each occasion insufficient evidence had allowed him to walk free, despite his guilt being obvious to all and sundry.

The CID had worked hard on the latest break-in and luck had been on their side when a pensioner who lived on the opposite side of the road had witnessed him leaving the property at the time the crime was committed. The fact she came to the station and picked him out from the video portraits they put before her, was the icing on the cake. He was sure they had him this time.

At court, he had suffered the usual nerves he experienced at such events but felt he had handled himself well in the circumstances. When the jury foreman finally announced those magic words of *guilty,* he was ecstatic. Following this, the confirmation from the judge of a prison sentence of three years was magic to all their ears.

Riding on the elation of his success, he had returned to the station at lunchtime with the courage to execute an invitation he had promised himself for several weeks. Finding his probationary officer, Yvonne Foster, in the staff room, he had asked her directly if she fancied joining him for a meal sometime in the future. The look of delight immediately swiping her face told him his intuition had been correct. That they had finally settled on this very evening, had been too good to be true.

Like a schoolboy on his first date, he could not remember when he was last so thrilled. Just twenty minutes now to the end of their shift and he would be off home, shower, and change to start what he believed could be a new and exciting chapter in his life.

Driving southwards towards the town centre, he found himself humming a tune that Girls Aloud had put top of the charts not so many years ago. Yvonne looked across and caught the joyful expression on his face.

"You sound happy," she said. "Who's the lucky girl?" She was trying her hardest to disguise the smile she knew wanted to escape her lips. Letting the mood take him, John gave her a skirting grin and keeping his eyes firmly on the road ahead, moved his left hand to her lap. Making contact with her hand, he gripped it lightly and squeezed. She responded likewise.

"Something tells me I'm into something good," he recited, not knowing from where the words had come, but knowing he had heard them somewhere in the past. Whatever, he felt they were appropriate and were obviously having the right effect.

While still gently caressing his hand, she suddenly froze, a look of incredulity flashing to her face as she uttered, "That's the red Jaguar stolen just minutes ago."

Out the corner of his eye, John caught a fleeting glance of the Jaguar as it sailed past in the opposite direction. Slamming the brakes on, both hands came to the steering wheel as he prepared himself for action. Yvonne thumped the siren button on the dashboard and was immediately rewarded with the familiar wail from above.

The road was busy with the evening traffic but the siren had a startling effect with brakes being applied in both directions as the nearby traffic screeched to a halt.

John quickly saw his chance, using a gap ahead he shot forward fiercely, slammed on his brakes and immediately shunted backwards, his head swinging rapidly left and right as he manoeuvred into the yawning gaps before braking again, changing gear and taking off in hot pursuit of the Jag. Several of the drivers and their passengers in the immediate vicinity breathed a sigh of relief on his departure.

Now in pursuit, Yvonne was quickly on the radio.

"Car NT to HQ," she said, once through to the control unit, her voice calm and measured despite her heart beating double. "We are in pursuit of the stolen red Jaguar on the A1101 making towards the A47 at Elm and request urgent assistance."

"OK, Car NT. Your situation is noted, will come back to you shortly. Keep me in the picture please."

"Roger and out," Yvonne replied, keeping the transmitter in her hand as she concentrated on the action ahead.

It was obvious the driver of the Jag had picked up on their manoeuvre and was already making a break, dangerously overtaking a lorry as he approached the roundabout to the A47. They both clearly heard the brakes applied from the oncoming vehicle as the Jag dangerously swerved back to the left-hand side of the road.

Their siren had a chaotic effect on the surrounding traffic as cars either came to a halt or climbed the footpath in confusion, some opposite each other, so there was insufficient space to go between. John impatiently sounded his horn, the harsh cacophony of sounds only adding to the confusion. By the time the Jag hit the roundabout, it was a good hundred metres and at least a dozen vehicles ahead.

"My God, what bloody idiots," John bawled in frustration as a driver in the car ahead slowed to a halt and opened his window to wave a perfect overtake hand signal just as the road narrowed further, leaving him an almost impossible gap between the stationary car on the opposite side of the road.

"Well, here goes," he said boldly as he put his foot down and went for the gap, screwing his eyes up in anticipation of possible contact. How he made it, he would never know, but he did and was offered a further reward when the oncoming traffic cleared for some fifty metres ahead, giving him the opportunity of overtaking three cars on his side of the road in one swoop.

Hitting the roundabout, Yvonne's radio crackled back into life. "Calling Car NT…there is help on the way. The chopper will be in the air almost immediately and will be with you in five to ten minutes. Several pandas are also closing in on the area. Will keep you informed."

"Thank you, we can do with all the help we can get," Yvonne replied with some relief.

***

Wayne couldn't believe the scintillating power under the bonnet. No more than a gentle touch on the accelerator pedal and the car shot smoothly forward with an almighty response. It was a monster. He had never driven anything like it.

No sooner had they passed the police car cruising in the opposite direction than he realised they had been identified. The shrill sound of the two-tone siren came to them almost at once. It was a shame they had been spotted so quickly but, never mind, he told himself, it gave him an earlier than expected chance to see what the Jag could do.

A quick glance in his mirror at the turmoil behind, with the police car trying to extricate itself from the traffic, confirmed the chase was really on. Only a short distance from the roundabout ahead, he knew the faster A47 offered more scope to the powerhouse under his control.

At first, stuck behind a huge lorry, he had little sight of the road ahead when he pulled out and forced his foot to the floor. The automatic gears performed smoothly so that he glided past the vehicle and quickly dropped back to the near lane before an approaching car was upon him. The driver of the vehicle was not so impressed and sounded his horn loudly before flashing his lights in annoyance.

"Up yours," Wayne responded verbally as he leant forward in his seat, the adrenaline coursing freely through his veins.

Taking the roundabout at speed to meet the A47, it felt as if the car was riding on tramlines, so secure and steady its action. The new road, although non-restricted, was unfortunately for Wayne, single lane for traffic travelling in their direction. He couldn't wait to open her up. However, the volume of advancing traffic prevented this with a convoy of commercial vans, cars and several articulated lorries impeding his immediate path.

Seated alone in the centre of the back seat, Tom felt a yearning for his seat belt which, up until now, had not crossed his mind. Blindly, he ran his fingers along the glossy leather of the seat until they touched the cold metal of the clasp. Pulling it over his shoulder, he felt a little more secure as it clicked solidly into position.

After several similar escapades with the 'lunatic', as he had named him, he had now acquired a strange confidence in Wayne's driving. The fear he originally held of having a serious accident seemed to have receded somewhat to be replaced with a thrill for the speed and excitement accompanying each adventure. Only that morning, he had joked with Danny that he could now understand why it was called *joy riding.*

Looking in his wing mirror, Wayne noted with some satisfaction the clear flashing blue beacon emerging from the roundabout was now a good two hundred metres in arrears. He knew from the beginning he had the speed to outrun it providing he had a clear passage ahead.

At this very moment, he was stuck behind a female driver with two children in the back seat. He was waiting as patiently as he could for the opportunity of a clear space in the oncoming lane so that he could overtake.

Always on the alert, the large P sign signifying a lay-by just a hundred metres ahead caught his attention. As he changed his position on the road, moving from the right-hand side of the car in front to the left, Danny woke up to the anticipated manoeuvre and immediately encouraged the obsessed Wayne.

"Go for it, Wayne, now's the time," he gushed excitedly.

Waiting just a few seconds more, Wayne then swung into the lay-by, accelerated sharply along the slim fifty metres of tarmac and swerved back on the road in a matter of seconds ahead of the lady driver. Tom noticed her look of surprise turn to disgust as they stormed past. He had to smile.

"Wow," yelled Danny in a further ecstatic contribution. "This car's amazing!"

"Told yer so," Wayne calmly added.

The road ahead was still busy so that Wayne had to bide his time in overtaking each vehicle. On every occasion, he did so, however, his confidence in the car's ability was fortified. So smooth and effortless, by now, he felt the only thing it couldn't do was fly.

The fanfare of hooters and flashing of headlights that invariably followed his rather dexterous actions only added to his ego, like applause for a virtuoso performance. Every few moments, he was checking his mirror for sight of the chasing police car only to conclude it was making little progress on closing the gap between them.

Once off the A47, the traffic was a lot lighter and he was able to accelerate for longer periods. In no time, they had reached the sleepy village of Chatteris where he reined the Jag down to a cruising speed purposely along the narrow high street to allow his pursuer to close on them.

"Come on, you buggers," he coaxed as they appeared from the bend. Patiently, he waited for the white BMW to approach within fifty metres before hitting the accelerator.

"Now we'll show them a clean pair of heels," he shouted excitedly, as he bathed in the vroom of the engine and the immediate bite on the road with the injection of pace.

At the same time, several spots of rain splattered noisily on the windscreen. Casually, his left hand moved to the steering column and found the desired knob. The large wipers arched smoothly across the screen vanishing the accruing drops and leaving a crystal clear view. Knowing he had the open country lanes across the Fenlands ahead, he felt confident the police car would be left in his wake.

***

"My God," yelled John Hislop to Yvonne as he accelerated round the sharp bend into Chatteris and caught sight of the Jag again in the High Street, no more than a hundred metres ahead. "I do believe they are giving themselves up."

The Jag, cruising slowly past the line of shops ahead, looked as if it could be stopping. John reduced his speed as he approached. He could make out one passenger in the front and he believed, one in the back, but couldn't be sure. Yvonne's first reaction was to reach to the dashboard and cut the siren.

The Jag had almost stopped and they were now closing down rapidly. Only fifty metres apart, there was a guttural roar as if an aeroplane was opening its engine to a clear runway. At the same time, the Jag gunned into action, tearing off with an ear-piercing screech, leaving a cloud of burning rubber in its wake. John was left gob-smacked.

"Christ," he bawled at Yvonne in total shock. "Did you see that?"

The reaction from the Jag of slowing and then accelerating away on their approach, however, triggered in his brain an old wound that had festered for several weeks. With this, he shared his thoughts with Yvonne.

"Do you know, I have a feeling this is the same driver who smashed my mirror and we chased through Wisbech a few weeks ago." It was just the fillip he needed, an extra boost stoking him up to the gung-ho mood he was now experiencing. All of a sudden, the chase ahead took a new perspective.

Before Yvonne could reply, her phone came to life. "Car NT, helicopter should be with you any time now," the voice told them.

At the same instant, both became aware of a loud grating noise above, like a giant cement mixer in the sky. A burst of static announced a new caller. "Car NT, Flight-lieutenant Colin Dawson of the air support unit here, we have the Jag in our sights so they can't get away. Keep as close as you can please. There are three other cars moving in ahead so we can hopefully direct all of you and set up a trap." Despite the drone of the blades, the voice came strong and clear. Yvonne thumped the siren back into action.

"Now we have them," John confirmed.

He had realised some way back his BMW did not have the power of the Jag. In his favour though, was his knowledge of the road to Erith they were now taking. It had been adapted and developed through the years to skirt the various farms, thus offering lots of twists and turns, many of which could be described as deceiving and dangerous if taken too fast. With this in mind, his confidence was increasing in leaps and bounds.

Ahead, the Jag powered on. Every so often, they saw the red taillights in the distance come alive as the brakes were applied. John wondered just how well the driver knew the area and in particular, the bends, and was hopeful that he would misjudge one at any time and skid off the road. Crouching over the wheel, he was now in pursuit mode, his driving instincts sharp and alert. With the help of the helicopter, knowing it could move at speeds up to 125mph, this time they would not lose them for sure.

Over the next three miles of open road, he held his own, gaining on the bends and losing on the straights, so that the deficit was still no more than two hundred metres. John was well pleased with his driving skills and the BMW which was giving him a feel of power he had not experienced for some time. They had heard nothing from the helicopter for a few minutes, when the red light flashed on and the now familiar drone came to them clearly preceded by the voice of Flight-lieutenant Colin Dawson.

"Hi there again," he reintroduced himself. "Well done, you're holding him fine. The driver's got quite a machine there."

"You're telling me," shouted John, loud enough for Colin to pick up. They heard a burble of laughter in response.

"As you will probably know, we are approaching Erith where he only has the choice of two routes, one to Ely and one to Willingham. Hopefully, he will choose the latter because we are setting up a reception committee with a stinger across the road. If he chooses Ely, we will make other plans."

John had to smile at the thought of the stinger. He had attended a two-day course in Warwickshire only last year which had included a demonstration of the spike strip in action. He had witnessed a car driven at speed into the instrument which had shredded its tyres and brought it to a halt within twenty metres. He had been highly impressed.

"Let's hope they choose the Willingham route," he confided in Yvonne, a bemused expression on his face.

160

All three occupants of the Jag were on a high.

Wayne, still electrified by the performance of his mighty monster, felt he was becoming more adept at handling the twists and turns. Braking earlier and coaxing it round the bends, before accelerating again, seemed to be the answer. Once the roads straightened out, the power was unbelievable. With his eyes darting from the road to the wing mirror and back again, he felt in complete control. The wet surface was not a problem, the tyres gripping the road firmly, even on the most hazardous of bends. There had been times when he had completely forgotten the pursuing BMW, his concentration and admiration for his new friend paramount in his mind.

Next to him, Danny sat rigid, bent forward in his seat, enjoying every moment of the aggressive driving. Occasionally, he would look back at Tom with an animated grin to share the enjoyment of a sharp bend or the thrust of the car as it bombed into a new stretch of open road. From time to time, he would shout words of encouragement to the possessed Wayne.

Only when the low drone of the helicopter came to their ears was there a change in the atmosphere. Wayne pressed the button to lower his window only to change his mind when the driving rain hit his face

"Blimey," he announced. "They've sent the air force out now." Danny laughed heartily.

"We can lose it, no worries, mate," Danny volleyed in support, massaging Wayne's ego to even greater highs.

In the back, Tom was beginning to fret. He had seen several police chases involving helicopters on the television in recent months and all with the same result. There had been no escape for the tearaways, even when they had deserted their respective cars. Wiping his sweating palms casually on his jeans, he was beginning to consider the seriousness of their actions.

"I think we should give ourselves up," he stammered.

Danny was on him straight away. "Don't be a prat, mate, we can outrun them. Can't we, Wayne?"

"Of course, we can," replied the egotistical Wayne.

As they approached the village of Erith, Wayne made no attempt to cut his speed, shooting through the High street at 60mph. One old aged pensioner, balancing precariously on her walking stick, was about to tackle the zebra crossing. Fortunately for her, she decided to delay her venture for a few seconds longer, because there is no doubt she wouldn't have made it. She cringed in fear as the draught from the passing Jag hit her unexpectedly. Wayne gave her a mock wave but all she saw was a blur.

Coming out of the village, the roundabout was soon upon them.

"Do we want Ely or Willingham?" Wayne asked his two passengers as he studied the routes on the post ahead.

"Ely sounds good," said Danny, having little idea of what either offered.

"I still think we should call it a day," Tom added ruefully from the back seat.

"Idiot," Wayne shouted with obvious contempt. "Okay, then, it's Ely."

A further glance in his wing mirror as he approached the roundabout confirmed sight of the blue beacon emerging from the village. The police car had closed a little. Taking the roundabout with the intention of going straight across to the Ely road, it was at the last moment he changed his mind for some reason and continued via the next exit to Willingham.

A surprised Danny looked across at him. "I thought we were taking the Ely road? He questioned.

"My choice, ain't it?" he answered in an arrogant tone. He wasn't really sure why he had made the decision. It was just one of those things you do at times on the spur of the moment, he told himself.

It would be true to say the beauty of the surrounding countryside was lost on all of them. The serenity of the working lock, long boats manoeuvring themselves through the narrow gates, went unnoticed as they raced on, transfixed only by the road ahead and the thrill of the chase

Once past, the drone of the helicopter reached them again.

"Bloody hell, that's getting on my nerves," Wayne said in anger. He had slowed for the bend at the loch but now his foot fell again on the accelerator and his passengers sensed once more the surge in power.

For the next mile, the road hugged the river dangerously before breaking away at a dogleg bend. Here, just half a mile ahead, the police had set up their roadblock. A row of thirty-six three-inch solid metal barbs spread across the whole width of the road between two police signs awaited the Jag's arrival.

The four constables who had arrived only minutes earlier were already soaked to the skin, their heavy-duty overcoats providing little protection from the squally wind and rain that came at them in sheets. Once the stinger was in place, they stood around in the car park just off the bend, chatting nervously, each wondering what the outcome of this imminent drama would offer. They knew many a driver, seeing the barrier ahead and realising the futility of the challenge, would come to a halt and give himself up, but you could never tell.

***

Halfway along the river road they were now travelling, Wayne experienced a strange foreboding, a peculiar inner emotion he was at a loss to understand. With the realisation that there had been no oncoming traffic for some time, he sensed danger and rightly so, for as he closed speedily towards the end of the strait of the riverbank, he could see there was trouble ahead. The road appeared closed and barricaded by several police vehicles and various obstacles which were not yet clear. A quick glance to his rear mirror confirmed the approach of the BMW so there was no escape there.

"Right, lads," he addressed his passengers. "We'll teach these buggers a real lesson."

Another surge of power from the Jag, taking the speedometer back over the 60 mark, made it clear as to Wayne's intentions.

Danny was motionless, his shoulders hunched forward, his eyes fizzing with the excitement of the event about to unfold. In contrast Tom was so scared sick he considered undoing his belt and jumping out the door.

Wayne was beyond recall, his mind was on a mission and that mission was destruction. As they approached the barrier, a lone police officer stood five metres before it, waving his arm up and down in a signal to slow down. This riled Wayne even more so that he aimed straight for the officer. The man's nerve quickly snapped as the Jag bore down on him at what looked to be a suicidal speed. Comically, he turned and hurdled the stinger before sprinting to the safety of the parked cars and his colleagues.

With a maniacal grin, Wayne changed direction and aimed the car for the kerbside of the stinger. It looked weaker was his theory and offered the extra room of the car park entrance for manoeuvring back on the road after impact. He was about to find out.

With only twenty metres left before hitting the barrier, Tom grabbed Wayne's shoulder and shook him violently as he screamed, "Stop, Wayne, please stop. You will kill us all."

His pleas were lost in the impact of the crash, an impact so devastating that it was etched on the mind of all those that witnessed it forever. So frightening, so terrible, a cacophony of heart-stopping sounds as almost simultaneously the tyres burst, the police sign was forcefully catapulted across the road and the deflated tyres tried to bite into the gravel of the car park, thunderously throwing a smokescreen of dust, stones and dirt high into the air.

***

In the Jag, Tom was hysterical.

Amidst the throes of his panic, thoughts of his father came to him. What if he never saw him again?

He must persuade Wayne to pull out of this crazy lunacy. From behind, he could see he was bent forward in concentration, seemingly determined to smash directly into the obstruction ahead. Not even the deafening drumming of the rain on the roof could eclipse the intensity of the moment. The Jag was almost upon the barrier that had been erected to stop it.

As a last resort, he stretched forward from his back seat despite the restraints of the belt and grabbed for Wayne's shoulder, shaking it frantically in a final effort to try and instil some sense.

"Stop, Wayne, please stop, you will kill us all," he pleaded, almost crying, but to no avail. At the same time, they struck the barrier with a sickening metallic crash that shattered all their nerves. Beneath them, they sensed the tyres puncture as the car shuddered and swerved wildly from the reduction in speed.

As if all of a sudden it was its own master, carried by the force of its momentum, it skidded into the car park still at a frightening speed, not the smooth traveller it had been but a rocking, shaking, mass of uncontrollable metal.

In the driver's seat, the frenetic actions of Wayne's shoulders confirmed their plight as he tried unsuccessfully to bring it to a halt. He was the first to be aware of the giant tree that lurched up before them, the car swinging broadside to take the impact directly on Wayne's door which collapsed inwards with an ear-splitting crunch, caving in his chest and lungs before rebounding onwards across the small expanse of turf and the river beyond. Neither appeared to have any effect on its speed as it surged for the bank.

From his seat in the back, Tom had sat dumbstruck by the sheer ferocity of events, his face screwed up in a mask of horror as each atrocious element of the crash unfolded. His eyes wanted to close, to avoid the unbelievable horror he was witnessing, but they stayed open, if only by half, to witness each phase as it occurred. He wanted it to stop but the nightmare just went on and on. As the Jag hit the tree and the driver's door collapsed towards him, he thought it was the end for all of them but the warrior car continued its path of terror.

"Oh, no…" Tom cried as he saw what was ahead. He had forgotten Danny but suddenly his friend made a grab for the wheel despite Wayne's limp torso slung heavily across it. He forced his hands under his chest to seek a grip but too late as the Jag shuddered on meeting the rising bank and took off for the river beyond.

The silence that followed lasted just a split second. It was followed by a resounding splash as the Jag landed on the surface of the water, amazingly still upright. For just a moment, it stayed afloat but with those frightening seconds came the jets of water, cold, fierce and terrifying, as they burst through the floor, the windows and the damaged door.

"God, please help me," Tom uttered in a voice so low it quivered to a silence. His eyes closed in surrender to his fate.

There was no time to think as the car dropped rapidly below the surface, bonnet first with the weight of the engine. The brightness of the sky disappeared, to be replaced by the dull green opaque nothingness of the riverbed. Tom panicked as the water level rose quickly up his body. But, with the chill of the water came a new reaction. An urge to survive overcame him. *I have to get out of here,* he told himself. Subconsciously, he took one huge breath, inhaling the last trace of air to fill his lungs to capacity before the water flooded his vision.

Panic took over as he realised he had only seconds to live. By now, the car had landed bonnet first on the riverbed, the thick reeds taking much of the force. The rear dropped gently, the car settling at a slight angle on its right-hand side leaving the doors on the passenger side free.

He struggled with the seat belt, finally pressing the clamp to release himself so that he was lifted inside the car with the buoyancy of the water. His first reaction was to open the door. With his head pressed against the roof, he scrambled forward. He tried the electric window button but no response. His hand frantically traced the side of the door for the lever that would release him from his watery tomb. He found it and pushed downwards. With a mighty thrust, he threw himself against it and it gave way. Forcefully, he prised it open, giving himself sufficient room to make his escape.

His lungs felt as if they were exploding, collapsing under the throbbing pain biting at his chest. It was so dark he could barely see the outline of the car. The reeds grabbed at his legs as he took a step along the riverbed. All he could think of was swimming upwards to meet the air his lungs so badly needed. He felt his body had little more to offer.

About to take the first stroke of his ascent, a faint blurry movement from the passenger seat caught his attention. Drawing closer, he could see Danny fumbling with his door from within, air bubbles dribbling intermittently from his mouth.

Forgetting his own plight, he waded to the door, grabbed the handle and yanked it towards him as forcefully as he could. It gave way. Danny looked up in surprise, his eyes, bulging with fear, catching his and spelling out the gratitude he could not express.

He looked to be on his last legs as he fell out, his tortured and bloated face confirming his condition. Realising his problem, Tom grabbed his arm at the same time thrusting upwards. Danny came with him but so slowly, he feared that they would not make it. His brain told him to release his load but he would not. Feeling himself close to death, all he could do was to keep kicking in the hope that he would break the surface. The faint light from above was growing brighter. Then darkness overcame him.

Chapter 13

"What do you mean had an accident? What sort of an accident?"

David had woken up with a start to the intimidating jingle of his mobile. It was 2:47 in the morning. Up until then, he had slept well. Now, still drowsy, he was patiently trying to absorb the words that Rachel was throwing at him in an emotional tone that did little to assist him. She seemed to be struggling to find the right words to explain the situation clearly.

"The police said he had been involved in a chase."

"A chase with whom?" David cut in, the tone of his voice sharp and angry but at the same time choked with concern.

"I don't know the details, all they said was he was in a chase and had ended up in the hospital."

"In the hospital," David repeated, his brain working overtime to piece together exactly the details presented. Completely lost to comprehend the facts, he found his frustration rising to breaking point. Already, a fierce ache had developed in his chest as the tension gripped him and he was sure it wasn't going away.

"What time did he go out and with whom?" he questioned her, hoping to clarify the situation with a little understanding.

"He wasn't in last night, he was staying with Danny."

"But it was Monday, he doesn't stay at Danny's on a Monday. *He has school.*"

"He didn't come back after the weekend," she stalled, her voice tapering to a husky whisper.

"When did you last see him then," David demanded, his voice now bearing an edge that was starting to frighten her. She had not seen this side of him before. He was normally so calm and gentle.

"He hasn't been home since Thursday," she finally surrendered, hopeful that his Gestapo questioning would cease.

"Thursday," David barked at her in disbelief, so fiercely she felt her eyes welling with tears.

"Yes," she shouted back, feeling a slight release of the tension as she prepared to share with him the secrets that had haunted her for several months. Before she could begin, David took control.

"And you never told me, you just let him disappear for days and thought that was okay?"

"I wanted to tell you but—"

166

"But nothing," he shouted. "You've shocked me, Rachel. I thought my son was safe with you and look what's happened?" She started sobbing.

"Well, have you anything else to tell me that I need to know before I try and get home? Did they say what hospital he was in?"

"Kings Lynn, A&E Department," she answered solemnly through her snuffles.

"Right," were his final words. There was a sharp click and the line went dead.

For a few moments, David sat on the bed to calm himself. His hand was shaking uncontrollably as he replaced the receiver on the hotel phone. He felt numb, his head was in a whirl. The tightness in his chest was ever present.

Firstly, he would phone Charlie. Presumably, he would be at home in bed and therefore, the nearest on hand to rush to the hospital. After that, he would phone a local taxi firm and book a cab for hopefully a speedy journey to Kings Lynn. Then, if he had time, he would phone the police to see whether he could obtain some fuller details than the sketchy ones Rachel had passed on.

After dialling Charlie's number, it was no time before the phone came alive and the drowsy tones of Charlie's voice echoed to him.

"Charlie, it's David. Tom's been in some sort of an accident and is in Kings Lynn Hospital."

"Good God," Charlie sounded as shocked as he had been. He quickly told him all he knew. "I went to Danny's yesterday evening to try and see Tom but his mother said the boys were out, and she didn't know when they would be back. To be quite honest, she didn't sound as if she was too concerned. I was going to call around this morning about eight, and try and catch him before he went to school."

"So you knew he hadn't been home for several days?" David asked.

Not sure how much David knew of his son's recent behaviour, Charlie didn't want to cause trouble for Rachel and decided to answer with caution.

"I only found out a few hours before and that's why I wanted to talk to him to see if I could find out what was going on."

"Well, thanks for that, but it would seem it was a little too late."

The tone of sarcasm was quickly digested. David was seriously on edge. This was the sort of calamity Charlie had been trying to avoid. First thing, he needed to calm him down.

"Look, David, we mustn't jump to conclusions, it could just be something minor and he could be home in a matter of hours. I'll go to the hospital now and see what I can find out, and then I'll phone you straight away. Okay?"

"Thanks, Charlie, I'm so worried," said David, his voice breaking up with emotion.

"I know," Charlie said with feeling. "But as I've said, it could be nothing."

"God, let's hope so," came the forlorn reply.

"Calm down, find a local car firm and get home as quickly as you can," Charlie advised. "In the meantime, hopefully, I will be able to phone you and give you some good news."

"Will do, Charlie, you're a brick."

167

"No trouble," Charlie said flatly. "See you soon and don't worry, it will be all right, I'm sure."

Dropping the phone into its cradle, Charlie sighed heavily. This was the last thing he wanted so close to the big day. Hoping he had pacified David just a little, he gave the matter a few seconds thought before preparing himself for the journey ahead.

***

A policeman, seated sentry-like in front of the two curtained cubicles at the A&E Department, did little to improve Charlie's state of mind. The officer was happily reading a magazine, browsing the pages in a lazy carefree manner that gave the impression the contents were of little interest to him. An empty teacup on a saucer lay untidily under his chair.

At this early hour of the morning, the room had a tranquil air to it, only the hum of the fans and a distant mumbling of soft voices further down the ward having any impact on its serenity.

Travelling to the hospital, Charlie had tried to conjure up in his mind different scenarios as to why Tom could be in hospital following a car chase but was at a loss to come up with anything feasible. Details from David had been very sketchy and like David, he was a little lost as to the background of the situation they were now facing.

Charlie's nerves began to jangle somewhat as the officer stood up smartly and smiled. He was young, fresh and police friendly, was his early assessment.

"Hello there," Charlie introduced himself. "I'm here to see Tom Lucas."

The officer smiled in acknowledgement. "Are you family, sir?" he asked.

"Well, not really, I'm a close friend. Can you tell me what's happened exactly?"

"I cannot do that unless you are family, sir. What I can tell you is that the lad was pulled from the river unconscious and he is still in that state at the moment. You are welcome to go inside and have a look at him if you wish."

"The fact is, the lad's father is currently in Manchester trying to get home. Obviously, he is aware of the situation and is terribly worried. I have told him I will find out the details and phone him as soon as I can. His father is running in the Olympics in a few weeks' time and this is just what he doesn't need."

With the mention of the Olympics, Charlie could see the policeman's brain quickly churning over and with it he sensed a recognition that would hopefully benefit his request.

"You're that coach, the one who's been on the TV recently," the officer said, now smiling broadly as if in the presence of royalty.

"Charlie Greaves," Charlie replied, gripping the hand thrust at him.

"Pleasure to meet you, sir."

Charlie sensed a change in the man's attitude. There was a short pause before he spoke again, this time in a hushed conspiratorial tone that amused Charlie. "In the circumstances, sir, I will fill you in with what I know."

The constable started to tell the story in some detail, covering the chase from Wisbech in the stolen Jaguar, highlighting the assistance of the helicopter, the roadblock utilising the stinger, the carnage that followed and the car careering out of control into the river. It all seemed pretty bleak as far as Charlie could see.

The only relief from the chilling climax of the tale was the news that, after what seemed an impossible time, when everyone present had thought there was no hope of anyone surviving, Tom had surfaced in an unconscious state, gripping another boy whom they had assumed he had dragged from the sunken vehicle.

He went on to explain that the driver of the pursuing police vehicle and his co-driver had, by then, arrived at the scene, and had immediately dived in at a risk to their own lives and pulled the two boys out. By this time, both were unconscious and not breathing. They were given artificial respiration by the officers present and fortunately, both lads came round.

However, soon afterwards, Tom dropped back into unconsciousness and there had been no change since. As he understood it, everything had been done by the hospital staff and they could only hope he would recover in due course. In the meantime, all they could do was wait.

As an afterthought, he mentioned he believed there had been a third member in the car who did not survive. He understood, at the moment, they were dredging the car from the riverbed and they would know more when this was accomplished.

On hearing this, Charlie felt completely deflated. He had heard stories of similar situations where the victims had not recovered consciousness and often, where they had, there had been brain damage.

"Would you like to see the young man?" the officer asked Charlie as he drew the curtain back at the entrance.

When he saw Tom lying on his back with a mass of tubes and wires attached to what would seem every conceivable part of his body, he was more than shocked. He looked so weak and vulnerable as he lay there motionless. His eyes were closed tightly, his face ashen and lifeless.

His first thoughts were of David's reaction when he arrived shortly. If he was shocked, how would it hit his father? Very hard, was the obvious and only answer.

Beside Tom's bed, a screen flashed up various figures, one his pulse, he guessed, the others he was not sure of.

"Are the other lads parents here?" Charlie asked.

"No," answered the officer. "They don't appear to be at home and we are still trying to contact them."

"Can I go and have a word with him, please?" Again, the officer gave the matter a little thought before replying.

"I guess it will be all right, sir, but don't take too long please as someone may turn up to relieve me." Charlie was thankful for the concessions the officer was making and made up his mind to be brief. He pushed his way back through the curtain and entered the adjacent cubicle.

Although he also had little colour in his face, Danny's weak but impish grin was a tonic compared to Tom's current state.

"Hi, Danny. I'm Charlie Greaves, a friend of Tom's," Charlie introduced himself.

Danny held his expression in place. "Tom's told me about you. You make him laugh."

"That's good," Charlie said, pleased to learn that he had made a mark with the boy. "You have been very lucky, you know. You could easily have lost your life."

"I would have done, if it hadn't been for Tom," he answered with some verve. "How is he?" There was a sharpness about his question that Charlie read as genuine concern.

"Not too good, I'm afraid. He's still unconscious."

"Oh, Christ," was Danny's response. Charlie noticed his eyes welling. "He will be okay, won't he?" It was said with a strength of feeling. "We can only hope so, at this stage," Charlie replied.

The lad seemed to want to talk so Charlie pulled up a chair. It was a further but more detailed account of the evening's escapade with the lad again making a big issue of Tom's heroics. After five minutes, Charlie sensed he was exhausted and decided it was time to let him rest.

"I had better get back to Tom," Charlie announced as an excuse to make his departure. "As soon as he comes round, we will let you know." On leaving the bed, Charlie gave the lad's leg a gentle squeeze through the blanket in a friendly gesture.

"Take care and get yourself better."

"Thanks, Charlie," said Danny in a voice that failed to hide his grief. No sooner was Charlie clear of the curtains than he heard a muffled sob. The officer was back on his seat. Charlie thanked him for his kind assistance and left the ward to return to the car park.

Once outside the hospital in the fresh air, he took a deep breath. It was only a partial relief. He was shaken to the core with what he had seen and heard. Taking a seat on a slatted bench under a friendly lamp, he was dreading the phone call he knew he had to make.

He gave the matter a few minutes of careful thought before dialling, not wanting to increase the distress he knew would follow on telling David the news but at the same time pondering any small points that would help to lessen the impact. As far as he could see, at the moment, there was very little good news. If only he would regain consciousness; that was the miracle they needed.

No sooner had David answered his call than Charlie realised the nervous state he was in, popping questions at him so fast that Charlie found it difficult to answer with any clarity in his own exhausted state. He was in the back seat of a hire car passing through Corby only forty miles away as he spoke.

"Hold on a moment, Dave, don't jump to conclusions," he pleaded with him at one point after being bombarded with a spate of negative assessments. "The medical staff are confident he will regain consciousness but they are not sure when."

"I can't understand what got into him, I would never dream he could do anything like this. Why didn't Rachel let me know what he was up to?"

"Boys of his age do stupid things and often don't consider the consequences," Charlie tried to console him. "I'm sure Rachel had her reasons. Perhaps, she didn't want to worry you?" He had decided it would be better to let Rachel explain her side of the story in her own time, especially as he knew little of the background that had brought this catastrophe about.

"Worry me, bloody hell, Charlie, worry me," he repeated. "She's more than bloody worried me, she's frightened the life out of me."

"They seem to think Tom pulled the other boy from the wreckage and could be a bit of a hero," Charlie added, hoping the slight change in tact might defuse his tension somewhat.

"Could be a dead hero, that's bloody useful," David came back at him with full sarcasm.

"Did you manage to speak to the police?" Charlie asked.

"Yes, and a lot of good it was too. I finally got through to the March station. There was only a skeleton staff on duty, and I think they put the cleaner on to talk to me because he was absolutely useless and knew nothing. I gave up after a few minutes."

Charlie was finding the task of conversing too heavy in David's current state of mind. He was tired, stressed out by the scenario he had just visited, his eyes felt gritty from lack of sleep and his knee was aching with a vengeance.

"I think they are expecting me back in the ward, Dave, so I had better make a move," he said, excusing himself.

Reluctantly, David let him go. "Okay, Charlie, I'll hopefully be with you very shortly."

Charlie cringed at the thought.

Chapter 14

Predictably, the remainder of David's journey took just a couple of minutes under the hour. As Charlie saw the hire car approaching, he stood up and steeled himself, ready for the anticipated ordeal ahead. No sooner had the car stopped than David jumped out the back door, a light bag in his hand.

Charlie could not believe the difference in his appearance since he had last seen him only two days ago. His face was gaunt, strained beyond all belief. His eyes had an intensity Charlie found quite worrying. It was difficult to believe he could change so much in such a short time.

"Hi, Dave," he said as calmly as he could. His first reaction was to offer his hand but thought better of it. "This way," he added, pointing to the main entrance.

They had barely taken a few steps when Charlie realised the driver had not been paid. The man looked as if he was about to lean over and call through the opened passenger window when Charlie caught his eye.

"I'll pay the driver," he advised David, much to the man's relief. David looked openly embarrassed but quickly dismissed his oversight and continued in a hurry towards the lights of the entrance hall. Charlie peeled off sufficient notes to settle what he considered a not too costly bill in the light of the circumstances and added a fiver for a tip that was more than appreciated.

"Ta very much, guvnor," said the thankful driver as he pulled off with a wave of his hand. "Hope he gets some good news."

"So do I," Charlie murmured to himself as he took off after David. He caught up with him just inside the reception area, grabbing his arm briefly to let him know he was there.

"Sorry about that, Charlie, I'll pay you as soon as I've seen Tom."

"No problem, Dave," Charlie responded. They were almost running down the corridor now towards A&E when Charlie caught his arm again and reined him down so that they came to a complete standstill. David's face registered his annoyance. Pulling him gently to one side so that he could look him in the eye, Charlie told him straight.

"Remember, Dave, your son is unconscious, so prepare yourself for that. It shocked me, so I'm sure it will shock you."

For several seconds, they stared fixedly at each other, Charlie searching David's eyes for some clue as to what he was thinking. All he read was fear and he had little idea as to how to handle it. They started walking again towards A&E, albeit at a slightly slower pace. Charlie felt his nerves tingling on the very edge.

He was hoping the officer may have retired from his sentry duty but it was not the case. He was still seated outside and unfortunately, looking more authoritative than he had done previously.

Again, he arose on their arrival and threw them a genial smile.

"This is the lad's father," Charlie explained as he led David in. The man nodded in acknowledgement and moved to one side.

David's reaction was more acute than Charlie could ever have imagined. At the moment he saw the boy, his eyes widened as if in disbelief. The pain seemed to instantly paralyse his face so that, in a stroke, he looked wizened and aged. He just stood there staring, lifeless and dumbstruck, in the face of this mortifying catastrophe.

Gently, Charlie caught hold of his arm and shepherded him forward towards the chair by the bedside. In trauma, his eyes were glued to the boy's face, his expression remorselessly dead. He dropped on to the chair, at the same time grabbing Tom's hand as he fell forward across the bed, crying pitifully with a rawness of grief that was totally heart-rendering.

"My boy, my lovely boy," he wailed helplessly as he smothered his face in the pillow close to Tom's face. Charlie found it difficult to contain the tears stinging his eyes. He quickly wiped his hand across both before moving to David's side and placing a hand on his shoulder. David's pain was all too obvious and he wished he could take it from him.

"Dave, he's going to make it, I just know he is," he said with as much conviction as he could muster, at the same time trying to prise David from the bed. It was useless. For what seemed ages, he just released all his grief, crying fitfully, his sides shaking visibly with the exertion of his dreadful convulsions. Not until he was close to exhaustion was there any sign of it coming to an end and even then, the recovery was gradual.

Finally, he seemed to pull himself together, raising his head from the bed and looking up helplessly to Charlie. With his eyes ringed raw red, his hair stuck untidily to his brow, the channels of his tears marking his cheeks, he looked a poor soul. Charlie's heart jumped out to him. "We're going to win this race, my boy," Charlie consoled, trying to reassure him, hugging him tightly and kissing the top of his head.

It was several minutes before David stood up.

"Sorry, Charlie," he said with a hint of embarrassment whilst wiping his eyes.

"No problem, Dave, I'm sure if it was my son, I would have reacted in the same way. I'm glad I was here for you. That's what's important." Once on his feet, David massaged his shoulders which were tense from his weeping. "I think I could do with a bit of fresh air."

"That's fine," Charlie confirmed. "You go out to the car park and I'll stay with him for a while."

"Thanks, Charlie, you're magic," David said with a forced hint of a smile.

In a solemn mood, David passed along the wide corridors towards the exit and the car park, his thoughts so dark that if death had been an option he would have offered little resistance. Racked with guilt, if Tom should die, he could see no future and would gladly join him.

Since receiving the devastating news in Manchester, a terrible guilt had surfaced, a deep throbbing guilt that had punished him with its insistence. Selfishly, he had pursued his own career, ignoring the needs of his son who had lost his mother so recently. Why had he done it? Why hadn't he shown the lad more consideration? The questions kept coming at him thick and fast with not one satisfactory answer. His mind was in turmoil, his thoughts in disarray. He had never felt so distressed.

Pushing the main door open with excessive force, it flew back on its hinges hitting the protective stopper with a jolt. He had no sooner tasted the cooler evening air than he recognised the slim figure approaching him through the hazy light of the car park. On sight of her, a red mist of anger surfaced. She looked sheepish, smiling nervously as she came towards him.

"How is he?" Rachel asked, when close enough to see David's eyes clearly.

"Unconscious, thanks to you," were the few stark words that immediately ruffled her calm. His eyes drilled into hers with a ferocity she found frightening. There was no time to think.

"If you had just told me what he had been up to, this would never have happened," he bawled at her fiercely. She stood before him dumbstruck, the power of his anger so extreme, she thought he was about to strike her. Totally confused by the unexpected aggression, she could not think clearly, her mind a jumble of mixed emotions. Like everyone else, the lack of sleep was taking its toll. Any reasonable words of defence escaped her.

"I'm sorry," were the only words she could finally deliver as she felt her eyes bubbling with heavy salty tears that started to drop to her cheeks. This seemed to infuriate him even more so that he grabbed her by the shoulders and almost lifted her from the ground. As this violent action caught her by surprise, she gasped with the shock. Her eyes widened in disbelief as his bored into hers with an intensity.

"I'm sorry, Rachel...would you please go home, I don't want you here." He held her before him for a short while, his eyes penetrating hers with what she read as a mixture of pain and sorrow.

"Please, David, let me stay and help you," she pleaded miserably.

"Go," he shouted at her, at the same time, pushing her away from him. She stood before him, her face a picture of grief. For a few moments, his eyes held a threat of malice but then his whole demeanour seemed to relax as though a spirit had left his body and returned him to his normal self.

"Please, go," he said in a voice much calmer but at the same time final.

For a brief moment, she wanted to run to him and throw her arms around him, to offer some comfort in this moment of need, but she could not. His actions had been too severe, too destructive to ignore.

He turned from her and walked back to the hospital, his head bent low with the weight of his torment.

She watched him the whole way to the entrance, hoping, she guessed, for just the hint of a glance of regret but it never came. Resignedly, with tears still dripping down her face she also turned and started her journey back to the cottage, temporarily lost as to what the future held.

Chapter 15

The hours that followed were some of the darkest Charlie could ever remember. Only the death of his son, Daniel, came anywhere near this trauma.

David returned from the car park looking more haggard than ever. Entering the cubicle, he made no effort to raise his mood, his eyes immediately falling to his son's poor frame before acknowledging Charlie.

"Rachel just turned up but I sent her home," he said meekly, as if of little consequence.

Once again, Charlie had an urge to fight her corner but thought better of it in the circumstances. The time was not right and he could see any words in her defence possibly aggravating the situation. No doubt, the two of them would sort themselves out once, hopefully, everything was back to normal.

He got up from his chair next to Tom's bed and offered it to David. With a faint gesture of thanks, he slipped into the seat and immediately gathered his son's hand in his. Leaning forward, he rubbed it gently with his other, at the same time wistfully staring at the fragile face before him.

Charlie was spent. The anxiety of the last hours was beginning to take its toll. In recent years, living on his own, he had been lucky enough to be able to programme himself to the luxury of at least eight hours sleep most nights and found it difficult, especially in recent years when his body was beginning to tire more easily, to function properly, if this routine was broken.

"Do you want a coffee, Dave?" he asked, as he moved towards the exit. David appeared preoccupied and didn't look up.

"No, thanks, Charlie, I'm okay," he said in a voice that lacked any shade of emotion.

Charlie hoped he had taken some refreshment during his journey from Manchester, but doubted it. Tiredness quickly dismissed any further concern as he made his way to the drinks machine.

A break from the desperate atmosphere of the A&E department was a relief. He felt he could not leave David on his own for any length of time and resigned himself to spending the next few hours in attendance if necessary.

For once, a black coffee had some appeal, the extra caffeine would hopefully help to keep him awake. He added two sugars instead of the usual one.

Returning to A&E, he was surprised to see a new officer seated outside. He was much older with a balding head and broad sideburns.

"Hi there," Charlie greeted him as he passed. "Just starting, are we?"

"Afraid so, sir, six hours before I'm free," he replied with genuine warmth.

It was six o'clock as Charlie settled himself again in the seat closest to the entrance. A nurse was checking the various instruments with meticulously care, adding the figures to a log of statistics attached to a clipboard at the side of the bed. On Charlie's arrival, she looked up and offered a comforting smile to which Charlie readily responded.

By this time, the morning light was just starting to spill across the ward from the broad windows high above the walls. Studying the scene before him, Charlie could not help but wonder what the day had in store for all of them.

Within a few minutes of his settling down, David had fallen asleep in the armchair, his head drooping sideways. He didn't look particularly comfortable but at least he was sleeping, which would do him good.

It took some time to sip his way through the coffee, pondering as he was on the events of the day. He was in no hurry. Once finished and the empty cup carefully placed on the floor, he finally relaxed and found himself drifting uncontrollably away into a peaceful sleep. Twice, he woke himself as his chin dropped to his chest. Despite his efforts to ward off the pressing tiredness he finally succumbed, falling into a deep sleep that carried him almost two hours into the morning.

He awoke with a start, his mind playing havoc with him as a cacophony of noises left him in a state of confusion. To the forefront of these, the harsh screaming of a frenzied patient some way off down the far end of the ward, grabbed his immediate attention. "It hurts, don't move me, *please*…don't…" The words, tapering off to silence, left Charlie cringing in suspense for a few moments as he waited for further activity.

It never came, so that his concentration refocused on David who was still slumbering peacefully, his head slumped firmly on his chest and his legs now splayed loosely in front of him. He definitely didn't look comfortable but Charlie had no intention of waking him.

Still a little sleepy, Charlie gave some thought to the current scenario. As he studied David, he wondered just what effect this catastrophe would have on their Olympic preparations. With the start of the Games only six weeks away, the timing could not have been worse.

For one thing, the story was bound to reach the papers in the next few hours and what would they make of it? If nothing else, the local paper would have a field day. He imagined front page would be favourite. There was a chance, of course, that Tom may have been an innocent party, drawn into the crime by the urgings of the older boys. This could provide a little comfort. Hopefully, he would be too young to be named in their report.

If Tom didn't come round, God forbid, he already accepted, that would be the end. From their months together, working closely day after day, he knew the boy was David's life and without him, there would definitely be no immediate future.

As these thoughts washed drearily through his mind, David came awake, stretching his arms in the air in a lackadaisical manner.

At first, Charlie's attention was focused on David as he shook himself to seek some comfort in the chair but as he did so, his eyes were drawn to the bed and Tom. What he saw, he could not at first believe. So shocked was he that, for a few seconds, his breath caught in his throat, his eyes staring fixedly in need of proof that the sight before him was real. Tom's eyes were open. Open. Yes, they really were.

"David! Look!," he bawled, jumping from his seat as he rushed to the red alarm button above the bed and pushed it with meaningful intent. The alarm blasted in response, creating an immediate reaction as the whole ward appeared to come to life. David was out of his chair in a flash, his face sealed with a look of surprise as he fell on his son's bed.

"Tom, Tom, can you hear me?" he shouted as he cradled the boy's face gently in his hands. The response was immediate, a slight suggestion of a smile wavering on his lips for a brief moment before his eyes closed and his face contorted frighteningly. There was a tension to his body as if he wanted to raise himself, and then his mouth split open and he spewed weakly down his chin.

David looked anxiously around the bed for a tissue but before he could move, a nurse had arrived on the other side of the bed and had the matter in hand, quickly wiping his chin with a towel and lifting him up so that he could retch more comfortably. The nausea continued for several minutes, each effort seemingly draining him of the little energy he had left. Finally, it came to an end and he closed his eyes peacefully.

"Is he okay?" David asked anxiously whilst watching the nurse take his pulse. By this time, two other nurses were present, mechanically dealing with the various duties that were part of the recovery procedure.

"He's going to be fine," she confirmed, smiling sweetly as she pulled a pen from her lapel.

Overcome with relief, David fell back on to the bed and kissed his son's cheek for the second time. "My lovely, lovely boy," he just kept repeating, the tears from his eyes smothering the boy's face and soaking the pillow.

Throughout David's display of emotion, Charlie found it difficult to control himself, sharing, as he was, every tinge of pain and relief with his friend as if he was the father. He now found himself in need of a tissue as further tears found a path down his cheeks. Embarrassed at such behaviour in the presence of the nurses, he surreptitiously moved to the bedside cabinet and pulled a couple of tissues from their box.

Turning around, he was faced by David, a David that had the face of a man reborn, a jubilant face he had not seen since leaving him two days ago. Their eyes met. They didn't speak. They didn't have to. They just rushed at each other and hugged fiercely, both crying openly as the relief washed over them. It was an act that carried its own message.

"Thanks, Charlie," David said, his voice quivering just slightly. "I thought I was going to lose him, you know?" This set him off again so that Charlie felt him shudder as he tried his best to stem his emotions.

"He's okay, Dave. He's going to be fine," Charlie said, rubbing his hands across David's shoulders. Slowly, he sensed the tension draining from his body. A strength had returned to his face, a revitalisation that shone with a challenge of what the future now held.

"Hi, Dad," a voice came weakly from the bed as they drew apart. Their eyes dropped to see Tom looking up at them with a thin smile on his face.

David couldn't control himself. He just fell back on the bed once again and kissed his son's face so emotionally, one side and then the other. Not until the nurse returned did he move. By this time, Tom had closed his eyes. She put her hand to his brow. Realising David and Charlie were both studying her actions, she looked over and smiled.

"He'll be fine, give him a day or two," she reassured them.

Chapter 16

"Dad, you can go home now and get some sleep you know, I'm going to live."
Despite the relief from such a remark, David found it difficult to smile.

It was late afternoon and he had spent most of the day with Tom. The only time he had left him was to buy some food and drink from the hospital shop and pay a visit to the loo. He just couldn't bear to leave him for any length of time. Twice Tom had fallen asleep during the day but David had not been able to join him, despite his lingering tiredness.

"Yes, I must get back and see Rachel," he finally replied.

He had phoned her twice on her mobile and once on the landline, but all had been fruitless. He had left a message on each occasion but as yet, he had heard nothing. He felt an urge to make his peace with her.

Since Tom had come round and the medical staff were confident he would make a full recovery, the anguish, and subsequently, his anger, had subsided. They still had a lot to talk about. After all, he had relied on her to care for his son during his absence and she had let him down. He was disappointed with her but there may have been more behind it than he realised.

At the same time, she could have made him aware of any problems she was having. He still found it difficult to understand why it had turned out the way it did. The more he puzzled over the implications and the events as he knew them, the more stressed he became, so he decided to drop the matter for now. Besides, he was too tired to give it any further thought. In the words that Charlie regularly used, he was truly knackered.

Charlie had gone home two hours previous under protest. He had wanted to stay and drive him home but he could see how exhausted he was. Normally, Charlie was alert, responsive and garrulous, to say the least, but by the afternoon, he had looked dishevelled and worn-out, occasionally falling asleep and snoring noisily. He insisted he should go home and have a good sleep, and he told him he would catch a taxi and make his own way in due course. Despite some resistance, he had finally agreed.

In the middle of the morning, whilst Charlie was still with him at the hospital, a senior police officer had arrived at the ward to speak to Danny. Charlie had advised the youngster earlier of Tom's recovery and he had been elated by the news. David had refused to speak to him saying he had no wish to talk to someone who could have helped in killing his son. Charlie thought this a little unfair on the evidence they had so far heard, but once again, decided to keep his views to himself in the circumstances.

The officer had put his head round the corner and introduced himself, at the same time, it would seem, taking a careful note of Tom's condition. He was asleep at that time. Obviously, the doctors had filled him in as to the medical situation.

After some formal pleasantries, he added in a more serious tone, mainly addressing David.

"You will appreciate, sir, that the situation your son finds himself in is very serious. A death has occurred from this episode, and there will be a post mortem and charges may follow when all the evidence has been collated. I trust you will let us know when he has recovered enough to give us his side of the story?" David nodded perfunctorily.

Seemingly satisfied with Danny's story, the police guard had been removed soon after the officer's visit. This had the welcomed effect of relieving some of the tension. However, the officer's stern remarks stuck in David's mind for quite some time.

A little later, Danny made an appearance in the room after being discharged from hospital care. At first, he stood at the entrance looking sheepishly at Tom's prostrate form. The bravado that usually accompanied him had somehow dissipated under the experiences of the last few hours. Charlie quickly identified his embarrassment.

"Hi, Danny, feeling better?" he asked.

Moving his weight nervously from one foot to the other, he looked up at Charlie. "I'm good, Charlie, thanks. The doctor has been round and discharged me, and my parents are on the way to pick me up."

"That's great news," Charlie had said, recognising the boy's awkwardness as his eyes seemed glued to Tom's bed.

"He's going to be okay, old chap. Don't worry."

When the lad's trance finally broke, his nervousness returned. Charlie could see that he wanted to address David but the icy response to his presence, the lack of any acknowledgement, made him feel uneasy. Finally, he steeled himself to the task ahead, cleared his throat and found his voice.

"Mr Lucas," he began politely. "I can't tell you how sorry I am that this has happened. I encouraged Tom to join in the stupid games and I deeply regret what happened."

He was still addressing David's back. A palpable silence followed whilst Danny collected his thoughts. Charlie found it quite appealing and smiled at him supportively. He responded with a weak smile before continuing.

"Whatever 'appens," his voice strengthened as a surge of emotion carried him forward. "He saved me life. I wouldn't be here now if it weren't for your Tom and I owe him...owe him big, sir, so if he ever needs me, I'll be there for 'im. I promise." Charlie felt the emotional electricity charging the room. The *sir* came as a bit of a shock to Charlie and to David too. It took a while for David to show any reaction but he finally turned and faced Danny with a look on his face that signified the remorse had, at least, been acknowledged.

"Thanks, Danny," was all David was prepared to say. It was sufficient reward for the boy's bravery in speaking up, Charlie thought. Danny turned, nodded to Charlie and disappeared to find his parents.

An hour later, just after Charlie had departed, Tom had opened his eyes again. He had slept solidly for almost two hours and looked much better for it. Although still very weak, there was an awareness in his eyes that had previously been lacking. On seeing him stir, David pulled a flannel from a bowl of water by his bed and after screwing it tightly to remove the surplus water, mopped it across his brow. A knowing smile was the reward.

"How you feeling, Son?"

"Better, thanks, Dad."

"That's good. You look better. Do you want something to eat?"

"No, thanks. I'm not feeling hungry but I could do with a drink."

David poured a half-glass of water from the flask and set it down on the bedside cabinet. Leaning over Tom, he pulled him up from the bed, at the same time grabbing the two pillows and stuffing them quickly behind his back. He didn't look comfortable so, not satisfied with his handiwork, he pulled him forward again and removed the top pillow. Plumping it up with both hands, he dropped it behind his son's head and was finally happy with the result.

Tom smiled. "All this for a sip of water."

Holding the glass to his lips and with a tissue in his other hand, David did his best to get most of the liquid down his throat with little spillage.

"Thanks, Dad," Tom said, wetting his lips with his tongue.

"Not a very good nurse, I'm afraid, Son, so you had better recover quickly."

"You're the best dad in the world and I'm so proud of you competing in the Olympics." It was the first time that Tom had openly acknowledged his achievements on the track, which came as a shock.

"Well, I'm pulling out after this and dedicating all my time to you, Son." The look of anguish immediately swiping Tom's face was a further surprise.

"No, Dad, you can't," Tom pleaded in such an agitated state that David feared for his health in his current state.

"Okay, Son, don't get excited," David said calmly, rising from his seat in response.

"But…Dad…you have done so well in winning your place in the Olympics, you can't just give it up, it's the chance of a lifetime!" The appearance of tears in his son's eyes emphasised the message so plainly spoken. David was somewhat overwhelmed.

"All right, Son, don't upset yourself. I'll think about it. I promise."

"I'm so proud of you, Dad, and my mates at school think you're a hero. They are so envious. They think you can win a medal and I really want to see you running at the Olympics with all the great athletes like Jessica Ennis and Mo Farah. It will be fabulous. Please don't chuck it away now. Not because of me, PLEASE, Dad."

"My head is getting so big, it will explode in a minute," he laughed at Tom. With so much praise and enthusiasm from his son, there was really only one decision he could make but for some reason, possibly the lingering tiredness, he wanted to delay such a commitment for a little longer.

"I promise you I'll speak to Charlie and I'm sure we will come up with a positive decision."

"You will let Charlie down if you don't run and he's done so much for you. You have told us that many times." He could see Tom getting quite heated with the conversation. As he started to struggle with his breathing, he knew it was time to call a halt.

"Relax, Son," he told him, again wiping the flannel across his brow which seemed to have the right effect of calming him down.

"You will run, won't you, Dad?" The force of Tom's eyes strengthened his plea.

David knew he couldn't hold out any longer. "Okay, I will run. I promise." The beam of a smile that came his way had its usual reaction with David. With this, the boy seemed to relax and settle to the comfort of his bed.

"You look tired," David told him, mopping his brow for the second time.

"I am," he sighed. Within a few minutes, his eyes were drooping and David decided it was time to leave and return home. A little snooze himself would be very welcomed. He rose from his chair, careful not to scrape the legs on the floor for fear of waking the boy. He had just reached the exit when a familiar voice stopped him in his tracks.

"Dad."

"Yes, Son," he replied, looking back with an exaggerated sigh. Tom's eyes opened and looked at him with sincerity. There was something very compelling in his voice.

"I'm sorry." The words hung in the air for just a moment.

"No, Son…I'm sorry…for leaving you in a situation where this could happen. It's my fault and it won't happen again." He moved back to the bed and leant over Tom, kissing him on the forehead. "You're alive, that's the main thing, so now you have to get yourself right, young man, and first of all, you need some sleep, so go to it," he commanded, tucking the sheet over under his chin. Tom smiled cheerfully and watched his father make his way to the exit again.

"See you later."

"See yer."

Chapter 17

As his cab drew up outside the cottage, David sensed a foreboding, a premonition something was amiss. It was probably the absence of Rachel's car outside the property that started his mind racing.

On the journey home, he had given some consideration to his fiery reactions at the hospital and was now feeling he may have been too harsh in the circumstances. Hopefully, she would understand he had been under a lot of pressure and the news that Tom had made a full recovery would placate the situation. He certainly hoped so.

After paying the cabby, he thanked the man and found his keys in his pocket. The jingling of the bunch just outside the door was sufficient to set Tammy alight so that before he had the key in the lock, she was yelping her welcome and throwing herself against the door in heavy blows. Opening the door, he wedged himself in the gap to stop her escaping to the front garden, a skill he had now practised to perfection. As usual, he was given a wet reception, Tammy dousing him with her tongue until he could stand it no longer.

"All right, girl, that's enough," he told her as he pushed her to one side. Reluctantly, she wagged her tail and headed for the dining room.

"Hello, I'm home," he called aloud to the empty hallway. There was no response. He followed Tammy in. Immediately, the sight of the room in a state of untidiness sent a shiver of concern through his body. His eyes settled on the dining table where an envelope together with Rachel's business phone and a bundle of keys looked ominous. Anxiously, he moved towards it, reading his name on the front as he approached. The writing was Rachel's.

Nervously, he split it open and pulled the foolscap out. Dreading what the contents may hold, his eyes scanned the lines of neat writing rapidly, each one compounding the pain he was already feeling. Once he had finished, he felt numb.

Tammy came to his side and nuzzled his hand. Harshly, he shoved her away. He dropped to the sofa and read it again, more slowly this time. It was important that he understood its full significance.

Dear David,

I am so sorry I have let you down. There were many times when I realised I wasn't looking after Tom like I should but I guess I didn't want to admit it. I should have told you what was going on and I am sure you would have sorted it out. I feel I should never have come between you and Tom. It was much too soon after the death of your wife and I am so sorry that I forced myself upon you. I realise now that we should never have let the relationship develop as we did.

When I saw you at the hospital only a few hours ago, I realised the pain you are going through. I so hope that Tom recovers fully and you can pick up your lives together. He is a good boy and I know you are really proud of him. I wish you luck in the Olympics and will watch your races with great interest on the TV. I know what you and Charlie have put into it, and should you win a medal, you will truly deserve it.

I know you haven't had much time to involve yourself with the business but when you do, I hope you will be pleased with the results. Brenda is quite capable of running it for you and I know she will be more than delighted to take over where I left off, especially with the extra money I know you will offer her and which she badly needs. My set of keys are here together with the mobile phone on which I keep all the business numbers. Tell Brenda all my connections are on it.

Finally, I want to say thank you for all the love you have shown me. I feel I have been truly loved and you can't always say that after a relationship. You are a wonderful man and a great dad, and I know you will find someone one day to replace what you had with your first wife. You deserve every success in life and I am sure you will find it. Please don't forget me too quickly because I will always love you.

Love you, my darling,
Take Care,
Rachel
XXX

"You silly girl," he yelled in anger to the empty room. "You didn't force yourself on me. I fell head over heels in love with you."

Even Tammy looked shocked, her ears raised sharply in confusion. David rose from the sofa and slung the letter ferociously on the floor. Still talking to himself, he paced the room like a mad man.

"Rachel Forbes, I love you. Please come back," he kept reciting as his mind tossed through the repercussions of her actions. He had already phoned her several times at the hospital but she hadn't answered. He tried it again now only to receive the same response.

For the first time, he realised in the eighteen months they had known each other, he had never met any of her friends or family. She had occasionally talked about a cousin living in London but discussions concerning her parents were few and far between.

Still in a state of panic, a fresh idea came to him. He rushed to the drawer of the dresser and withdrew the telephone book, frantically searching its pages until he found the number he wanted. He dialled it quickly and only had seconds to wait.

"Brenda," he shouted into the mouthpiece. "Have you seen Rachel today?"

"No," she said. "She phoned me this morning, and said she wasn't well and could I open the nursery today. I told her to go to bed and rest herself, and let me know when she felt better. I haven't heard from her since. I was going to phone her this evening to see if she was any better."

"You don't know where she's gone then?"

"What do you mean *gone?*"

"Oh, nothing," he said, not in the mood to go into any detail. "She's disappeared and I'm a bit worried about her, that's all. She will probably turn up." He tried to sound light-hearted but feared his voice was telling her otherwise. "To be honest, we've had an argument and I think she's walked out on me," he said, feeling rather foolish. "Are you okay in the shop for a few days if she's not back?"

"Yes, I'm fine," she said with more than a touch of enthusiasm.

"If she phones you, will you ask her to give me a ring please?"

"Of course, I will."

"Sorry to trouble you and thanks for your help," David added. "Goodbye for now."

Once he had put the phone down, he made himself a cup of tea and sat down, his mind slowly filtering through the different aspects of their relationship, searching for some small clue that would give him a lead to anyone who could help.

He knew her parents had lived in Tunbridge Wells, Kent, but was sure she had told him they had recently moved. Her father had been ill and retired early and her mother worked for a local charity but he could not remember which one. He was sure it was a fairly obsolete one in any case. Unfortunately, they were not that close. As far as he knew, she had only seen them once in the time they had been together and that was when he had been engaged at an athletic meeting and could not accompany her.

For a few moments, he sat in silence juggling with the various ideas that came to his head. It was then that his mobile rang. He stood up smartly and extracted it from his pocket, hoping against hope it was Rachel. Charlie's name came to the screen.

"Hello," he said, rather flatly.

"Hi, Dave, how's things? Are you home?"

"Yes, I am, Charlie, but Rachel's left me and I don't know what to do." The tone of David's voice was so desperate it pulled Charlie up in his tracks.

"Dave," Charlie said, as calmly as he could. "That's bad news but I know she loves you, she told me so only the other day. She will be back, I'm sure." As usual, Charlie's words of comfort meant something to him but at that moment, his doubts were strongly negative.

"I don't think so. The note she has left me sounds pretty final and I don't have anybody to contact who might know where she is."

"How about Brenda?"

"I have already spoken to her. Rachel asked her to manage the shop but she has no idea where she is."

186

Charlie had phoned hoping to discuss some positive plans for encouraging David's interests back to his Olympic target. On the back of the joy of Tom's recovery, he thought the timing could not have been better but he soon realised his mistake. Charlie listened for several minutes as David unloaded his feelings. Finally, he decided to change the subject.

"How's Tom?" he asked.

"He woke up after you left and was a lot better. The sister hinted that he could be home tomorrow, God willing. I think he is just tired and needs a good rest."

"That's great. Are you going back to the hospital tonight?"

On Charlie's words, David skimmed his eyes over his watch to see it was almost half past seven.

"Crikey," he shouted. "It's time to leave already."

"Do you want me to take you?" Charlie offered.

"No, I'm fine, but thanks once again."

"Okay, but you know where I am if you need any help and don't worry about Rachel. She'll be back."

"I hope so," said David solemnly with little conviction.

Chapter 18

The next twenty-four hours gave David little time to mope over Rachel's disappearance.

On returning to the hospital in the evening, he found Tom had been moved to another ward on the far side of the building. Despite the multitude of signs and arrows plastered on the walls, he managed to lose himself in the labyrinth of corridors before eventually arriving at Marlborough ward. No sooner had he opened the door than he found Tom immediately inside, sitting in a chair beside his new bed. He almost looked his old self again. A big grin on the boy's face was the best tonic anyone could have prescribed.

"Wow, you look as if you're ready to go home," he said in shock.

"Actually, sister said you can pick me up tomorrow morning any time after eleven o'clock," came the unexpected reply. "They want to keep me under observation for a little longer just as a precaution and then everything should be fine." It was good news. With so many ups and downs in such a short period of time, at least the day was ending on a positive note.

"I'll be here eleven o'clock on the dot," David promised.

"You'd better be," Tom said with a casual smile.

***

Having Tom home was such a relief after the desperate experiences of the last few days. He had picked him up from the hospital at the promised time and they had travelled home in an atmosphere of joyful expectation. For the first time in what seemed ages, he felt he could at last relax and enjoy his son's company. That evening he cooked for the first time in several weeks, a special meal of fillet steak, onions, chips and peas, a favourite of both of them which he enjoyed preparing and presenting. As he watched him wolf it down and show his appreciation with a thumbs up, it was like old times.

It was not until they had finished eating and taken their drinks into the lounge that David mentioned Rachel.

"When I came back to the house last night, there was a letter on the table from Rachel," he began. "She seems to think it was her fault you got involved with the boys you did and therefore, she feels responsible for your accident. Consequently, she has left us and it does not look as if she intends to come back."

It was said in such a sorrowful tone, it immediately pricked Tom's heart with a deep sense of remorse. He looked at his father and read the pain so clearly showing

"Dad," he said, taking a deep choking breath. "It's all my fault. I treated her badly right from the start. When you were not here, I was rude to her and encouraged my friends to do the same. It's my fault she's left you."

Confused by what he was hearing, David just stared at his son in disbelief. "I never wanted her here, I just wanted you and me together." As he forced the words out, the tears came with them so that he broke down completely. David realised it was probably the first time he had seriously considered the emotional turmoil the lad had been feeling since his mother's death.

"It's all right, Son, don't get upset," he said, hugging him warmly to his chest.

"Dad, I'm so sorry."

"No, Son," he said, slowly and thoughtfully. "It's my fault. I should never have dated anyone so soon after your mum's death. It was not fair to you."

Pulling himself from the embrace, Tom turned to look his father in the eye. "But, Dad, I want you to be happy. I really do. Please find Rachel and we will start again. I promise I will be kind to her and respect her if she comes back."

It was a plea, delivered with such sincerity, David could not help but take strength from it.

"We'll see, Son, but her letter sounded rather final."

They sat together on the sofa for a few minutes longer, both wrapped up in their thoughts. Tom eventually prised himself from his father's arms and stood up.

"Have you told Charlie yet that you're back in training for the Olympics?" he asked in the somewhat relieved atmosphere they both sensed now prevailed.

"No, but I will phone him tonight and let him know, providing one thing." There was a short pause.

"What's that?" Tom asked cautiously.

"That you promise me you won't get involved in any more pranks like this last one. Without Rachel around, I want to know I can trust you when I'm out."

Tom's smile dissolved so readily to a further look of sheer sincerity David had no qualms as to his reply.

"Dad, after what I've been through, I can assure you I have no intention of taking any risks or doing anything stupid in the future. I feel lucky to be alive. I promise I will never do anything again to worry you." The undisguised frankness David read in his eyes and his voice was quite touching.

"I will speak to Charlie in a while and let him know," David said simply. "In a few weeks' time, we are due in London for a training programme before the big event so we will have to think about that."

Only minutes later, David was on the phone to Charlie.

"Hi, Charlie," he began. "Do you think you can call around so we can discuss the future, please?"

"That sounds ominous," Charlie replied in a serious tone.

"No, it's all good, I can assure you."

"That sounds better," Charlie said, clearly relieved. "I'll be with you in no time."

True to form, the bell rang within what seemed minutes and Charlie was at the door.

"Who's that?" David asked Tammy as she leapt out of her basket and darted for the front door, her tail wagging dangerously as she passed a glass tumbler left precariously on a low stool. David followed and caught her collar before opening the door to Charlie.

"Hi," said Charlie as he entered.

Tammy's tail broke all records as it lashed about in wild abandon. David held her down so she couldn't jump up whilst Charlie made a fuss of her ears. Gradually, she settled and David released her.

They went into the lounge where Tom was sprawled full length across the sofa, a cushion behind his head. On Charlie's appearance, he had no difficulty in smiling.

"You look better, young man," Charlie greeted him.

"Thanks, Charlie," he replied, a little shyly.

"Given us nightmares, you have."

"Sorry," he said with a look that again confirmed his remorse.

"Good to see you home and safe." Tom grinned back at Charlie's genuine warmth.

While David arranged some drinks, the chatter continued. Finally, the more personal issue of David's participation in the Games came to the fore.

"I realise after the recent traumas, Dave," Charlie said calmly before they got fully started. "You may feel you are not in the right frame of mind to continue with the huge challenge you will be facing. If this is the case, I shall truly understand, I promise you."

A short, almost dramatic silence followed. David sensed his son's eyes boring down on him.

"Charlie, old friend," he said. "I only have to look at my son's face to realise there is no way out. I have to compete or it would appear he will lose face at school with all his friends. Isn't that right, Tom?" he added, looking up at his son. The humour was not lost on Charlie who could not keep a straight face and smiled openly.

"That's right, Dad, and you had better win as well."

"So there you are, Charlie, straight from the horse's mouth. Not only are we back in business but we have to win as well."

The relief on Charlie's face was obvious. It was more than he had hoped. If he was honest, only hours ago, he had resigned himself to the fact there was no way David would want to continue. It seemed out of the ashes of disaster, the phoenix of a new chapter had arisen and with it, unbelievably, a rejuvenated sense of purpose that seemed more positive than ever.

"The fact that we are going to win has never been in doubt," said Charlie, tongue in cheek. "But I have to admit I had my doubts about your participation after the events of the last few days."

"Let's have a drink," said David, snapping the lid off a bottle of lager and offering it to Charlie. Once David's glass was in his hand, he clunked it loudly against Charlie's bottle. "Cheers," they both said simultaneously.

"So it's back to work Monday morning then?" Charlie asked after a short sip of the amber fluid.

"You bet, mate, I can't wait."

They both felt the future had never promised so much as it did at that moment.

Chapter 19

Monday morning was special. Or so it felt to David.

With the traumas of the last few days behind him, he was back doing what he really enjoyed. Running and training with Charlie, the epitome of pleasure and self-satisfaction.

Mondays had always been one of his favourite days of the weekly training cycle. The beginning of another week and the platform for further improvement in his speed and stamina. He was always pleased to learn what new challenges Charlie had in store for him. In his current mood, he felt he was capable of tackling anything. He could not wait to get back on the track with Charlie and re-establish the standards they always set themselves. It had all been going so well in Manchester and he was sure it would not take long to pick up where they left off.

He had woken early at seven o'clock after the first decent night's sleep for several days. A half hour later, he was sitting at the table in the kitchen with a bowl of cereals and a glass of orange juice in front of him. Over the weekend, he had had little time to study anything. In this short moment of relaxation, he caught sight of the local Gazette peeping from under a pile of assorted papers and letters that had been strewn haphazardly across the table. He pulled it out.

The headline immediately caught his attention and with it came a deep feeling of inspiration. ***Wisbech Embraces the Olympic Spirit*** was splashed powerfully across the front page, accompanied by a collage of pictures of local characters carrying the Olympic torch through the town.

There was a young soldier, no more than twenty-one he would guess, holding the lighted torch aloft and smiling proudly as he made each courageous step on two prosthetic legs. The look of admiration and encouragement from the surrounding crowd of onlookers and helpers added real passion to the event.

In another frame, a ninety-two-year-old pensioner, who had earlier in the year completed his tenth London Marathon, was tackling a less strenuous distance, again with the famous torch in his grasp. There were also a few younger stars who had been chosen for their various achievements or special qualities, all providing a personal and memorable contribution to the last hundred or so miles that the flame would complete on its path to the Olympic Stadium in London.

The accompanying article had been written by the Gazette's leading sports writer. David read it avidly. It highlighted the fact that the torch relay would last seventy days and visit over a thousand communities.

It was heady stuff. David found himself immersed in the paper whilst sipping his fruit juice. The article was spread over the first five pages of the weekly. He had only reached the second page when his own name jumped out at him.

Local athlete, David Lucas, from the Wisbech Athletic Club will be representing the country in the 1,500 metres at the Olympic Championships next month. David is coached by past Olympic competitor, Charlie Greaves, who has been coaching at the club for over thirty years and has achieved much success, particularly with the youngsters.

David's success in gaining a place in the Olympic squad is a remarkable achievement considering he only took up athletics seriously eighteen months ago at the late age of twenty-nine.

The circumstances of their partnership are even more extraordinary. They met whilst out running a year last February, during one of the worst fogs the area had experienced for many years. Following an attack from an unknown dog, David accidentally fell in the River Nene and was at the mercy of the tide. Fortunately for David, Charlie was running nearby and thanks to the frantic barking of his dog, Tammy, was alerted to David's perilous circumstances.

By this time, David had pulled himself to the temporary safety of a branch but then passed out in the very austere conditions. Balancing precariously on the holding branch and with little thought for his own safety, Charlie reached the unconscious David and pulled him to the safety of the bank.

Despite his sixty-five years, Charlie then carried the unconscious David a good half-mile to a local residence where the ambulance was called and David removed to hospital.

The events that followed were even more sensational when David joined our local athletic club to discover he was soon beating many of the seasoned athletes. With Charlie's experience and coaching, his performances continued to improve, culminating in his now famous but controversial second in the British championships in June when he gained his place in the Olympic team.

David has stated many times that he owes his life to Charlie and his success at the Games would go some way to what he obviously feels is a huge debt. What a tremendous achievement it would be for David to win a medal in what many people consider the elite event of the Games, the 1,500 metres.

"Not much pressure then," David murmured to himself, at the same time, smiling with a sense of pride on realising the full impact of the paragraphs he had read. Although a bit dramatic, he thought to himself, basically correct. His concentration was broken when the kitchen door slipped open. Tom's head appeared, a huge grin on his face as usual. It was so refreshing to see his son in the old light. He felt their relationship was back to full strength which was the biggest bonus.

"Hi, Dad," he said as he strutted into the room still wearing his pyjamas.

"I see you're ready to do a good day's work," David said sarcastically, with little reaction. "You can have this week off in view of the circumstances, then you're back to school next week, young man." Tom's face screwed up in response. The lack of any verbal reply David took as an acceptance. He pulled the chair beside him from under the table and tapped the seat with his hand.

"You going to have some breakfast?" he asked.

"Yep, I guess so," Tom replied, springing onto the proffered chair with boyish enthusiasm

As he sat down, David looked at his watch. "I'm off in ten minutes, meeting Charlie nine o'clock at the track. I trust you will be okay on your own?"

"Of course," Tom replied boldly. After a short pause, while he put a spoonful of corn flakes in his mouth, he added with sincerity. "I hope I haven't damaged your training programme."

"I shouldn't think so. Charlie will probably make me work a bit harder, but I'll live."

"Sorry, Dad." There was a tone of contrition in his voice that David found quite appealing. He cuffed the back of his son's head with a gentle swipe and they both grinned fondly.

"You may like to see your dad's name in print here in this article," David said passing the newspaper over to Tom with the pages fully spread. Tom seized the paper and started to read with enthusiasm.

"Cor, Dad, you're really famous!" David had to laugh at the boy's intensity.

"Not yet, Son, I have to win a medal first."

"You could be the Sports Personality of the Year if you win a gold medal."

"I think that's going a bit too far."

"Charlie thinks you can do it."

"Well, Charlie's thinks I'm Superman. Don't build your hopes up, lad. You could be disappointed."

"I don't think so." There was a sense of the highest respect in his voice.

David stood up and bent over his son's head, kissing him lightly on the pate before running his hand through his unruly mop of hair causing the fringe to droop over his eyes.

"Thanks for your confidence. If nothing else, you've charged my batteries for the day." Tom pushed his locks back in place and looked up as his father left the room.

"See you later and be good," David told him as he closed the door.

"Good luck, Dad. Love you."

"Love you too, Son."

Chapter 20

"Well, I'll give you another few days off if this is result," Charlie addressed David as he walked off the track. David straightened his back, pulling himself up to his full height. He couldn't contain the smile that forced its way to his lips.

"What time did you say I did?" he asked in astonishment, his furrowed brow an indication of disbelief.

"One fifty-two. The fastest time you have ever run for eight hundred metres."

"I don't believe it. You're pulling my leg."

"No way, my boy. I only tell you the truth when it comes to your training and you know it. I told you your performance would improve in the last few weeks and this is it. This is the beginning of your final preparation. We have built the stamina over the months, now we add the finishing touches and you will be ready to enter that mighty Olympic Stadium and do your stuff. You will be amazed at what your body is capable of achieving over the next few weeks. You wait and see."

The track session had passed like a wonderful dream. After the lengthy warm-up preliminaries, they had started the serious work with some 100 metre sprints, ten in all. As David finished each one, he jogged back to the start and repeated the exercise until the full number were completed. As usual, Charlie recorded the times with some precision. They were roughly on par with previous performances. During the brief discussion that followed, both agreed that in view of David's absence from the track for a few days they were quite satisfactory. Another break and another phase, this time six 400 metres which he completed again at times holding up well to his usual standards.

It was now time for a full 800 metres.

"This is where your few days break may possibly take their toll," Charlie told him as he prepared himself for the final piece of work. David's only response was a shrug of his shoulders. He really had no idea what to expect. In his heart, he knew he would give it his best shot, as he always did, and what that threw up remained to be seen. He failed to see missing a few days training could interfere with his progress and this was foremost in his mind as Charlie's command sent him on his way.

After two hundred metres, he felt comfortable, dropping into a nice stride which allowed him to settle into an economical rhythm. It felt so good to be back in training. The track was now his life. Running was a gift that had been given to him, he was sure. The flush of pleasure was transferred to his legs, so that their action seemed effortless as he approached Charlie and the end of the first lap.

The old pro stood just beyond the starting line, his eyes glued to him as he hit the lap marker for the first time.

"Great, Dave, great," he yelled as his finger hit the button of his stopwatch. Spurred on by a strange intuition, David was encouraged to sprint earlier than he had intended. Winding it up from three hundred metres out he knew was foolhardy, but feeling as he did, he had to go for it. His stride lengthened, he felt good as he hit the final bend. It was not until the home straight his over-enthusiasm took its toll, his legs turning to jelly in a few strides. With his strength rapidly waning but the finish in sight, he closed his mind to the pain as always, and just kept pushing and pushing through the red mist, until he was there and it was over once again.

"One fifty-two point three, the fastest eight hundred you have ever run," Charlie yelled, punching the air with his fist. To improve his speed, they had been concentrating on the two-lap distance over the last few weeks and it was certainly beginning to pay dividends. As David recovered, Charlie ran to him and gave him a hearty slap on his back.

"That's great, just what we need to go into our final preparations," Charlie enthused, so much so that David was forced to push him away when he tried to ruffle his hair. There were times when Charlie could overdo his passion. Recovery mode was not always the time for such extravagance.

Once his breathing was back to normal, they sat crossed-legged on the lawn beside the track and discussed the remarkable results the day had thrown up.

"You kept telling me to expect crap times," David led. A lopsided grin was Charlie's immediate response.

"I should have known better. I'm an old fool." As he spoke, the grin broke to a full beam. "I should know by now not to challenge the Wisbech Wonder." There was a certain glint in Charlie's eyes and David immediately read its true meaning. Out of the blue, a fresh notion clicked in his mind and he couldn't restrain his thoughts.

"You did that purposely," he accused, his voice raised. "You purposely told me that I would run slower because you knew I would make every effort to ensure it wouldn't happen." Charlie said nothing, just stared back, the smug look of self-satisfaction splashed on his face sufficient to confirm the charge was close to the truth.

"You old sod," David added in mirth. "You know more tricks than a trained monkey."

"Years of practice," Charlie concurred, winking openly to mitigate his cheekiness.

Chapter 21

Tom could not have been happier. Two weeks had passed since he had returned to school and what a difference those weeks had made. All of a sudden, he was a hero.

His story had made the front page of the local paper under the bold heading of ***Local Boy Saves School Friend from Drowning after Runaway Caper.*** The paper's story gave a rather exaggerated view, or so he thought, of the event, but when he reached the final and climatic paragraphs, he could not help feeling so proud as the paper extolled the virtues of his bravery with such enthusiasm.

He found himself reading it over and over again, especially the paragraph that read, ***His bravery at this stage was exceptional. In a final effort, he fought his way to the surface, still clutching his friend, only to pass out at that point. Fortunately, police constables, John Hislop and Yvonne Foster, were on hand and, without a care for their own safety, dived in to pull the two boys from the water.***

It appeared the criminal element of their escapade had been glossed over in favour of the drama and heroics of their escape from the sunken car, which had been emphasised at length and in detail.

On his first day back at school, he was a little wary, not knowing what to expect. His dad had warned him that in view of the death involved people may take a dim view of his act. However, it was not the case and within minutes of his arrival in the playground, he had been surrounded by not only his personal friends, but many others, several of whom had completely ignored him in the past.

They were all eager to hear his story, which he told, on each fresh occasion, with more confidence and fluency. His audience listened attentively, hanging on to every word, so engrossed by the telling he found no need to embroider the facts, but just tell the story as it was. The feeling was great. He was the school hero and enjoying every minute of it.

Even the girls, who would normally collect in conspiratorial groups around the outskirts of the playground, watching the boys with sullen looks, wanted to be his friend. There was one in particular, a tall blond girl in the year above, who had never given him the slightest glance as far as he was aware. She had approached him coyly and asked him if he had been scared. His mature reply that he imagined anybody would be, was rewarded with the cutest of smiles.

From then on, she seemed to find excuses to talk to him at every opportunity, appearing several times in the corridors and the playground to waylay him as he changed lessons. On each occasion, she would raise her eyebrows in a friendly gesture he found most appealing. Her name was Lauren which he thought suited her. A pretty name for a pretty girl, he told himself.

Danny, for some reason, had taken a further week to return to school but when he did, it set the whole hero worship scenario off again. They had spoken several times on the phone in the intervening period. Tom had finally ceased phoning him when he decided he had heard the words *thank you* too many times. The truth was, he found it embarrassing and wished he would stop.

"You don't have to keep saying thank you all the time," he told the gushing Danny.

"But, mate, I just feel so lucky to be alive and I wouldn't be if it wasn't for you."

Tom couldn't find an answer. He had hoped his fervour would subside by the time he returned to school but this was not the case. In the playground of all places, they met for the first time since the incident. Tom felt every pupil had their eyes on them as Danny rushed forward and embraced him so forcefully, he was sure he stopped breathing.

"Thanks, mate," Danny shouted loudly for the umpteenth time as he danced him round in a rough bear hug, much to the amusement of their fellow pupils, who shouted and whistled their appreciation. In the staff room, headteacher, Mrs Doreen Phelps, called her staff to the window to witness the compelling scene. Only Tom wanted the action to cease. It was several minutes before the heat ebbed from his cheeks.

His dad's publicity from the Olympic furore which had been growing strongly over the past few weeks with the approach of the Games, added further to the charisma currently surrounding him. The national papers were building the grandeur of the Olympics day by day and the momentum was surging towards the Opening Ceremony in London.

It would seem even the least sporty in the country were waking up to the event which was about to explode. Only last week, his dad had featured in a half-hour television programme covering some of the lesser known competitors from a range of sports varying from athletics to triathlon, beach volleyball and table tennis. Most of them were unfamiliar names to the television audiences but it was obvious from the various interviews there was growing optimism for the forthcoming weeks. The following day, he had been bombarded with new friends who just wanted to say hello, to meet the son of a television personality. Everyone wanted to know him.

***

It was Saturday. No school, no early morning start.

Tom decided to stay in bed and just relax. Three weeks had now passed since the trauma of the car chase but, if he was honest, he had not yet recovered from the repercussions of that day. Nightmares of those awful few minutes as the car hit the water kept recurring with frightening regularly, punctuating his sleep with painful effect. He had felt a strange lethargy since and guessed it was just the

198

legacy of a near-death experience. Even young fit minds and bodies take time to recover from such events, he imagined.

Earlier, his dad had tapped his door lightly and stuck his head into the room. It was just before nine o'clock.

"I'm off now, back about four," he announced. "If you can find time, will you take Tammy for a short walk please?"

"Okay," he told him. "See you later, Dad. Good luck with the training."

He fell asleep then. Not a deep sleep but just a long comfortable snooze that carried him through the morning to twelve-thirty. Whatever, it had done him some good; he felt quite refreshed when he woke up. After a quick wash, he dressed and ventured downstairs to have some breakfast. Tammy was his only obstacle on his route to the kitchen. She waylaid him for a good few minutes in her usual boisterous manner before he finally pushed her aside to find the cereals in their respective cubbyhole.

A leisurely late breakfast followed whilst he read both the daily and local paper. Again, he noticed the emphasis on the forthcoming Olympics with several pages covering various aspects of the changes Londoners would experience during the fifteen days of competition. And then, just over two weeks later, the Paralympic Games would follow the same procedure. *What a feast of sport*, he thought to himself, *and to think my dad's a part of it.*

In particular, he was amazed to learn certain major roads throughout London would have designated lanes only approved vehicles carrying competitors, officials and foreign dignitaries would be allowed to use. The fact these special cars would override the numerous traffic lights in the big City, changing the lights to green on their approach, was even more awesome. Security at the Games was another issue he found interesting. Already, the estimated cost had doubled with the threat of terrorism always prominent.

Just after two o'clock, his mind clicked into the promise he had made to his dad to walk Tammy. It was no hardship. In fact, a chore he enjoyed. To see the old girl romping through the fields, with the occasional squawk of a pheasant or the sight of a scurrying rabbit escaping her path, was great fun.

Slamming the front door firmly behind him, he was pleased to see the sun peeping benevolently through the thin clouds with a promise of better things to come. It had not been a great summer for weather with well over the average rainfall hitting East Anglia and the farming industry particularly hard. In anticipation of the muddy fields ahead, he was wearing his old trainers. Unfortunately, they were no longer waterproof.

In no time, Tammy was through the gate and christening her favourite patch of grass. There were several large puddles along the lane and, like a small child, it was not long before she was paddling in the dirty water. A wry smile touched Tom's lips as he imagined his father's face on seeing Tammy caked in mud. He would hopefully have time to put her in the bath and give her a good dousing with the shower attachment before his return.

From the lane, the fields on both sides looked waterlogged. He knew the farmers were complaining they were having difficulties harvesting their crops and on studying the conditions he could understand why. The field to his left, in particular, looked to have been partly lost to a vast area of surface water, like a small lake amid the verdant crop. And this was summer.

To avoid the fields and the wet grass, he stuck to the farm lane up to the riverbank. His decision to return through the orchard was probably a wise one. This would take him longer but hopefully, it would keep his feet dry. In any case, there was no hurry and he was enjoying the exercise. As he reached the orchard, a bird of prey, some thirty metres ahead, caught his attention. It looked like a kestrel. Dipping its wings to maintain its stability, it glided on the air currents like a well-balanced kite. From that height, Tom imagined it could easily pick out a mouse or other small creature in the field below.

Tammy was her usual excitable self. Splattered with mud, she didn't look the same dog that left the house only twenty minutes earlier. Now deep in the orchard, she disappeared for a while, returning a few minutes later with a loose branch broken off from one of the trees. Far too big for her to handle, she could barely drag it across the grass. Growling in frustration, she was rocking it back and forth. Tom had to smile at the effort she was making. Realising she was not going to give up on it, he went to help her.

"I've kept myself dry all the way here and now you're going to ruin everything," he told her as he stepped cautiously onto the wet turf. Immediately feeling his feet sinking into the mud, he bent down and rolled his trousers up at their bottoms before reaching Tammy who was now shaking the branch with renewed vigour. Taking it from her, he quickly broke off the side shoots and greenery leaving a solid rod some two foot in length. Once finished, he held the projectile up for Tammy's inspection.

Her tail thrashing wildly was sufficient proof of her approval. Lowering her chest to the ground in anticipation of the game ahead, she couldn't wait to make a start. After squelching back to the tarmac of the lane, Tom threw the rod as far as he could with all his strength. Instantly, Tammy leapt after it, all the time, her tail keeping up its fierce momentum. In no time, she had retrieved it and was back, the fond glint in her eyes telling him she was enjoying herself.

They continued their game until reaching the orchard gate. Nearly home now, they were back on the farm lane when the sound of an approaching vehicle caught their attention. Restraining Tammy by her collar, Tom looked up to catch the eye of the driver who had politely slowed to pass him. He recognised the car as a local taxi and saluted the driver with his free hand. He noticed a face peering from the back window but had little time to discern any features. The driver returned his greeting before accelerating towards the bend ahead.

With Tammy still in a boisterous mood, it took several minutes to reach the bend themselves but when they did and had sight of their cottage, Tom was surprised to see the taxi parked outside. From a distance, it looked as if a man was at the front door whilst the driver remained in his cab. Tom quickened his pace. By the time he was close to the cottage, it appeared as if the man had abandoned any hope of finding someone at home and was returning to the car along the path. On seeing Tom approaching, he looked up.

"Hello," Tom said politely, catching the man's eyes with a friendly smile. "Can I help you?"

"Oh, you live here?" said the man in a quizzical tone. Tom's immediate reaction was that he looked very feeble. Dressed smartly in corduroy trousers, white shirt and a lime green jacket, the clothes failed to disguise the frailty of the body beneath. Tom took pity.

"Yes, my name is Tom Lucas and I live here with my dad."

"Your dad is David, I presume?"

"Yes, that's right," Tom replied with growing interest. "Do you know him?"

It was the question that Frank Lucas knew he had to face at some time. He had rehearsed so many introductions in the last few days. So many possible questions, and so many answers had riddled his brain by day and by night. In the end, he decided there was only one way to tackle the situation. Just answer any questions truthfully. If nothing else, it saved a lot of complications. You tell one lie and then you have to tell another had been an adage he had tried to carry throughout his life, not always successfully. If it failed, he would at least have no regrets.

"Yes," he said hesitantly, a little wary of proceeding. By this time, Tom had come closer so that he stood in front of him. He studied the boy thoughtfully. He looked a handsome lad, bright-faced, full of character and charm. With his cheeks glowing rosily from his exercise, he looked the epitome of youth; full of health and vitality. Frank was finding it hard to contain himself. Although a few years older than David when he had last seen him, the resemblance was unmistakable.

"I'm his father," he finally uttered in a gust of emotional release, so forceful he sensed tears welling in his eyes. He felt his heart thumping in his chest as both stood speechless, staring into each other's eyes, their thoughts in limbo as they fought to analyse their feelings.

"I'm your granddad," Frank whispered huskily, as though a further explanation was required. With this, he held his arms out in a plea to come forward. Tom did so, not through any pressure, just a response of his heart that drew him to the old man. He hugged him fondly, at first with some strength but then withdrawing that strength as he realised the frailty of his body.

"My dad thought you may be dead," Tom told him.

"I'm not really surprised," was all Frank could say in response. They remained locked together for a while longer, no further words spoken, just a bond of love gelling in the void of silence. It was Tammy who finally separated them. Not to be ignored, she snuggled between them and looked as if she was about to jump up.

"Don't you dare," Tom threatened, fearing for the old man's safety. "This, Granddad, is Tammy," he continued as an introduction. Tammy looked up fondly, her tongue hanging loosely from one side of her gaping mouth, her tail making its usual robust movements.

The word *granddad* pricked Frank's heart. "Hi, Tammy," he said, feeling a lump in his throat. "You look as if you're a bit worse for wear," he added referring to her state as he smoothed his hand across her back. Not only was her body and legs completely caked in mud, but it was now splashed vividly across her nose and head as well.

When Tom looked again, he realised the old man was crying, the tears visibly rolling down his cheeks. He looked embarrassed.

"I'm sorry," he said, seeing the concern on Tom's face. "I'm just a silly old man."

"No, you're not," Tom countered as he placed his arm round his granddad's back. Frank pulled a handkerchief from his pocket, then for some reason he started to laugh. It was a joyful laugh as though a great weight had been lifted from him. It was catching and Tom found himself joining in, laughing genuinely for no particular reason other than a warmth he felt inside. Only the old man's sudden coughing fit brought it to an end. It was a hacking cough, harsh and chilling. It bent him over with its ferocity as he struggled to control it.

"Come inside, Granddad," Tom told him, taking his arm and leading him gently back up the garden path. They had taken just a couple of steps when the old man stopped. Fumbling in his chest pocket, he withdrew a twenty-pound note and pushed it into Tom's palm.

"Here, pay the cabby," he instructed him. "I think that should be enough. Tell him to keep the change."

Tom walked back to the cab, the driver oblivious to the emotions close by as he sat reading his newspaper to the sounds of Radio One. "Thank you, young sir," he said pocketing the note with a broad grin. With a gentle wave, he closed his window and drove off.

Tom hurried back to his granddad, concerned for his health as the wheezy coughing continued.

"Come inside, Granddad," he repeated, once more catching the old man's arm and escorting him up the path to the front door. Inside, he sat him down and made him a cup of tea which seemed to settle him. Eventually, the old man's coughing ceased and they were soon chatting comfortably together.

One after another, Tom threw questions at him, some quite searching, so he realised father and son must have discussed him at length over the years. Knowing this, at first, gave him a warmth. Occasionally though, with a particularly delving but innocent question, the guilt that had plagued him for so long would resurface to dampen his burgeoning spirit. Nevertheless, there was a naivety about the boy that was so refreshing. Sitting with him and talking so openly filled him with a joy he had not experienced for some time.

***

The afternoon on the track had passed in a series of challenges for David and he felt he had met them all with credit. He had not been able to match his best 800 time of the previous week but the run was still impressive. As he climbed into his car to make the journey home, he was still on a high.

A twist of the ignition key set the engine in motion and with it the radio came to life. The soulful strains of *I will always love you* filtered through the car, pricking his heart with a strange reaction. It was a tune that always held him spellbound, so poignant and engrossing he immediately found himself listening intently, hanging on every word as the singer emptied her heart. With it, thoughts of Rachel came to him. He realised, not for the first time, he was missing her, missing her terribly.

With each line of the doleful ballad, memories of their short but meaningful romance came flooding back, in particular their first date, a day so memorable, yet, so unexpected. The unfortunate events of one autumnal day last year had set the wheels in motion.

After dropping Tom off at school, he had been in his van, half-way to his first job in Whittlesey, when his mobile rang. He picked it up and put it to his ear.

"It's me, Dad," Tom's voice crackled into clarity. He sounded worried.

David pulled off the road and stopped. "What's up, Son?"

"I've forgotten my English homework book. I've left it in my bedroom."

"Can't it wait until tomorrow?"

"No, I'll get into trouble. I need it this afternoon," he pleaded.

For a moment, he considered refusing, briefly relishing the thought such action may help to make his son more responsible in the future. Such thoughts, however, were soon dismissed as he remembered so clearly his own shortcomings at the same age. Occasionally, he wondered whether he was too lenient with the lad, often giving in to his requests at a whim. He found it difficult to say no, but again, he realised their circumstances were different to many parents. After all, the lad only had him to depend on.

"Right, I'm turning around. I'll leave it with the school secretary before lunchtime."

"Thanks, Dad. You're the best dad in all the world." He had heard it many times before but it still touched his heart. "By the way, have you remembered I'm staying at Danny's tonight and won't see you until tomorrow evening?"

"Yes," he had said, not really sure whether he had or not. With Tom not around, he imagined he would be fast asleep in his armchair most of the evening.

It was a good hour later, after returning home and visiting the school, he started the grouting on a client's patio, a job he had originally promised would be completed a week earlier. Unfortunately, the dark fluffy clouds that had ploughed the sky all morning finally released their cargo, the rain slapping down with some insistence on the plastic sheets he had had the foresight to unroll only minutes earlier. He sat in his van for almost two hours listening to the radio and casually munching through his sandwiches before deciding the rain was unlikely to relent. He had a ton of boulders and a pond liner to pick up in Wisbech for a job later in the week so decided to use the next hour for that purpose.

Taking the back roads and subsequent farm lanes to save time, he drove at speed, the gusty rain still lashing at the windscreen with some force. When the engine cut unexpectedly twenty minutes later in the middle of nowhere, he couldn't believe his bad luck. Twice, he turned the starter key to be met with an unfavourable metallic click and no response. Surrounding him on all sides was the familiar Fenland scenery, vast expanses of fertile farmland, probably some of the richest arable land in the country but dense, flat and boring in the rain.

Climbing out of the van into the wet, he swiftly raised the bonnet. Car mechanics had never been his forte so there was little chance of finding the fault. To his untrained eyes, it all looked fine. After briefly playing with the plugs, he decided none were loose, dropped the bonnet and returned to the cab.

Drawing his mobile from his pocket, he phoned the RAC to be told they were exceptionally busy and there could be some delay. Resigned to a long wait, he decided to phone Rachel to catch up on the news of the day. Although she had only been with him for six weeks at that time, she had already impressed him with her intelligence and efficiency. The fact he found her damned attractive was a further bonus. By this time, it was a few minutes short of 4:30 P.M.

"Have you remembered Mr and Mrs Buxton are coming to see you at five?" she asked on hearing of his predicament.

"Oh, God," he moaned. The problems of the day had wiped it clean out of his mind.

"Can you phone them please and apologise on my behalf. Ask them whether they can make it later in the week or even next week?"

"I'll see what I can do," she said chirpily. "How about you?" He was pleased she was concerned.

"Oh, I'll be okay," he told her. "Hopefully, the RAC man will be with me shortly and, fingers crossed, it's not a big problem. I'm sure he'll get it going in no time. You go home when you've phoned the Buxtons and I'll see you tomorrow."

"Are you sure? I could come out and try and find you."

"I don't think so, but thanks for the offer. I'm in the middle of nowhere and it would be difficult finding your way here, I can assure you." He knew she was having difficulty finding her way around the area at the moment so finding him where he was, had to be a bridge too far.

"No, I'll be fine. You just sort the Buxtons out and I'll see you tomorrow," he repeated.

"Okay, good luck."

As soon as he put his phone down, the traumas of the day caught up with him and he thumped his fist down on the steering wheel in a show of temper.

"Sod it," he swore to himself. The whole day had been a complete disaster. He had wanted to meet the Buxtons who had been introduced to him by one of his delivery drivers. Apparently, they were a wealthy couple living in Castle Rising, a Norfolk village close to Kings Lynn, renowned for its elaborate and substantial properties and dominated by a 12th-century castle.

True to their word, it was almost an hour to the minute before the RAC mechanic made his appearance. Pulling up in front of his van, the driver gave him a mandatory wave before jumping out of his cab. He was a jovial lad, which was good, because when he returned from what looked a very thorough inspection, he announced the cam belt was broken and his efforts to restart the engine may have caused untold damage. With a shrinking smile, he passed on the news that the cost may be in the region of five hundred pounds or more.

Towed home, needless to say, he was not a happy bunny. When they finally reached the nursery, to his surprise, the lights in the office were still on and the front door stood slightly ajar. After supervising the drop off of the van, he thanked the lad for his assistance and they said their goodbyes. Entering the office, he was amazed to see Rachel seated at his desk looking more than a little exhausted. On his appearance, she raised a meek smile.

"I couldn't get the Buxtons on the phone and they arrived just before five o'clock," she explained, rising from the chair. "They only left a few minutes ago." She looked relieved to express herself but at the same time drained of energy, her face a mask of total fatigue. He had never seen her like this.

"Sit down," he gestured with the palm of his hand before she had time to leave his desk. "I'll get you a coffee." She slumped back into the chair obediently.

He filled two cups at the machine and returned to take the seat in front of her, pushing her cup forward across the table. A couple of sips of coffee seemed to revive her a little. She took a deep breath and prepared to tell him the full story.

"The Buxtons looked a little perturbed when I told them you had broken down and would not be back to see them today. They are going up to Birmingham tomorrow to spend a few days with their son and family, and from there, they are off on one of these twenty-eight-day cruises around the world and won't be back until nearly Christmas."

"How the rich live," David chirped in.

"Anyhow," she continued. "In the circumstances, I thought I had better try and deal with them myself. I hope you don't mind?" She eyed him coyly, looking for a response.

"No…no," he stuttered, fascinated by her story.

"Well, I showed them the two books," she continued, pointing to the two albums of colourful photos spread on the desktop. He had put them together from the various jobs he had completed in the past. "I tried to explain, as best I could, the various stones and designs they could consider. I have watched you do one or two presentations and tried to use the same format, but it wasn't easy."

She began to perk up as she relaxed, sipping her coffee and reminiscing on her sales pitch.

"They really liked this one," she said, opening the larger album and thumbing through the first few pages with enthusiasm until she came to a page with several photos depicting a large front garden with a high wall, wrought iron gates and an extensive brick patio which stretched all the way to the house and beyond.

"That's one of my most expensive creations to date," David said with a wry grin.

"I was hoping you would say that," she replied, her eyes now sparkling with enthusiasm. "They also liked a couple of your ideas for the back garden but would like you to see it before they make a firm decision. I think they would appreciate your views on a particular project they have in mind. They are going to phone you on their return to the UK and hopefully, you will be able to call on them?"

"Of course," he answered. "Do you think they appreciate the likely cost?"

"Probably not, but they gave the impression if you come up with the goods, the cost is not a problem." She was positively beaming at him now.

"Well, it sounds as if you have done a great job on my behalf."

"I was nervous at first," she admitted. "But they are lovely people and once I got going, I was quite enjoying it." She was obviously pleased with herself and it showed. Her expressive brown eyes were still fizzing with the excitement. If she impressed the Buxtons as much as she was impressing him, he could understand their reaction.

"Well, I owe you," he said locking his eyes to hers with a force clearly reciprocated. "Can I take you out to lunch?" As the words tripped from his lips, he was actually amazed at his own boldness.

A fleeting waft of surprise passed quickly across her face to be replaced by an intensity of her eyes that answered his question immediately.

"That'll be wonderful," she said breezily, on regaining her composure. "When are you thinking of?"

"Tonight," he said spontaneously, almost as a joke.

"That's ideal," she said calmly. "My flatmate is out at Zumba."

"I'll pick you up about eight-thirty then, if that's okay?"

"That'll be fine," she confirmed after a quick glance at her watch. "Just gives me time to take a shower and put my glad rags on."

When he arrived outside her flat in town exactly on the dot of 8:30 P.M., he was feeling nervous, his stomach knotted with an ache of expectancy he found hard to control. It was some time since he could remember such an experience. With slight trepidation, he pushed the bell button and waited. After what seemed several minutes, he could hear the firm approach of footsteps descending the stairs. When finally the front door opened and she stood before him, it felt as if his heart bounced against his ribs.

Within the short time since they had parted at the office, she had transformed from the conservative yet sophisticated secretary to the epitome of young womanhood at the height of her beauty. A jewel to his eyes, she wore a tight-fitting red dress that fell just above her knees, provocatively accentuating the contours of her model figure. Her hair was scraped back off her forehead and neatly held in a tight bun by a decorative red ribbon. On her feet, high-heeled sandals seemed to give her legs extra attraction. He had never seen a woman look so stunning.

He took her to the *Old Barn,* a restaurant just off the main thoroughfare in the centre of Wisbech. Apparently, it had been completely refurbished over a year ago and was very popular with the local community. Dimly lit, it seemed the ideal venue for such a promising evening. It was only half full but just cosy enough to create the atmosphere he had visualised.

Excusing herself from the starter, she was tempted on the main course by the well-advertised guinea fowl breast stuffed with mushrooms, sage, dolcelatte cheese and red wine sauce. He went for a traditional lamb shank with French fries and vegetables. Between them, they shared a bottle of Beaujolais. When the meals arrived and were tasted, both agreed the restaurant's reputation was well deserved.

Throughout the meal, they talked comfortably, unveiling details of themselves that had been lost in the past but now dusted off for fresh deliberation. David always found it difficult to talk about his mother's life, her dependence on alcohol and subsequent early death leaving a scar on his life that had failed to heal. He mentioned his father briefly, skirting over the six years he knew him, with little feeling.

Her life had been a little more settled, a reasonable happy childhood as an only child with parents that were, if anything, a little too pushy, expecting of her to follow their dreams rather than her own. These had included ballet and piano, both of which had little attraction. From the age of eleven, she had attended regular piano lessons with an old spinster teacher in her home town of Tunbridge Wells, achieving a grade 2 certificate before rebelling in her late teens, much to the disgust of her parents. A series of disastrous relationships then followed, understandably none of which she was keen to share with him at any length.

By ten o'clock, the restaurant was filled to capacity, the noise quite deafening as the alcohol took effect. For the two of them, it mattered not, oblivious as they were to their surrounds. It was as if they were the only occupants. They chatted all evening, finding common interests that drew them closer together. Her personality, and clear outlook on life sparked in him fresh ideals and ambitions, a path to the future promising so much, a path he was more than eager to pursue.

When finally they returned to her flat, a half-hour from midnight, they kissed hotly and at length in his car, their passion only subdued by the unexpected flood of light from her flatmate's bedroom window. Laughing at the simplicity of the situation, they kissed again fondly before saying goodnight.

***

As the song drew to a close, the singer's voice seemingly cracking as she whispered her final words of endearment, his thoughts returned to the present. With the Games now so close, he had tried to forget her, push her to the back of his mind but it was not easy. He regretted so much their falling out, regretted his behaviour and the deplorable manner in which he had dismissed her. A lingering guilt had replaced the anger that had so quickly paralysed their relationship. He wondered again whether she would make contact in time. He had phoned her several times each day but she had made no effort to return his calls.

As he pulled away from the car park, he consoled himself with the thought he had quite enough on his plate at the moment. The next number on his radio, a far more boisterous and earthy tune, shook him from his melancholy thoughts. By the time he arrived home, the selection of more up-tempo tunes had reversed his mood and he was back in a joyful frame of mind. He was looking forward to the evening with Tom. Since the accident, every evening he spent with him had a new meaning. He would cook a nice meal for both of them before they settled down to the television for a few hours.

He put his key in the door, expecting the usual salvo of a greeting from Tammy but it did not come. She must be out in the garden, he thought to himself. Once in the hallway, he could make out voices from the lounge. He recognised one as Tom's. The other was a mystery.

He opened the lounge door to see Tom sitting in the armchair facing him. In the other chair, he could make out the back of someone's head, a bald pate with thin wispy grey hair. They were talking avidly until his entrance when they both came to a sudden halt.

Tom looked up, his eyes lit with a beam of happiness as he announced, "Dad, Granddad's come to see us!" At the same time, the visitor rose from his chair.

David faced his father for the first time in almost twenty-five years. Despite the gaunt emaciated features, he knew it was him straight away. There was a familiarity about the eyes, the droop of the jaw. It came back to him in a flash as the memories of his departure flared in his mind.

He was stunned, shocked to the core, so that he just stood staring as Tom had done only half an hour previous. The silence was heavy, the tension palpable, begging some action. Frank was the first to make a move. He smiled a nervous smile, all the rehearsing gone out the window as he struggled to find some words.

"Hello, Son," he said, stepping forward intuitively to close the gap between them, his hand held out in greeting.

David's initial reaction was to ignore the gesture, yet, something inside forced him forward. He took the hand feebly, restraining the strength in his grip. Frank was aware of the lukewarm reaction.

"What do you want?" David asked with indifference, holding his father's eyes with a fixed stare.

"Just wanted to see how you were after all this time," Frank said, feeling quite pathetic but trying to ignore the heat of embarrassment flushing his collar. "I had no idea you were living so close to me until I saw you on the TV the other day. A chap down your athletic club gave me your address when I said I was your father."

The voice quivered slightly, his breathing heavy. David realised he was struggling to express himself.

"He shouldn't have done that," he said flatly. "I find it quite intimidating that I come home to find you in my house alone with my son without my knowledge." For the first time, he caught Tom's eyes. The boy looked troubled, his face locked in an expression of numb bewilderment. He was obviously struggling to come to terms with the situation.

"I asked Granddad in because he wasn't feeling well," Tom offered in a tone of annoyance. He had imagined his dad would be pleased to see his father after all the years and their reunion would be something joyful, not the aggressive stand-off that he was currently witnessing.

"You come back into my life after all these years and just expect me to welcome you as if you've been here all the time?" David asked his father as a question.

"Your letter telling me you didn't want to see me anymore, didn't help, Son," Frank replied in what he felt was a rather pathetic attempt at defence.

"What letter?" David responded sharply.

"The letter you wrote to me when I asked your mother if I could come and take you out every so often. You said you didn't want to see me again and when I questioned your mother, she said I was upsetting you and making you ill. I decided, at that time, I should leave you alone. At least, for a while. Then things changed. I lost my job. I had to move away. I had some problems with my health. I was in and out of hospital. One thing led to another and I sort of gave up. I'm sorry for that, but it's the way it happened." There was a touching sincerity in his voice. For some reason, he had no doubt his father was telling the truth.

"I didn't write any such letter, I swear, "David answered abruptly, his face masking the surprise he obviously felt. "I didn't know anything about you wanting to see me."

There was a silence. A silence so solemn as both digested the implications of the facts that had been so forcibly laid before them. The realisation that David's mother must have forged the letter to make it look as if he had written it seemed beyond normal decency.

Any respect David had held for her had been eroded bit by bit over the endless years of her alcoholism. It had left him with only pity for her wasted and debauched life. As he now came to terms with the evil of this unfolding saga, his pity quickly turned to something stronger. With anger simmering through his veins, he raised his eyes to his father, only to witness the same reaction there. In fact, the old man looked totally destroyed. All of a sudden, the papery skin of his face seemed to hang from his cheeks, creased and sagging around the bloodshot and watery eyes staring back at him with a longing.

The truth of the woman's act had unfolded at that moment, the impact for both men quite destructive as they weighed up the lost years and what might have been. In a stroke, David wiped any animosity towards his father from his mind. He was the first to break the silence.

"I'm sorry, Dad," he said with a heavy heart as he seized the old man by the shoulders and hugged him to his chest. It was an action that took Frank by surprise.

"No...you have nothing to be sorry for, my son, I'm the one to blame. I should not have let you go so easily. I should have fought for you. I am in the wrong." As Frank buried his head deeply in his son's chest, the floodgates of his emotions opened with a force he was unable to control, releasing the painful and poignant regrets of twenty-five lost years. David felt the wet caress of his tears through his vest and hugged him closer.

"She was a difficult woman, my mother. No one could blame you for the way you acted, Dad." These words seemed to help Frank recover his calm. Feeling foolish, he pulled himself from his son, drawing his handkerchief from his pocket and dabbing his eyes as he did so. David could not help but notice the flecks of fresh blood on the white cloth.

"I'm sorry," the old man said, smiling through his embarrassment.

"There's nothing to be sorry for," David told him as Tom joined them, his face sparkling, sharing with them the relief and happiness of the occasion.

"I've got a granddad!" he shouted as he went into a farcical dance, raising his arms to the ceiling and throwing his hips from one side to the other. It had the effect of releasing the tension. With a smile on his face, David looked at his father, a look that ignited a spark almost twenty-five years in the making. With both men laughing hopelessly at the boy's antics, David seized his father for the second time and hugged him fondly, aware at the same time of his frailty as Tom had been.

When the excitement finally ebbed, they all fell into an armchair and relaxed in the buoyant mood the bittersweet traumas of the last few minutes had left them.

"I think this calls for a drink," David announced. "What will you have, Dad?" It felt so good to hear the word *dad* that Frank paused for a moment to let it sink in.

"Er…I'll have just a small lager, Son," he eventually replied.

"And you're having a fruit juice, I guess?" David addressed Tom, who nodded enthusiastically.

It was a few minutes before David returned with the tray of drinks. When they all had a glass in their hand, he thought it appropriate to say a few words.

"Dad," he began, his eyes resting comfortably on his father's, "Tom and I are really happy you have come back into our lives but you will appreciate my life for the next few weeks, at least, is very full with my Olympic preparation. However, in two weeks' time, I have to move to the Olympic village, and I'm sure Tom would be more than pleased for you to come and stay with him until the end of the Games."

"Yes," Tom shouted, jumping up from his chair and thrusting his fist high in the air. "Please say you will, Granddad," he pleaded to Frank who looked slightly taken aback by the suggestion.

Witnessing Tom's enthusiasm, he felt he had little choice. Only the condition of his health held him back. Memories of his recent fainting attacks played on his mind. He was not sure whether he should mention this.

"Please say yes, Granddad," the boy almost begged for the second time, his face so imploring Frank could not deny him.

"All right, I'll come," Frank finally agreed, feeling an immediate warmth from the action.

"Right, that's settled then. Here's to a very happy new future for all of us," David said raising his arm. All three glasses clinked together sharply.

It was a further two hours later that a tired but extremely happy Frank Lucas was driven back to his flat in Wisbech by his son. They had eaten together, the two steaks shared comfortably between the three of them. From the back seat of the car, his grandson kept up a continuous bombardment of questions, some easy to answer, others, a little more difficult. One or two needed some careful thought and a little tact. He was not hiding anything, he had made his mind up on that, but sometimes certain situations could be interpreted in different ways, especially with the young.

It had been a memorable day for all three of them.

Part 3
Fame and Glory

Chapter 1

Resting for a short while on his bed, David studied his surroundings with a mixture of pleasurable surprise and fascination.

The apartment was not quite what he had expected. Both his and Charlie's bedroom were a generous size, the pine bed and accompanying furniture giving the impression they were of a high quality. The lounge had a spacious settee, a table and four chairs, a wooden cabinet with drawers, a television and internet access. The small kitchen was well-equipped, providing adequate needs for any basic catering. In his opinion it was very comfortable.

Over the last few days, he had felt a strange release from the tensions of recent weeks. The feeling was as if a long and exacting journey was finally drawing to a close. He guessed it was the realisation the gruelling months of training were almost behind him and the fruits of all their work hopefully now so close. He felt relaxed, fit and ready to give the performances he was sure the next fifteen days would ask of him.

The whole place had an invigorating whiff of excitement about it and he breathed it in deeply with a sense of satisfaction. The Olympic Village was magical. They had arrived at two o'clock, just an hour ago. Entering the city of London and making steady progress through the traffic, they both sensed the air of expectation that seemed to have infiltrated the capital city over recent weeks. The faces of Britain's leading athletes, cyclists, swimmers, boxers and oarsmen, smiling from the posters at every lamppost, captured the spirit of the promised extravaganza that would follow.

"Your picture could be looking down on us shortly," Charlie had joked as he noticed David's gaze sweeping continuously from one side of the road to the other.

"Considering it has been over sixty years since the last Olympics in this country and will probably be the same before the next one, I think it very unlikely."

"But think how lucky you are to be making your debut in your own country. I bet not many athletes have had the luxury of that."

"Yes, I know, Charlie," David replied after considering the remark. "I definitely feel we have a big advantage over the visiting countries."

"Don't feel too sorry for them. They will have had ample time to acclimatise, I'm sure. Many have been here for the last few weeks, and some, months, I understand."

For the first time in several days, it had stopped raining, which seemed a novelty in itself. The media had detailed the plight of the Lake District and other areas of northern England, in particular, where the excessive rain had brought floods that were devastating villages and farmlands, leaving people without homes, food or electricity. Many were already predicting this year could be the wettest on record. In recent weeks, the volume of rain had done little to change that forecast.

On reaching Stratford and the Olympic Village, they had been amazed by the sheer magnitude of the whole thing as the complex loomed so immense before them. After parking the car and passing the strict security registration, they had dawdled in wide-eyed astonishment through the thoroughfare of paths criss-crossing the lush lawns laid generously across the expansive outdoors. The feeling of space was amazing. Without being too ostentatious, the grounds had been set out with palm trees, fountains, pools and figurines, giving the area a relaxed and holiday-like atmosphere.

With their cases in tow, they had slowly threaded a path through the throng of new arrivals, most of whom were in a similar state of wonder at the sheer enormity of what they were witnessing. Everywhere, the mood was light, just smiling faces and excited voices as everyone wallowed in the thrill of this initial experience. Many were already taking photographs with their phones and cameras, asking their friends to pose in front of some valued background souvenir or requesting the favour of a snap of themselves.

In no time, they had been made aware of the multitude of nations present as so many languages and dialects hit their ears, each group that passed seemingly talking in a language foreign to their brain.

Occasionally, they had caught sight of a familiar face from Team GB. Poster girl and ladies team captain, Jessica Ennis, had been talking garrulously to a teammate as they passed one of the many fountains. She nodded brightly at them in recognition. Both Charlie and David wondered how such a slight frame could hold the secret of the strength and stamina required to compete in the energy-sapping seven events that made up the women's heptathlon. The fact she had arrived at the event presumably in peak condition after so much publicity and commercialism throughout the previous twelve months seemed a miracle in itself.

They had paid a fleeting visit to the food hall, just to give themselves an idea of what was in store for their stomachs. Like everyone else, they had been pleasurably surprised at the variety of the different menus. It would seem every diet had been catered for, from traditional British to Halal, Asian, African, Caribbean, a fruit bar brimming with grapes, watermelons, raisins, dried fruit, nuts, seeds and a salad selection of the broadest range imaginable.

"Don't get carried away, Dave," Charlie had warned him as he rubbed his hands together at the sight of the delicious feast of goodies. "Remember to stick to your diet."

"After my last race, I'm going to stuff myself crazy," David had promised.

Visiting the gymnasium, they were positively aghast at the vastness of the well-appointed complex of running, cycling and rowing machines, backed up with weights and sauna rooms. Next to this, there was an entertainment and relaxation area, sporting games rooms of billiards, pool, snooker and table tennis. An imposing stage took its place at one corner, the microphones and covered drum kit suggesting live entertainment would be forthcoming over the following weeks. It was all so exciting.

As David stretched lackadaisically on his bed, he remembered the four envelopes handed to him by the security guard on their arrival at the registration area. He had immediately opened his case and tucked them inside.

Now in his hand, the stiffness of the contents told him they were all cards. He studied the handwriting on each. Recognising the familiar scrawl on the third envelope, he smiled and split it open. The picture on the card was scribed in rich colours depicting an athlete standing on a rostrum receiving a huge trophy with the bold words of **WINNER** engraved across its front. Hoping he looked nothing like the smiling figure on the front, he opened it up. Inside, Tom had written in large blue marker pen letters.

DAD, YOU ARE SO COOL. I KNOW YOU ARE COMING HOME WITH THE GOLD MEDAL. I WILL BE THERE TO SEE YOU. ALL MY SCHOOLFRIENDS WILL BE SHOUTING FOR YOU.
LOVE, Tom. XXX.

He felt his eyes welling and closed them to regain his composure. He realised this reaction just endorsed the love he held for this other life, this young man he was so proud of, and such an important part of him. God, how he loved him.

He swallowed and forced his concentration back to the other letters. Through his watery vision, he studied the top one with no immediate recognition. He pulled the enclosed card out of its envelope to see the words GOOD LUCK set in silver capitals on a shiny red background. As he unfolded it, the spidery writing inside took him by surprise. It lacked any real clarity.

Dear Son,

You have made me the proudest father in the country. Thank you so much for taking me back into your life, and giving me the opportunity of spending some time with you and my wonderful grandson. I really don't deserve it but let's hope I can make it up to you both. Good luck in your races. I know you will make us all very proud.

Your loving father,
Frank

He studied the writing anxiously, aware the letters were weakly scribbled in a manner that could have been achieved by a six-year-old. For a few moments, he reflected on the fact his father had had a good education and held down a demanding job with a top insurance company. To witness such a poor hand was a little puzzling. He had realised he wasn't well but with so much going on had not given it any deeper consideration.

For the first time, it came to him his father's condition may be quite serious. At the same time, it compounded his desire to see a lot more of him in the future. The idea of asking him round for lunch every weekend surfaced again and he made up his mind to put it in to practice once the Games were over and things were back to normal. Hopefully, they would be able to catch up more fully on each other's lives.

Only this morning, he had witnessed again the bond that had so rapidly developed between Frank and Tom. Not only did Tom rise at the unheard of time of six-thirty but accompanied him in the car only forty minutes later to his dad's flat. On his father opening the front door, he witnessed the love between them. Seeing them hug each other so warmly touched his heart. Knowing his father would be there to oversee him during his coming absence was a further bonus.

Later, back at their cottage, after Charlie had arrived to start their journey, he had left them in Tom's bedroom with the youngster enthusiastically exhibiting his Manchester United memorabilia. They had both shouted good luck to him at the tops of their voices on his departure, their enthusiasm so overwhelming, he had to smile as he closed the front door.

The writing on the penultimate card again gave no clue to the sender, so he just tore it open. It was a larger card than the others. It had been sent by the Wisbech Harriers and signed by what looked like every club member. It would not have been possible to add another word, the signatures and short expressions of good wishes so compacted together on the two centre pages. It was a further boost to his pride.

Occasionally, in recent months, he had reflected on his good fortune in finding himself in the elevated position he now held. With this, he had made his mind up, when it all came to an end, he would want to give something back. The club would definitely be at the top of his list of beneficiaries.

There was now only one envelope left. The writing looked vaguely familiar but he could not for the life of him think who may have sent it. He puzzled over it for a few seconds before splitting it open. Again, the card was quite plain, similar to his dad's. Just the words GOOD LUCK embossed on a blue background. He opened it up and read:

Dear David,
Just had to wish you good luck.
Thinking of you,
Love,

Rachel
XX

Without realising it, his eyes had filled again. Instantly, a tear trickled down his cheek. He closed his eyes to stem others that wanted to follow but without success. He couldn't control his emotions any longer.

"Rachel, why did you have to leave," he half-mouthed, half-uttered as he rose to his feet. "I'm so sorry."

At the same time, a familiar voice from the adjoining lounge cut short his burgeoning rant.

"Are you okay, Dave?"

The voice had its usual calming effect. Almost immediately, he pulled himself together.

"Yes, I'm fine, Charlie. Will be out in a minute." After wiping his eyes, he took a deep breath, gave it ten seconds and opened the door into the lounge area. Charlie was standing across the room, a smug grin stretching his face.

"The accommodation is great, I'm sure you will agree?" he asked simply.

David, still carrying some embarrassment, avoided eye contact.

"Yes, it's all brilliant," he said keeping his gaze to the floor. In his hand, he held the four cards.

"Had some good luck cards from Tom, Dad, the Club and Rachel," he explained as he took each card in turn and opened them out so they stood upright on the cabinet.

"That's nice," Charlie said. "Have you heard anything from Rachel recently?"

"No, don't even know where she's living." Charlie picked up from the tone of his voice the weight of his grief and decided not to pursue the matter further.

"Give it half an hour and we will go down the track for a short session. Tomorrow's the Opening Ceremony so we will have two short visits to the track early and then have a good rest before the big event. From what I hear, it's going to be amazing. You okay with that?"

"Yes," David confirmed, returning a smile as he let Charlie temporarily chase his blues away.

That evening, after David excused himself at ten o'clock and went to bed, Charlie's curiosity got the better of him. He collected all four cards together and sat down to study them. He imagined they all had an impact in one way or another but one in particular had upset him. Examining them one by one, he soon realised it was the card from Rachel.

Chapter 2

The big day for London had finally arrived. The vault of well-kept secrets, the fruits of seven years hard work for so many, was about to burst open and dazzle the world with its brilliance. It was 8:30 P.M. on the evening of Friday, 27th July and the Opening Ceremony of the XXXth Olympiad was only minutes away.

Eager not to miss any of the excitement that had blissfully snowballed towards this point since the capital had opened its eyes in the waking hours of the morning, Charlie and David had arrived at the stadium just after 5:30 P.M.

During the morning they had paid two short visits to the training area, David going through the motions with several short pieces of work, all of which seemed to meet with Charlie's approval.

"We have done the hard work. All we need to do now is keep you ticking over," Charlie had said, not for the first time. The message was accompanied with his usual confidence and a pat on the back.

In the afternoon, David had taken to his bed for a short rest and had woken refreshed for the evening's extravaganza. The morning had seemed to pass very slowly, the afternoon even slower, for Charlie especially, so there was a certain feeling of relief when the time eventually came to don their Olympic uniforms.

At the tailors, two weeks previous, they had tried on their white and gold suits and following just a couple of minor adjustments, both were satisfied with the results. When David had arrived home, he had been forced to dress again for the benefit of his very proud son who had shown his approval with a complimentary, "Wow, Dad, you look the business." What that meant exactly, he was not sure but it left him feeling good nevertheless. Tom immediately took a picture on his phone to show his envious schoolmates the following day.

After some time dressing in their respective bedrooms, Charlie and David finally faced each other across the lounge in their new attire.

"You look the McCoy," Charlie beamed at David as he stood adjusting his collar in front of the mirror.

"Well, I'm getting a lot of compliments, Charlie, so I can't look that bad. You look pretty good yourself. Makes you look younger," David responded on studying his mentor.

"What! Forty, you mean," Charlie laughed.

"No, seventy."

Charlie was sixty-six

In the competitors' stadium, David took a seat on one of the benches next to his good friend, James Thompson. The seats had been neatly arranged under the huge marquee in the warm-up area adjacent to the main stadium. Team GB were rapidly gathering.

No sooner had they arrived than Charlie was confronted by an old friend at the entrance. Following their initial introductions, Charlie had advised David he would catch up with him later. There had been no sign of him since and David imagined he was seated somewhere amidst the hordes now surrounding them.

Each country had its own assembly area where all competitors and officials had been asked to congregate at least two hours before the start of the ceremony. Organisation appeared to be of the highest level as team after team grew in size under their respective banners. Strategically seated in their teams so they could be assembled in alphabetical order once the parade was underway, Team GB, being the host nation, were at the rear, which had made the job of locating the team a lot easier. Marshals, positioned every twenty or thirty metres apart, had been a godsend.

"It's a shame it's starting so late," James said to David, almost shouting to ensure he would be heard above the volume of background noise. "I understand quite a few of the competitors are miffed that it is taking place so late and they can't attend because they are competing tomorrow."

"You can't blame them, can you? How do you think we would feel if we had to miss *this*? It's a once in a lifetime experience." David's enthusiasm summed up James' feelings exactly.

"I think they are mainly the swimmers, but I guess the organisers have to take account of all the other countries and the television coverage, of course," David added. "We're lucky we have another week to go."

James nodded in agreement. "How's your training going, by the way?"

"Fine, thanks. Charlie seems to be happy with me, at least. How about you?"

"I've had a few twinges from the old ankle earlier this week but a couple of sessions with the physiotherapist seems to have done the job."

"That's good," David added, grinned and followed up with, "the other night, I dreamt you and I finished first and second in the final."

"Who was first?" James said with interest, a look of amusement creeping to his face. David never replied, just shrugged his shoulders and returned a blank smile that said it all. "I see," James laughed. "I'll settle for second." It was all part of the friendly banter they now shared so warmly.

It would seem the entire population of London, including its multitude of visitors, could not wait for the greatest sporting occasion in the world to commence. For once, the weather was behaving kindly, the sky now darkening rapidly but still cloudless above the complex. Even the temperature seemed to have climbed a few degrees.

A buzz of expectation lay heavily in the air, as if a great Messiah was about to descend. To David, it felt strange, ethereal in a spooky sort of way he could not really define. Just odd. Peculiar. To enjoy every moment had been his intention and that was what he was doing, drinking in every last detail.

Around the competitor arena, several large screens relayed the BBC television coverage. Next door, in the main arena, you could sense the excitement spilling over as the sixty thousand crowd were rapidly filling to capacity. The request for tickets to the Opening Ceremony had been over-subscribed by tens of thousands and it looked as if those now present, who were lucky enough to hold a ticket, were determined to enjoy their good fortune to the full.

A stereo effect, produced by the sounds from the screen's loudspeakers mingling with the actual hubbub of activity floating in from the main arena, was quite extraordinary. A cacophony of sound, so extreme, it was almost frightening.

"Good job they are friendly," David laughed as they both listened to the tumultuous noise in wonder.

All of a sudden, it went quiet as everyone's attention was drawn to the screens where the countdown had begun. One minute to go. The figure sixty appeared on a stopwatch, then fifty-nine, fifty-eight, reducing rapidly. The silence lasted just a moment before the spectators picked up on the count.

"Fifty-seven, fifty-six, fifty-five..." resounded around the arena, the voices rising in unison as they counted down together. David and James looked at each other, smiled and joined in the fun, adding their voices to the expanding volume.

The figures sped up down the fifties, into the forties, the thirties, twenties, many numbers portrayed by a defining subject of British life. The famous Thirty-Nine Steps, the celebratory twenty-first birthday cake and candles, the black door of Number 10 Downing Street, the red Number 9 London bus, each cleverly edited.

Following this, the screens transported the world along the River Thames from its source to London and finally the stadium where reality took over. Within no time, the arena came alive to the sights and sounds of hundreds of actors portraying a pastoral scene of Great Britain in the eighteenth century. Horse-drawn farm vehicles, a rural cricket match, maypole dancers, a competitive rugby session, all added to the magic.

"Wow, this is amazing," David shouted to a similarly enthralled James.

"You're not kidding, mate," was his instant response.

The roar of the crowd rose to titanic proportions before simmering to the first announcement.

"Ladies and gentlemen, welcome to London and the Games of the XXXth Olympiad. To open our ceremony, please welcome Olympic cyclist, a member of Team GB and Britain's first winner of the Tour de France, BRADLEY WIGGINS."

And there he was. The tall slim figure of Britain's latest hero, Bradley Wiggins, who only days previous had been the first Englishman to win the coveted Tour de France, one of the most gruelling sporting events in the world. Wearing the traditional Champion's yellow jersey, he sprang on to the raised stage with his arms waving wildly as a tidal wave of applause rained down from the excited crowd. There was no chance of any let up as Bradley made his way to the rear of the stage where the giant Olympic bell, a sturdy rope dangling from underneath its dome, awaited his attention. Grabbing it with both hands, he quickly gave it a firm pull to release the balloons carrying the symbolic Olympic rings. They floated smoothly into the air to a further surge of appreciation from the crowd.

Totally mesmerised, David could not believe the unfolding depiction as a cast of some two and a half thousand volunteer actors portrayed scenes from the Industrial Revolution. Throughout the performance, lasting several minutes, a thousand drummers kept up a pulsating beat which finally came to a climax when six huge chimney stacks appeared from the ground as though by magic.

"Good Lord!" James exclaimed. "Where did they come from?"

"God knows," David replied, spellbound by the sights before him.

With no time to catch a breath, all attention was refocused on the screens where a taxi was seen travelling to the Queen's famous London residence, Buckingham Palace. After passing through the giant gates, it stopped at the main entrance where one of the palace staff rushed forward to open the door. Out jumped actor, Daniel Craig, smartly attired in evening dress and portraying his most famous role as master spy, James Bond. Unaccompanied, Daniel passed through the hallowed passages of the palace meeting the royal corgis on his way. Finally, he came to another footman holding a door open and he was ushered inside. Anticipation had already reached boiling point as a rear view of the queen sitting at a desk filled the screen.

"Mr Bond, ma'am," the footman calmly announced.

Bond waited respectfully for a response as the seated figure completed some paperwork, her back still towards him and the camera.

"I bet it's that woman who looks like the Queen," David said to James in a whisper that probably echoed the thoughts of a whole nation. "Surely, the Queen wouldn't take part in such a frivolous sketch?"

Finally, she turned.

"It's her!" David gasped in unison with a vast proportion of the crowd as all could see it was truly the Queen in person.

"Good evening, Bond," she said before coolly rising from her chair.

"Good evening, your majesty," Bond replied. Accompanied by her corgis, the Queen led the way to the main door with her famous bodyguard respectfully in tow. In the forecourt a helicopter awaited their arrival. The Queen and Bond climbed aboard, the rotors fired and they were soon in the air heading for east London and the Olympic Stadium.

Minutes later, back in the complex, all eyes raised to the sky as the drone of the helicopter hit the ears of the crowd. On the screens, you could see the queen fitting her harness in preparation for a parachute jump. Bond was similarly attired. No sooner were they ready than both had ejected from the circling craft, their chutes billowing in the wind as they fell slowly from the sky.

"That's definitely not the Queen," said David, as the two parachutes calmly floated down to earth, disappearing behind the rear of the stadium from the eyes of the audience and the television cameras.

"I should imagine it's not Daniel Craig either," replied James with a bemused expression. Whether it was her Majesty or not, the unexpected show of such unusual behaviour from a royal was greatly appreciated with applause breaking out from all corners of the stadium.

As it slowly petered out, her Majesty appeared in the royal box with her husband, the Duke of Edinburgh, raising the volume of affection to even greater heights. Enjoying her Jubilee year to the full, the look of pleasure she had exhibited on so many occasions over recent months seemed even brighter, as she waved gracefully before taking a seat, the adoration of the crowd still ringing loudly around the stadium.

To follow such a performance was not an easy task but the standard was faithfully maintained. The ensuing tributes, to the National Health Service, English literature and the music and film industries, were of the highest quality. So wrapped up in the spectacular displays, David was unaware of the time.

"Are you getting nervous?" he asked James on looking at his watch. He sensed the time for the parade was fast approaching.

"Not really," James replied, sucking thoughtfully at a straw protruding from a can of lemonade. "I just feel excited, I think. I guess the old butterflies will start to flutter once it's time to go."

As James spoke, they both realised there was something going on at the front of the mass of people who now filled the holding area to what seemed its capacity. Just a ripple of activity to start with, you could sense the wave of excitement slowly approaching the swollen British camp.

"I think this might be it," James said with a sigh of relief. Around him, others were becoming animated, looking around inquisitively at the sea of heads before them. All sensing that, perhaps, the moment they had dreamt of for so long, would shortly be reality.

Whilst seated, the numbers had not seemed so vast but now, with everyone standing and preparing to move, it felt like a tidal wave of humanity ready to roll.

In the background, Scottish singer, Emeli Sande, touched every heart with an inspirational rendition of *Abide With Me,* her soulful voice clearly drawing the emotion from every word. Once again, the crowd rewarded the performance with an ecstatic ovation. Before it had time to diminish, the announcement that sent the crowd wild was finally delivered.

"Ladies and Gentlemen, the athletes of the XXXth Olympiad."

With trumpets blaring harmoniously, the procession was on its way. A tall sturdy Greek flag bearer led his team proudly into the arena, his broad smile and bearing drawing a sensational response from the crowd. Unbelievably, the reaction eclipsed all before it. The energy was so intense. For many, it was a moment that would be etched in their minds for ever. Around the arena, a multitude of cameras flashed simultaneously, creating an impression on the screens of one huge blinding light.

A team of over a hundred Greek athletes, coaches and managers followed, their inherent charisma lighting the arena with a vivacity that would be a hallmark of every team following. It was a scene of pure joy as the members, inhibited in their actions, danced, waved and gesticulated to the beat of the drummers' rhythm, some holding video cameras above their heads, others using their mobile phone cameras for a memento of the reception that truly exceeded all expectations. David and James watched spellbound as the screens portrayed the hiatus of excitement.

Close on the heels of the Greeks, the team from Afghanistan entered to the same rapturous response, the alphabetical cycle now in full motion as the teams streamed purposefully through the entrance. Incited by the drummers beat, a marching rhythm was maintained that kept the procession moving at a lively pace.

As each country entered, highly esteemed delegates, often royalty, prime ministers and other leading government figures stood in the Royal Box and waved excitedly as their athletes acknowledged their presence.

In the British camp, Team GB, energised by the raw response of the crowd, were initially frustrated by their inactivity. They could not wait to meet the baying crowd. Small groups had formed within their numbers, chatting amongst themselves to pass the time. The mood was light and joyful. Very gradually, the multitude before them was decreasing, disappearing country by country down the awaiting tunnel, a slight adjustment to their position as each team shuffled forward. Now and again, there would be a major shunt, maybe a few metres and then it would come to a halt and they would all be stationary for several minutes before another rally came along.

"Patience is the name of the game," David half-shouted, half-whispered to James, who checked his watch.

"It's now an hour since the parade started," he informed David.

"Doesn't surprise me when there are so many athletes. Anyhow, we're nearly there now."

Before David had finished speaking, there was a sudden surge.

"Must be the Yanks speeding things up," he added with a grin, as they were swept up with the team and carried into the tunnel.

Despite the muffled sound, they could sense the magnitude of the awaiting reception well before meeting the stadium entrance. In just a few minutes they were clear of the tunnel and out in the open, the atmosphere beyond imagination. Almost frightening, pandemonium prevailed as the crowd let their emotions run free. The lights were blinding in those seconds before adjustment and the noise, a sonic boom blasting their eardrums.

David quickly cast a wary glance at James who was mouthing something to him, his eyes lit brightly with the excitement he was experiencing. Yet, he couldn't hear a word above the noise. A quick shrug of his shoulders was sufficient indication he was having trouble understanding and James turned away with a smile to concentrate on his own experiences.

They were positioned halfway down the team, but on the outside, so they could see the crowd in the front rows clearly, their actions almost manic as they waved and shouted joyously. In no time, any semblance of order in their initial ranks had been lost so the whole team moved freely, some in small groups hugging each other whilst waving fanatically in all directions. Others were dancing, jiggling their hips and wildly throwing themselves about with the beat, all the time smiling in total bemusement as the appreciation continued to rain down on them.

As Team GB reached the far corner of the arena, the procession came to an end. Efficiently, they were shepherded to their new position in the centre of the track to await the final proceedings of the evening's schedule.

Totally inspired by the whole scenario, David turned to James. "Well, that's something I'll never forget," he confessed.

"I know what you mean, mate. I absolutely agree. We will take it to the grave."

The last half hour was as stirring as anything they had yet witnessed. From the mound at the top of the arena, Chairman of the Olympic Committee, Sebastian Coe, welcomed the world to London with an inspiring speech to which the Olympic President, Dr Jacques Rogge, enthusiastically responded.

It would seem that every aspect of the evening was a jewel in a very precious crown, one memorable event following another. The Queen's speech of welcome, the reappearance of the Olympic flag carried by a distinguished group of sportsmen and women, peacemakers and philanthropists and then the appearance of Muhammed Ali, considered by many to be the greatest sportsman of the modern era. Now in ill health, the old warrior looked a pitiful replica of his former self but the rapturous response from the crowd as he struggled out to the centre of the arena was quite remarkable.

"My dad says he was definitely the greatest boxer he has ever seen," James bawled to David who nodded in agreement.

"A great man all round, from what I understand. Apparently, he stood up for his principles, refusing to fight in the American army and was thrown out of boxing for several years only to come back eventually and win the World Heavyweight title."

"Twice, I believe," James added.

With all the teams now in position, the scene was set for the climax, the arrival of the Olympic torch. On cue, the man toasted as the greatest Olympian, Sir Steven Redgrave, winner of five consecutive rowing gold medals, entered the arena holding the torch aloft. As before, the response was unbelievable with the applause rising again to gargantuan heights.

Sir Steven made his way to the far end of the stadium where six youths, chosen for their potential in their respective sports, awaited his arrival and the transfer of the flame. In no time, they were holding their lighted torches aloft ready for the final act.

Now was the time to realise the function of the copper kettles which had been deposited on to stems in the arena by a representative from each country on their arrival. The kettles now stood, the centrepiece of attention, before the young athletes. Ceremoniously, they set their torches to a few, each one transferring its flame to the next so that within seconds all of them were ablaze.

With the music now pumping loudly, the kettles rose from the ground converging to form one of the closest kept secrets of the evening, the Olympic Cauldron, a jaw-dropping spectacle that sent the crowd wild. Simultaneously, fireworks sprouted colourfully from the turrets of the stadium completing an unforgettable event. Once again pandemonium reigned.

The honour of closing the ceremony was left to singer and composer, Paul McCartney, who put on a show fit for such a great occasion. Seated at his piano and surrounded by a group of trusted musicians, he treated the audience to a tuneful selection from his Beatles repertoire.

The conclusion brought with it almost a feeling of relief as the whole crowd seemed to draw breath, the spectacle having aroused so much emotion and energy. Everyone present felt drained but joyfully satiated. As the lights rose and the crowds gradually scattered from their seats, each member of Team GB were struck with the awareness that the starting tape had been raised. They were about to face the challenge of their life, a challenge so intense they would probably never see the like of it again.

"Wow," David enthused as he strolled with James amongst the dispersing competitors, "that was some show." Both considered the day a monumental event in their young lives.

"I took a few photos with my phone," James replied. "I hope they come out all right."

"I'm sure they will, mate."

"Feels like it's getting close now, doesn't it?" James added. "Exciting and what?"

"Bloody frightening," said David, his face contorted in response.

It was another hour before David was back at his apartment. Charlie was already home sitting on the settee watching the television as he entered the lounge. He smiled fondly. David thought he looked a little weary.

"Well, my boy, what did you think? Glad you made it here?" Charlie asked.

"Sure am, Charlie. Still in a dream, can't believe it's happening. I feel I could wake up any time soon."

Charlie laughed. "You will believe it when you're on the starting line. Well, I hope you do, or we have wasted the last twenty months."

It was said in fun but both realised the seriousness of those few words.

Chapter 3

As the days unfolded, the British public were treated to a feast of sporting glories never experienced before in the one hundred and twenty years of Olympic competition.

After the threat of possible failures in security, transport and general administration, the smoothness of proceedings at all the many centres provided a welcomed reward to the discipline, teamwork and enthusiasm of so many.

The roll of medals for Team GB started slowly, a silver on the third day, followed by a bronze on the fourth and another on the fifth. Cycling, one of Britain's strongest sports, was favourite to provide the first gold but this never materialised when the fancied British road racer had problems with his bike and failed to finish.

Britons had to wait to the fourth day for that elusive gold which came, quite unexpectedly, from two young ladies in a rowing pair on the water at Eton. This opened the floodgates to a feast of successes that seemed to multiply with every event. The newspapers were having a field day.

Every morning, Charlie and David would find a table in the dining area, and study the sports pages enthusiastically whilst eating their breakfast. James and Ross would often join them, leading up to some varied discussions as to the main hopes for the day's performances.

"We seem to be doing well at the rowing and cycling," Charlie had commented at the end of the first week.

"I think it's the French President who said we always do well at sports where we sit on our arses," James responded to a hearty burst of laughter from all present.

By the time the athletics programme started in the second week, the medal haul was beginning to swell. There was a buzz in the GB camp that was strangely frightening, an inexplicable feeling something extraordinary was about to happen and happen it did.

The Saturday opened with all interest centred on ladies team captain, Jessica Ennis and her attempt to win the heptathlon. Team GB's pin-up girl had gone into the second day of competition with a comfortable lead, only to struggle with the shot put which had never been one of her strongest events. A reasonable performance followed in the javelin which gave her a commanding lead going into the final event, the exhausting two laps of the 800 metres.

"She looks so determined and focused," David addressed Charlie as they sat watching the event on the large screen in the complex.

"So you will be in a few days' time," said Charlie with some emphasis, as he leant forward to concentrate on the proceedings. "Although she has a good few points in hand, she can still lose, anything can happen out there. She has to run it sensibly and watch the girls that matter." By this time, a large crowd had congregated, some taking seats but many standing to watch the defining moment.

Much to Charlie's surprise, Jess led right from the gun and opened up a gap of several metres from the chasing pack. Bravely, she held her advantage into the second lap and beyond. Only as she approached the final bend did it look as if she was going to pay a price for her bold run when two of her opponents started to close. Caught and passed in the final straight, she was not prepared to surrender and with a gutsy effort, responded with a sprint that carried her back into the lead and victory. Immediately, there was an avid response from the surrounding crowd.

Charlie released the air from his puffed cheeks. "That was a brave run, especially as she must have realised she had the event sewn up well before the final straight," he said in a tone emphasising the admiration he held for the girl.

"That's the way she is, always wants to give her best," David added, enjoying, along with everyone else, watching her ecstatic reaction as she crossed the line. "Not happy to settle for second best. That's what makes a great champion." The look of release from the tensions of the past few weeks was clearly showing on Jessica Ennis's face as she smiled brightly, grabbed a Union Jack from a spectator and started trotting around the arena with a multitude of photographers in tow.

"Does something to you when you see that sort of thing," David said with some deliberation. "Sort of boosts your desire to perform well. It's inspired me."

"That's good, just the job to get the juices going, my boy." As Charlie was about to return to his newspaper, the list of competitors for the next event caught his attention. It was the final of the men's long jump. He noted the name Greg Rutherford of Great Britain.

"Met him at Birmingham," Charlie said matter-of-factly.

"Who?" David enquired

"Greg Rutherford. Nice lad, quite confident but don't think he has a chance of getting amongst the medals, unfortunately."

"He's done well to get to the final," David remarked on studying the names of the competitors. Both were soon buried in their papers, Charlie in the sports pages, David pondering over the crossword.

It was a good half-hour before Charlie raised his head from his paper and glanced at the screen again.

"My God, Greg's taken the lead," he yelled, seeing the tall red-headed lad from Milton Keynes jump for joy on realising his achievement. Charlie and David were suddenly glued to the event, willing Greg to hold his lead through the remaining rounds. It was early days in the competition and there were still four rounds to go.

Greg, with the crowd now fully behind him, was responding well. In the fourth round several of the competitors bettered their best performance, but so did Greg, adding ten centimetres and holding the lead. Now it was a case of catch me if you can as each looked for that special jump. Despite the target distance being well within the capabilities of several, one by one they tried and failed. The tension was gripping.

"Come on, make a foul jump," David spoke aloud as the final competitor, a Norwegian, started his run. The crowd were temporarily hushed to silence. That was until he made his jump, his feet hit the sand and it was obvious that he was short of the distance required. Greg had the gold medal. The stadium erupted.

Throwing his arms in the air, Greg couldn't believe the fairy tale result. It was all over and he was Olympic champion. A Union Jack appeared from the crowd which he quickly wrapped around his shoulders as he took off on a lap of honour.

"Well, that was a surprise," said Charlie with a broad grin on his face.

"Good for him," David replied breezily, happy to witness a further and what's more, unexpected success.

The crowd's mood remained buoyant as Greg completed his circuit of honour. Only as he prepared to leave the arena was there any sign of a lull and then, for only seconds, as the appearance of the 10,000 metre hope, Mohamed Farah, revived their enthusiasm. Known as Mo to his many fans, the twenty-nine-year-old, born in Somalia, had moved to England in his early years. He looked every part the distance runner. Of average height at five foot nine inches, with a slender but sturdy frame, his shaved head completed the hard man image he portrayed.

"Looks fit and strong," said David, his eyes set firmly on Mo.

The gun sent them on their way. With almost thirty competitors in the field, there was bound to be a lot of jostling, arms flaying about wildly as each runner searched for a rhythm that would hopefully carry him through the twenty-five laps.

As the early laps were played out, it was soon obvious that records were not on the cards. It was to be a tactical race to the end. With three laps to go, Mo was safely positioned in the leading pack of twelve runners. Moving with a rhythmical stride, he looked strong and in control. Making his move approaching the final lap, he drew the Africans from Ethiopia and Kenya with him, together with his training partner, the American, Galep Rudd. On the final bend, he held a comfortable lead over Rudd with Ethiopian, Tarika Bekele, in third place. Lengthening his stride in the straight, it was soon obvious no one was going to catch him. The crowd roared their approval as he crossed the line and threw his arms up in triumph.

"Wow, what a day," David exclaimed on watching Mo drop to his knees and ceremoniously kiss the track. "What can top that, three gold medals in one day?"

"David Lucas winning a gold in the 1,500 metres," Charlie responded with a wry grin.

Chapter 4

David was amazed at how well he had slept. His big day had finally arrived. It was Wednesday and the morning of his first heat. On previous nights, he had struggled to toss the thoughts of competition from his brain and invariably they had kept him awake for what seemed ages. Last night, to his surprise, he had no trouble, falling asleep almost as his head hit the pillow. Relaxed and refreshed, he felt ready for the ultimate test before him.

The excitement in the British team had magnified over the past week as so many athletes, right across the spectrum of events, seemed to be performing well beyond their expectations. Personal bests were becoming the norm as one by one the British competitors returned to their camps overjoyed with their success. An atmosphere of achievement was permeating the whole team and was not for stopping. The British public, glued to their television sets, were looking for medal hopes in events they had not even realised existed until the televised Games hit their homes.

The reception on the track for GB athletes was close to hysterical. David's race was set for 2:40 P.M. and now only minutes away. It was the opening heat in his event with the first four competitors home moving through to the semi-finals tomorrow. Four other heats would follow today. The two fastest losers from all the five heats would join the semi-final line up.

There was a certain relief to finally reaching this point and, surprisingly, he felt quite cool under the pressure. He had completed a short workout with Charlie earlier in the morning which, together with his warm-up, now left him feeling loose and relaxed.

"Just treat the race like any other," Charlie had advised in his pep talk an hour earlier, advice which tickled David as he entered the arena to a barrage of adulation, the intensity of which seemed decibels above even the Opening Ceremony. At the sight of his British tracksuit, the response was ecstatic, so powerful and stunning, he was temporarily mesmerised. Like everything else over recent days, it was almost unreal.

Strangely, he felt a confidence hard to define in the tense atmosphere of the moment. At first, he found himself questioning his own calm and wondering whether it could have a negative effect on his performance but immediately, he dismissed any such thoughts, telling himself firmly his new self-confidence had to be a bonus. He was actually enjoying the moment and perhaps, that was the reason for this feeling.

Throughout the previous week, he and Charlie had studied the performances of most of the competitors in his event, at least where any form was known. They had spent hours sitting down in the evenings sifting through the web seeking information and video recordings of the relative meetings from the last few years. He felt as though he knew more about some athletes' careers than he did his own.

Of his immediate opponents and there were ten, he had two Kenyans who stood out on their current form. Charlie reckoned he could look to them for the pace. They enjoyed running from the front, he told David, possibly sprinting from the last lap in the hope of burning off the opposition.

Charlie's assessment was they would run together as a team at a good pace, accelerating if challenged, forcing any opponents to run wide to pass them. Both had competed well throughout the year. Nixon Kiplin, probably the most dangerous of the pair, had won at two of the main meetings and Silas Cheboi, his compatriot, had been in close attendance. They were dangerous opponents in Charlie's estimation and needed watching. American, Douglas Bennett, was another with some recent form, winning the Grand Prix at Basle only two months ago. Of the others, Charlie had picked out the Frenchman, Andre Gasgoine and another African, Caleb Margat, both young men with growing reputations.

As he was called to the starting line, his mind was honed to the task ahead. One hundred per cent concentration. Charlie had taught him well and he was about to reap the rewards from all the work he had invested. This was it; the beginning of the greatest challenge of his life. A date with destiny, he hoped.

The sharp report of the starter's gun was a welcomed relief from the tension of the preliminaries. Immediately, all eleven runners scrimmaged for their initial positions on the track. David fell into fourth place as the two Kenyans made their expected move at the head with Andre Gasgoine in front of him. The pace was reasonable and David found himself relaxing into a comfortable stride. No worries so far.

The chasing field seemed content to let the two Kenyans take the pull at the front so the order remained unchanged until the beginning of the third lap. At this point, there was an injection of pace, a move which David and Andre immediately covered, going with them into the bend. The Kenyans' tactics were beginning to pay off as a gap opened up to the rest of the field.

Realising the damage they had done, the Kenyans kicked again. Andre was now struggling to go with them and David passed him to fall in three metres behind, still going smoothly and feeling full of running. Over the next half lap, he moved majestically closer. Through the blinkers of his concentration, he could sense the enthusiasm of the crowd willing him on with every stride.

Running into the penultimate bend, he felt confident but reined back his enthusiasm with a tinge of caution, saving his energy for a later burst. He felt in control and was savouring every moment. It was a great feeling. In the straight, with the final bend in sight, he made his move, initially dragging the two Kenyans with him, but not for long. He lengthened his stride, determined to hold them off should they make a counter-attack but it never came. Half-way into the bend, he took a quick glance behind him to see the nearest challenger a couple of metres in arrears. He hardened on again, feeling relaxed and strong as he covered the final thirty metres to the finishing line. It was all over and he had come through it successfully. Around him, the crowd released an adulatory roar that blew his ears. They felt they had witnessed something special and his time confirmed their confidence.

Dazed by the moment as the press appeared to emerge from everywhere, David felt the need to exit the track as soon as possible. Looking around, he spied the other competitors heading towards a gate at the side of the track.

Politely dodging the photographers, he made the move, reaching the gate at the same time as a pretty young girl smiled sweetly at him in an attempt to catch his attention.

"David, we need you for a television interview, if you don't mind. Would you follow me, please?" she requested. There was little chance of escape and he followed meekly. She led him to the broadcasting area where the interviewer stood patiently awaiting his arrival.

"And here comes David Lucas fresh from his first heat in the 1,500 metres," he announced to the public whilst smiling professionally.

"David, that looked fairly comfortable and a very good time?" he questioned, pushing the microphone towards him.

David felt his usual pang of nerves when put in these situations. He coughed and cleared his throat.

"I felt good," he confirmed. "But didn't expect to pull away quite so easily, I must admit."

"Did you realise you were so far ahead as you came into the straight?"

"I looked across at the screen and thought they were on my tail so I concentrated on the finish, and just put my head down." There was a slight grin from the interviewer.

"So that was the reason for the acceleration, was it? You opened up about five metres, you know?" David didn't know. He had not had a chance to watch the replay.

"I haven't seen it yet," he replied, with a look of the utmost honesty.

"No doubt, you will be interested to see how your teammates do? I think James Thompson is in the next heat."

"Yes, I am."

"Well, I'll let you get going and thanks for talking to us."

"Thank you," David answered politely, pleased to exit the ordeal.

No sooner had he left the platform than he saw Charlie pushing his way through the throng of spectators in his direction. As they met, both threw their arms wide and hugged fiercely.

"Well done, my boy, that was brilliant," Charlie shouted into his ear.

"Thanks."

"And it looked quite easy?"

"It was really, I guess," David replied, lowering his voice so that only Charlie was able to hear.

"Your time was magnificent in the circumstances. There is so much more to come."

"Yes, I've just seen it on the screen and thought they'd made a mistake."

"No mistake, my boy and it's only the beginning. A world record is on the cards, I can tell you."

"Good old Charlie, always the optimist," David quipped in response.

Charlie laughed. Throwing his arm around David's shoulders, he dragged him down the aisle in the direction of the competitor enclosure.

"Let's go and watch the others."

Whoops of congratulations seemed to come at him from every direction as he entered the Team GB viewing area. Shyly, he raised his hand as a token of acknowledgement.

"I think you have a greyhound there, Charlie, so you had better feed him some rabbit tonight," a comedian shouted from the back of the room.

"I think you're right, mate," Charlie replied before settling down to watch the four other heats.

No sooner had they taken their seats than they could see the dozen competitors for the second heat lined up for the start.

James was in the middle of the field as they took off in response to the starter's gun, immediately dropping to the rear as the leaders set a good pace. David was surprised at how nervous he felt watching his teammate. The funny thing was, he had felt more relaxed before his own race.

Initially, the order remained unchanged and stayed that way for the first two laps. Then halfway through the third lap, James made his first move, passing the group at the rear effortlessly to settle behind the leading four runners who were starting to accelerate towards the final lap. James went with them giving himself room to attack on the outside when necessary.

David found himself carried by the euphoria of the moment as he bawled loudly for his mate in anticipation of the expected performance. With two hundred metres to go, the lead changed as Tunisian veteran, Abdul Farli, sprinted to the front and opened a gap of some five metres followed by the Australian, Dan Nelson and James, moving smoothly close behind. By the final bend, all three had pulled clear of the rest of the field who appeared to be struggling to maintain contact. By the time they reached the final straight, all three runners looked in control holding their positions, happy not to exert themselves too much at this stage of the competition.

Once James had crossed the line with his place in the semi-final secured, David could at last relax. He was amazed at how tense he had become. His throat felt quite sore from shouting. The British supporters were again magnanimous in their approval.

Grinning broadly, he looked around at Charlie who was gazing at his stopwatch in deep concentration. After a short while, he looked up with that familiar glint in his eye. "Three seconds slower than you and old Abdul was flat out right up to the line," he whispered. It was not David's interpretation of the race exactly but he said nothing.

Without a GB representative in the next two heats, there was a discernible lapse in the crowd's participation. Nevertheless, Charlie gave both races his full attention, watching carefully to note the performance of all the leading competitors, his stopwatch accurately recording their times.

"You are going to have to watch that Yusef Farga, the Syrian," Charlie told David in a serious tone after the fourth heat. "His time was nearly as fast as yours and he was moving deceptively well. It looked to me as if he could have gone a lot quicker and he will be in your semi tomorrow." David nodded mindfully.

The final heat was now upon them and you could already sense the buzz from the crowd. The emergence of Philip Rhodes from the tunnel, leading his group of competitors, set the arena alight. It was a special reception for the crowd's champion, a message carried with the gusto befitting an athlete of his standing. A true hero in their eyes, Philip raised his arm in recognition of their generous welcome.

Three tiers below where they were standing, Charlie could see the back of Freddie Stokes's head as he watched every move his star pupil was making. He imagined his nerves were as taut as his had been.

The tension seemed to gain momentum as the runners moved to their starting positions. The athletic pundits had given the impression this heat would be nothing more than a formality for the current British champion and the crowd were seriously looking for him to deliver.

David was considering how it must feel with this weight of expectation on your shoulders when the gun sent the runners on their way. Quickly sorting themselves out, Philip settled in third place behind the green vest of the Irish contender, Aidan Frost, and the Spaniard, Rafael Dennes, who had made a name for himself when winning the 3,000-metre event at the Crystal Palace Meeting in June. As always, David's eyes were drawn to the fluency of Philip's action. He almost gave the impression of floating over the track as he trailed the leading pair lazily through the first two laps.

Into the third lap, the race started to heat up with several runners from the rear of the field moving up to challenge the leading threesome. Sensing the move, Philip strode to the front.

There was an invincibility about him, his stride lengthening as he opened up a gap of some three to four metres from his nearest rival. The mighty roar of the crowd carried him onwards into the final lap as the leading pursuers panicked to close the deficit which had opened to a good six metres as he came off the penultimate bend.

Along the far straight, Philip looked to have the race sewn up when the feverish crowd witnessed a change in his rhythm. The sparkle of excitement lulled with frightening effect. There was an audible gasp of disbelief as the stride that looked so majestic disintegrated before their eyes leaving him lumbering forward in what looked to be an effort to maintain. Like a car sucking its final dregs of petrol, he was losing momentum. Behind him, the chasing runners picked up on the change of pace and surged forward in response.

Battling on into the final straight, Philip still held the lead but only by a diminishing couple of metres as a group of four moved in behind him. In a swift surge, he saw three of them pass him. His legs were treading water as he struggled to hold his coveted fourth position to the line.

He was almost there as he sensed a body beside him. Intuitively he gave it one final effort but it was not enough. He had lost his coveted place by half a metre. Desperately, he fell and vomited on the track.

The crowd were hushed in suspense as all eyes were targeted at the scoreboard. Slowly, the statistics unfolded and finally a sigh of relief as Philip's time confirmed he had made the semi-final by a fraction of a second, one of the two fastest losers. The British champion was humbled but still in the fight.

Charlie's reaction was a slight nudge to David's ribs for his benefit only. He looked below to see a troubled Freddie climbing the stairs towards him, his face screwed up with the agony he was obviously feeling. Charlie's heart went out to him.

"Hope he's okay, Freddie," were the only words of condolence he could find on seeing the look of devastation written on his friend's face.

Once Freddie was out of sight, he shared his feelings of the race with David.

"The winner was two seconds slower than your race so I don't think we have anything to worry about there," he informed him in a soft voice. Charlie's dreams were beginning to materialise.

Chapter 5

Only his second day of competition but already David was enjoying the routine, the thrill of the track and the excitement that accompanied it. Like a nervous contestant on a talent show who had wowed the public with a spectacular debut performance, he couldn't wait to get back on the stage. It was semi-finals day and another challenge to face.

It had come as no surprise to the public when an announcement had been made earlier in the morning that Philip Rhodes had withdrawn. There had been rumours after his poor show in the previous heat that he had been suffering from rheumatic fever and it was generally felt this could be the answer.

Once again, David had slept well. The previous evening had been shared with Charlie for a sociable dinner, twenty minutes with his physiotherapist and friend, Geoff Hunter and a visit to the shower room where he had undertaken a most unwelcomed ice bath.

He was feeling good once again as he lined up for the start of his heat, the first of only two this time. The confidence he had so recently discovered was prevailing. His concentration was sharp as the gun fired and despite a slight scrimmaging with the runner on his inside he held fourth place as they covered the first bend. The pace was quicker than the previous race but he felt at ease as they pushed through the early two laps, keeping himself clear of trouble and running well within himself.

As Charlie had predicted, Yusef Farga, the Syrian, made a break well into the third lap, quickly opening up a few metres from the field. David was prepared for this and manoeuvred himself to the outside, passing the two runners in front fairly comfortably as he set off in pursuit of the leader who was pushing on at pace. He cautioned himself not to try and close the gap too quickly, advice Charlie had dispensed many times.

There was still a good five hundred metres to go as he lengthened his stride. The gap between him and Yusef began to close. Coming into the straight to tackle the final lap, he snatched a glance at the big screen to see the chasing group clustered together but a good few metres in arrears.

By the time he had covered the length of the straight, he was in Yusef's slipstream, just a metre behind and full of running. Once again, he was amazed at how good he felt. Coming off the bend, a feeling of overpowering energy consumed him. He could wait no longer. With a mighty effort, he sprinted past the bewildered Syrian, who could offer little resistance.

Along the far straight, he opened up three or four metres and looked to be moving further ahead. It felt so comfortable. As he came into the finishing straight, he realised he was well ahead. Consumed by the euphoria of the moment, he had no intention of letting it go and sprinted to the finishing line, much to the appreciation of the crowd.

"What a magnificent run," bellowed the commentator from the plethora of loudspeakers spaced strategically around the stadium. Over-excited, he sounded as animated as the thirty thousand crowd who roared their approval for the performance they had so joyfully witnessed.

"Just missed the world record by half a second," he added to the drama of the moment, raising the applause another notch.

On the track, David was bent over double, his arms dangling loosely to the ground as he recovered from his exertion. When he straightened up, he was once again facing a barrage of photographers eagerly jostling for a position to capture his picture. Their requests to smile were easily met as he felt more than happy with his performance. A feeling of satisfaction was glowing warmly inside him. It could not have gone better and had him longing for the final.

Even his interview session seemed less stressful, although the interviewer's assessment that the gold medal was almost his, seemed a little presumptuous, he thought. Slowly, he was waking up to the ways of the media.

No sooner had it ended than Charlie was there to congratulate him. With his eyes glazed with tears, he grabbed him around the waist, lifted him bodily from the ground and swung him around a couple of times, kissing his head fondly in the process. The cameras caught the action and relayed it willingly to the watching public.

"My wonderful boy, you did it and so comfortably. I can't believe it," Charlie shouted, almost breaking down with emotion. David had seen him excited with his results many times but never in this state of animation.

"Hold on, Charlie," David told him, breaking loose from his clutches. "I haven't won yet, you know, there's a final to come."

"You'll win it, Son, I know it," said Charlie exuberantly, wiping the corners of his eyes.

"Let's hope so," David added with a smile.

As previously, they remained at the arena for the second heat and were rewarded with the sight of James holding his position along the final straight to finish third and join David in the final.

***

"He's done it, Grandpa, he's done it!" Tom yelled excitedly as he jumped up in front of the television and rushed wildly towards his granddad who was crouching forward in his chair rubbing his eyes under his glasses. Tom dropped heavily on to the arm of the old man's chair and hugged him fondly with his usual passion.

"Careful, Tom," Frank said, raising his arm weakly to restrain the lad's enthusiasm. "Not so rough, your granddad's not so young as he used to be." He looked up at the lad and smiled. Tom noted a tear dribbling down his cheek and wiped it away with his hand.

"I know I'm a sentimental old fool," Frank said quite sheepishly, "but to see your dad doing all this is just amazing."

"I know, Granddad. He looked so good and won so convincingly. Do you think he can win the final?"

The old man struggled to pull a tissue from his pocket before answering. "I don't see why not. He looks pretty good to me." Removing his glasses, Frank gently wiped his eyes.

"And you will be there on Saturday to see him."

"I know," Tom confirmed. "I'm so excited. Are you sure you won't come, Grandpa?" Tom asked eagerly. "I know Charlie will get you a ticket if you want one."

"No, no. It's too much for me, lad. I will watch it here and see you when you get home."

They had spent the last two weeks together, both enjoying each other's company. Frank had really valued the time to regale his grandson with tales of his youth, a few amusing stories of various adventures in his life and a little background on his recent illness.

The boy had asked questions of his wife, the boy's grandmother, and he had answered with caution, not wanting to blacken her name too much in the eyes of someone so young. With Tom's help, he had organised much of the cooking. It had not been too difficult with the selection of pre-packed meals that David had left in the freezer. Each evening, they had sat in the lounge with a tray on their lap, a novelty that appealed to Tom as much as it did to him.

He had never felt such happiness. His grandson was the epitome of youthful enthusiasm and it was such a pleasure to fuel his passion for life and knowledge. He felt twenty years younger in the last week.

"Look," Tom shouted, pointing to the television as his dad's face came full screen. They both watched in total fascination as David was interviewed. Although a little nervous with his answers he came over well, giving the impression that a medal in the final was well within his capabilities.

Woken from her sleep with the shouting, Tammy stood up in her basket, shook herself and sauntered over to Frank's side where she fondly nuzzled his hand.

"Do you recognise your master's voice, old girl?" he asked, seeing her head angled slightly to one side.

They both laughed as it did look as if she was actually listening, her eyes peeled on the screen and her tail wagging gently.

"Look at Charlie!" Tom yelled, as they witnessed David's eccentric coach grab his charge and lift him forcibly from the ground before swinging him wildly round in a circle. They both laughed heartily at the bizarre antics.

"I wonder what my school mates will make of that," Tom giggled. "Roll on Saturday."

Chapter 6

"Dad, you were amazing, really amazing."

For the umpteenth time, Tom was waxing lyrical on his father's performance in the semi-final two days previous. Charlie had arranged for a cab to pick him up from the house and he had arrived at the visitor's reception at the Olympic Complex thirty minutes ago after a two-hour journey. Since then, he had never stopped talking, the excitement of the day ahead so euphoric his mind was doing cartwheels. David was happy to see him so full of energy.

"Loads of the kids at school have phoned me up. They all think you are going to win a gold medal."

"Here, sip this," said Charlie, presenting him with a banana milkshake in a tall glass in the hope it would calm him down.

"Thanks, Charlie," Tom said whilst steering the straw to his mouth and sucking enthusiastically.

"Nice one, Charlie. That should keep him quiet for a few minutes," David commented. They looked at each other and smiled.

"How's Granddad?" David asked as he watched the level of the milkshake dropping rapidly to the bottom of the glass.

"Not very good, Dad," Tom replied. The gravity in the lad's voice didn't go unnoticed. "He has trouble getting his breath, keeps falling asleep and taking pills all day long." David studied the sad expression on his son's face.

Picking up on the solemn pause, it was not the atmosphere Charlie was looking for at this crucial moment in David's preparation. He decided it was time to move on.

"Our car will be here in twenty minutes," he announced. "So I suggest we start getting ready. We will drop your dad off at the competitors' entrance and then maybe we can tackle the ice cream parlour before finding our seats in the stadium." The twinkle in Charlie's eye was sufficient incentive to encourage Tom to take a final gulp of his drink and make his way to the door.

"Wow, Charlie, that sounds great."

"Don't you want your bag?" Charlie asked, pointing to the back satchel hanging from the arm of the chair Tom had vacated.

"Oh," Tom cried with a tinge of embarrassment and ran back to pick it up. "I've got my autograph book and camera in there."

"Hope you've got your dad's autograph?" Charlie questioned.

"What do I want that for?" Tom replied, with a mischievous grin.

Saturday, the 20th of August 2012, the final day of the athletic events and what a day it was turning out to be.

News of Team GB successes had been arriving all day. In the velodrome, less than four hundred metres away, the cyclists had added another two gold medals and a silver to the tally; at Greenwich, the GB equestrian team had won a further gold and several of the boxing team were moving to their final bouts and guaranteed medals.

In the stadium, the crowd were frenzied with anticipation. Within the next few minutes, they felt they could be heralding another gold medal, a new champion and possibly a world record. David Lucas was favourite to win the final of the 1,500 metres in both the eyes of the public and the press. He would deliver, they were sure.

Seated on a bench in the holding tent within the warm-up arena, David waited patiently for the call to join the other competitors for his final.

After leaving Charlie and Tom at the arena entrance, he had had a half-hour to spare before changing and then undergoing his warm-up. Finding a quiet corner in the building, it was a welcomed chance to read the papers. Much to his astonishment, he found his picture staring back at him from the sports pages on several of the daily issues. He had even made the back page of the *Daily Mail* with a full picture and the caption, ***Golden Boy Aims for World Record.***

"I guess I'll just have to get used to this new world of celebrity," he told himself.

Not particularly enamelled with their choice of pose, he thought the close up of him nearing the finish of Thursday's race could have been a little more flattering. His eyes were closed tightly and his mouth contorted in the weirdest of grimaces. It gave the impression he was dying rather than winning, he thought.

As usual, Charlie had dispensed his final words of wisdom in the car. They had basically been a shorter version of their earlier discussions. Again, the emphasis had been on the importance of relaxing and, of course, tactics.

He was confident with so much at stake, like Mo's race last Saturday, it would become more tactical than a race against the clock. But as Charlie said, anything can happen out there, so he had to keep his wits about him and just see how it panned out.

Up to that moment, he had kept his emotions under control, that was, however, until Charlie dropped him off at the competitors' entrance. Charlie and Tom had both climbed out of the car to wish him good luck.

Despite trying to display a calm exterior, the serious look on Charlie's face could not disguise the affection and nerves he was feeling as he grabbed his head, with tears in his eyes, and kissed his neck passionately.

"This is it, Dave, the big one. Just keep your head and all our dreams will be realised."

"Thanks, Charlie. Thanks for everything," he said, the words underlining the importance of what this race meant to him, and Charlie, of course. He had difficulty in controlling the emotions about to escape. No sooner had he pulled himself together than Tom jumped at him, folding his young arms tightly around his neck. With his feet dangling off the ground, he gave him the biggest hug he could ever remember.

"Good luck, Dad, I just know you're going to win."

"I hope so, Son. I'll do my best, I promise." After such a send-off, he made a quick escape to the warm-up area.

"Will the competitors for the final of the 1,500 metres please go to the marshalling area at the entrance to the arena."

This was it, the beginning of the final chapter, the date with destiny he had dreamt of for so long. *Just do your best*, David told himself before setting off to join his fellow competitors who were already assembling in a group under the supervision of a marshal. James rushed forward to meet him as he approached and held out his hand. They shook firmly.

"Good luck, mate," he said with just a hint of nerves as their eyes scanned each other searchingly. Both harboured the strange concoction of fear and excitement for what was to be the biggest challenge of their young lives.

"And you, mate," David replied.

Once all twelve competitors for the event were present, they formed a line ready for their entrance to the main arena. David was positioned behind the lanky Kenyan, Nixon Kiplin, who was to lead the group, with James three places behind him. By now, they were familiar with all the competitors from their event. A few nods and pleasantries were exchanged as they stood waiting for their instructions to move.

At last, they were on their way through the tunnel, the now familiar drone of the crowd increasing with every step as they drew closer to the entrance. As they broke out to the daylight, the reaction was extraordinary. A swell of sound seemed to descend upon them like a tropical storm. Shouting, shrieking, clapping, all merged into a cacophony of bedlam that was both uplifting and ecstatic. It continued unabated for what seemed minutes.

In the front row of the main stand, Charlie and Tom joined the throng in the celebration of the Team GB competitors. Charlie had purchased a sizeable Union Jack flag on a pole for Tom which he was waving frantically as his father paraded in front of them.

"Come on, Dad!" he yelled joyously, whilst turning to Charlie to share a beaming smile. It was definitely the greatest day of his life, one to be etched in his brain forever.

David thought he had witnessed the ultimate warmth of the crowd in the last few days but this was something really special. Both his and James's names were being chanted around the arena as they marched to the starting area. Once there, they had a few minutes before receiving instructions to remove their tracksuits.

No sooner had the competitors lined up along the starting line in the same order as their entry than a cameraman was before them and they were, one by one, being introduced to the crowd and the television audience across the world.

Nixon Kiplin was first and smiled proudly as a torrent of applause drifted down from the stands. He raised a hand in acknowledgement.

David was next. The crowd anticipated his call, so that, no sooner had the announcer began reading his name than his words were obliterated by the sheer outburst of response, a true breath-taking roar of fanaticism, love and expectation, which permeated the arena from every corner. The crowd had definitely taken David to their hearts and were looking for him to deliver the ultimate prize, a gold medal. It continued for an embarrassingly long time before the announcer could move on. Totally stunned but highly delighted, David had to remind himself of the job in hand. Shyly, he gave the camera a gentle wave before refocusing his concentration on the race ahead.

Again, when the time came for James's introduction the crowd raised their response to titanic levels which were now becoming the norm for Team GB competitors.

Finally, the preliminaries were complete and the focus was now on the runners as they stood hunched at the start waiting their final instructions. The air seemed to crackle with anticipation.

"Get ready," the starter commanded, setting off a slight stutter of movement along the rank. The sharp report of the pistol unleashed a crashing roar from the crowd that shook the arena with its force.

The runners took off in a disorderly break with Nixon Kiplin sprinting to the front for an early lead. His compatriot, Silas Cheboi, followed suit and dropped in two metres behind. At the first bend, David found himself in fifth place with Dan Theobald of the USA on his inner. Although the pace was reasonably fast for the first lap, there were no visible signs of discomfort from any of the competitors.

Entering the second lap, Nixon Kiplin had stolen a five-metre break from the rest of the field who seemed content to let him go at what appeared to be a breakneck pace at this stage. Bunched together quite tightly, the general feeling was that he would come back to them as the race progressed.

The order remained unchanged throughout the lap but the long languid strides of Nixon Kiplin were carrying him further ahead. With the third lap approaching, he was now ten metres clear and still moving strongly.

David, although running wide at Theobald's shoulder, was happy with his position and the pace at this stage. Like the others, he felt Nixon Kiplin was pushing his limits at the head of the field. Entering the third lap, he was moving comfortably but decided it was time to close up. He felt this would give him more opportunity to manoeuvre in the latter stages. At the back of the field, several were beginning to find the pace too hot with a group of four gradually dropping away.

Lengthening his stride just slightly, David moved ahead of Dan Theobald, past Yusef Farga and into the slipstream of Silas Cheboi, who appeared to be struggling. The crowd, sensing the ease of his movements, urged him on with a roar of approval. The energy levels were raised a further notch as David took

Silas Cheboi in a couple of strides and looked to be setting his sights on the leading Kenyan, who still appeared to be running well within himself.

The announcement from the commentator that the pace was opening up the opportunity of a world record, sent a fresh buzz of anticipation through the crowd

Hitting the back straight for the third time, Yusef Farga fell away to be passed by a group of three which included James Thompson. Seemingly with little effort, David lengthened his stride again and began closing the gap between himself and Nixon Kiplin. Stride by stride, he was gaining on the Kenyan. The crowd were going wild as he came to the home straight for the penultimate time and cruised to the Kenyan's shoulder.

Nixon was not, however, willing to surrender tamely and increased his pace in response, an action that drew further effort from David as they hit the final lap in perfect symmetry, each testing the other to the full. All eyes were now firmly fixed on the leading pair.

"They're neck and neck," confirmed the commentator breathlessly, before raising the crowd's anticipation further with the announcement: "This could definitely be a world record?"

Along the back straight for the final time, they ran as one, seeming joined together, not willing to concede an inch as an epic battle of mind and body was played out to the full. Stride after stride, they were eating the track on their way to a common dream that neither was prepared to concede.

In the hope the intimidating pace would take its toll on the Kenyan, David collected himself for one last effort as they drew to the final bend. He kicked hard into it. Nixon went with him for a few strides, but then David sensed the break, just slightly at first, but then, a feeling he was away, drawing two, three metres clear. He felt so good as he moved into the straight, the gap now opening with every stride. For the first time he sensed victory.

"David Lucas has a world record in his sights," the announcer shouted excitedly. The joy of the crowd was contagious, escalating, it would seem, with every stride.

With forty metres to the line, David spurred himself onwards, a feeling of invincibility growing with every stride. The gold medal was now his for the taking. The feeling was, however, short-lived. Without warning, the pain hit him. So sudden, so excruciating, so extreme, it was as if an arrow had penetrated his calf. He was thrown to the ground with the reaction. A shock wave of emotion blasted the stadium. As one, the crowd, struck dumb in disbelief, were hushed. Even the announcer was temporarily silenced in bewilderment.

On the track, Nixon Kiplin could not believe the scene before him. As David, with seemingly the race in the bag, moving strongly and five metres clear, keeled over on to the track holding his right leg. Unbelieving of his good fortune, Nixon maintained his waning stride and fell over the finishing line with his arms aloft. Two metres behind, the unknown Brazilian, Carlos Ponte, finished strongly as did James Thompson to snatch the bronze medal in the last couple of strides.

But all attention was on David as he struggled to his feet in stunned disbelief. Clutching his leg, he staggered painfully down the track towards the finishing line in an effort to complete the race. The crowd, realising the heroics of his actions, were now behind him all the way as he wobbled precariously on his damaged leg. The applause of the crowd, the raw emotion of what they were witnessing, was of another dimension.

The drama, however, had not completely played out. From seemingly nowhere, a man appeared and ran towards David. Throwing an arm around his back, he gave him the support he badly needed.

"Lean on me, Davy boy, and we will finish this together," Charlie said, breathing heavily, as they started to cover the final twenty-five metres to the line.

"It's Charlie Greaves, David Lucas' coach," the announcer gustily shouted.

The crowd, lulled temporarily by the unfolding event, renewed their enthusiasm to its extreme as the heart-wrenching scenario was played out to the full.

With Charlie's assistance, David hobbled painfully towards the finishing line, each step an agonising reminder of his injury. When finally he made it, he collapsed to the ground, Charlie unable to support him further.

Within seconds, photographers were everywhere, swarming around in an effort to catch what was likely to be the most dramatic story of the day. David, traumatised in agony, his head spinning, thought he would pass out in the surrounding havoc as he lay on his back, looking up at the sky. When a stretcher team arrived only minutes later, they had difficulty in forcing a path through the throng of pressmen, all so eager for a slice of the action.

It was several minutes before he was lifted to the stretcher and carried from the stadium, his face etched with pain. Charlie remained by his side. There wasn't a single person seated, everyone was on their feet, applauding the passion of the scene they had just witnessed.

Sadly, the mood of the crowd had been numbed despite the gain of a further bronze medal. A deathly blanket of sorrow hung heavily over the stadium. In a split second, unquestionable success of a world record and a further gold medal had been snatched from their countryman. The applause continued long after David's departure.

Chapter 7

In the seclusion of the medical tent, away from the frenzied atmosphere of the arena, David was able to collect his thoughts and consider fully the implications of the disastrous event that had befallen him. Charlie was still by his side as the two bearers lowered his stretcher to a cradle.

As soon as the men had left, David raised his eyes to Charlie, the pain of defeat written so clearly on his face.

"I'm so, so sorry, Charlie," he said, his voice quivering as he tried desperately to control his emotions. He felt like crying to release the heart-felt pain but even that would not come. Charlie only had to look at him to see the torment he was suffering. He caught hold of his hand and gripped it tightly.

"Davy, you were magnificent out there, absolutely magnificent," he said, with the truest sincerity. "As far as everyone watching that race today is concerned, you were the winner. A world record was on the cards. It was all yours and only the quirkiest act of fate has stolen it from you. So don't beat yourself up. I'm proud of you. As proud as I would be if you had actually won it. There was nothing more you could do. It looks to me as if you have torn your hamstring and from my experience of this it may be several months before you will be able to run again."

David felt his eyes stinging with tears. "Charlie, we did it together, it was a partnership all the way," he said with the same deep feeling. "Who won it?" he asked as an afterthought, suddenly realising he was oblivious to the outcome of the race

"Nixon Kiplin finished very tired to take the gold, closely followed by the Mexican, Carlos Ponte, with James snatching the bronze."

"James took the bronze!" David shouted excitedly, the smile on his face highlighting his pleasure in hearing this news.

"I thought you would be pleased to hear that," Charlie added.

"He'll be over the moon," David confirmed, the welcomed news raising his spirits a notch. "That makes me feel a bit better." It was a few moments before he spoke again as he gave some thought to what the success would mean to his friend and his family.

"I should imagine they'll take me to hospital for an X-ray, Charlie. So, can you take Tom back to the hotel tonight as we originally planned. Hopefully, I'll be brought back to the apartment after the hospital. I'll stay there tonight and phone you tomorrow morning to see where we stand. I would still like to stay for the Closing Ceremony if possible but I'll see how the leg feels. If that's all right?"

"Yes, that's fine, Dave," Charlie replied with a smile, a sad one at that. "I'm enjoying my time with Tom."

"I hope you're not spoiling him too much?"

"Would I do that?" said Charlie with a twinkle in his eye which confirmed he would and probably already had.

"Tell him I'm sorry I didn't win. They won't allow him in here so I can't see him before I go, but I'll phone him as soon as I can," David said.

"I'm sure he will understand, especially as you are the new Team GB hero."

"Some hero, without a medal."

"As I said, Dave, don't beat yourself up."

"I'll try, Charlie, but it won't be easy."

Charlie could see that. He was finding it difficult enough to hide his own disappointment but he smiled again all the same.

Chapter 8

David couldn't remember when he had ever felt so low. For the umpteenth time, he closed his eyes but, as before, the images of the fateful seconds of his race just kept reappearing. Finally, accepting the situation, he pulled himself up from the pillow and turned on the bedside lamp. It was 5:20 A.M.

He had returned to the apartment from hospital just after ten o'clock with the unfortunate news the injury to his leg was the most serious, a grade 3, whatever that meant. Apparently, it was a complete muscle tear and likely to take three to four months to mend before he would be able to undertake any serious exercise. Heavily bandaged just below the knee, the support provided some relief from the continuous throbbing. He thought a couple of paracetamol would help him to sleep but it was not the case.

He was suddenly aware a huge chapter of his life had come to an end. The gold medal had been the ultimate target. In fact, he and Charlie had spoken little of life beyond yesterday's event. Was the daily routine of training, which he had thrived on for eighteen months, about to cease? The joy of running he had discovered in the last few years would never leave him, he was sure of that.

The truth was, he had come so close to winning the gold medal. It had been a pipe dream in the early days, maybe not to Charlie, but to him, but as the months passed, the confidence Charlie gradually instilled in him, gave him the belief that the target was possible and it was, as yesterday proved. But why did it have to go wrong? Why was the golden goose stolen from them in those final seconds? Lost in his depression for a few minutes, thoughts of his son came to his rescue.

"Unbelievable, but I have to move on," he told himself in an effort to inject some positive thinking to his current mood. Focusing on Tom had always been a good way of clearing his mind and setting new targets, and this was the direction his heart was telling him to go.

During his two-hour stay in the A&E Department of the hospital, whilst waiting the results of his scan, he had phoned Tom on his mobile.

"Hi, Son, sorry I lost," he announced simply as a casual introduction.

"Dad, you were magnificent. Everybody knows you would have won. Loads of my mates from school phoned me to say how unlucky you were. They all think you were so brave to get up off the track and walk to the finish. You're an absolute hero in their eyes."

"Walk! I think it was more of a limp," David joked.

The enthusiasm in the lad's voice did wonders for his then current frame of mind. Tom was obviously on a high from the whole day, running off, one after the other, the names of celebrities he had seen and the different events that had caught his imagination.

"Charlie's looking after you all right then, I take it?" he asked at one point.

"He's brilliant, Dad," was the enthusiastic reply. "We're playing on the X-Box at the moment."

"Charlie won't know what to do," was David's immediate response.

"You're joking, he's already beaten me once."

Speaking to Tom had provided a little light relief from his melancholic thoughts, a feeling further enhanced, ten minutes later, when he phoned his father.

"Hi, Dad, just thought I'd give you a ring to see how you were after watching your son flop on the track," he opened the conversation light-heartedly.

"Son, don't say that," Frank immediately admonished, the tone of his voice quite severe. "My boy, you were so unlucky. I was so proud of you, I can't tell you." He sensed his dad choking with the words.

"Guess I was a bit unlucky, but, that's life," he said, trying to lighten the conversation. "Anyway, how are you?" he asked, changing the subject purposefully.

"I'm fine, I've been really enjoying myself with Tom. He's a great little lad, you know?"

"I know," he replied calmly. They spoke for ten minutes, Frank regaling him fully with stories of various episodes that had taken place during the last week. They had obviously enjoyed their time together. After a while, the old man started wheezing as though he was having difficulty in breathing, and David thought it best to say goodbye.

"Tom and Charlie will be home tomorrow, and I may stay for the Closing Ceremony."

"That's fine, Son, enjoy yourself," were his final words before a further fit of coughing brought their chat to an abrupt end. With his father's health now a priority, it was his intention to investigate it a little more fully in the future months.

Ten minutes after making this second call, the results of his scan were presented to him. His heart sank with the news.

**

Reaching for the floor from his bed, a shot of pain from the back of his calf brought the doctor's words flooding back. *It will take several months to heal fully.*

He decided to forego shaving but even a wash from the bowl took ages in his current state of incapacity. It was almost seven o'clock by the time he was ready to leave the apartment. The hospital had given him a crutch and with a little practice, he soon found the advantage of taking the weight from his damaged leg. Not really hungry, he thought the short walk through the village to the food hall would do him good. He would have a bit of breakfast, see how he felt and then make a decision as to whether to stay for the evening ceremony.

It was a beautiful morning, the sun already at its summery best. A few harmless clouds could not spoil the perfection of the turquoise sky.

There was no one about as he closed the main door and made his way through the village to pick up the path leading to the food hall. The fresh air worked wonders on his mood as he hobbled slowly along reminiscing on the events of the past two weeks. Memories of the friendships, the camaraderie of so many nations brought together under one roof, would remain with him throughout his life, he was sure. By the time he reached the entrance to the food hall, he felt his spirits finally rising with the thoughts of a new day and some new challenges ahead.

Inside, he had never seen it so empty but realised it was possibly the first time he had visited the food hall before eight o'clock. There was a small group seated around a table to one side as he entered. From their accents, it was obvious they were French and in vigorous discussion. Two other couples were present on separate tables and looked to be enjoying the pleasure of a full breakfast.

After closing the door behind him, he made for the English bar on the far side of the hall. Leaning heavily on his crutch, he had only taken a few steps when he heard someone clap. This seemed to be the cue for a full show of applause as one after the other the party of French contestants stood and beaming eagerly in his direction, clapped him across the floor.

Totally embarrassed, he had to stop and wave. "Thank you very much," he said courteously.

"Well done, monsieur, you were very brave," the young man who had started the clapping replied boldly. "You should have won. We feel so sorry for you."

"Thank you. That's very kind."

He turned to continue his passage across the hall only to notice the other two couples were also adding their applause from their respective tables. He nodded in acknowledgement.

Selecting a tray at the entrance to the food queue, he added a plate, knife, two pieces of toast, some butter, marmalade and a cup of cappuccino coffee before finding himself a table by the wall. Now feeling tired from his cumbersome walk, he chose a chair facing the wall and stretched out his damaged leg. He hoped his anti-social behaviour was not too obvious but a little solitude suited his mood, especially after the reception a few minutes earlier.

Over the next thirty minutes, the hall began to fill out as the early risers arrived for their morning nutrition. With only a few events remaining, most were now free to sample the less healthy diets their training programmes had prohibited for so long. As the tables were occupied one by one, you could sense from the atmosphere the excitement building for the Closing Ceremony now less than twelve hours away.

Taking a final sip of his coffee, David stretched out lazily in his chair before contemplating the strenuous return to his apartment. He was about to move when he was aware of a young girl in a black dress arrive at his table.

"Hello," she said politely whilst stretching her hand towards him. "My name is Fiona Bach and I'm from the BBC." David shook her hand. "I'm so sorry about your unfortunate accident yesterday. We would like to invite you to join the morning programme to give us your side of the story. If that's okay?"

"At the moment, it's pretty poor," David joked.

"I'm sure you are really disappointed, I know I would be, but the public would like to hear from you. You're front page on most of the Sunday papers, you know?" He didn't.

Public relations was a big part of Fiona's job and she was very good at it. It was not long before he had agreed to return to the stadium for a 9.30 slot on the morning programme.

With half an hour to kill before his appointment with the BBC, he had visited the shop and purchased two papers, both of which had a full front-page picture of himself, as Fiona had told him. He was lying on the track in agony whilst feverishly gripping his damaged leg. The headline on one was *British Hero Denied Gold* and the other *The Agony of British Hero.* The look on his face was testament to the ordeal he had suffered. A wry smile came to his lips as he thought he couldn't imagine Tom's friends hanging one of these pictures on their bedroom walls.

Much to his surprise, he enjoyed his interview with the BBC. Sitting in the green room beforehand, he had felt a little nervous but with a glass of wine inside him, once on the couch, facing the two highly skilled interviewers, he had felt relaxed and confident. Like everyone else, they were full of sympathy for the terrible tragedy that had befallen him and wished him well for a speedy recovery and his return to the track. The whole thing had been a warming experience.

By the time he had returned to his apartment, the day had caught up with him. He was feeling tired, the leg was aching continuously and he was longing for a good night's sleep. He quickly dismissed any thoughts of attending the Closing Ceremony. He would return home with Charlie and Tom, and they would watch the final embers of what had been a truly memorable but heart-wrenching period of their lives on the television in the comfort of his own lounge.

Chapter 9

Seven days had passed since his fateful day on the Olympic track, seven heavy days that David would describe as some of the cruellest he had ever experienced. Not as black as those hours waiting at Tom's bedside, of course, but days filled with regrets for what might have been. The scar on his mind was still very fresh. There was a bleakness about his life he could just not dismiss, however hard he was trying.

Eating his breakfast in the kitchen when the phone rang, he picked it up half-heartedly.

"Hi, David. I've got some good news for you," Carol Thorson conveyed excitedly.

"That'll make a change," David responded coldly with little thought, immediately realising how rude it could have been interpreted. "I'm sorry, Carol, I didn't mean it to sound like that."

She laughed loudly. "I know you didn't, no offence taken I can assure you."

Carol had been a brick since Rachel's departure, taking over the reins of the business with little assistance and running it with what appeared to be meticulous efficiency. With him absent for most of the time, she had received very little help. Rachel had left her the details of companies and tradesmen she did business with and Carol just took it from there.

Obviously, the substantial rise he had promised her had been a warm incentive but even so, there were always other factors to consider. He knew she was a single mother with two young daughters to care for and wondered how she was coping with the extra burden.

"Listen," she continued. "One of our delivery men came in today and said he saw Rachel a few days ago waitressing in a pub in Sussex."

"Really," said David, suddenly alert to every word.

"Yes, but the only thing is, he doesn't know the name of the pub. He went on a stag-do with a group of his mates to a race meeting at Plumpton in East Sussex. Not driving, it sounds as if he had an awful lot to drink. They stopped at the pub on the way home to have a meal and there was Rachel apparently serving at the tables. He was sure it was her because when he spoke to her, he swears she recognised him. Although he had no idea of the name of the pub, he said they stopped about an hour after leaving the racecourse before reaching the M25. He thought they were possibly still in Sussex but couldn't be sure."

"Well, that's wonderful. I'm sure you realise I miss her—"

"I know you do," Carol cut in. "I see it in your face every time you come down here."

"It's that obvious, is it?" David asked sadly.

"I'm afraid so. But I can tell you, David, she really loved you, she told me so many times and I should imagine she still does. She was so lost trying to understand Tom's behaviour and with you having so much on your plate with the running, she was afraid to talk about it. It's a great shame but I'm sure you can put it right."

"Thanks, Carol. It sounds as if it might be a needle in a haystack job but I'll certainly try my best."

"That's good. I'd love to see you both back together again. You make a lovely couple."

"Thanks for that," David said pleasantly. "And thank you for all your efforts in the business. I don't know how I could have managed without you in the last few months."

"I've enjoyed every minute. It's a new life. I've had to make some changes to my lifestyle but it's all fitted in quite nicely and I have money to spend on my two girls which is great."

"That's good," David said. "Well, I had better set about my detective work and see if I can find Rachel."

"That'a boy, go and get her," was Carol's enthusiastic response.

No sooner had he put the phone down than he had his mobile in his hand searching the Maps application for Plumpton Racecourse. It told him the journey was 153 miles south, the other side of the M25. The racecourse was clearly marked but his problem was deciding which route they had taken on their return journey to reach the M25. There were two main A roads as far as he could see, either of which looked a possibility but also a B road that ran almost directly to the motorway. Which route would they have taken? It was a pin job as far as he could see but he just had to give it a go.

Chapter 10

Looking at his watch, it was almost four o'clock. David was tired and hungry.

He had left home just after 8 A.M. but a delay on the M11 had increased the journey time by a full hour. The four-mile queue that had welcomed him just after Stansted Airport had shunted along at infrequent intervals for what seemed ages. Not until the Chelmsford junction had it cleared, leaving the traffic to speed away to an open road. As so many times before, there was no sign of road works, accidents or in fact, any incidents that would cause such a hold-up, leaving the motorists mystified. Fortunately, the M25 had been a lot more friendly and he had made good time crossing the Thames at Dartford and heading for Sussex. He made a mental note to pay the toll charge for the bridge first thing in the morning.

He had finally arrived at Plumpton Racecourse just before twelve o'clock after taking one of the two main A roads. Despite his mind being elsewhere, he was impressed by the beauty of the surrounding countryside. The leafy lanes, open commons, scenic valley woodlands and the dainty villages adding a charm to an area that seemed to be blessed with a tranquillity nothing short of majestic.

From the racecourse, he had retraced his route northwards for forty-five minutes, purposefully keeping to a comfortable speed around forty miles an hour. Possibly, young men on a day out would have driven a lot quicker but he had to cover as many contingencies as he could.

From here, his search began. The first pub he came to was the *Old Friar,* a wide fronted building with a large car park, patio and a dozen or more wooden benches sporting over-sized umbrellas. Most of the seats were occupied with an assortment of young and old. Being Tuesday, the young were likely to be businessmen and women from the local village enjoying a quick break before their afternoon work session and the old, just pensioners enjoying the fruits of their retirement.

Weaving his path around the outside tables, he made his way to the main entrance. Inside, it was even more crowded and the noise so loud that your initial reaction was to cover your ears. Every seat and table seemed to be taken with people talking garrulously in groups whilst sipping at their drinks and taking occasional bites at the food in front of them. Politely jostling through the throng of standing customers, he finally reached the bar where a young man with a Mohican hairstyle, tattooed arms and a painful looking ring through his lip gave him a welcoming smile.

"Can I help you, sir?" he asked.

"Yes, I'm looking for a young lady called Rachel who I am hoping may work here," David said openly.

The young man gave the matter some thought before replying. "No, I'm afraid there's no one here of that name."

"I suppose you don't know anybody of that name, early twenties, who works in *any* of the local pubs?" David said casually, fishing for a possible lead.

"No, I'm afraid not, mate, nobody comes to mind. There's lots of pubs around. You will 'ave to keep trying."

"Well, thanks anyway," David said on leaving.

"Good luck," followed him out the door.

By four o'clock, he had tried the same approach at twelve different pubs all the way along the two main A roads and was now just two miles from the M25. There had been a Rachel at the sixth one and for just a moment, his hopes had been raised. That was until she had appeared from the kitchen. At forty years old, six foot tall and fourteen stone, he could only apologise for the inconvenience.

Tired and hungry, the inspiration that had carried him through the day was slowly ebbing. His bad leg was beginning to throb mercilessly. He had dispensed with the crutch mid-week, a move that would probably not receive the approval of the hospital.

After ordering some food at the bar, he found a table in a small alcove of his latest and possibly last visit of the day. Aptly named *the Golden Swan*, it overlooked a millstream where two of the birds and their young were gracing the tranquil waters. It was pleasant enough with an airy feeling, stone flagged flooring, a mahogany bar and comfortable high-backed wooden benches. At least, it was peaceful, with just one young couple making eyes at each other on a table in front of the mullioned windows.

He had to attend to some office work at the nursery tomorrow but would return on Thursday and go through the same routine on the other roads he had marked as possible routes to the motorway. No way would he give up until he had investigated every pub in Sussex and Surrey if necessary.

It was nearly twenty minutes before his food arrived.

"Sorry for the delay," the young waitress apologised as she placed a generous plate of fish and chips on the table. "Our chef likes to go out for a smoke about this time."

"No problem," said David. "This looks worth waiting for," he added, on eyeing the delicious meal before him.

"They tell me your looking for a young girl called Rachel who's a waitress in one of the local pubs?"

"Yes, that's right," said David, raising his eyes with interest.

"Well, my girlfriend shares a flat with a Rachel who works in *the Farmer's Arms* at Nutley which is about twenty miles from here."

"How old is she?"

"I would say early twenties. Very pretty."

"Light brown hair?" David further questioned.

"Last time I saw her, yes."

"Do you know how long she's been around?"

"Only a few weeks, I'm sure."

David had suddenly lost his appetite. "Can you give me directions to get to *the Farmer's Arms,* please?" he asked, feeling a sudden jolt in his stomach.

Carrying the detail in his head, he paid the young girl for the meal, adding a generous five-pound tip to the bill. After thanking her for the information, he made a rather hurried exit from the pub.

***

The Farmer's Arms was not quite what he was expecting. Smaller than the majority he had visited during the day, his first reaction was that it could do with a good coat of paint. Two of the letters, the *a* and the *r*, had almost disappeared from the sign which was drooping sadly at an angle from its supporting beam. Outside, two old men, scruffily over-dressed in thick coats as if it was winter, sat chatting amiably whilst taking occasional sips from their pint glasses on the table.

David parked his car in the rather ill-kept area at the side of the pub, backing into a large bunch of tall stinging nettles in an effort to leave sufficient space for cars to pass between his front bumper and the pub. Nodding at the two gentlemen on passing, he made his way inside. It was empty apart from a man behind the bar. As he walked towards him, he looked up.

"Yes, can I help you?" he asked in a tone lacking any warmth.

"I understand a young lady is working for you by the name of Rachel?"

"Are you the police?" the man asked, a sudden look of fear clouding his face.

"No, I'm not," David laughed. "I'm an old boyfriend." The man looked slightly relieved. With a sigh, he looked at the clock on the rear wall.

"She'll be in about half-six and don't hold her up because she's here to work," he growled. "And if ye're staying here you can buy a pint or bugger off. Do yer understand me?"

"I'm so overwhelmed by your charm," David replied in a caustic tone. "I'll have a pint of lager please."

The man scowled, his bleak watery eyes showing little emotion above the dense and untamed beard that covered the bottom portion of his face. David sensed an air of roguery about him.

"That'll be three pounds and fifty pence," he said as he thumped the glass down purposely on the bar so that a splash of liquid bounced over the rim and dribbled down the side.

"Not cheap," David said as a final come back before taking a seat at a dirty table just inside the door. Looking at his watch, it was only half-five and an hour to kill. However long the wait, he was determined to make the pint in front of him last. He caught sight of a discarded newspaper on the chair beside him and started reading to pass the time. It was yesterday's issue but he found a couple of articles inside that were of interest.

Engrossed by a story of a young soldier who had lost both his legs fighting in Afghanistan and was now part of a team tackling an expedition to the Antarctic, he was unaware of the time. Only when the barman spoke did he react.

"This man wants to see yer," he announced to the newcomer at the door.

David looked up. Standing just inside the door, Rachel stood rigid, her eyes wide in disbelief.

"Rachel...!"

"David...!"

Stunned, they both just stared at each other, their mouths tweaking a slight smile which rapidly grew to something more meaningful.

"What are you doing here?" she asked in a voice quivering with emotion.

"I've come to see you," he replied calmly, drinking in the warmth of her eyes. "To apologise for my behaviour."

"You haven't got anything to apologise for. It was my fault."

"No, it wasn't.! Look, just sit down for a minute," he said, drawing a chair from under the table. She did as he told her. No sooner was she seated than their eyes locked into each other's again with an intensity.

"Rachel, I'm sorry I behaved as I did. I was wrong to blame you for Tom's accident."

"No, you weren't," she corrected him. "I should have told you more about what was going on."

"Maybe," he conceded. "But I'm sure you weren't aware of the company he was keeping?"

"That's true," she agreed.

Looking deeply into her eyes, he felt the same prickle of excitement he had experienced at their first meeting. The sweet smell of her perfume filled his nostrils and made his senses swim. He fought back a strong urge to take her in his arms, and kiss her there and then.

"Rachel," the po-faced barman shouted gruffly. "You need to get to the kitchen." There was no response.

"Rachel, I've missed you so much. Will you come back to me, please?" David pleaded. They were drawn together like strong magnets. Their eyes held each other's with a force that wouldn't let go. Tears came to her eyes. She made no effort to stem them.

"Yes," she whispered huskily and then, "Yes, yes, yes," in quick succession, each one louder than the one before, so that she was almost shouting.

"Sod it," he swore, losing himself as he rose gingerly to his feet. Balancing precariously for just a moment, he put out both his arms to her and she came to him, her eyes shining with that old familiarity. He pulled her to him, and kissed her lips in a wild and spontaneous act of passion.

"Rachel, if you don't get to the kitchen, you don't have a job." It was a final warning in a voice as hostile as the pub. There was still no reaction as they remained locked together, lost in the tenderness of their kiss. Eventually, they separated and David took her hand firmly and led her to the door. Before leaving, he turned to face the barman who was glaring viciously at them both.

David caught his stare and returned it with one sharper. "Up yours," he said simply as they took a step outside.

Chapter 11

The three runners and their dog approached the bank separating the flood plain from the farmland beyond. The dog, a golden Labrador, led the way, making the ascent with ease, and on reaching the summit, turned to watch the humans make their effort up the steep incline, all the time her tail wagging feverishly, showing her pleasure.

The young woman was the first to start the climb, already breathing heavily as she prepared herself for the challenge. Close behind her, the boy, just a few months short of becoming a teenager, put in a determined effort to close the gap.

"I'll beat you to the top, Rachel," he shouted joyously as he sprinted towards her in pursuit. The man at the rear watched in amusement as the two of them scrambled excitedly up the bank, the boy passing the woman with some ease before she grabbed his leg and brought him down.

"That's not fair," he shouted, laughing as he picked himself up and took off to close the slight advantage her action had given her. Half way up, both were struggling for breath as the boy drew level. Not willing to concede victory, she gave it one final effort, pumping her arms and legs vigorously to hold her ground. A few paces and they were almost level. Reaching the top, both stopped simultaneously, laughing at their foolishness, their bodies bent forward as they fought for air in long breathy gasps.

"I would have beaten you easily if you hadn't have grabbed my leg," Tom told her with a wide grin on his face.

"At least, we beat your dad," she said, still panting heavily from the effort of her climb. They both looked back towards the lower ground where David was just starting the ascent. With long comfortable strides, he came towards them smilingly broadly as he closed on the path where they were now standing.

"Like a couple of kids you two are," he said breathing easily and showing little sign of exertion.

"How's your leg?" Rachel asked.

"Considering I only started running a week ago, very good. Feels a little tight in the calf but the consultant said it will wear off."

Tom looked at his watch. "Are we opening the presents when we get home, Dad?" he enquired in the hope of a positive response.

"If Charlie's arrived, we can," David told him.

"That's good."

"I thought we would eat about three o'clock if that's okay with everyone. The turkey should be nicely cooked by then," Rachel said, eyeing the two males.

"That's fine with me," Tom confirmed.

"And me," David added. "Eating our Christmas lunch while we watch the Queen's Speech is just the job." With this, he threw his arm around his girlfriend's neck and pulled her gently towards him before kissing her neck. "You're running well for somebody who has only just started."

"You don't know my talents, my love. I keep myself fit running the business. It won't be long before I'm beating you." She had the familiar sparkle in her eye that had a way of reaching right inside him. He hugged her fondly.

"We had better get back to Granddad," said Tom, inspecting his watch. "He'll start worrying if we're much longer."

"Where's Tammy?" David enquired realising he hadn't seen her for some time.

"She won't be far away," Tom said with confidence before calling her name. Immediately she bounded out of the bushes and threw herself at him. "No chance of losing you, is there, girl?" he said cheerfully as he fondled her ears before pushing her away.

"Okay, let's go," said David, breaking into a steady jog.

All three of them started running comfortably side by side with Tammy leading the way a few metres ahead, enjoying the musky scents of the pathway. A hundred metres on and the old stile came into view. By now, Tammy was a good way ahead. They were all watching her closely, anticipating her disappearance through the gap in the tall grass under the wooden structure when, quite unexpectedly, she came to a standstill as if frozen in her tracks.

As they approached, they were amazed to see her body tensed rigid facing the stile, a low guttural growl escaping her jaws, her lips pulled back to expose her teeth.

"What's up, girl?" David asked her. He was shocked. He had never seen her behave in this way before. Once at her side, he rubbed his hand along her back. There was no response. She just remained in the same stance, her eyes fixed rigidly on the stile as if she was seeing a ghost. All the time, the growling continued.

Lost as to the cause of her behaviour, David climbed the stile. Standing on the bottom rung, he was surprised to see what looked to be an old man sitting on a tree stump some twenty metres ahead. In front of him, a large dog was sprawled out cleaning himself.

"So that's what frightened you, is it, old girl?" he said smiling bemusedly. "I didn't think you were scared of anything." With this, he went over to her and slipping his hand through her collar, pulled her gently towards the stile. He sensed straight away she was not willing to move as her back stiffened in an effort to retaliate.

"Don't be silly, girl," he told her as he drew her lead from his pocket and attached it to her collar.

"What's up, Dad?" Tom asked on realising there was a problem.

"I don't really know, Son, but Tammy seems to be scared of a dog on the other side of the stile."

"That's strange," Tom confirmed.

"I agree. If I go the other side, can you pass her lead through the gap and I'll pull her through?"

"Will do."

David climbed the stile and bent down to receive the lead from Tom. Tammy did her best to hold her ground, stubbornly refusing to move, so that Tom had to use all his strength to drag her forward. Seeing his dad's hand appear from the other side, he dropped the lead into it.

"Got you," David said as he started pulling. It needed all his strength but eventually, her head appeared, her eyes still pop-eyed as they glared frighteningly at the dog ahead. She cowered to David's side, keeping her body low to the grass as she was forcibly moved. By this time, Rachel and Tom had climbed the stile and were close behind.

The old man remained seated as they approached, the dog still at his feet. David smiled in a friendly gesture. "I don't think our dog likes yours," he said as an explanation of Tammy's behaviour. There was no response, no eye contact. It was as if they didn't exist. "Happy Christmas," David added, partly in fun, as a reaction to the lack of politeness.

Only when they had passed, did the old man rise and coughing violently, make a move towards the stile. "Come on, Castro," he said gruffly between deep intakes of breath. The dog gave him a steely look, before dragging himself off the ground and following in close pursuit.

The three of them huddled together not wanting to talk too loudly whilst he was still within hearing range.

"What a strange man," Rachel said eventually.

"You're not kidding," David agreed.

"Have you ever seen him before?"

"Never," David said with some certainty but as he spoke, a thought came to him. "I wonder if that could be the dog that attacked Tammy when I fell in the river last year."

"Well, he's certainly got a lot to answer for if it is," Rachel said in a serious tone.

"We're nearly home," Tom announced as they reached the farm lane. "I can't wait to see Charlie and Granddad." With this, the old man and his dog were soon forgotten. David had to smile as he picked up on Tom's remark.

"What are you smiling at?" Rachel enquired.

"Do you realise, eighteen months ago, I didn't know I had a father and now I seem to have two."

"And…eighteen months ago, you didn't realise you were the fastest 1,500 metre runner in the world," Rachel added.

"But, alas, you will never see my name in the *Guinness Book of Records*," David said with a tinge of sadness.

THE END

Apology

The final of the 1,500 metres at the London Olympics 2012 was won by Taoufik Makhloufi from Algeria in a time of 3 minutes 44.08 seconds. In second place was Leonel Manzano of the USA and in third place, Abdalaati Iguider of Morocco.

My apologies to these fine athletes.

Graham Sheppard